Famiglia Fabrasia

To Fran
My favorite Aunt!
Thanks for the support
Dom

Famiglia Fabrasia

Domenic Pugliares

Library of Congress Control Number: 2011962116

ISBN:	Hardcover	978-1-4691-3102-3
	Softcover	978-1-4691-3101-6
	Ebook	978-1-4691-3103-0

This book was printed in the United States of America.

To order additional copies of this book, contact:
Xlibris Corporation
1-888-795-4274
www.Xlibris.com
Orders@Xlibris.com
107741

Acknowledgments

This book was a cathartic process that took many years to complete. I want to thank my parents, who truly made me believe that I was capable of achieving whatever I wanted in life. Apparently, writing a book now is one of those achievements. I need to thank three lovely women who transposed my hen scratch into legible typed text. First, my battle-ax assistant, Mary Bell, who passed on unexpectedly in the beginning of this process. Had she stuck around, this book would have been done years ago or I would have been the one to pass on early. Many thanks to Rebecca Eltzroth, who finished transposing the book, and Jennifer Greenlaw, who did all the final editing.

Finally, I thank my wife Serena and my sons Ben and Dan. They have supported me in all my crazy endeavors, both good and bad.

Chapter 1

Luke pulled his black S550 Mercedes with bulletproof glass into his parking space in front of Fabrasia's restaurant. No one from the neighborhood would ever dare park there. Lucas Fabrasia, "head of the famed 'Fabrasia' crime family," was visibly shaking his head as he parallel parked his eighty-thousand-dollar car. How many lives did he actually have? He had just beat a federal racketeering charge that the feds were convinced would stick. They finally had him and half his crime family. It would have virtually crippled crime in this part of Little Italy. Inexplicably, one of the lower-level FBI agents, Joe Stone, had disclosed the whereabouts of the fed's star witness, Joe Ambloni, to one of Luke's captains, Johnny Gombramsi.

In a bold high-noon attack, eight brazen, gun-wielding hired guns stormed the shitty little motel where four feds were guarding Joey until the trial. Two feds were killed immediately and the other two feds seriously wounded, but unable to protect Joey, who was shot an incredible two hundred and ten times. In the attack, two of the thugs were also killed; the other six escaped without injury. Since they were out-of-town talent, nothing could be traced to Luke.

The feds, although seriously pissed off, and obviously carrying a grudge against Luke, having lost two of their own and the other two never ever being able to wear a badge again, had no choice but to drop the charges without their star witness.

Luke, shaking his head, half because he couldn't believe he had (figuratively) yet again dodged another bullet, was puzzled as to why one of their own would give up Joe Ambloni? Who was this Joe Stone and what did he want? Should he take him out? No! Two feds in one week is enough. The pressure, if you could believe it, would be worse than it was now. Luke hated loose ends, but this guy could also be a huge asset. Without even asking, or better yet, not asking for money, he saved Luke many long years in jail. He would have to meet this Joe Stone, but not now. He'd wait until things cooled down in a little while.

Luke walked into his restaurant to thunderous applause from most everyone who was anyone in the underworld. Luke's three lieutenants—Jerry "Fat Hands" Melazia, Luciano "All Business" Caprisi (also called "AB"), and Giovanni "Johnny" Gombransi—were in the front, leading the applause. Then, one by one, they physically kissed Luke's ring as a sign of respect and dedication. Luke quieted the crowd with a swipe of his hand. It still amazed him how much power he had. One swipe of his hand immediately quieted two hundred or more people. Not that he was uncomfortable with his power. He knew that because of his famed ruthlessness with adversaries, people took him seriously. What was sometimes overlooked was his business cunning. He took a small-time racketeering business and made it into a three-state multi-hundred-million-dollar Mafia franchise. Luke, had he been born with a silver spoon in his mouth, could have easily been a Fortune 500 CEO.

With everyone's attention at hand, Luke spoke to the crowd. He, with a different upbringing, could probably have been a great orator as well, but under the circumstances his tough-guy inflections were just about impossible to hide, which, by the way, also worked to his favor. "I want to personally thank all of you that stuck by our family over this trying time. Trust me, I know who my friends . . . our friends are, and may nobody ever fuck with them." This was greeted with great applause. When it subsided, Luke, who by now was holding a glass of grappa, held it high. "God bless us, our families, and, most importantly, our children." Johnny reaffirmed with "Cent' Anni," and they all drank a cheer to freedom.

Giovanni "Johnny" Gombransi was strutting around just a little more cocky than usual. Justifiably so, since it was to Johnny that the Fed Joe Stone reached out to with Ambloni's whereabouts.

In the seedy underworld, anyone who is anyone knows who's doing what. Therefore, everyone knew that Johnny saved Luke's ass, as well as probably half of those in the room. What they didn't know was that Johnny didn't do anything special to get Ambloni's whereabouts; it just fell in his lap. Johnny's opinion was who the fuck cares. There are no pictures on the scorecard! The fact is, he got the info, and with that info he saved the family. Luke, of course, knows that Stone contacted Johnny. Luke was happy that it was Johnny because if Johnny was nothing else, he was as loyal as the day is long. He would be happier to stand in front of a truck to protect Luke than to step out of the way and profit millions. Luke liked that, so even though Johnny wasn't always the sharpest knife in the drawer, he would rather have ten Johnnies than a smart guy he couldn't trust.

The restaurant was exactly what you would expect from an establishment owned and operated by Luke. Big enough to hold two hundred, if you added tables, but cozy enough that when there were only twenty-five or thirty people, the place didn't seem empty. Large frescoes adorned the walls, which were trimmed in dark mahogany. Many small stained glass partitions divided up the restaurant, which gave that cozy feel and also doubled as quiet spots to dine and talk business—family business. A large bar, which ran almost the length of the building with dark mahogany and small marble pillars and mirrors, adorned the back wall. It's always nice when you're far away from the front door should any trouble enter the building. The ceilings were Italian plaster. The hand carved plaster was just as it was in the old country. Luke saw to that by flying the artisans over from his family's hometown in Calabria.

Tonight, the restaurant was hopping with excitement and cheer. Luke, to his family, both paternal as well as fraternal, was as generous as a man could be. Tonight, the best of wines and hard alcohol would be flowing as well as cigars from Luke's private stock. At one point you could hear Luke call to one of the waiters—a cousin of a cousin, he was sure, "Montecristo, for our family members, pronto."

Luke milled around for about a half hour making sure the proper food, wine, and cigars were being enjoyed. When he was confident that everything was under control, he sought out Johnny to speak to him privately.

Luke, a big man, caught Johnny's eye from across the room with just a tip of his head. Johnny immediately knew that the boss wanted to see him in the infamous deaf room. Johnny, a very independent and stubborn man, was neither when it came to Luke, dropped everything when told to do something by his superior. He went immediately to the deaf room. If nothing else, he was loyal and dedicated. It took Luke a little longer to get there, stopping occasionally to exchange pleasantries. He had the social graces of a politician if he so chose to use them.

The deaf room was named because of its design to deaden all sound from the inside because of its rubber ceiling and floor with four bullet proof glass walls. Four freestanding glass walls stood in the center of the basement, making it impossible to bug. This, coupled with sophisticated metal-detecting devices at the door, even eliminated the need to pat people down as they entered the room, although many were just as an added precaution. In the mob, your guard can never be down.

When Luke entered the deaf room, Johnny was waiting, smoking a Teamo cigar. Johnny was a forty-two-year-old bull. Although not that tall, maybe five feet ten or five feet eleven inches, he was all of two hundred and twenty pounds, most of which was solid muscle, other than his small pasta gut. Tattoos covered both forearms and biceps. He had them mostly for effect. They rounded out his tough guy appearance, not that he really needed help. Johnny was blessed with that nice thick black Italian hair which was just now starting to show specks of gray. For an Italian, his features were not as pronounced as you would have imagined. Were it not for the noticeable scar on his chin, his facial features would not draw that much attention.

Luke shut the door behind him, extended his arms, and hugged Johnny for nearly thirty seconds. When they separated, Luke said, "Johnny, great work. I . . . we all owe you a debt of gratitude. Now give me that fucking rope you're smoking and let's celebrate with a real cigar," as he pulled out two Romeo and Juliet Churchills from his pocket. After lighting the cigars, Luke went to the corner of the small room where, on a glass shelf (nowhere to hide a transmitter), he poured two glasses of grappa, an Italian version of bad moonshine. Luke cheered their good fortune and then from his other inside pocket pulled out an envelope with one hundred hundred-dollar bills. As a look of gratitude crossed his face, Johnny tried to decline, but he knew there was no way to say no to the boss. Even when he wanted to say no, like when he had to whack his childhood buddy, Joe DiSisto, because his gambling debt got him talking with the feds, he did it because in this business the boss is the boss and you do what he says or pay the consequences. So Johnny did it and he accepted the money because in this gig you take the good with the bad. This definitely was part of the good.

Luke spoke. "Johnny, as happy as I am with the way everything turned out, I'm still bothered about this Joe Stone guy. Why did he give up Ambloni? He had to know it would cost some, if not all of his own, wasting Ambloni. It just doesn't make sense. He couldn't have done it as a plan to deeper infiltrate us because Ambloni had enough on us and me, in particular, to hang half of us. They certainly wouldn't put their own in harm's way. What's his act?" "Boss, I only met him once and he didn't say much. Basically, all he said was Ambloni is at the Stargate Motel, Room 14B. There's a front door and a back door. There will be four agents, heavily armed, and then he said his name was agent Joe Stone and that he was sure Mr. Fabrasia would appreciate the info. Luke, as you know, we quickly used our contacts to check out the story and two days later, after it checked out, ba da bing, ba da bang, an out-of-town hit and we're now all home free." "Johnny, nothing is for nothing. When things die down, I'm going to need to meet this Stone guy, but not for a while."

Little did they know it would be sooner than they ever expected.

Chapter 2

Luke, sleeping the best sleep he'd had in months after leaving the celebration party, was awoken by the brutal ringing of the phone. He was slightly hung over, if not from the grappa, certainly from the Cuban nicotine. Luke cleared his head to hear the gruff voice of one of his other Lieutenants, Jerry "Fat Hands" Melazia. "Jerry, what the fuck—it's 6:00 a.m. in the morning." "Bad news, boss. I thought you would want to know. Stevie's been whacked, execution-style, back of the head in his Camaro."

Stevie DiAmbrosio was a low-level soldier. A nice enough guy, but a heavy drinker who liked the ladies and by all accounts wasn't real nice to them. Not a great loss organizationally, but what were the ramifications? Luke's brain, not quite functioning well, was still quick enough to wonder if this was the beginning of war with a rival family. Maybe one of the families expecting Fabrasia to go down had intentions of moving in. Now that he's still around, maybe they want in anyway. Unlikely—he was too powerful, but maybe? "Where did this happen?" "Three blocks from the restaurant, probably right after the party." "Call the crew and have them meet me in the deaf room in an hour. Send over four of the boys and a car to escort me. Tell the boys to watch their backs on the way in case we have a war brewing we don't know about. God fucking help them if someone thinks they can fuck with us . . . pricks!"

He slammed down the phone and jumped in the shower. Jerry quickly started making calls following the boss's orders. Like Johnny, Jerry was more loyal than smart. Luke, maybe to his detriment, held loyalty over everything which gave him a secure feeling about whom he surrounded himself with as direct reports. In this business, if you were smart you really trusted no one, but Luke was different. He would rather die for his three direct reports rather than sell them out. He knew, the way all great leaders know, who is loyal and who isn't. His three were loyal to the death. He hoped beyond hope he would never have to find out differently.

Jerry "Fat Hands" Melazia was a mountain of a man. Smaller in height than Johnny, but bigger all around, a slightly smaller version of a Sumo wrestler's physique with the most enormous hands you've ever seen in your life. Hands that had been used to choke the life out of no less than nineteen men, either traitors, suspected traitors, thieves against the family and, in two cases, just assholes that said the wrong thing at the wrong time to obviously the wrong guy with a wicked bad Italian temper.

Jerry had a thin head of hair with one of those comb-over-the-scalp hairdos. He was thick in the middle with a bulbous nose and huge ears. If you didn't just know by looking at him that he would break you in two for looking at him cross-eyed, you'd probably just laugh at him. Thankfully, few had made that mistake. What most people didn't know about him was that he was the most caring guy in the world to his wife and two kids and he had the softest of touches while tending his small, but beautiful, garden. Nobody knew about his gardening prowess, even Luke, because that would be a sign of weakness.

Jerry made all of the calls with the messages, one of sadness about one of their own. The second was an immediate command from the boss to safely, but quickly, get to the deaf room.

By 7:15 a.m. most of them, on less than four hours sleep, were assembled in the deaf room, sitting on two simple benches on either side of a glass table. The only chair was for Luke. None had pads or any other clever places to insert a bug. Assembled beside Luke on his right were his three direct reports, Jerry (Fat Hands), Luciano (AB), and Johnny. To his left were three higher-ups in his organization: Louie "No Luck" Lombardi, his brother Matthew "Lucky" Lombardi, and Benny "The Kid" Bambino. At the end of the table were the other set of brothers, Ronnie and Richie Scandora.

Luke started by dispensing with the pleasantries. "What the fuck is the word on the street? Is it one of the other families? What are we dealing with?"

Louie "No Luck" Lombardi spoke first. "I called all my men from the cell on the way here and nobody knows nuttin."

Agreement came from around the table. Nobody seemed to know where the bullet came from or, more importantly, where the next one will be coming from.

Luke said, "How do we fight a ghost? Someone out there took out one of us and it was execution style. No accident! We need to call in all our chips on the street and find out."

Luke suddenly blurted out, "What the fuck!" Through the bulletproof glass door of the deaf room, Luke saw two of his henchmen, Bruno and Sal, dragging a guy down the basement toward the deaf room. Bruno and Sal each had an armlock on the guy in the middle whose feet were hardly touching the ground.

Johnny stood up, hand on his 9 mm Berretta, and said "Boss, that's the Stone guy. You know, Joe Stone, the guy who tipped me off where they had Ambloni stashed!" "What the hell is he doing here?" Luke said. "I don't know, but I don't like the feel of this. It can't be good." Lucky opened the door. "Let's find out what's going on."

Lucky, by mob standards, had truly lived the charmed life. He had never so much as had a parking ticket, never mind ever being pinched. Also, unlike his brother, he was one of the most gifted gamblers of all time. He just seemed to know when to bet the favorite or when to go with the underdog. Some said he just waited to see what his brother "Unlucky Lombardi" was going to bet on and he would bet the opposite way. That probably wasn't too far from the truth, because as lucky as Matthew was, his brother was equally unlucky.

Lucky opened the door just in time for Sal and Bruno to come crashing into the room with the Stone guy. It would have been interesting to see what would have happened if Lucky didn't open the door just in time. Bruno and Sal probably would have slammed into the door with Stone. Remember, Luke treasured loyalty, not necessarily brains.

Bruno started stuttering, "B . . ., B . . ., Boss, this guy, gu, guy came bu . . . bu . . . bursting in, in, in." "Bruno," Luke interrupted, "Thanks." "Let Sal tell me what happened." "Boss, this guy comes busting in and he demands, can you fucking believe, demands to see you. We were just going to beat the shit out of him and throw him in the alley but he showed us this." Sal threw an FBI badge on the table. Me and Bruno think it's fake. We also took this from him," placing a 9 mm Berretta on the table.

Stone suddenly spoke up, "Luke . . ., I mean, Mr. Fabrasia, we need to speak . . . alone." "Mr. Stone." "Joe, please." "Joe, then, is this official business? Am I under arrest?" "No, you're not under arrest and this may not be official, but it certainly is a matter of grave importance."

He then slowly reached into his pocket with all eyes watching and many fingers already placed on ready triggers. Joe slowly pulled out a cassette tape and lightly threw it on the glass table in front of Luke.

"Please get a tape recorder and listen to this tape with me in private." Luke looked at the tape, then up at Bruno, and with hardly a flick of an eyebrow Bruno was off in pursuit of a cassette recorder.

"Stone, you got a lot of balls coming here to my place alone without a warrant or backup." "Sal, did you check outside?" "Yeah, boss, when we first grabbed him, I sent out four of the boys to scour the neighborhood. He came alone." "Like I said, you got a lot of balls. Can't you see I'm having a meeting of my restaurant's executive committee." Stone, all of a sudden looking more like a lion rather than the cowardly lion, said, "Maybe you might want to take a break from your meeting to hear what I got to say about Stevie?" "Stevie who," Luke said with as much conviction as any Oscar-winning actor. "Stevie DiAmbrosio, one of your soldiers who was killed about six hours ago." "Well, Mr. Stone . . . Joe, I don't have any idea what you're talking about—soldier, I'm not in the army." "Fabrasia . . . I'm sorry. Mr. Fabrasia. Can we dispense with the bullshit? Can you get a tape recorder and ask your associates to leave us alone for five minutes?"

Fabrasia, again with just a light tip of the head, sent the message to his men to leave. As they obediently filed out of the deaf room, Jerry "Fat Hands" said, "Are you sure, boss, you don't just want me to squeeze his neck?" "Jerry, let's be hospitable to our guest . . . at least for the time being."

As Jerry was last to leave, Bruno stepped in and handed Luke the tape recorder. With another tip of his head, Bruno knew that meant thank-you and leave all at the same time.

"OK, Mr. Stone, your tape better be good." Luke placed the tape in the recorder and pressed the play button. Immediately, Luke recognized Stevie DiAmbrosio's voice. "If you promise me a new identity and no jail time, I can give you enough shit on Luke Fabrasia to put him away for good this time." In a voice that was definitely Stone's, Luke heard, "What kind of shit is that, Stevie, because we have enough on you that you'll be on Social Security by the time you see daylight again." "All of it, gambling, prostitution, drugs and, of course, hits." "Well, we already know . . . suspect Mr. Fabrasia's on all of that, but what kind of proof?" "How about direct orders from Luke himself for me to kill Alex Samalia?"

Luke zoned out for a second. Two things raced through his mind. Stone was going to blackmail him, and second, he very seldom makes big mistakes and he never directly gives orders. He only gives them to one of his three direct reports and lets them do the dirty work. It's that extra layer of insulation that ensures longevity in his field of endeavor. But he let his temper get the better of him one night when he found out that not only was one of his lower-level guys, Alex Samalia, skimming off the top of his collections, but he was bragging about it while he was drinking. Stevie had told Luke, and Luke made the decision on the spot to have Stevie whack him right away to send a message. He quickly focused back to the tape. He must have only zoned out for a split second because he heard Stevie say on the tape, "I recorded the conversation just for insurance in case I ever got pinched bad like now."

Stone pushed the stop button and again very slowly pulled out of his pocket another tape. He switched one for the other and again pressed the play button. Luke felt his heart go into his stomach when he heard his voice telling Stevie to whack Joey. This time Luke pressed the stop button.

"OK, Joe, I see your point, but without Stevie alive, you've got nothing, so your plan to blackmail me ain't worth shit! Whoever whacked Stevie unknowingly did me a favor, and when I find him, I'll have to thank him." Luke was feeling better now that the feds' case was worthless.

"Mr. Fabrasia, I'll accept your gratitude." "Why's that, Joe?" "Because I killed Stevie!" After a brief pause, Luke said, "You know, Joe, that this room is bug proof and you've been searched for a wire even though it wouldn't work here anyway. So no one can hear this conversation if you're trying to set me up." "Mr. Fabrasia, your guys already checked to make sure I was alone. If I wanted you in jail, I wouldn't have dropped the dime on Joe Ambloni and you'd be well on your way to jail right now. You were very lucky that I happened to be the guy who collared Stevie or you'd be back in a world of trouble now." "Well, I guess I haven't had a chance to officially thank you for the Ambloni situation. Yet I guess now you've got my attention, how much is it going to cost me for my gratitude? Oh, and of course, to get all the copies of the taped conversation you had with Stevie?"

"Mr. Fabrasia, you've misconstrued my intentions. I'm not looking for money. I think, though, I've given you enough to ponder on today. Don't call me, I'll call you." He tossed the tape to Luke and said, "Keep these as a souvenir. There's more where these came from." Stone got up to leave and turned toward the door when a clamp clenched down on his triceps. Pain rocketed up his shoulder but he never turned back toward Luke. Luke, with sour breath mixed from cigars and grappa from the night before and coffee this morning, spoke directly into Stone's ear. "I don't know what your fucking act is yet, Stone, but God help you and your family if you're fucking with me." "Trust me, Mr. Fabrasia, you won't be disappointed, and I don't have any family." Luke let him go and again, with a flip of his head, the boys on the other side of the door knew to let Joe Stone leave untouched.

Once Stone was safely out of the building, Luke reassembled his meeting. He said to the guys, "Keep turning over stones to find out who put the hit out on Stevie and to Luciano "All Business" Caprisi, his third direct report, "Find out everything you can about this Stone guy! I want to know what his grandmother had to eat on this day in 1941. Capisce?" Johnny, who could never keep his mouth shut, said, "What did Stone want this time?" Luke said, "Johnny, you go do what I told you and when it's time to know about Stone, I'll tell you guys and not until then."

Stone left the building with more than just a little adrenaline flowing through his veins. He could hardly contain his smile. He knew he had Luke's attention. More importantly, he was convinced Luke was intrigued enough by what he had done so far that he was assured he could lead Luke down the road to achieve Stone's purpose in life.

Although it was far into spring, this early morning it felt more like fall than the coming summer. With very little sun and a better-than-half chance of rain, one could easily be depressed by such a day, although Stone couldn't be further away from being unhappy. Stone's mind was turning a mile a minute; his feet were barely touching the ground. Stone, who was an excellent FBI man with extraordinary instincts, was so intoxicated with his encounter that he didn't even realize he was being followed. Not that he would care even if he knew. Actually he would have been disappointed if he wasn't being followed. He knew once he decided to go along this path, his life would never be the same. He not only wasn't afraid of that, he welcomed it.

Stone had taken a right out of Lucas's restaurant and had walked two blocks through Little Italy. He then turned right and walked a block to where his nondescript dark blue Ford Taurus was parked. Although the outside of his car was nondescript, the inside was anything but. Stone, a self-taught techno guru, had every imaginable electronic tracking, listening, crime-fighting, or possibly crime-committing device ever invented. All courtesy of our tax dollars. Nothing but the best for our men and women working the underground for our country.

Stone wasn't an easy guy to miss if you happened to be following him. Six feet tall, broad shoulders, and a big square jaw that had movie star written all over it, except for the deep worry lines that adorned his face and particularly his eyes. They were lines that developed from many years of lamenting over something very troubling. Regardless of his troubled eyes and his government-issue clothing, you could easily be watching him on TV. Probably one of those daytime soap operas.

Stone put his key in the car door. Unlocking the door acted as a catalyst to snap Stone back to reality. As he opened the car door, he, for just the briefest of seconds, caught one of Luke's goons probably fifty yards behind him half crouched between two cars.

Stone thought to himself this was too easy. Couldn't Luke have sent someone with a little more stealth to keep tabs on him?

Stone started the car to a cacophony of electronic beeps and blurps as the ignition-dependent services came to life. Stone casually adjusted his rearview mirror to catch both the goon crouched behind the car on foot and now he also spotted two more goons in a Lincoln at the corner, a block away, behind him. Boy, he must have been walking on air not to notice them behind him before. They might as well have been sending up flares behind him with how obvious they were.

Stone decided to go home for a while now considering they must already know where he lived anyway. No need to bring them on a wild-goose chase. Stone, always the solid citizen, by appearances anyway, put his blinker on and pulled out of the parking space to head for home. In sync with Stone leaving, the two goons turned up the street to follow at a safe distance, stopping long enough for a slightly overweight goon to tumble between the two cars he was hiding behind and climb into the back seat of the Lincoln.

As the two cars disappeared up the long, congested city road, directly across the street from where Stone was parked, a spent cigarette was discarded from the shadows of the doorway on to the sidewalk. A man dressed in jeans with a baseball hat and a coat with the collar up stepped out of the shadows, turned right, and walked back in the direction of Fabrasia's. From his perch, he was able to watch all that just happened without being noticed.

Chapter 3

Luke had made his way upstairs to the kitchen area of the restaurant. With cash money to burn, as Luke had, because of his many illegitimate business activities, he could afford to have state-of-the-art kitchen facilities—equipment that could never be afforded by a restaurant the size of Fabrasia. Even with its seating capacity of two hundred or more, it was really operated like a small Italian restaurant that seated less than fifty with everything cooked to order.

Luke had one of the goombas make him espresso and he sat on a stool leaning on a stainless steel table that was used to prepare dinners. He wasn't sure if he was pissed or amazed at what had just happened. No, he decided, he was definitely pissed! Luke didn't like surprises, not even as a kid on his birthday. He would always go to the store with his mother to pick out his present. Although as pissed as he was, he owed Stone a debt of gratitude if not money for saving his ass, not once, but apparently twice. Stone was very clear, though, he wasn't looking for money! Luke slammed his fist down on the stainless steel table three times hard enough to make the two hundred and fifty pound table dance up and down. Why! Why! Why! Not being able to answer his own question and nobody willing to offer any assistance for fear of the repercussions, if they were wrong, just left Luke alone.

Luke then did what he does whenever he doesn't have an immediate answer. First, he eats until he can't eat anymore. Then, out of a sense of remorse, he goes to his personal gym in the basement of the restaurant and works out to the brink of a heart attack.

Luke is a big man, probably about six feet, one inch tall. If it weren't for his constant ingestion of rich Italian food and his favorite grappa, he would be a chiseled specimen at forty-four years of age. But when you couple his eating habits, since most mob business is done over the dinner table, with his vigorous workout schedule, you get a guy that's probably twenty to thirty pounds overweight, although not an ounce of flab. He was just massive muscle under bulk. Not that he has to do any of his own dirty work anymore, but he's certainly capable of it and on rare occasions like now, when he's full of pent-up hostility, he would enjoy doing some of his own dirty work.

After Luke had a huge breakfast and just as huge a workout, he showered. Now with his head clear, it was time to sit down for a late lunch. Luke, much calmer now than he had been just a few hours ago, had made up his mind on what to do. Regardless of what this Stone guy had on him, Luke figured he was still the mountain and Mohammed, no matter how powerful he was, had to go to the mountain. Whatever Stone wanted, he would have to come to Luke one way or the other.

Therefore, Luke had decided to do nothing. Patience, they say, is a virtue, and it's something that was long coming for Luke who could tend at times to be impatient.

Luke, now reveling in his maturity, decided to let things run their course instead of deciding to grab the bull by the horns. Luke had decided to let his guys find out whatever they could about Stone and keep a tight surveillance on him to track his every move. He was also confident that he could waste him at a moment's notice. Dead men have a hard time testifying as all concerned found out with Ambloni just a few days ago. Luke had Lucky Lombardi call Jerry, Luciano, and Johnny, his three direct reports, to come have lunch and discuss the last few days' happenings and how he has decided to handle it.

Chapter 4

Stone drove through the downtown traffic wondering why the goons were following him so closely, never getting more than three blocks behind him, but mostly less than two blocks. His confusion stemmed from the meter installed under his dash that registers with a slow beeping sound if there is a tracking device on the vehicle. When he parked the car this morning, there weren't any devices on the car at all. He was sure of it. Clearly, one of Luke's goons had placed it there sometime between when he entered the restaurant and when he got back to his car. This whole mockery of being trailed so close must be a ruse to throw him off guard if and when he tried to shake them.

In the Lincoln, Louie "No Luck" Lombardi was driving with his hands so tight on the steering wheel that his knuckles had turned white. Ronnie and Richie Scandora weren't helping the situation, constantly telling Louie to change lanes, speed up, slow the fuck down! Ronnie said, "If you lose him, Luke will have our asses." No Luck replied, "No fucking shit. Don't worry, I won't lose him." Richie said, "Yeah, more importantly, don't let him know we're following him." Louie mumbled to himself, "Lose him, don't lose him, speed up, slow down, what the fuck, do I look like a yo-yo?"

Stone, sensing a problem by watching the Lincoln's erratic driving, slowed down and made it easier to be followed the remaining few blocks to his house. Stone was bothered by both their incompetence and by the thought that they were trying to outsmart him. Neither one sat well with him.

Eight blocks behind all of this, a nondescript Chevy slowly tracked their progress with a GPS tracking system.

Chapter 5

Luke had ordered antipasto for everyone and assorted other appetizers—calamari, mussels, and bread with oil—enough to fill the table. When everyone was comfortable eating and drinking Chianti, but before their entrée arrived, Luke started to talk business. "No one, and I mean no one, is to touch Stone unless I give the order. I'm not sure yet what his act is, but we got enough guys digging into his past that we're bound to pick up something. He's either stupid which I doubt, or he's the best worm I've ever seen, although I doubt that as well because I doubt the feds would order a hit. Unless of course it was one of our rivals and Stone's just being opportunistic telling us he whacked Stevie. If that's true, then we still could have a potential war on our hands, so don't let your guard down. Third, and in my mind most likely, there's some reason why this guy wants to be one of us. Something doesn't smell right about it, but you know what, boys, time will answer this question. Either, we'll figure it out or he'll tell us. When we know, we'll deal with him. Like I told him, God help him and his family if he's fucking with us." Just as Luke was finishing, the entrees were arriving. Luke, with a big smile on his face, hands in the air, just like a good Patriarch, “Mangia.”

As the lunch progressed, conversation turned to the other pressing business matters of the day. Who owed them money, who was making them money, what businesses were doing well, which ones weren't, and what needed to be done to make them more profitable? The outside world would never believe how much this meeting was similar to any “legitimate” business strategy meeting. The only major difference was that most meetings like this happen in Fortune 500 boardrooms instead of a mob guy's restaurant. Of course, most of Luke's businesses dealt in, if not illegal, at least illegitimate business ventures and always had to hide cash from the government. Having said that, some people may think there was no difference other than where the meetings took place, since most big corporations are always looking for ways to reduce their tax liability.

The last espresso, having being finished, signified the end of this high calorie meeting. Everybody was feeling better a short twelve hours after the disturbing calls they all received this morning. All of them felt a sense of business as usual, and business as usual it was for the next two weeks, almost to the minute.

Even a mob boss needs a day off occasionally and for Luke it was typically Sunday. Sundays were mostly shot anyway because by the time he took his family to church, then to brunch, the day was all but gone anyway. Luke, like almost all his guys, was a big churchgoer. Luke's church, St. Anthony's, where most of his guys also belonged, was probably one of the most financially stable churches in the whole Catholic diocese. Luke knew at some deep level of himself that what he did for a living was wrong. There probably isn't a person in the world that can rationalize dealing in murder, extortion, prostitution, theft, and drugs can be good or wholesome, although rationalization is the tool of all evil. They say the road to hell is paved with good intentions—bullshit! The road to hell is a yellow brick road called rationalization.

Rationalization is what Luke and the mob are all about. He figures someone is going to do it, so it might as well be him. At least when Luke is involved, it will be done with style and grace and as fairly as this business can be conducted. Not like the Asians who, in his mind, are ruthless killers without reason. Or the blacks and Spanish who are unorganized and commit organizational genocide and will never become a true underworld power. Then there are the Russians who just lack class and don't get the ways of the Western world. They may be ruthless but at the end of the day they lack the organizational structure and discipline to rival the Italians. Therefore, it was left to the Italians to deal with and manage the underworld. Rationalization—murder needs to be committed to keep out intruders to the business or traitors, or deadbeats who owe and can't or won't pay. Those people in particular need to be eliminated so more people won't try to undermine the mob's power. Send a message—kill so more won't need to be killed—rationalization.

If there weren't prostitutes, more unwilling women would be raped and abused—rationalization. People are going to gamble and if it isn't run fairly, people would be killing each other over welched bets—rationalization. The worst in Luke's mind was drugs. This he just can't understand because he never understood the need for recreational drugs. Just the idea of losing control of his senses was tantamount to giving up his dignity. Nonetheless, people—a lot of people every day—want and need drugs. Therefore, someone needed to supply them. At least if it were him, the drugs would be guaranteed to be high quality so if people got sick or died, it would be from abuse, not from poorly manufactured drugs made with inferior chemicals. That's probably why his drug trade was such a big part of his business—rationalization. Nonetheless, Luke truly believed that he was one with God. Why wouldn't he be? He's managing all of this filth with style and grace. Wouldn't God want it that way? Who better than him to deal with the dregs of the earth and keep control of them to keep them out of normal society? Hell, the law shouldn't persecute him; he should be given a medal by the governor for managing all this shit and not taking the resources of the government to deal with all these problem people. It takes a big organization to run his little government. Just as the real government needs taxes to run their organization, Luke needs not to pay taxes to run his—rationalization.

There also must be redemption for sharing wealth with God. The Jews have been doing it for years and look how successful they have become. Luke by far is St. Anthony's largest benefactor. Father Landini must also feel the same way as Luke. Why else would he accept all the cash he's received from Luke over the years? Luke had personally donated over a million, five in the last ten years. Typically, he sends over a bag with ten grand a month to Father Landini, with more around Christmas and Easter—rationalization.

Like all good leaders, Luke leads by example. His generosity to the church and his sense of rationalization has transcended to his people. Father Landini has a seemingly endless supply of paper bags showing up at the rectory door—mass rationalization.

After Mass that day, Luke was relaxing in his backyard around his brick patio pool, Sunday being a family day at the Fabrasia's. That is, of course, if business doesn't require his presence. Luke loved his family and would do anything for them. In his mind, unless he could provide for them, he wasn't worthy of them, so business always came first. Family, though, was as close a second-place finisher. That is as close as a photo finish at a horse race. Luke had three children—Luke Jr., seventeen; Nick, fourteen; and his baby and sparkle of his eye, ten-year-old Donella.

Luke Jr., although his namesake, other than in looks wasn't much like his father. A tall, wiry kid, he was much less physical than his father and much more cerebral. Luke Jr., just a sophomore in high school because of Luke starting him late in school, had already been the lead in two plays. Luke, as proud of his son as an actor as he would have been if his son had been the star quarterback of the football team, realized that Luke Jr. was much more like his mother. Luke actually preferred that his son be the intellectual that he knew he could have been had he taken a different road in life.

Nick, on the other hand, was everything that Luke Jr. wasn't. His build was much thicker. Although two years his junior and at least three to four inches shorter, Nick weighed as much as Luke Jr. did. Nick would have loved to be the star quarterback, but that wasn't his calling in life either. Nick was built and acted like a lineman. The fourteen-year-old already had the body of a man and had already used physical intimidation much like his father had to early in his career. Nick actually loved to fight and had little, if any, remorse at leaving his victims bloodied and hurt. Luke feared a career of crime for Nick following in his footsteps. Time will tell, though. Who would have ever thought Michael (Al Pacino) would have followed in his father's footsteps.

Then there was Donella. Princess, as Luke often called her. The queen pain-in-the–ass, as the boys often called her when obviously Luke wasn't around. That type of behavior would receive an immediate backhand, and Luke's hand wasn't one you wanted to receive backhand, forehand, or even in a strong handshake. Donella was petite and strikingly beautiful for a small girl. She had olive oil skin and light brown, long curly hair, always with a bow in it. She typically wore frilly clothes which were as feminine as can be. There was not a tomboy bone in her body. She would much prefer a make-believe tea party than a game of kickball. It was a sight to view Luke sitting at a miniature table and chair set drinking make-believe tea with his princess. This would not bode well for him to be seen in such a position from either his own people or, God forbid, his rivals. Such, though, is a father's love for his only daughter.

His wife Teresa, pronounced Ter-a-sa, was not a thing of beauty in the "trophy wife" sense. Then again, she wasn't a trophy wife either. She was Luke's high school sweetheart. Teresa did though possess beauty. Beauty in the best sense of the word, both inward as well as visually. She was of average height but very curvaceous. A figure that men would have raved over in the forties, but not in the new millennium. Hard bodies that border on the physiques of adolescent boys seem to be more in vogue. Luke, for the life of him, could not understand why.

Teresa had beautiful features that were in perfect proportion to her oblong face. Tight, light brown skin, with hardly a wrinkle for a woman in her early forties. Teresa was always meticulously dressed. Never would she be seen without perfectly applied makeup and polish on both her hands and feet.

One of the steadfast rules of the mob has always been to never tell your wife or girlfriend (in most cases, both) anything that has to do with the business. There were many reasons for this, not the smallest was to have a disgruntled significant other turn state's evidence.

Luke was completely different in this respect. Teresa was his true partner in life. Not only were they romantically compatible, they were also intellectually in sync. Luke had been faithful to his wife since the day they met and fell in love in high school. To the best of his knowledge, all of Luke's men, with the exception of Luciano "All Business" Caprisi, had a piece on the side. Luciano's only reason for not having one was purely financial: he hated to waste money. Luke never had any interest in being with anyone else but Teresa. A deeper love just didn't exist. Not that there weren't plenty of opportunities for Luke to stray between all the whores in his employ and the borderline whores that didn't do it for money, just for the power of being a mob girl. There was an endless supply of pussy at his disposal—to no avail, because it held no interest for him.

On this near perfect day, Luke sat in his lounge chair taking in the rays, enjoying his gin and tonic, and smoking a fine Cuban cigar. His boys were floating listlessly in the pool, while Donella, the apple of his eye, sat on the pool steps playing with her small water toys.

Teresa was puttering around the pool looking to Luke utterly fantastic in her one-piece bathing suit. Although she could easily have worn a two-piece suit, Teresa was much too reserved. Luke, getting lost in the moment, began fantasizing about Teresa. The fantasy was so real he could actually feel her soft skin as he slipped off the shoulder straps of her bathing suit revealing her more than ample breasts. Then, for some odd reason, she began slapping him. He couldn't understand why when it occurred to him that he had fallen asleep and Teresa was lightly tapping his cheeks to wake him up.

"What? What? What the fuck?" "It's Johnny on the phone and he says it's important." "It better be. He knows how I hate to be bothered on Sunday." She handed him the phone. He was able to sneak a quick peek at her cleavage as she leaned over to hand him the phone. He knew he got caught red-handed doing it and in return he just got a big smile from Teresa. She knew she was the only person in the world who had his number and she loved it.

"Johnny, this better be good. I'm trying to have downtime with my family." "Boss, don't you think I know? I'd like the fucking day off today too. I thought you might like to know Stone called me fifteen minutes ago and wants a meeting today at 5:00 p.m."

"Tell him I'm busy." "Boss, he says it's important." "Tell him I don't jump for anybody. I'm busy today. I'll meet him at 5:00 p.m. tomorrow in the deaf room." "But, boss," he says, "It's." "Johnny, who's the fucking boss here?" "You, boss." "Great, I'm glad you realize that. Now go set it up and tell him how to come in the back door. We don't need feds walking in the front door. It's not good for business." With that, Luke hung up.

He knew the rest of the day and night was shot. He probably should have just met the prick today and got it over with, but no fucking way. The mountain was not going to Mohammed. His great mood had just disintegrated to shit. His fantasy, his good mood, his relaxation.

Luke barked, "Lucas, Nick, get your asses out of the pool and help your mother do some yard work now." Family day just turned to family hell.

Chapter 6

The human mind is an incredible thing: the way it can just block things out that you want to block out; its ability in the right body to multitask and never confuse the eight things that are going on simultaneously and also the ability to ignore potential dangers that are not immediately at hand. That is how Luke always functioned—running on all eight cylinders at once, never skipping a beat.

Luke went to work on Monday as if all was perfect with the world. Talking to this one on the cell phone, yelling at that one in person, scaring the shit out of a high stakes gambler who owes him twenty large, giving him a twenty-four-hour deadline or pay the consequences, fencing of some spectacular hot diamonds. He almost forgot his meeting coming up at 5:00 p.m. with Stone.

Then almost as if an alarm clock went off in his head, at 4:50 p.m. Luke stopped what he was doing and poured himself some grappa. He called Lucky over from whatever he was doing and told him when Stone shows up, frisk him good, then escort him down to the deaf room. Lucky just shook his head, knowing when to speak, when not to speak. Lucky noticed a little edge in Luke today, so his opinion was a nod was better than trying to strike up a conversation and getting himself in trouble by saying the wrong thing.

Luke went down to the basement of his restaurant trying to mentally prepare himself for his meeting with Stone. What bothered him was how he had no idea how to prepare for this meeting. "Who was this guy and what did he want?"

He had called Luciano "All Business" Caprisi today to find out what he had turned up on Stone. A. B. told Luke that so far nothing unusual had turned up. Only that he had no brothers and sisters. His mother had recently died about one year ago and his father apparently before he was born. He had been a local cop for a couple of years, a real climber making sergeant within three years, then leaving abruptly to join the feds after being accepted on his third try. Since becoming a fed, his career had been less than stellar. Nothing bad, but nothing spectacular either.

Luke was good at most things he chose to be involved in, but he was great in a few endeavors. One area where he was great was in sizing up people and doing it fast. He hadn't been able to size up Stone yet, which bothered him, but he was convinced after his last meeting that Stone was going to be prompt. He would bet money that Stone would not be late. This guy ran his life by the numbers even if they were apparently screwed up numbers. He was hoping the rest of Stone was going to be equally as easy to figure out.

Luke looked down at his diamond-encrusted Rolex. The little bet he had going with himself, he bet fifty grand at 5:02 p.m., was that Stone would be led down the stairs by Lucky. Stone would arrive by 4:55 p.m. Lucky would frisk him, break his balls a little, and so as not to keep the boss waiting, he would then quickly bring him to the boss.

Luke, sipping his grappa, looking at his watch, just as his Rolex slipped from 5:01 p.m. to 5:02 p.m., saw a slightly disheveled Joe Stone being led down the stairs to the deaf room.

At the flick of Luke's head, Lucky knew it was time to leave. They didn't call him Lucky for nothing. As soon as the glass door behind him was shut and Stone knew that they were alone, Stone went into a rage. "Luke, didn't I send a message that I wanted to meet with you twenty-four hours ago?" Luke, still sitting down and as cool as a cucumber, said," So, it's Luke now, not Mr. Fabrasia." Stone, who was turning a little red, replied, "Don't fuck with me. I wouldn't have called for you if it wasn't important, and yes, after the shit I've pulled you out of, I've earned the right to call you Lukey if I want." All the time Luke was just sitting with his hands folded, grappa in front of him, just shaking his head with a small smirk starting to form on his lips as if this whole thing was beginning to amuse him. That look just added fuel to the fire for Stone as his rant took on even a higher pitch as he continued, "I saved your ass not once but twice, you ungrateful shit! I have a mind to turn you in myself." Luke never flinched or wavered during this whole episode, just continued with his ever-widening smirk and slowly shook his head. He never would have allowed this if any of his men were present to witness. The deaf room was soundproof, so there was also no chance of them being overheard as well.

Stone continued on for about another forty-five seconds. When he finally stopped to take a breath, Luke slowly stood up. "Mr. Stone . . . Joe, if you're done, would you please take a seat?" Stone, expecting any kind of a response other than this, sat down like an obedient puppy dog. Luke walked around to Stone's side of the room and sat on the corner of the glass table facing Stone who was still flushed and breathing heavy.

Luke slowly smiled, "Stone, let's get something straight right now . . . if you ever demand that one of my men contact me to see you at your convenience or if you ever raise your voice to me or disrespect me ever again," and, just as smooth as silk, Luke slid a 38 Smith & Wesson Chief's Special from the small of his back, cocking it as he brought it forward. Before Stone knew what had hit him, he was staring cross-eyed at the muzzle of the nickel-plated gun placed squarely between his eyes. "I will blow your fucking head off your shoulders. Do you understand me?" Stone, who was still flushed, became even redder knowing he was literally staring death right in the eye. How could this be? How did he screw up so bad as to put himself in this position? Deep breath—OK—you know you have something he needs. Calmly, he thought, talk your way out of this.

"Luke . . . I I mean Mr. Fabrasia." Luke, who now had a deadly sneer on his face, wondered whether or not it would just be easier to kill Stone, grind him up, and make him disappear out of his life as quickly as he had entered. "Luke is fine so long as you use it with respect." "Luke, I apologize, but I assumed . . ." "Don't assume!" "I figured because of my prior good deeds that you would be interested in what I have for you." "Maybe I am, but not at the expense of my appearing to pander to you by coming at your beck and call." "Well, after I tell you what I have, Luke, maybe you'll change your mind." "Stone, most people never get a single chance to disrespect me—you got your one and only chance, which in my book makes us even."

Luke slowly released the hammer of the 38 so as not to have it go off accidentally in Stone's face. He got up and walked back to his side of the table, sat down, and threw back what was left of his grappa. "What kind of business do you want to talk about?"

"There's a huge shipment of cocaine coming into the docks tomorrow night at 11:00 p.m. These two low-level Colombian thugs are going to make the pickup. There will be at least five kilos with a street value of about $2.2 million. The following night at 10:00 p.m. there will be a transfer from the #2 Colombian, Juan Helamus, to the head of the Russian mob, Vladimir Polanski, and his top two henchmen. The FBI doesn't give a shit about the three low-level Colombians or the boat operator. They are just pawns in the big picture. They want the top Colombian and Russian. They are the trophies the FBI looks for—kinda like when they thought they had you." "Stone, what does all this have to do with me?" "Well, I know where these guys will be hiding out for the twenty-four hours between the pickup and the transfer. Since the Feds are only interested in the transfer, we have a window where these guys won't be watched. We can swoop in, lift the cocaine, come out $2.2 million ahead, and most likely start a war between the Colombians and the Russians, which will open up more drug trade for us." Luke sat back in his chair, his head beginning to spin a little. He put his hand up to stop Stone. "This is all very interesting, but please explain to me what is all this "us" and we" about? Do you have a fucking mouse in your pocket? I don't have any we! What you see around here is me and only me."

"Luke, don't you see why I've saved your ass twice? This is only small potatoes compared to what we can do together." "I don't have any partners." "I'm not asking to be your partner." "What are you asking?" "I could be an integral part of your organization." "I already have three lieutenants. I don't need anymore." "I don't give a shit what you call me. I'm your guy on the inside, and everything I give you, we split fifty-fifty." "I told you, I don't have partners." "I'm only your partner on the stuff I bring you." Luke paused for what seemed like an eternity. Luke, now turning over the 38 special in his hand, said, "Then thirty percent and you are my sometimes associate." "Forty percent." "Stone, you're going to learn two things today. Don't ever disrespect me, and I don't negotiate!" "Then thirty percent it is and you won't be sorry." Luke, though, wasn't so sure he wouldn't be sorry.

Chapter 7

Stone spent the next ten minutes giving Luke the details of where and when to intercept the cocaine. The mood in the room had changed from charged energy to a more businesslike atmosphere as details were exchanged and discussed. On Stone's departure, Luke stood up and shook Stone's hand. Luke made sure that he grabbed first and also made sure he grabbed mainly Stone's fingers, not the meat of the hand. Luke applied continual pressure as he shook his hand and leaned over and whispered into Stone's ear, "There will be no place to hide if you're trying to set us up. This will be the beginning of a financially beneficial relationship and nothing else!"

As Stone's fingers were methodically being crushed second by second under Luke's tremendous force, his face never wavered.

Stone's thought was that Luke would have to physically amputate his fingers one by one before he gave Luke the pleasure of showing any weakness. Luke was impressed by Stone's control. Stone stole the opportunity with Luke being so close to him. Before Luke knew what happened, Stone kissed Luke on both cheeks in the traditional Italian style of family and friendship. Speaking into Luke's ear, he whispered, "You may want me to become the partner you never had or thought you never wanted."

Luke was so surprised by the double kiss on the cheeks that his iron fist melted, allowing the blood to once again flow into Stone's fingers.

Luke, still somewhat in shock, croaked, "Whatever. Let's see how this deal goes down in thirty-six hours and whether or not you've made yourself $660,000 or you're setting us up and you've become fish food. Capisce!"

"Luke, you won't be sorry. You just send your best men and this will be like taking candy from a baby." Luke replied, "Don't worry. I'll send my best. If everything goes well, I'll see you here in forty-eight hours sharp to split the cash. Now get out of here before I change my mind."

Stone again left "Fabrasia" with his feet barely touching the ground. He left through the back door the same way he entered through the alley, which was kept immaculately clean, probably at Luke's direction in case of a hasty departure. Better not to be tripping over garbage cans and winos. At the end of the alley, Stone turned right where he had parked his car, not attempting to hide it anymore.

The act of turning the key in the lock brought him again back to reality. He thought to himself—that was pretty stupid getting so hot, but at least Luke now knows he's not a pansy (as if putting a bullet in the back of Steve DiAmbrosio's head wasn't enough to show his higher-than-normal testosterone level.). Thirty percent! He kept screaming to himself. He had gone in with no higher expectations than twenty percent. He shoots, he scores! Although money was typically the farthest thing from Joe's mind, in his plan an extra two hundred and twenty thousand would go a long way considering his total yearly compensation was only about sixty-eight thousand before taxes. Six hundred and sixty thousand for not a lot of work seemed pretty damn good.

Joe started his car to the multitude of beeps and blurps he had become accustomed to. The sensor on his dash indicating the tracking device beeped as it had since his last meeting with Luke. Stone wanted to continue to play dumb and wait for the perfect opportunity to dislodge it and hand it to Luke. Then the strangest thing started to happen. Instead of the constant beep, beep, beep, it changed to beep—beep beep—beep—beep beep. Stone had to shake his head for a minute. That sound pattern could only mean one thing. There were now two tracking devices on his car. What idiots! Are they afraid the first bug is going to fall off and this is insurance? When I get further into my plan and into Luke's inner circle, I am going to have to tell him what baboons he's got working for him.

Stone didn't have time to worry about it now. He had a lot to do before Luke's guys ambushed the Colombians. Everything had to be perfect, although this should be so easy two fifteen-year-olds could pull it off. Little did he know that organized crime was never that simple.

Stone pulled away from the curb and headed to his office. When he got two blocks away, Luke's same three goombas pulled out in their Lincoln to follow Stone, much more comfortable now that they had a tracking device on Stone's car. They would have to suffer Luke's wrath if Stone were to shake them because now they could follow him anywhere with their GPS device.

Stone watched the idiots pull out two blocks behind him. He thought to himself the least they could do was wait until he was out of sight. With two tracking devices, they should be feeling pretty confident. He was tempted at the next light to dislodge one and throw it in the back of a pickup truck to confuse them and have some fun. It sounded great to him, but he didn't' want to raise any eyebrows with Luke until after they made their first couple of scores. So, off to the office for some reconnaissance work for tomorrow evening.

Eight blocks behind, a nondescript car followed, not one but now two tracking devices on two different vehicles: the prior one on Stone's car and the new one on Luke's guys' car. When watching them on the video screen mounted in the vehicle, it showed equidistant blips traveling north.

Stone had a ton of work to do. He not only had to keep up appearances at work, he also had to make sure everything went well with his own decisive plan. Stone was working on four cases either solely or in conjunction with fellow FBI agents. The one taking the most time was a counterfeit operation run by a high tech group of MIT radicals. They were using a software program combined with a scanning device they had developed on their own. They were producing copies of currency that were virtually undetectable. The uniqueness of their process was that they could duplicate an old bill. The new one was as old and worn looking as the original, which raised very few eyebrows when passed at local department stores.

The fact that they weren't greedy and only copied each bill just once and didn't stay in any one area too long made them almost impossible to catch. Stone was placed on this case, as he was with most of his cases, because of his high tech prowess. Most of Stone's work was therefore white-collar related. High tech extortion from banks, internet commerce crimes, mostly the kind of stuff that requires a chess player's thought process. He was teased by his fellow FBI agents that he could use the paper Chinese finger handcuffs that kids play with to apprehend his perps. Stone's need for a gun was almost nonexistent. His brain was a much better tool for tracking down those people who were just in it for the money and not the power like Luke.

That afternoon Stone pushed around a lot of paper on his desk, not accomplishing much but looking busy. What he did do that was important to him was sit in at a 3:00 p.m. meeting to get updated on everything that was hot at the FBI, kind of like the old roll call on Hill Street Blues, only with more detail.

Stone could hardly contain himself, fidgeting during the whole meeting like he had a bad case of hemorrhoids, only sitting attentively while the FBI Chief Inspector detailed the plan for this evening's surveillance of the cocaine transfer from the *Argo Manchada*. "There will be no intervention on the transfer," bellowed Chief Inspector Donnelly. "I only want two agents, Ned Dimico and Shawn Turner, observing from a distance of no closer than one-half mile with infrared telescopes. We know through our mole Valdez exactly what the plan is. Our only concern is that the two Colombians holding the dope don't make a run for it and become overnight entrepreneurs. Dimico and Turner, just watch them make the pickup, keep in cellular touch with Agents Tim Cooper and Louis Bracket who will be stationed inside the vacant warehouse building across the street from where they intend to spend the night with the dope. They have direct orders not to move from that location until after the perps leave the following morning. They will call ahead to the rendezvous location where we will have a tactical SWAT team in place. Both the SWAT team and Cooper and Bracket are already in place so as not to raise any eyebrows."

Stone hoped that his face didn't show any undue emotion and strain while listening to the plan. There had been a change of plans since last week's meeting. Once the exchange took place, Dimico and Turner were to keep their distance and only make sure that the perps made it to their overnight safe house in the warehouse, then disappear so as not to raise any flags. Now Stone was in a quandary. Call it off or find a way to deal with Cooper and Bracket? "Screw it," Stone thought, "I've worked too hard for too long and although I need to be careful, I can't let this opportunity pass. This is not a high alert surveillance for Cooper and Bracket. They will have been cramped up for almost thirty six hours by the time this all goes down and not expecting anything to happen." It's basically a dimwit watch as Stone's workmates called it.

Stone couldn't wait for the meeting to be over but he had no choice. The last thirty minutes or more of the meeting covered assorted other cases they were working on. Stone hardly heard a word they were saying, his mind turning over and over on how to deal with this new and potentially catastrophic twist.

Chapter 8

Luke, ever the strategist, was taking no chances. He immediately called Luciano "All Business" Caprisi after his meeting with Stone. "AB," "Yeah, boss." "Get over here now, dress in black, and bring enough smokes, food, and drink that you can stuff in a knapsack to pass two days, pronto" and hung up.

"AB" knew never to question and he also knew that of Luke's three Captains he was by far the smartest and most levelheaded. He knew immediately that this had something to do with that Stone guy. He could tell Luke was a little spooked by his presence and, quite frankly, so was he. This whole thing didn't add up.

"AB" was a little older than the rest of the guys. He was in his early fifties. He definitely would have been the heir apparent of the family if he weren't almost ten years older than Luke. As most rulers believed from the time of Caesar they would live forever, very little went into succession planning, especially in the mob, because the school of thought was that once everyone knew who the successor was, things mysteriously happened to the leader. Both Luke and "AB" knew that if anything happened to Luke, "AB" would step right in. He was the logical choice. "AB" hoped and prayed that this never would happen. He was more than happy with his lot in life. He had more than enough money and money-making ability, thanks to Luke, and one-tenth of the stress that Luke had to deal with.

Although "AB" was older, he was no less a menacing figure. At five feet ten inches, under his accountant's façade clothing, was a rock solid individual that had been in weight training since his early twenties. It was hard to believe that, under his baggy, unostentatious clothing and wire-rimmed glasses, there was such a powerhouse. "AB" really preferred to have his men do his dirty work, but on occasion (which is how you build your reputation in this world) he would have to do his own enforcing. "AB," just like in his business practices, wasted very little time and effort. Some of the guys liked to draw out their torture slow and hard. "AB" used his time wisely and didn't waste anything, especially time. When he knew he had a problem he had to deal with, he would just "get down to business." If he had to kill someone, unlike Jerry "Fat Hands" Melasia who would slowly choke someone to death enjoying every second, AB would just grab their head and spin it until he broke off their neck at the top of the spine, an act that would take approximately two-tenths of a second. Quick and concise, that was "AB's"s way.

"AB," after Luke's call, grabbed a knapsack and filled it with fruit, PowerBars, some Parmesan cheese, and four bottles of Gatorade. He stuffed a pair of underwear and socks, two 9 mm guns, a small infrared telescope, two pairs of rubber gloves in case he needed to erase any remnants of his stay wherever Luke may be sending him, and six cigars. "AB" kissed his wife Lucia. What a couple Luciano and Lucia, the masculine and feminine derivative of the same name. Two peas in a pod, both as tight as the day is long. He rubbed his Rottweiler "Machine Gun"'s head. You be a good boy now, "Machine Gun." If anyone comes near Mommy, you bite his head off. He said it in jest but he knew it to be true. "Machine Gun" lived up to his heritage as one mean dog to anyone other than "AB" and Lucia.

Lucia was a perfect mob wife who never asked questions. She just understood the less you knew the better, although she was a little suspect because rarely did Luke send "AB" anywhere overnight. He usually reserved that type of job for his other two goombas. At least that's what she thought of them. No one else in that organization could hold a candle to "AB" except maybe Luke. No, definitely Luke. She had a great respect and trust for him. Luke had that power over people.

"AB" arrived at Lucas through the back door and went discretely to the "deaf room" knowing that was where Luke would want him. He was surprised though to see Luke waiting for him. Usually Luke, by intention, always kept everyone else waiting. He didn't look good, ever since this Stone guy showed up. Nothing you could put your finger on, just that sense you have when you know someone real well.

"AB" let himself into the room and as was his style cut right to the chase. "What's up, boss, and I hope you have a bag of cannolis ready for me if I'm going away for a while."

"I'll give you a fucking cannoli right up your ass." They both chuckled. Then the air got real serious again.

Luke cleared his voice and took a deep drag on his cigar, blew it out, and began. "Stone wants to be our guy on the inside. He told me about this drug deal between the Colombians and those pricks, the Russians. You know I'm not sure which of the pricks I hate worse, the Colombians or the Russians." He thought a second and said, "The Russians and the Colombians provide us with drugs, but they both suck and you can't fucking trust either of them. Nonetheless, if Stone is right, we can fuck them both and hopefully start a war between them and save some of our bullets." Luke went on to describe in detail what Stone had laid out for Luke. "OK, boss, what's my involvement here because I got to tell ya I don't trust this guy and that much hooch would put me behind bars until they take me away in a bag, but you know I'll do whatever you want." "AB," I would never knowingly put you in harm's way. You're too important and I, too, don't know if I trust him, so this is the plan. He expects I'm going to send him my best guys to do this. What I'm going to do is send Sal and Larry. If it's a setup, they'll go down shooting because they're not smart enough to give up and, on the off chance they get caught, they know we'll kill their families if they give us up."

"So, what about me? What do you want me to do?" "You're going to be safely hiding in an abandoned building just waiting and watching with an infrared pair of binoculars, and "AB," I don't give a flying fuck what happens, do not, I repeat, do not leave your post. You're too important. No heroics. Your job is just to watch them. If they fuck up, let them sink. If it's a setup, stay low until the heat cools off and then get the fuck out of Dodge . . . Capisce?" "Capisce. I'll go tell Sal and Larry, boss." "No, I want you there long before anyone gets there if indeed anyone is going to be there. I'll handle Sal and Larry so they understand, especially about our code of silence." "Color me there, boss." Luke watched as "AB" left with thoughts only of pride, love, and trust.

Luke then called for Sal and Larry, both of whom were big on brawn and small on brains. He picked them especially for this job because they were tough and ruthless, didn't talk much, and they were totally loyal to Luke. There was also one high card Luke had to dangle in front of them. They weren't yet "made" official wise guys, so to speak. This was Xanadu for all aspiring thugs. Being "made," especially being made by Luke and being in his family was like winning the lifelong lottery. The family always protects its own and no matter what happened in the line of duty, their families would always be taken care of—kind of an underground pension plan. Luke explained how he wanted this deal handled. Quietly break into the building, kill the three Colombians, and leave a Russian-made 9 mm on the floor to make it look like the

Russians were to blame. Get out quick and leave no other evidence. "No problem, boss," said Sal. "Consider it done." Luke put up a single finger and they both stopped in their tracks. "You boys have worked hard and I'm proud of you. Complete this job and you'll become 'made,' so don't fuck it up!"

They could hardly control their emotions. In their minds, they had already hit the lottery. Larry and Sal said almost in unison, "Don't worry, boss. Consider it done." Little did Luke know that winding the boys up like that was a fatal mistake.

Chapter 9

Stone was wound up like a top as he sped toward the docks with no clue as to how he was going to handle this new situation. What was he going to do with Cooper and Bracket? They obviously were going to see Luke's guys take out the Colombians and most likely would have to act, or, at the very least, it would put Luke squarely back in the FBI's sights. Worse than that, Luke would think Stone was setting him up. Should he call Luke and call it off? What a fucked-up situation. Think and think fast! Then, just like that with the force of a ton of bricks hitting him, he had it. Not only did he figure it out, but he also had everything he needed with him. Luke's a smart guy and I told him to send his best and I'm sure he will. Chances are they'll never even see Luke's guys go in and they'll surely use silencers, so chances are they won't be any wiser. Bracket and Cooper will probably sleep this one off anyway given their orders.

Should anything go wrong though, he had the solution. He had the technology in his car to block radio and cell waves for anything within three hundred yards of his location. Should anything go wrong he could block transmission, which would keep reinforcements away and give him enough time to figure out his next move.

Within minutes and unknown to each other, "AB," Cooper, and Bracket showed up and took their positions. Cooper and Bracket drove under the building directly across from where the Colombians were located. With their car safely hidden under the building, they took up their position inside the abandoned warehouse. Cooper, the responsible one of the two, made sure they had their radio, food, cigarettes, and, most importantly, fold-up chairs so they could be comfortable while settling in for what was supposed to be a boring night. Little did they know.

Stone parked behind an abandoned dumpster in the parking lot just to the left of the building that Cooper and Bracket were hiding in.

Almost simultaneously "AB" walked into the building to the right of Cooper and Bracket. Taking Luke's advice, he was super careful and parked eight blocks away and walked to his location to make sure there was no sign of him. He was already wearing leather gloves knowing he could never be too careful. "AB" found two wooden boxes, one to sit on and one to use as a table. He carefully set out his binoculars, one of his 9 mm's, and some of the food he brought. He figured he might as well grab a bite while the getting was good because he had a real bad feeling about tonight.

The *Argo Manchada* had been in dock for about thirty-six hours now. The cursory customs check almost thirty hours ago was nothing more than a couple of US Custom agents walking around the ship with clipboards checking off boxes on a standard custom's form. Appropriate forms signed and stamped, the ARGO now had clearing to unload its cargo of fruits, vegetables, and exotic woods from South America. Now, with everything unloaded, any and all activity around the ship was quiet.

Louis and Ramone pulled up to the gangway of the ship, Louis in a new black Lexus ESC/100 with the lights off. No need to attract any attention. As they left the car to walk up the gangway, Louis pressed the alarm button to lock the car. It obediently beeped and flashed its lights twice briefly. So much for traveling in stealth Ramone quipped to Louis and they both chuckled. They boarded the ship, instinctively knowing exactly where to go. They turned right, then left, down a flight of stairs, hung another left, and then went into the ship's fairly vast laundry room.

They entered without knocking and both stopped dead in their tracks gasping as they both stared straight down the muzzle of an automatic assault rifle. It was the shock of the barrel that struck them. They held their breath for a split second, then burst out laughing. "Mo Capitan, como esta?"

Captain Rodriguez was a slender, small man with a well-groomed mustache and jet black hair of a man fifteen years younger, but with sea worn skin which gave away all of his fifty years in this world. The captain was standing behind a stainless steel table used to sort laundry behind three duffel bags, so only the top of his head and the muzzle of his automatic rifle were visible. "Louis, Ramone, you're getting soft in your old age. I could have blown both your nuts off before you knew your dicks were gone." Then he laughed the hearty laugh of one who knew he was on the giving side of a practical joke.

"What the fuck are you trying to do? Scare the shit out of us, Captain? It's a good thing we like you or we would have had to kill you." "Ha, ha, ha. Kill me and kill the golden Argo that brings the golden smack that makes us rich, amigos. By the way, you're fucking late and I got a hot mamacita waiting for me. Two weeks at sea is a long time with a bunch of ugly muchachos."

Agents Dimico and Turner were stationed in a warehouse about thirty yards to the right of the *Argo Manchada*. Dimico was the fuck up of the pair, always was, always would be. Turner, on the other hand, was Mr. Responsible—dotted every i and crossed every t. He always ended up doing all the paperwork, because as partners what one does reflects on the other and he couldn't, no wouldn't, allow his name on a report that fuck up Dimico would scribble. It's kind of like when you first get married and you try to be nice and do the laundry, only you purposely fuck it up and make your newlywed's white bra and panty set pink. That's a job you lose forever. But, forgive the pun, I guess it all comes out in the wash because you end up with trash duty because she breaks a nail and draws blood the first time she tries to surprise her newlywed by doing a "man's job." However, it never quite worked that way with Dimico and Turner. There was no give and take, only take with Dimico. He would give nothing and take everything, and Turner knew if he didn't do all the dirty work it wouldn't get done and if it didn't get done, they would both get a black mark on their record and a black mark just wouldn't do for a lifer in the FBI. Turner wanted to be the man one day, whereas Dimico started counting the days to pension the day after he was inducted into the "I."

Here we go again, another usual day at the office thought Dimico as he pored intently, or more exactly, studied the current issue of Penthouse and Playboy while memorizing each curve and dimple of Ms. April, much the same way a Harvard MBA student would be memorizing the case study of the first huge LBO of Phillip Morris Tobacco. Turner calmly said to Dimico, without ever moving from his stance, that the subjects had entered the ship at 10:22 p.m. "Make note of it." Dimico, with as much intentness, didn't so much as move his eyes from his "subjects," nodded obediently, and just said,

"Yea, yea, when I get up, I'll get a pen and write it down. What time did you say it was again?" "10:22, shit for brains—ten fucking twenty-two. Write it down!" "Yea, yea, whatever." But Dimico was only thinking about what had just arrived in his pants.

The captain, as jovial and accommodating as was his nature, knew the fun was over. He had a hot date and he wasn't so sure how long she would wait, although with the money he spent on her while he was in town, he felt pretty secure. "OK, boys, same as always. Check the stuff, call your boss, and have him wire the dineros into my Cayman account." Ramone opened one of the three laundry bags, ruffled through some dirty laundry, and pulled out a bag of pure white smack. He opened his switchblade and slid it into the bag of smack with the deftness of a surgeon, smoothly pulling out the blade with a thin white residue still clinging to it as dust inevitably clings to furniture. Carefully he licked the razor sharp blade. A small smile, one of knowing, crosses his face. "It's goooood! I won't even bother counting it, Captain. You've never shortchanged us and you know if you did, boss man would eat your daughter for breakfast." "Ain't that the truth? He really is a crazy fuck, but I am not a greedy man. I do what I promise and ask only for the fair payment me and the boss man agreed to."

With that, Louis and Ramone picked up the three white duffel bags of pure smack with a little bit of dirty laundry for good measure and started off for some long boring hours of cards in a shitty warehouse building. Louis said, "Ramone, I'm driving, you carry the extra bag." It was amazing how much two million dollars of smack weighed. As they walked out the laundry room door, Captain Rodriguez yelled, "Hey, watch out when you go into the third bag. It has some of my dirty underwear and I had hot tamales last night, mama mia, I near shit myself." The three burst out laughing—probably the last real laughter for Louis and Ramone.

As Louis and Ramone walked down the gangway, Turner got his own hard on of sorts.

Hey, hey, shit for brains. I've got them back in view again heading down the runway to their Lexus at 10:45. No, no, make that 10:46 p.m." Dimico, still totally enthralled with Ms. April, was nodding his head but really not paying attention to anything other than what a great ass Ms. April had. "Hey Turner, do you think they really airbrush these pictures to make them look better? I don't. I just think she was born as perfect as the day is long." "Fuck you, pervert," Turner mumbled as he wrote down the times as he knew he would have to but never taking his eyes off the Colombians until their black Lexus turned the corner and disappeared out of sight. Without ever turning back to look at Dimico whom he despised, he picked up the radio, called Cooper and Bracket and simply said "baby carriage is rolling to the overnight babysitter." "Ten to four, big eyes," came the crackled response. Turner and Dimico were done for the night or should we say Dimico was done as if he ever started. Turner still had an hour's worth of paperwork to get done. His only happy thoughts were once he became boss, he would make Dimico's life miserable.

Louis and Ramone drove away laughing at their encounter with the amiable Captain Rodriguez with the quiet air of confidence knowing now that they had the hooch, they were in control. The golden rule: He with the hooch has control. After Louis turned the corner from the *Argo*, he flipped his lights on, although he could have driven there without them. The moon and stars were out and it was only four or five blocks to the safe house. Well, actually, it was a safe warehouse, but who's counting? A perfect place to hide out before the meeting with the Russians tomorrow morning. All they need to do is show up tomorrow. The big boss and about twelve Colombians will already be there with the Russians if we get texted "A1," we know everything is OK. If we get texted "11 2," it means trouble. Don't bring the hooch, call Jimmy the big boss's second-in–command, and we raid the Russians with a hundred guys and whoever dies, dies. Guaranteed though, there will be more of us and the Russians will go down.

The warehouse is perfect. You can drive in the door on the right of the building and out on the left. Louis has a garage door opener so he doesn't even have to get out if he doesn't want to. There are only two other doors—one in the front which has a dead bolt and one in the back that is completely blocked off. The beauty of the building is that from the outside it looks just like all the other abandoned buildings. No one other than someone who knew would ever look for anyone there.

"AB" was munching on some capicola, cheese and bread when the black Lexus slowly rolled down the deserted street. With one hand on his sandwich, the other deftly and immediately found the infrared binoculars and brought them to his eyes. The black Lexus pulled to the right side of the building and disappeared. He could tell the car entered the building by the reflection of the headlights against the milky wire and glass factory windows of the warehouse. Knowing now that things were now going to get interesting, he wolfed down his sandwich and packed everything back up in his knapsack except his 9 mm and his binoculars just in case a quick escape was necessary.

Cooper and Bracket had just finished baloney and cheese sandwiches that Cooper's wife had made. Louis Bracket was thankful for Tim's wife, not just because she was easy on the eyes even after having two kids but because he was an irresponsible bachelor. His idea of a balanced meal was Fritos and a diet Coke. Susan Cooper always made enough stakeout food for both of them. Although they had just eaten four sandwiches between them, Louis hoped there was more for later because this was supposed to be one of those boring all-nighters where you just watched and recorded in the log every hour or more often if something happens. How wrong could he be? How could he ever have imagined the hell that was going to besiege him, actually not only him, but both of them?

"All right, Tim, log them in, and I'll take the first watch. See if you can get some shut-eye. We're in for a long boring night. Oh, and by the way, what else did that wife of yours pack for food?" "Hey Louis, do you mind if I claim you on my taxes as a dependant this year?" which gave them a good laugh, actually their last.

Sal and Larry had stopped at Rosie's, a local joint where only people with baggage hung out—people with drinking problems, past and present, ditto for drugs; divorced, looking to get divorced, people with social, behavioral problems of every make, shape, and model; and, of course, wise guys galore. Believe it or not though, it was one of the safest bars in town because everyone knew everyone was bad or more screwed up than them. Therefore, everyone pretty much stayed to themselves.

They knew that if Luke caught them drinking before this job, they were in big trouble. That's why they chose Rosie's on the outskirts of town where they wouldn't be noticed as much blending in with the other misfits. As much as they knew they shouldn't be there, they just had to have a shot and a beer to calm down. They were so excited they could literally shit themselves, which is almost what Sal did, barely making it to the john to drop his watery load.

Sal went to the table in the corner where Larry had already got them two Buds and two shots of Jack. "Sal, I already ordered another round. We don't have much time and I'm so hopped up I need to calm down. Sal, can you just fucking believe it, made? You and fucking me! Cheers, my good friend. We've busted a lot of heads for this. Enjoy." Sal and Larry drank both shots, chasing them with two Buds each, and promptly left Rosie's, one of them never to be seen again.

Sal and Larry bounced into Larry's Monte Carlo SS, black of course. What other color car would a self-respecting, soon-to-be made guy drive? Larry thought of this as he drove toward the dock.

He also thought as teenagers do as they pass on to more mature ages, "I need a more self-respecting mode of transportation. A Lincoln Town Car," Larry said aloud. "What the fuck are you talking about," Sal said. The first thing I'm doing once I'm made is buying me a big-ass Lincoln Town Car, black, of course, so you better pick a different color, Sal, if you want one too." "First and secondly, make mine a Cadillac Seville, not some old man Town Car." They laughed and then almost magically they both focused in on the job at hand. It meant everything for them.

"OK, let's go over this one more time," as the nice little buzz settled into Sal's head. "We take that door barrage thing that we stole from the drug guys that time they were having lunch at TGIF's. As I understand it, Larry, it's just two guys in a warehouse. You swing the door barrage and knock the door in. I'll go in, guns blaring, since there should be no one around. We scare the shit out of them and get them to surrender. We act like we're only there to rob them and let them go. They give us the goods in case they got it hid. Then we tell them to lie down on their stomachs so we can tie them up. We then ba-boom, ba-boom pop them in the back of the head with this Russian piece of shit and drop the gun and let the games begin between those jerk-off Russians and asshole Colombians. Perfecto! And if it goes bad, we blow them the fuck off the face of the earth and hope they didn't hide the dope that well." They smiled and high fived each other.

Stone, like any great chess player in his time alone in his car, played out every possible scenario in his head hoping for the best, but fortunately expecting the worst.

Larry and Sal, with all the stealth of a freight train running through a quiet town at two in the morning, pulled to a stop right in front of the building. If Stone could have only seen his own face, he surely would have laughed or possibly cried or maybe even both. Never, in his wildest imagination, did he expect to see two of Luke's guys pulling right up to the front door! What were they going to try to do—act like Jehovah's Witness and just ring the bell to gain entrance? Just as you could be reading his lips mouthing: "What the fuck," "AB" was simultaneously mouthing the same words, following it up with "and the boss wants to make these guys—is he nuts?"

Now "AB" was at full alert. This was going to go down fast and hard and it wasn't going to be pretty. As he subconsciously grasped and tightened his fist around his 9 mm, his eyes were glued to his infrared binoculars, expecting the worst and continually reminding himself of the boss's last words—"Do not get involved and by all means do not be seen!" Bracket had begun to doze off after he was convinced the Colombians were hunkered down for the evening. Cooper, being the more responsible of the two, was taking the first shift. When he saw the black late model car pull up in front of the building, he just had one of those bad feelings and immediately shook Bracket to wake him out of his sleep.

"We've got company and I know we're supposed to lie low, but I don't think this is in the plan. Radio ahead to have backup standing by in case what I think is going to happen, does." Just as Bracket was shaking himself back into reality and reaching for the radio to call in backup, the radio mysteriously spoke to him, "Cooper, Bracket—this is Inspector Stone. I've been tailing two Russians and it looks like they've come to crash the party. I've already called for backup and if anything goes down before they get here, I'm right behind you." Bracket pressed the radio button and spoke back to Stone. "Are you sure they're alone?" "Absolutely." "I had a hunch after our roll call meeting and I've been on these two guys all night." Stone, very comfortable with his radio transmission, because after his initial dismay and Luke's idiot guys pulling up to the front door, immediately jammed their signal so the only people on the frequency was the two of them. Everything that was in place was in place and whatever shit was going to happen was going to happen. Now, eight eyes were all intently watching two half-in-the-wrapper thugs set in motion a chain of events that would change eight lives, some of them permanently.

Since Larry was driving, Sal jumped out of the car almost before it came to a stop with the battering ram in both hands and two pistols stuffed in his belt. Larry jumped out of the car and rolled across the hood of his car (not really giving a shit about his pride and joy now that he had his sights on a new Lincoln), with a pistol in each hand. "AB" was shaking his head, wondering if they thought they were Butch Cassidy and the Sundance Kid.

Meanwhile, inside, Louis and Ramone went into an immediate defensive mode as soon as they heard the rumble of Larry's car come to a screeching halt in front of the building. Throwing over the table they had been playing cards on and drinking Jack Daniels, they cocked their weapons and crouched behind the table in expectation. The expectation didn't take long.

Sal crashed through the door headlong and fell flat on this face with the momentum making him hit the floor and roll. This clumsy move inadvertently probably saved his life since it took him out of the line of fire. Larry came right through the door with both guns blazing, initially shooting in the air until he realized that there were two guns pointing at him from behind a turned over table. His last thoughts were, "Oh shit, I didn't think they would be shooting back." He was able to fire off three rounds from each pistol before being shot first in the chest and then in the head by Louis. Larry, out of sheer luck, with the last of the six bullets he fired, took the top half of Ramone's head right off with blood seemingly exploding everywhere, though not before Ramone set his sights on the sprawling Sal and unloaded two direct hits—one to Sal's shoulder and the other to his lower side sending burning flames through his body.

Cooper and Bracket, knowing backup was on its way, were down the stairs and out the door just as the shooting seemed to be over. They ran to either side of the doorway with guns drawn and held high. Bracket yelled, "FBI, drop your weapons." Cooper carefully showed his badge through the doorway to give credence to their claim.

Ramone, not believing they were FBI, for a minute decided to play possum. Ramone yelled, "Please, FBI, save me. They tried to kill me and my friend is dead." Bracket, knowing that Cooper had a wife and daughter, always went in first since it was a kind of his payback for all the free food. Bracket slowly went in the door. Ramone was moaning, "He shot me in the arm. I can't move it." When Bracket went in the door, Ramone was standing there with one arm in the air and the other hanging down, mostly covered by the turned over table. In the dimly lit room, Bracket had the illusion that Ramone was actually hurt and giving up. Ramone could sense the tension leave Bracket's body and that was when Ramone's right arm came out from behind the table and as precisely as he shot Larry, he shot Bracket dead, exploding his nose in the middle of his face. By now Cooper, who was infinitely more cautious and paranoid than Bracket, was now also caught in the building and the firefight began. Cooper rolled to the right, beyond the moaning and bleeding Sal and forced off nine quick rounds in Ramone's direction, rolling all the time to make a more difficult target. After his last shot, with the deftness of a surgeon, he dropped the spent clip and, with one smooth movement, inserted a full clip from his belt.

Ramone, intently focusing on shooting and killing his last intruder, fired off three shots in between ducking from the oncoming shots. His mistake was to take his eye off the front door. Stone, with a look on his face to match his name, stepped in the doorway, squeezing off two shots into Ramone's heart, killing him instantly.

Stone, scanning the room right to left with his pistol at full alert, yelled to Cooper, "Are you hit?" Cooper shakily replied, "I'm fine, but I think Bracket's . . ." "Yeah, Coop, I don't think he felt a thing, poor bastard." "Stone, where the fuck is the backup? Those lazy fucks. Bracket's dead and I probably would have been too if you hadn't shown up." "They should be right here any minute. Why don't you go outside and wave them down so we don't get shot by accident by some green yahoo?" "Sure, anything to get out of here," Cooper says. "Look out for that greaseball. He's not dead yet." Stone walked over to Sal as Cooper started for the door. As Stone bent down to check on Sal on the floor, he put his finger to his lips so Sal knew through all his pain to shut up as Stone took the Russian revolver out of Sal's belt.

Stone, quiet as a cat, followed Cooper out of the building. Cooper never expected anything until he heard a pop, saw a vision of his loving wife and daughter, then everything went black as the Russian bullet Stone fired entered the back of Cooper's head and exited with an explosion out of the front of his face.

"AB" watched all of this with total amazement. During the whole surreal gun battle, "AB" took his hand off his gun for only a split second, never taking his eyes off the happenings to take his portable scanner out of his knapsack to check for police activity. Surely one of the feds had to radio for backup. Amazingly, nothing was coming over the scanner other than a couple of routine traffic stops.

"AB" watched as Stone started to work quickly, without any hesitation. "AB" thought he looked as though he had been planning this his whole life. First, Stone went in and emerged in what couldn't have been more than a minute later with three laundry bags which he threw into the still running Dead Larry's Monte Carlo. Stone then shut the car off and took the keys to open the truck. He pocketed the keys and then went to retrieve the now very dead Larry. Stone, not wanting to cover himself in blood, dragged Larry to the back of the car. Without too much fanfare, Stone plopped him into the thankfully large trunk and slammed it shut.

"AB's" head, for a guy who was usually calm, cool, and collected, was spinning. He didn't know what to make of all this. His guys stupidly try to take the Colombians. Two feds who aren't supposed to be there show up; one gets killed by a Colombian and then Stone strolls in as cool as a cucumber and kills the remaining Colombian. He then suckers the other fed to leave the building and bang, he pops him right in the back of the head! What kind of cop, never mind cop, person is he? Now, he obviously has found the dope, and he puts it in Larry's car along with Larry. He must be going back in to get Sal so that it still looks as if the Russians are responsible. In the back of his head, he's hearing Luke say, "Under no circumstances are you to get involved." "AB," making up his mind, says aloud, "Sorry, boss, this couldn't have been part of the plan." "AB" grabbed his backpack and hurried down the stairs and outside to go help Stone clean up the mess and score the dope for the boss. Boy, he hoped he was making the right move—because he didn't want to spend the rest of his life in jail; even worse, if Luke got pissed at him, he probably would prefer to be in prison. Stone, working now with the precision of a watchmaker, had the situation scoped out and had decided his plan of action. He had already secured the dope and dead body of Larry. All that was needed to be done now was to plant the Russian pistol, get Sal out of the building, deposit the car, passengers dead or alive and dope into Luke's hands, and find a way to get back and get his car before anyone is the wiser.

When Stone got to Sal, he was moaning in excruciating pain. Thankfully for him, he was falling in and out of consciousness. Stone, still very cautious about not getting blood on himself, although not being successful, picked up Sal under his left arm. Since Sal was apparently shot in his right shoulder and right lower side, he probably had a stomach wound which would be very bad news. Sal was almost useless in helping Stone help him. Stone was basically dragging Sal with Stone's shoulder under Sal's left arm and with Stone's right arm, around Sal's waist, still holding the Russian pistol. Stone's mind was moving a hundred miles a minute not even realizing how pissed he was becoming at Luke for sending these two nitwits for such an important job. Stone was so wrapped up in his thought that when he looked up and saw a menacing black figure standing in the door, it took him by total surprise.

He instinctively went into a defense mode and dropped Sal while bringing up his weapon to shoot whoever had shown up, knowing that it couldn't be someone friendly. "AB" calmly but firmly said, "Stone, relax, I'm here to help. It's me, Luciano—"AB." Put your fucking gun down." "Who?" "AB." "The boss sent me. I wasn't supposed to get involved, but I saw the whole thing and if the boss had any doubts about you, he won't anymore." "How's Sal?" "Not good." He's losing a lot of blood, but I think he'll be OK if we get him to a doctor quick." "Don't worry, the boss has just the right guy." "Stone, don't forget to drop the gun. This ought to keep the Russians, Colombians, and the feds pretty busy for a while."

"AB" and Stone went about the business of loading Sal into Larry's car. Stone planted the gun near the doorway and then had the task of dragging Cooper back into the building. They both agreed that not having a dead fed lying in plain sight would buy them some time. With both of them working together, this took all of two and one half minutes and everything was fine until Stone started to get behind the wheel of Larry's car. "Stone, what the fuck do you think you're doing? Get out of that car!" "AB," look, if you weren't here, I'd be handling this. Now get out of the way before someone else shows up."

"Stone, I'll tell you one more time. I know now that you're cool, but now this is family business." "Well, if I'm not part of the family now, I don't know who is." "You're family when the boss says you're family. You've done good, so for now let me handle it from here and that's final. Capisce?"

Reluctantly, Stone slid out from behind the wheel. "Okay, I'll follow you. My car is just over there," pointing out the building across the street. "Madone! Your head is as hard as your fucking name. You're done for the night. Go home and ditch those clothes, just in case." Stone started to complain but knew it wouldn't do any good.

As they stood in the street, "AB" held out his hand for Stone to shake. As Stone shook "AB"'s hand, to Stone's surprise, "AB" pulled him forward and gave him a short but affectionate hug. "Good work, Stone. Now get the fuck out of here."

Stone, now moving quickly to his car, knew that even in a fairly deserted area such as this, he was pushing his luck. Just as he felt he was walking on air after he left his first meeting with Luke, he again had that feeling. The unexpected hug from "AB" gave him a sense of belonging that clearly was missing from Stone's life.

Chapter 10

Luke decided not to go home because, given what was happening, going home was not an option. His wife and kids would surely pay the price of his anxiousness. Instead, Luke decided to hang out at the restaurant. The non-mob people that were there to eat secretly loved to see him. Luke was a sort of local hero as bad guys sometimes are. Luke knew this and wasn't unhappy with his fame or, more correctly, infamous image. The crowd was thinning now that it was after 1:00 a.m. Non-mob people usually don't linger much after 1:00 a.m. because that's when, if there were any wise guys around, they would start filtering in. It was one thing to be in a public restaurant that just happened to be owned by a mobster and occasionally see him there. It was quite another thing to actually see the underbelly of the crime world start showing up en masse. That was just unsettling for people.

Luke was trying hard not to look unsettled, but was becoming increasingly agitated. He also should have been shitfaced considering he was doing shots of grappa about every ten minutes for the last hour and a half. Surprisingly, he felt as sharp as a tack. He was questioning his decision to send "AB." He was too important to put in harm's way, even though "AB" had explicit orders not to be seen or to get involved. Two more experienced guys might have been a better choice. "Fuck it," he said out loud startling Gino, the bartender, "What's amatta, boss?" "Nothing, Gino, just thinking out loud." Then Luke's cell phone rang.

Chapter 11

Stone got behind the wheel of his car with the obligatory bleeps and blurts of his computer system coming to life. Again, the signal from the tracking devices planted on the underbelly of his car began their pulsating song. Stone was totally confused and thought to himself, "Why didn't "AB" summon the goons assigned to track him to help with the cleanup of the feds and the Colombians?" He realized he was new to all of this, but how dumb could they all be? With an air of disgust, Stone switched off the machinery that indicated the tracking devices on his car and drove away. He figured they're so careless he'd see them in his mirror anyway and what's the difference—they already know where he lives and if Luke has any doubt about his loyalties, now he's got bigger problems.

Stone, always the planner, thought it might do him good to secure himself an alibi. He knew a little bar not too far from there that law enforcement types were known to frequent. Forensic science was good but not exact. They would only be able to pinpoint the time of death to within about forty-five minutes, which would place him at the bar if anything went afoul.

Since cops were the most frequent patrons of the "Owl View Bar and Grill," it tended to stay open later hours than most bars which ran the risk of being shut down or fined if they stayed open later than the blue laws allowed. Although he really wasn't the sociable type, he always ran into someone he knew there and that was all he really needed to do tonight. Stone drove about five blocks, pulled over, and changed into new clothes. Taking "AB's" advice, he placed his old clothes in a green plastic bag, drove another six blocks, found a dumpster behind a *7-Eleven* and threw away his old clothes. He then circled back another three blocks and parked as close to the front of the "Owl View" as he could, not knowing that his tracks had been followed and his very careful disposal of his clothes had all been for naught because they were now sitting in the trunk of a car with enough DNA to light him up like a Christmas tree with ten thousand volts from the electric chair.

Stone went to the more lit part of the "Owl View" at the bar versus the dark tables in the rear of the building near the restrooms. He obviously wanted to be seen. He ordered only a draft beer instead of the three shots lined up with three beer chases he really needed. Lenny, the bartender, had been there for years and was an affable enough kind of guy, tall and slender with a mustache, a pretty much stereotypical bartender. The reason he lasted so long at the "Owl View" was because he possessed the best trait a bartender can have. Speak when spoken to and that was Lenny's motto.

He lived by it, especially in a bar frequented by law enforcement types where what they did, more often than not, should be kept to themselves.

Lenny brought Stone the draft beer and would have been more than happy to just wander down the other end of the bar and just meld in until a patron summoned him.

"Lenny, pretty slow night, huh?" "It was busier earlier, but when it gets to be about an hour before closing, it always slows down. Plus there's nothing big going on since Fabrasia got off. Nothing brings in the boys in blue out like a good trial or an unsolved case for them to play Perry Mason with." "Yeah, I guess there's really nothing big going on now, but God knows in this town it's only a matter of time," Stone was thinking to himself as the words were falling from his mouth. Wait until tomorrow morning when all hell breaks loose between the Russians and the Colombians, not to mention the scorching heat from the feds when they realize two of their own were caught in the crossfire.

Dangerous profession of late being a fed

Lenny waited for an indication that the conversation was going to continue, and when it wasn't forthcoming from Stone, he just turned and wandered down the bar to blend into the surroundings. Stone was happy his whereabouts were confirmed. He would now just quietly finish his beer, have another for good measure, and leave as close to closing time as possible, thereby giving the illusion he had been there for an extended amount of time. Even though he had plenty of cash, he planned to pay by credit card to solidify his presence at the bar if need be.

Stone had just begun to dreamily settle into his second beer after an obligatory thirty-second conversation with Lenny. You never can be too careful. He truly was enjoying his brief time of solitude and the suds were beginning their magic when, out of the shadows of the bar, an obnoxious guy plopped himself beside Stone and said, "Stone buddy, isn't this past your bedtime? Lenny, what are you waiting for? Set me and Stoney up, will ya?"

Chapter 12

Luke jumped a little with the sudden ring of the phone, not enough for anyone to notice, but he did, and worst of all he knew it. He flipped the phone open with one hand. "Yeah?" "AB" was on the other end. "AB," always cool, in his normal tone, knowing full well that both his and Luke's lines were probably being monitored, not because of what was going on tonight, but just as a matter of course, said "I feel like having scrambled eggs." Luke, knowing the phone might be monitored, replied in a just as casual way, "Tonight, 'AB,' or for breakfast tomorrow morning, like when you should eat eggs." "No, Luke, I'm starving now and I can't wait until tomorrow morning." "'AB,' I was ready to go home, but for you anything, you know that. The usual place, my friend?" "Sure, Luke, I'll see you in a few minutes." They hung up. Luke, not wanting to let on to Gino or anyone at the bar that there was a problem, just looked at Gino and said loud enough for Gino and a couple that were still seated behind him lingering over their espresso, "That 'AB,' he's always fucking hungry. He's going to be as big as a house if he doesn't watch what he eats. Gino, I got to go. 'AB' wants to have breakfast. I'll see you tomorrow." "You got it, boss. I'll be here." With that, Luke casually walked toward the stairway, heading down to the basement with no more hop in his step than if he had all week to get there. Once Luke got behind the closed landing toward the basement, he jumped rather than ran three steps at a time to the basement and into the deaf room. He grabbed the scrambled phone and called Marcus Barolo, the "family" doctor, so to speak. Not really Luke's doctor, but the doctor that takes care of the family problems. In reality, he was not really a doctor either, but a veterinarian who flunked out of med school. Not because of lack of intelligence, but because of his love of the ponies and greyhounds, cards, and numbers. Basically, Marcus was a man of chance. Unfortunately for Marcus, his luck ran out after a string of bad bets and no way to pay them off. Luke had two choices, kill him or use him. He chose to use him.

Luke helped him finish school financially and kept close tabs on him, making sure he didn't get into hock with anyone else. Luke's deal with Marcus was that he could bet up to five grand a week. What he won he could keep and what he lost Luke would only collect in services. It seemed like a great deal for Marcus and, given the alternative, it was a phenomenal deal. Marcus had patched many a shallow knife wound, his share of broken bones, and, oh yes, four bullet wounds.

Marcus never complained, never questioned, and most importantly never, never mentioned his arrangement to anyone, not least of which to his wife, Margaret.

The phone woke up Marcus with a start. He groggily answered the phone with "This better be good." "Marcus, my friend, I know it's late, but my friend and I have this insatiable urge to have scrambled eggs. Why don't you wipe the sleep out of your eyes and meet us?" "You know it's funny. I was just dreaming about having some eggs. I really didn't have enough for dinner. Should we meet at the usual place?" "Excellent. I had a feeling you would be hungry." They hung up. Margaret rolled over and said, "Who's that, honey?" "Just a client whose dog just got hit by a car. I need to run. I'll be back for breakfast." "You're too good of a vet, dear. You should probably just let the mutt die. Be careful." And with that she went immediately back to sleep.

Marcus, ever grateful for his lot in life, wasted no time getting dressed and headed for his office. Luke had set Marcus up for just such occasions. It wasn't pretty and as well stocked as, say, South Central's Emergency Room, but it was private and very utilitarian. Marcus had everything he needed for anything short of major surgery, which he really wasn't capable of anyway.

Marcus was more than a little bit nervous as he sped toward his office. Scrambled eggs—shit—scrambled eggs. That was the code for bullet wound. For Marcus, in all of the times he was summoned—let's have a hamburger (knife wound), how about an ice cream (broken bone or bones)—scrambled eggs scared him the worst because he really wasn't a surgeon. He didn't have a team of nurses and the only time he lost one of Luke's guys was from a scrambled egg, or should he say a bullet wound, although that particular bullet had caught Tony Nirello in the neck. By the time he made it to Marcus's office, he had bled out almost half his blood supply and even South Central would have had a bitch of a time saving him. 45 caliber wounds were almost impossible to fix. That wasn't the point, though. The point was that Luke was so pissed that Marcus thought he was going to be the next one to bleed to death from the neck. Marcus was right because that's exactly what Luke had in mind until the better part of reason took hold. Luke, although emotional, knew that Tony was as good as dead when he made it to Marcus's underworld medical table. That didn't mean, though, that Luke didn't seize the opportunity to scare the shit out of Marcus. That he did. Marcus would never think of giving anything but his best effort.

"AB" was waiting when Marcus arrived. Sal had stopped screaming and was just in a continual moan. His coloring had gone to an ash gray. "AB" was concerned for him; the shoulder wound was one thing, but that hole in his side—oh shit, that was bad. The bleeding had slowed down some, but there was enough blood on Larry's velour seats to change the color of over half the front seat.

Marcus took one look at Sal and it was clear that this was not going to be an easy night. To make matters worse, Luke was just pulling in. Marcus briefly thought to himself, "Why couldn't I just buy the occasional scratch ticket? Then I could have been a real doctor with a golf club membership and a BMW." Those thoughts flew out of his head quickly once Luke jumped out of his car to survey the situation and immediately started barking orders. "Marcus, what the fuck are you waiting for? 'AB,' let's move him inside. NOW!" Marcus piped in ever so softly, "We don't want to move him around too much. He's lost a shitload of blood. We don't want to rupture anything else, or we won't have any chance to save him." Luke, not paying attention but hearing every word, carefully slid his arm around Sal's shoulder as "AB" grabbed him from behind his knees. Marcus was already moving to unlock the basement door. "No time to waste," he was thinking. Marcus, now in a zone, was working with the deft touch of the surgeon he should have been. He held the door open for Luke, and "AB" flicked on the lights and directed them to the operating table. Once Sal was lying face up on the table, Marcus put on rubber gloves, not bothering to formally scrub up. There just wasn't time. Marcus, with a very sharp pair of scissors, cut off all Sal's clothes, except his boxers. Luke was going to start barking orders when Marcus, sensing his need to gain control, calmly handed to Luke a very large gauze pad with a blog of antiseptic goop and guided his hand to Sal's shoulder wound. "Luke, this shoulder wound won't cause us too much trouble if we can stop it from bleeding. I need to get on this stomach wound right away or he's dead! Your job is to keep steady pressure on that shoulder wound so it doesn't bleed anymore." Luke, sensing what his place should be, coldly replied, "Right now, you're the boss. You do the right thing and 'AB' and

I will do whatever you need. Just don't lose him." Marcus, head down, knowing he had some semblance of control, started to work. He administered anesthesia, which was kind of fruitless considering Sal was already in shock, heading quickly toward coma.

"'AB,' hold these clamps open. I need to get in here and see what the damage is." Finally, some good news. Although the bullet didn't go straight through, it at least exited out Sal's back, which will require less work locating and removing the bullet. Also less of a chance of lead poisoning later. The bad news was that it did a number on his stomach and nicked his spleen. "This is going to require at least three or four hours of surgery. Settle in, boys, this is going to be a long night."

A long night it was, as Marcus, brilliantly, or as brilliantly as a vet could, operated on Sal's wound. He clamped and sewed, clamped and sewed, and had primarily "AB" as his nurse, dabbing blood and holding clamps to give Marcus more room when needed. Luke pitched in a hand now and then, but only one hand because he took Marcus's order to heart and for over three-and-a-half hours never let off steady pressure on Sal's shoulder. Marcus noticed Luke's commitment to keeping pressure on Sal's shoulder. Marcus probably could have let Luke stop after the first half hour but decided it would be better to keep him focused on the task at hand and keep him from walking around and looking over his shoulder, potentially distracting him. Little did Marcus know that Luke knew exactly what was going on but would rather have been right there watching to make sure the Doc didn't get sloppy. Luke also had a more ulterior motive. He desperately wanted to know what happened and wanted to interrogate "AB." He knew that if he pulled "AB" away and then they were needed, it could be a problem. Therefore, he took the temptation away by staying focused on the challenge at hand.

Chapter 13

"Mak, when did you get here?"

"That's Mako to you, Stoney Boy, not Mak, definitely not Martin, Not M + M, just plain Mako." "Well, then, Martin, you can call me either Joe or Stone but definitely not Stoney Boy."

"OK, Stoney Boy, what ya drinkin'?"

"Once an asshole, always an asshole, thanks, but I was just finishing up, past my bedtime, don't ya know?"

"Ah, come on, I'm even buying. I know ya don't know me that well but ya know me well enough to know I don't offer to buy that often." "Actually, Mak, last time you and I had a couple of beers, you went to the men's room and never came back, sticking me with the bill, asshole!"

"See, Stoney Boy, I truly do owe you a drink."

"Just one, Martin, then I'm off." "Don't call me fucking Martin or I'll leave ya holding the bill again."

"Lenny, girly boy agreed to stay for one more. Set us up with a couple of buds, real buds too, not that piss water girly light beer."

At first Stone didn't want anything to do with the newly arrived asshole. He just wanted to get home to sort everything that happened out in his head. The more, though, that he thought about it, the better it was for his alibi should he need one.

Mako was just the sort of guy you wanted to hate. Everything about him was despicable. He was above average height, but that was about the only thing above average about him. He had a scraggly face, too thin for his build. He dressed like a rerun from a bad seventies detective show. To the best of Stone's knowledge, he was the FBI's most obnoxious and disliked agent in the bureau. Partners, even if they don't always like one another, find some way to compliment each other—good cop, bad cop, or ones very detailed while the other sees the big picture. The only feature Mako brought to his many partnerships was being an asshole, not an asshole in a few cases, but all the time. FBI agents aren't much different than another branches of protective services you need to have at least a little edge in order to survive. Their motto seems to be "Nice guys finish last or, in extreme cases, dead."

Mako, due to his abrasive nature, had been through no less than twelve partners in his illustrious eight-year bureau career. One was killed in the line of duty, and eleven requested partner changes. Oh, and by the way, four of those eleven breakups ended in fistfights, three of them, believe it or not, won by the shaggy Mako, although we must mention, if you haven't already figured out, Mako won by doing something unsavory, dirty, underhanded, or all three at the same time.

Lenny, the bartender, promptly brought over the beers and melted into the woodwork, not wanting to get involved with Mako. Too many times, Mako had come in for a couple and since no one liked him, he ended up talking or in worst cases listening to him for the evening.

"So, Stoney, what ya been up to all night?"

"Oh, you know, a little of this and a little of that," holding up his beer to indicate that he had a few.

"Crazy shit about that Fabrasia guy, huh, we'll probably never get him now he obviously has someone on the inside, wouldn't ya think, Stoney?"

"Apparently, someone or something is on his side."

"Well, someone whacked one of his guys the other night. Maybe, we'll all get lucky and an all-out turf war will happen and all those fucking guineas will be dead! Come on, Stoney, let's drink to that," Mako said as he raised his glass.

Stone, already bored with all of this, lifted his glass about an inch off the bar, then just as unceremoniously dropped it back on the bar.

"Stone, weren't you working on something with those guineas?"

"I'm always working on something. Mako, do we have to talk shop?"

"What else would we talk about? We're FBI guys, Stony, it's what we do."

"Martin, I'm an FBI guy. You haven't had a decent collar in what eight to nine months?"

"Just a little lull in the action. I'm working on something big now, you know, drugs, extortion, murder, all that good stuff."

"Funny, Mak, I haven't seen or heard anything around the office about it."

"All in due time, my friend. Lenny one last round before closing time. So, Stoney, what is it you said you were doing tonight, a little of this and that?"

Chapter 14

Sal's fate now was with his maker. Marcus had done all that his trained veterinarian hands could do. Marcus's work was, by US standards, probably a little bit sloppy but by some third world country's standards pretty excellent. The operation got a little hairy at times because the bullet had made a couple of deviations on the way out. He had lost a lot of blood. The shoulder wound, fortunately for the tired Marcus, was a straightforward puncture wound simply in and out. All it required was some antiseptic and stitching. He wouldn't be using it soon if he lived, and that was still a huge question mark. His shoulder should heal just fine.

Luke made sure with Marcus that if it was OK for him and "AB" to take a minute outside alone. Marcus assured them that there was nothing they could do other than wait anyway. The next ten hours were critical but nothing they could do would make a difference. Luke thanked Marcus for what appeared to be a great job and promised him his gratitude and a special envelope.

Marcus said, "Luke, forget about the envelope for me. I need twenty-four-hour nursing care for him for the next seven to ten days and let's not forget I have a business to run and a life to live."

"Marcus, when you get a minute, call your secretary and have her cancel all your appointments for the day because you're not feeling well. Spend the day with Sal. By then, we will make the appropriate calls and get you the coverage you need . . . Capisce?"

Marcus thought about arguing and realized it would be futile. "Lucky for you I love the ponies. I'll call Jenny at 7:00 a.m. to rearrange my day."

"No, Marcus, lucky I like you and consider you part of my family."

They both smiled knowing smiles at each other. Marcus went back to admiring his work on Sal and Luke went outside to have a moment with Luciano.

Luke and Luciano walked out to the deserted parking lot. Luke looked around to make sure nobody could be listening. Once he was sure they were alone, the floodgates opened up. "'AB,' I specifically fucking told you under no—"

'AB,' with his hands in the air, tried in vain to stop the onslaught. "Luke, Luke, you don't understand." "AB" had been here before, and when the boss wanted to talk, it was better to just let him run his course.

"I fucking told you under no circumstances were you to get involved, and this is how you listen? How you repay my loyalty, my friendship? How long do you think they would put you away if you got pinched with two keys of coke and a dead guy in the trunk?"

"Wait! What? How did you know I had the coke and Larry was dead in the trunk?"

"You may have disobeyed my direct order, Luciano, but once you did, not for a second would I think you would leave any loose ends in particular if one of those loose ends was money."

"How did you know Larry was dead?"

"Sal and Larry were inseparable, so for him not to be in here means he is either dead or pinched. Had he got pinched, you wouldn't have changed coming out of hiding. Am I right?"

"Luke, you're amazing. The kid is in the trunk, the dope is in the back seat, and the front seat is soaked with Sal's blood. I really need to tell you what happened, boss, but first I best stash the dope and ditch the car and the body."

"Are you fucking nuts, 'AB'? Don't you think you took enough chances today? Call the brothers Lucky and Unlucky and have them come in one car. Whatever you do, have Lucky drive Sal's car. Drop the hooch off at our warehouse. Put it in the lead storage container under the floor. Then bring Larry to the sausage plant, grind him into nothing, and have him spread in the ocean. The car needs to be crushed into a 3 × 3 cube and sent to the melter today. No loose ends, capisce?"

"Capisce, boss."

"Go home, clean up, meet me in the deaf room for lunch. Then you can tell me the whole story. And it better be fucking good! Call Lucky on your way home. Get away from here and that car. You did wear gloves, right?"

"Boss, it's me, come on." Luke needed to let "AB" know he was still his man even though he was pissed. He opened his arms and hugged "AB."

"Now, go quick, I'm going to check in on Sal one more time and thank Marcus. I just might have to raise his line of credit after this one. Actually, if Sal lives, I just might have to send Marcus to real medical school."

Luke was feeling a little torn because his rational self was telling him to get as far away as possible. Should law enforcement of any kind show up, even he would have a tough time explaining a freshly operated bullet-ridden wise guy in the basement of a veterinarian and a blood-soaked car with two kilos of hooch. Nonetheless, his loyalty to his men far surpassed his logic many times.

Luke walked in to find Marcus sitting in a chair in the corner. His head in his hands rubbing the top of his head. Luke felt a burning sensation in his gut. That look could only be the look of a doctor who has lost a patient. Marcus, having not heard Luke enter the basement, jumped and let out a yelp when Luke bellowed, "What the FUCK happened to Sal?"

Had Luke taken the time to even look at Sal instead of over Sal to Marcus, he would have noticed that Sal was breathing, not like you or I, but at least he was still converting oxygen to carbon dioxide. "Luke, he's fine . . . well, not fine but still alive, God willing. Luke, I know I'm a fuckup and I'm lucky to live the way I do. Hell, I'm lucky you didn't kill me way back when. That hole I dug was just about big enough to bury me in. I owe you everything and then some. But Luke, I used to only gamble. You keep bringing me bullet holes and you're going to have a fucking alcoholic gambler on your hands. I just don't know how much more I can take. I think I want out." Luke though it best not to interrupt Marcus. Just let him rant a little. He'd been there before. This wasn't the first guy that wanted out once it got hot in the kitchen. Marcus also knew, just like everyone who's ever watched a second-rate mob movie: Once you're in, you're in for life. There ain't no getting out.

"Marcus, come here." Luke stood with his arms out. Marcus walked over a visibly defeated man. His body language said it all—his arms by his side, his shoulders sloped so low it seemed his knuckles were going to be dragging on the ground. He stopped eighteen inches from Luke, his head hung low so as not to make eye contact. Luke put his strong right hand behind Marcus's neck and his left hand on Marcus's right shoulder and pulled him close.

"Marcus, you should be proud of yourself, but not only for today. I truly believe that not even one of the high-priced Jew doctors down at South Central could have done a better job on Sal. You need to be proud about how you have turned your life around. A beautiful wife, family, practice, and, most importantly, you have stayed within your gambling limits which I have set up for you. Marcus, we both know in a different time and place you would have been a great doctor. So life isn't exactly what you want it to be, but whose is? Marcus, you are part of my family, and we are proud of you. Make no mistake, though. There's no retirement from the family. It's lifelong service with, by the way, lifelong benefits . . . or you know the alternative." Marcus, even though it just reiterated his position as a man without options, did like hearing how he was respected and part of Luke's family. In a weird way, he was starting to feel better about himself and his situation. It must have been the stress of the operation and lack of sleep that got the better of him. Then Luke spoke again, "I think you're due a raise, my friend. Your limit has been raised another fifteen hundred dollars a month. Remember, my friend, anytime you want the cash and just stop the betting, the money is yours to do with as you please."

"Thank you, Luke, I apologize. It's just that this was a bitch today and it all just hit me hard after I was done."

"No problem, Marcus, but listen time is running out for me here. I need to make myself scarce. I will call Lucy Storella. She is a former RN and wife of one of my guys. She will babysit Sal for as long as it takes. When she needs to go home and shower or whatever, you'll cover for her because I don't want him alone for a fucking minute, capisce?"

"He may be here a month or more, Luke."

"I don't care if it takes a fucking year. He took two for me and we'll do whatever it takes to get him back earning again."

"I'm with you, boss. Just see if you can get her here quick. I need a shower and Sal's going to need a lot of attention today."

"I'll call now." Luke opened his cell phone, went to the phone book, and found Lucy's number and autodialed it. "Lucy?" "Luke, how are you?" The requisite silence passed as Marcus listened to only one side of the conversation. "Yeah, Lucy, why don't you come down and meet me at the ice cream shop for a big sundae?" Again, there was the requisite silence . . ."No, not an ice cream, a big fat sundae!" One last silence . . ."Right away. Now you know how I am when my sweet tooth gets a craving . . . Ciao, Bella."

"OK, Luke, let me guess. The code for a long convalescence is a big fat sundae? My god, have you thought of everything? What the fuck am I involved in?" They both chuckled, smiled, and hugged again.

On his way out, Luke squeezed Sal's good hand, leaned over, and whispered to Sal for only him to hear; "You done good, Sal. Fight for your life because once you are better, we are going to celebrate when you become "made." You don't worry about anything, my friend. You just rest and get well." Although Sal was heavily medicated, Luke felt a small squeeze back on his hand. Words cannot describe the warm feeling Luke felt deep down inside. Always a sucker for his guys. The moment seemed to last an eternity to him. Luke left abruptly. Time to become scarce.

Chapter 15

No sooner had Luke pulled out of Marcus's Driveway, almost on cue Lucky and his not so affable brother Unlucky came wheeling into the vet's parking lot. What was it with Luke's guys that they all seemed to possess the stealth of a charging bull. The brothers may not have be the smartest characters but they were deathly efficient.

The plan had been set two miles from the vets at Denny's parking lot. "AB" upon leaving Luke rang up Lucky and told him to meet him at Denny's with his brother ASAP and hung up. Lucky knew that especially with "AB," when he called and didn't bother to say hi, bye, or anything else superfluous, that he better get his ass moving, which is exactly what he did. He woke his brother up who was asleep with a mob chick. Guess even Unlucky gets lucky sometimes, especially after dropping big money on a big night out. Lucky used the same pleasantries with his brother that "AB" used with him. The message wasn't received well by Unlucky and even less by his butana who grabbed at him incessantly as he got out of bed to the point where he backhanded her across the temple to make his point that he had to leave. There were rants and raving about what a useless piece of shit he was and that she wouldn't be there when he returned, but sadly they both knew she would.

A mere twenty minutes after the phone call, the rendezvous happened at Denny's. They all stood outside their cars not chancing anything. "AB," true to his nickname, gave only the salient points. "Sal's car is at the vets. Larry's dead body is in the trunk. Unlucky, there are two kilos of smack in the backseat. Take that and put it in Lucky's car, bring it to the warehouse and store it in the floor in the lead box, and then drive to the crusher to meet your brother. Lucky, your job is to get to the sausage plant and meet Benny. I want Larry's body to be ground up so small the fish are going to have a hard time eating it. When that's done, Benny will dispose of the body or what's left of it in the ocean. You then bring the car to Joe's Salvage. He will be waiting with Johnny. You must supervise this process. I want no loose ends! The car must first be crushed and then melted leaving everything in it. Don't take anything out of it except the smack. Capisce?" The only words the brothers spoke to "AB" on that cold morning was capisce in tandem. "One more thing. When you're done, burn your clothes. Don't just throw them away. Nothing to point back and I know I don't need to say this, but one word of any of this to even our guys and Luke will have you with the fish. When he wants the guys to know, he'll tell them himself."

Again, almost as if staged when the brothers pulled out taking a left out of the Denny's, Benny "The Kid" turned in from the other direction and got his orders to meet Lucky at the sausage plant. If only the government or big business could work this efficiently, the world would be a much more organized place.

Lucky and Unlucky wheeled out of Denny's. They didn't understand all of the ramifications of the potential, or should I say inevitable, war between the Colombians and the Russians or what Stone had done because they weren't privy to all that had happened. They did not know, though, that one of their own was most likely badly hurt at the vets. Unlucky had been there himself. He was one of those with stab wounds. Wasn't a real bad wound but one that required the expertise of Marcus. The real unlucky guy was the one that stuck him. He became one of the nineteen strangulation victims of Jerry "Fat Hands" Melazia.

Hey Lucky, what the fuck do you think happened?"

"I don't know, and right now I don't care but we got a big job to do and we better be focused because if either of us gets pinched in the next couple of hours, this will be the last time we'll be free men. So, brother, not one mile an hour over the speed limit, stay in your fucking lane, and don't try to beat any lights. Tonight, when this is all done, we'll have a real drunk fest." Lucky was saying that as they pulled into the vets literally just as Luke's car was out of sight.

The transfer literally took all of thirty-two seconds. Unlucky jumped out of the car almost before it stopped rolling, popping the trunk from the glove box on his way out. As per "AB's" direction, he went right to the backseat of the car and in two quick trips loaded the smack into his brother's trunk. By the time Unlucky was done, Lucky was behind the wheel and had the Monte fired up and ready to go fighting with his urge to floor it and just get this job done. He reminded himself the reason he got nicknamed Lucky was partly because he was legitimately lucky and partly because he thought things out.

Marcus watched all of this from behind the shades in his office, half tempted to call the police and anonymously turning the thugs in and potentially having the call traced back to him ending this horrible charade of a life he was leading. Then a sinister smile formed on his lips. Another fifteen hundred dollars a week, baseball season starting, and you thought Pete Rose had a gambling problem. Marcus left the window to go back down to Sal waiting for Lucy to show up. Now that the Red Sox had beaten the Yankees and conquered the curse of the Bambino, anything was possible.

The brothers, avoiding what could have been an issue with the vet, left cautiously in separate directions to accomplish their deeds. Let's face it. Unlucky had the easiest of all jobs as this was "AB's" design. Lucky, still nervous about his brother's tendency to fuck up even a free lunch, would be nothing but proud of his attention to detail this cool morning. He drove like a sixteen-and-a-half-year-old on his driving license test. Not even once did he violate a traffic ordinance. Unlucky drove straight to the warehouse and, not even having to get out of the car, used the remote garage door opener to open the twelve-foot overhead door in the back of the building.

This was a special and separate door away from the loading docks and the front entrance. This door was used infrequently and only for dubious purposes. Once inside, Unlucky had to move quickly. First, he had to jump out and disarm the alarm. By the way, the alarm didn't ring at anyplace as mundane as an alarm company or even the police station. It rang at Lucas's. There were a number of these places within Luke's empire, and 24/7 there was someone at the restaurant monitoring those alarms. A tripped alarm would bring an army of armed men. Just none of them would have badges, nor would they read you your rights. Once the garage door was shut and the alarm silenced, Unlucky, being extra careful, set the stay alarm in case anyone tried to get in after him, the guys at the shop would immediately come to the rescue.

There was a manual pallet mover in the garage which he used to move some very heavy pallets which were filled with nothing more than junk metal. Just a time deterrent, really. Once the pallets were moved, a faux floor plate was removed and then a digital combination needed to be input to release the heavy lead door helped open by hydraulically operated hinges. The door, although weighing well over a thousand pounds, opened effortlessly. Unlucky made quick work of unloading the smack, shutting and locking the safe, and then moving the pallets back in place. The whole process took less than twenty minutes. Sweating profusely, Unlucky then disarmed the alarm, opened the garage door, and reset the alarm which gave him twenty seconds to leave the premises and shut the door. By now "AB" was at Lucas's monitoring the alarm from safety within the restaurant, very pleased with Unlucky's work so far.

"AB" was rethinking his conversation with Benny "The Kid" Bambino thirty minutes earlier at Denny's right after his meeting with the brothers. "AB's" curtness hasn't always worked in his favor. He sometimes confuses the fact that he has above average intelligence. His directions, thoroughly well thought out and to the point, make sense to him. He doesn't see the need to discuss or explain. That's OK in an exchange between him and Luke because they are intellectually on relatively the same plane. "AB" gets it when it comes down from the top; therefore, he expects the same when he passes it on down. Luke is different in that respect. He, like all great leaders, communicates at the level of the person he is dealing with. They never sense condescendence in the conversation. A trait that more often than not is born and not taught.

Benny, still somewhat sleepy from a late night and a way too early wake-up call from "AB," was not anywhere as alert as the brothers. Benny was mid-fifties, overweight, and unlike most of Luke's guys older than his chronological years. "AB" was just as succinct with Benny as he was with the brothers when they met outside the car. No pleasantries were exchanged; they seldom were at the crack of dawn in Denny's parking lot. "Larry is dead. He's in the back of Sal's car. Lucky will bring him to the sausage shop in less than twenty minutes. You meet him there and get him chopped up so fine he could make it through a spaghetti strainer. Then I want the place steam-cleaned. Unlucky will be there and I want him to help clean up and the three of you take the boat and spread Larry over a large area outside, and I mean outside the harbor and not a word to anyone! Capisce?"

"Yea, boss, where's Sal?"

"Did I ask you to ask me any fucking questions?"

"But, boss."

"Did I fucking ask you to ask me any questions, you fat fuck! Time is wasting, now get the fuck over to the factory."

"Sorry, boss."

"AB" never heard the last word 'cause he was already in his car with the door shut and the car in reverse. "AB" wondered if he should have spoken more to Benny. Did Benny really understand what to do and not only what to say but, more importantly, what not to say? Too late, now he couldn't risk going over to the sausage factory and cell phones were out of the question.

Unlucky's job was done. He drove slightly faster to the sausage factory but not enough to garner any attention. Twenty to life for possession of two keys of smack behind him. Now on to disposing of a dead friend. By the time Unlucky showed up, his brother was helping Benny grind up what was left of Larry's right leg. You see, in Luke's organization, most everyone, if they even have a remote chance of becoming made, is cross-trained in a number of Luke's seemingly legit operations. "Knowing how to operate these businesses is good for the business," he was fond of saying.

Unfortunately Benny "The Kid" had an extended stint at the family's sausage plant. This had two very distinct disadvantages: one, this wasn't the first middle-of-the-night phone call to dispose of a body but the first time it was a friend, which made it even more difficult. The second, and in his mind the far more devastating by-product, so to speak, was for an overweight Italian who loved to eat sausage. His former favorite food will never ever grace his plate again. Unlucky nearly puked at the sight and smell of Larry's transformation to fish food. He sucked it up, though, and went right into working mode running hot water and pine sol into the slop sink. A good cleaning was needed, then a steam, then another good cleaning.

The body after being ground into minced meat was dropped into three extra heavy contractors' green garbage bags doubled up to avoid an untimely tear. Larry was one hundred and eighty pounds, and even though he was ground into a billion pieces, they still added up to one hundred and eighty pounds. Then it was decided that Benny and Lucky would take Benny's car to the marina and to discard Larry. Unlucky would stay and make sure there was no sign of Larry left anywhere on the floor, in the machine, not a molecule. Then he would take Sal's car to Joey's salvage. He knew Joey would be waiting, he always was. This part spooked him, because, should he get stopped in a blood-soaked car, it would be hard to explain. Although this was a slight deviation in the plan, that's why they got paid the big bucks. This was their job now and they had to make it work. The brothers once again parted, Lucky once again gave his brother the safety speech. That all changed when Johnny showed up when they were about to leave and took Sal's car by himself, thus allowing the three to continue their task without delay.

Chapter 16

Driving home from the vet's, Luke's mind was racing. He was having trouble focusing. He thought about the decision to send Sal and Larry. Hindsight is twenty-twenty, but maybe he could have lost someone even more important to his organization. Who knows? He should know, that's who, and regardless, he lost a guy and that bothered him deeply. He thought about Sal and whether or not he was going to live. Marcus, what if he snaps and calls the cops. Fucking "AB" disobeying his direct orders, even though he saved the day. Interspersed through all of these thoughts like the laces of a football, Stone fucking Stone fucking Stone! Luke then violently punched and cracked the dash of the S Class Mercedes. "Fuck, not again!" He'd done it before, so he knew it was going to be another thirty-five hundred dollars to replace it.

All of a sudden, a soothing thought came to his mind. Luke pushed the button on his steering wheel and spoke to his phone "Ter-a-sa."

"Dialing," the car responded.

"Hel . . . hello?" Teresa answered the phone, clearly still asleep. You already know that unlike most wise guys Luke has a true partnership with his wife. Although she never gives orders to the guys, she is an integral part of Luke's empire and, more importantly, she is his guiding light, his calming force, and his voice of reason.

"Teresa, sorry sweetheart, for waking you, but I thought you might like to have breakfast with your husband this morning?"

"Hmm, how about tomorrow breakfast at Tiffany's?"

"Ha Bella, you always make me smile. I'll owe you that one. How about just you and I at Fabrasia's?"

"You sure you don't want me to cook here at home?"

"No, see if Rosa can come a little early to help with the kids so you can get right down to the restaurant. My best guess is that I'm going to have a busy day. I'd prefer to stay close to the farm."

"Give me about an hour and I'll see you there."

"Ciao Bella."

Luke already felt better even though he realized there was much to do and even more to figure out. Teresa knew there were problems after being married to Luke all these years. She didn't need a telegram to announce her husband needed her. Teresa loved all the nice stuff, to be sure. The house, cars, pool, jewelry, and, oh yes, the power. More than that, though, she loved her man. She knew he could be ruthless, but all she really saw was a man that adored and respected her.

What usually took two hours to accomplish for her to leave the house took forty-five minutes. Her man needed her and nothing would stop her from going to his side.

Chapter 17

By the time Stone made it home, he was half drunk, pissed, confused, agitated, and half a dozen other emotions he hadn't even identified yet. The one thing he wasn't at this point was tired. He couldn't have slept if he took a dozen valiums. For an organized thinker and planner, this was sensory overload for him. Now the doubt was creeping in. Did he block Cooper and Bracket's transmission in time? He must have or the place would have been crawling with cops. Did he leave any DNA at the crime scene? He didn't think so but who knows? You only need half a piece of hair now. What a fucking mess! The likely ensuing war between the Russians and the Colombians wasn't an issue. That actually would be a great diversion that would help him with Luke. Give him time to become an integral part of Luke's family, show his loyalty, usefulness, and value. The two dead agents, that's a whole other story. The boss is going to be not only on a rampage having lost four agents in the last three weeks but now the head of the FBI is going to be questioning his boss, Lew Roland's, competency.

Stone, for the first time in a long time, was confused. His recent life leading him toward his new life had been well orchestrated. Tonight was a cluster fuck. He needed to talk to . . . explode at Luke for sending those buffoons. He knew damn right well exploding would be detrimental to his cause. Why, oh why, did he send those dopes? He still doesn't trust me, that's why he would. He will because I have laid down my career, hell, my life, for him three times now. But guys like Luke survive because they are overly cautious, paranoid even. Time, it will take time. Sleep, I need sleep because the shit is going to hit the fan tomorrow—Check . . . today when Damico and Bracket fail to check in and backup is sent to see what happened to them.

Lew Roland, a career FBI guy, although only just fifty years old, was a throwback to the FBI days of old—always in a dark shirt with a bad tie, never in a good mood, and always distant to his men. That was his way of showing who was boss. Lew was anything but incompetent—a social neophyte maybe, but incompetent, never! Make no mistake, he was still stinging from the Fabrasia Fuck up. Worse than even losing one of the biggest collars of his life. Having to visit the wives and families of the fallen agents. Someone was going to pay. Lew already went from A to Z in his mind. The unthinkable was already a trickle in his conscious mind. Did someone from the inside help Fabrasia? God help the poor bastard if that was the case.

Nobody in the world would suspect Stone; he had an exemplary record. Nonetheless, Lew Roland and the department were going to be even more under the microscope. Stone needed to get back in touch with Luke as soon as possible, but that was going to be virtually impossible for the near future . . . unless?

Chapter 18

Teresa showed up at Fabrasia's shortly after Luke. He was waiting for her at his corner table looking out at the front door. Some habits never die. Having your back to the door was one of them. As disturbed and agitated as Luke was when Teresa walked in, his facial expression immediately changed and softened. His love for his wife was evident and unmistakable. Teresa, knowing her man, noticed his smile when she saw him but her connection to her man was equally strong. She saw through the smile to the uneasiness that lay below the surface.

Teresa kissed Luke on both cheeks and then sat down close enough to him to almost sit on his lap. "Babe, thanks for the breakfast invite, you know I always love spending time with you, but this isn't social, is it? What's bothering you, what can I do to help?"

"Carda Mia, you know me too well. Certain things seem to be spiraling out of control. I need your woman's intuition. I have this situation with an outsider and I just don't get it." Luke then proceeded to tell Teresa the whole sequence of events from start to finish, which she already knew in bits and pieces. She never stopped him to ask questions. As close as he was with his top three guys, opening up like this would show weakness, which for Luke was out of the questions. Nor did she need to because Luke was very descriptive and did not leave out a detail.

Just as he was finishing, Jerry "Fat Hands" was delivering breakfast to the table. Jerry, an early riser, was always one of the first guys to arrive at the restaurant. Jerry, never too proud to chip in, was happy to play waiter for the Boss and Mrs. Boss. There was an unusually long silence as they both ate breakfast, when Teresa finally broke the silence. "There's no other solution than I need to meet Stone."

Luke's face flushed immediately, knowing his wife's stubbornness—he tried the calm approach first. "Teresa, out of the question. It is just too dangerous." "Luke," "What is he going to do, knock off a mob boss's wife? Please."

Luke then tried to rationalize. "Teresa, he's a fucking cold-blooded killer who knows what he is capable of. You can't be alone with him."

"Luke, half your fucking mob are cold-blooded killers and you let me be alone with them all the time!" She had a point, but this was different. They at least worked for him. So he went to his third and final approach, which always worked with everyone.

"I said, no, and that's final!" Well, it worked with everyone but Teresa.

"Too fucking bad, sweetheart. Now, eat your breakfast. I will go talk to Stone."

Chapter 19

Since sleep wasn't an option, Stone just showered, shaved, and put on some clean clothes. He proceeded to drink what seemed like a gallon of coffee. The coffee actually helped after the second full pot. If the caffeine wasn't doing the trick, the acid it was producing was clearly focusing his senses. He needed to get to the office before the place got busy. He needed to be in the office when the call came in from the docks when they figured out that Cooper and Bracket had a mishap. He needed to be the first one on the scene. That way, he could make sure that he didn't leave anything behind. More importantly, once he got there, he could contaminate the crime scene with his DNA. That happens all the time—crime scene investigators that are sloppy leave their stuff mixed into samples all the time. The networks' crime programs never show you those blunders.

Stone went down to his car. When he started it up, there were, as usual, all of the obligatory bleeps and blurps, then the unique sound of the tracking device in his car and that someone was close enough to be following him. "Fucking Fabrasia, he sends guys to follow me. I wonder if they are better than the fuck-ups he sent last night." Stone flipped the switch to turn off the receiver. "Fuck 'em. They can tell Luke I went to work early after saving him and his guys from another fucking mess." Stone drove directly to work a lot faster and reckless than normal. The coffee was working its cruel magic. Not enough, though, that his only stop on the way to work would be at Starbucks for a large, or was it Grande coffee, black? Not a chai or a latte or some other sissy drink. Just good old-fashioned high test black.

Stone made it to the office by 7:15 a.m. Not his usual 8:15 a.m. or so, but not early enough to raise eyebrows. Stone didn't even make it to his shitty desk when Mako came strolling down the corridor with a cup of coffee in his fat hands and a shit-eating grin with Dunkin Donut spittle spewing from his mouth as he greeted Stone with a "Long time no see, Buddy." The last person Stone had expected to see was Mako. He always came in late or, by his account, early, because he had to meet with some snitch or some other lame excuse. Stone, already on edge from the caffeine and lack of sleep and enough acid in his stomach to eat through a car bumper, wanted none of this.

"Stoney Boy—little early for you. Did you forget your homework or did you just want to put an apple on Lou's desk?"

"Fuck you—didn't you bust my balls enough last night?"

"Bust your balls—that was just some FBI bonding."

"Mako, are you even human? I'm running on fumes and caffeine. You look like you just had twelve hours of sleep after a two-week vacation."

"Practice, buddy. Just lots of practice. I know most of you guys don't like me, and really, I don't even give a shit, but, Stoney, old boy, of all the guys here, for some reason, I like you best."

"Aren't I just the lucky one?"

"Stoney, my friend, you and I are more alike than you think. We two are opportunists, aren't we?"

Stone, not knowing where this was going, just shut up and listened.

"You'll see—you and me—we're two peas in a pod, asshole buddies outcasts in a society of conformists."

Stone had enough of the metaphors. "Yeah, whatever you say, Mako, whatever you say."

Mako just said, "You'll see, you'll see." He said it eerily and walked away laughing and spitting Dunkin Donuts on the cubicle walls as he walked apparently having no clue—spittle flew from his mouth. Stone dismissed Mako as he always did, as everyone always did, shaking his head, went to his desk, waiting for the shit to hit the fan.

To Stone's surprise, once he got to his desk he actually got into character and started working—finishing paperwork, sending e-mails, and writing "to-do" lists, almost forgetting all else around him. When, as if he was being woken out of a trance, his phone rang. "Ha-ha, hello, Inspector Stone, may I help you?" he said anticipating a call to action for the mishap at the docks.

Instead, an unfamiliar sultry voice on the other end of the line said, "Inspector Stone, you don't know me but my boyfriend . . . aaahhh . . . my married boyfriend works for Luke Fabrasia."

A pregnant pause.

"Yeah."

"Well, the fucker is not only cheating on his wife, he also is cheating on me!"

A pregnant pause.

"Yeah."

Pregnant pause, only this time Stone is thinking how in the hell has Luke come so far without him cleaning up after his shit. This is just unfucking believable!

"Yeah."

"Well, don't you want the info or are you the wrong FBI guy?"

"No, I'm not the wrong guy, but exactly how did you get my name again?"

"I didn't, asshole. I called info, they gave me the main number, and you're the first extension that answered."

Now Stone's saying to himself, "Can I be this lucky?"

"Well, tell me what you know."

"Hey, I might be a mob chic, but I ain't a dope. You want what I have to give, I want a meeting in person in a public place, capisce?"

"If you really have that kind of info, why would you want to meet in a public place?"

"Luke has people everywhere, including in your building, and I said I'm no dope. I want to spill my guts, then be protected, can you guarantee me?"

Pregnant pause, Stone thought, "How many times am I going to have to mop up after this guy?"

Then he thought OK, where can I meet her and then dispose of her if necessary?

"Sure, I'll guarantee your safety. Meet me at the corner of Main and . . ."

"Fuck nuts, I said public . . . meet me at Marty's Diner around the corner from your office in twenty minutes."

"I thought you wanted public, not a place infested with feds."

"Safer than really being in public but not as claustrophobic as being in your office. Either my way or the newspapers. Deal or no deal?"

"Deal. What's your name, and how will I know it's you?"

"Lorraine, and I bet I'll be the only one with the big hair and a short skirt in the place . . . twenty minutes" were the last words he heard before the dial tone of the phone. Could his life get any more fucked up? Stone thought, "Great, this day hasn't even hit 10:00 a.m. and it's already gone to shit!" As he walked out of the building, his thought was, this time Luke can take care of the whore. He has done enough the last couple of weeks. Teresa smiled as she hung up the phone. She knew she put on her best mafia whore voice. Stone would soon be coming out of the Fed building walking toward Marty's diner. She would intercept Stone there.

Chapter 20

Luke sat at his table, swirling around some cold cappuccino staring blindly into his cup as a confused man would do.

Who is Stone? What is his game? Why did "AB" disregard my orders? Who is this Stone? Why did I send two idiots to do this last job?! Who is this Stone? What was I thinking to let my wife, the love of my life, go meet with him alone? *Who the fuck is this guy Stone?!?!??!?!?*

"Jerry, Vene Qua! Come here now!" Fat Hands and also quite a big body came running over as light on his feet for a big man as a jockey a third of his weight.

"Wha . . . what, boss? What's the matter? What do you need me to do?"

Acting more like an underling than the lieutenant that he was. "Call the crew, have them meet me in the deaf room at twelve o'clock. Have lunch ready in the room when we start. I don't want *no* interruptions once we start. Capisce?"

"Sure, boss, but will everyone be clear by then?"

"They better well be. You call them all. I'll be back at twelve noon sharp"

"Deal, boss, no worries."

No worries, right, was Luke's thought as he walked out of the restaurant. A hot shower and shave will help to clear his head, so home he went.

Chapter 21

Teresa sat in her custom Jag Vanden Plas pale green with white interior, a chic car if there ever was one. Teresa sat in the courtroom every day of her husband's trial, she knew. She made it her business to know who everyone in the court was. She knew Stone's face so there was no mistake when she saw him walk around from the back from the Fed building. She thought to herself, he wouldn't dare come out the front entrance and down the stairs. Not if his intention had been clandestine. She was right, and that actually made her feel better about him, that maybe he was for some strange reason on Luke's side. He walked head down as if not to garner any attention. Head down and deliberate as if he was a man on a mission who knew where he was going. Very similar to the way people walk in downtown Manhattan. Ask anyone from New York as soon as you seem lost or unsure of yourself, the creatures come out of the woodwork and take advantage of the unsuspecting and weak. Those New Yorkers who walk with a purpose are typically left alone and just blend into the scenery. That apparently was Stone's intention and good at it he was. So good, actually, that when he walked by Teresa's car, he barely if at all even noticed her presence.

Teresa had already moved to the passenger seat and had opened the window. When Stone was almost at the beginning of the front fender, Teresa said in a voice louder than conversational but clearly lower than a yell, "Stone, get in the driver's seat and drive." Giving credit to Stone where credit was due, in an immediate moment of recognition he understood the ruse played upon him. Almost without missing a step, he swung left around the front of the car and walked to the driver's door in the same manner he had been walking down the street, as if that had been his intention all along: to get behind the wheel of this blatantly feminine automobile and drive away. He no sooner got behind the wheel of Teresa's Jag than Teresa coldly ordered Stone: "Drive."

Chapter 22

The ocean was flat as any Midwestern lake. Good news, since Unlucky was still reeling from no sleep, too much alcohol, and the nasty deed of grinding up a buddy and putting him in garbage bags. Rough seas would have been the end of him. He couldn't have gone two miles out to sea when his phone vibrated in his pocket.

"Yo."

"Unlucky, you, your brother, and call everyone else, the deaf room, twelve noon." Click.

Well, I guess that about says it all, Lucky thought, and pushed the throttle to full so he could complete his task and be back for the big guy by noon. He told his brother, Lucky, the same cryptic directive; five similar calls were delivered by Jerry with the same curtness. Everyone understands business is business—no need for pleasantries, no offense taken.

Chapter 23

Luke, for some unknown reason, went from pacing like a penned animal to an almost Zen-like calmness. Luke wasn't manic; he just had his own way of dealing with issues. Quick sometimes, way too quick with a physical response to insubordination, or his determination of lack of respect. Did he dwell on issues too much or too long? Sure, sometimes. Did he snap to a certain situation some days and no reaction for the same situation on another day? Absolutely. That kept people off guard. Any leader that is totally predictable probably isn't a leader but more of a facilitator. Luke paces and mumbles because that's how he thinks, actually how most Italians think, and when he thinks if he wanted someone to help him, he has no problem asking. That is one area where he is consistent. His Zen state comes from making his mind up.

First of all, Teresa was his partner (welcome to Luke's mob). She was as cunning, smart, tough, and possessed that "oh so important" woman's intuition that men so sorely missed in the DNA dolling-out process at the beginning of time. She may not come back with the answer to who and what this guy was all about, but she would come back with nothing less than the right questions to figure him out. Secondly, it was no secret how devoted Luke was to his wife. Everybody knew fuck with Teresa, and Luke would not stop until the person who committed the offense and everyone remotely connected to the person would suffer untold torture. It happened once, and ten people, nine who had nothing to do with the offense, but were directly or remotely connected to the culprit, paid, and dearly, some with their lives, others with enough terror that they would never be the same. That is the fodder that legends are made of. No, Luke wasn't worried about Teresa and, more importantly, a clear vision path was starting to form. He might not know what to do but he knew what he had to do. Zen was good, he was feeling good, and in a few hours and lunch with the boys a plan would be born.

Then the phone rang. "Prego?"

"Boss, flat as a pancake out here, boat, maybe the Coast Guard, coming up fast." Used to this cell phone cat and mouse, Luke jumped right into character, "How far out there are you?"

"Three miles, give or take."

That's the perfect distance to start chumming for sharks. They like it when you spread it out fast over a large area. It attracts more of them, capisce?"

"Sure, boss, shark for dinner."

"Let me know when you got lines in the water."

Click.

Luke went from Zen to crazy in 3.2 seconds. What would the Coast Guard be doing chasing my boat? Assuming it was the Coast Guard. His mind screamed, "What the fuck was going on?"

Stone tips me off, Stone tips me off on the Russian dope, Stone kills his own feds in cold blood, then he sends the Coast Guard out to trap my guys. No fucking way! No fucking way! Can't be. Who knows? Who knows? The pacing began again.

Lucky yelled, "Boys, grab the bags, hang over the side, slice them up, put a weight in them and drop them next to the boat until most of the shit is gone, and make sure the bag sinks. Pronto! Pronto!"

You could say Luke's guys had many faults, but self-preservation wasn't one of them. They knew that there was a possibility that the boat gaining on them was the Coast Guard, so they went into hyper speed. They cut the bags over the side of the boat so not to put any DNA on the boat. The speed of the boat with the cuts in the bags acted as a great filtering system to empty the bags of Larry's pieces. As each of the three bags were emptied, a five-pound weight was tied to the bag and dropped overboard. This entire process took all of three minutes, and with the five-pound weights tied to the bags (a prerequisite for any good mob boat as well as being fast).

By the time the Coast Guard showed up, there was good old Benny at the controls slowing down, not because lights and sirens were blaring, but because they were slowing down to fish.

The Coast Guard captain spoke over his bullhorn, “United States Coast Guard, this is Captain David Trulane, Patrol Boat IP 12 conducting a random safety search. Captain, can you please show me your documentation?” “No problem, boss, want a salami sandwich?”

Chapter 24

"So your husband sends two dopes to do what should have been a job for his best and now he sends his wife to apologize for him?" Teresa, nobody's fool, and certainly not one to sit idly by while someone is clearly patronizing her, snapped quickly at Stone, "Shut up, you fool. Luke no more needs me to apologize for him than the Pope needs Rosary beads to pray. Besides, Luke's not big on apologies or thank-yous for that matter either. Luke didn't send me here, although he knows I'm with you. Trust me, he's no happier that I'm here than you probably are."

"On the contrary, I'm honored you took the time out of your busy schedule to have a spot of tea with me." Teresa had this immediate eerie feeling almost to the point of the hair on the back of her neck standing at attention. "How do I know you?" Teresa thought she saw a faint blush, not sure though, could just have been the morning light.

Teresa had this unexplained feeling of connection. "Mrs. Fabrasia, we do not know each other. Apparently, you must remember me from your husband's trial. I was there almost every day." Teresa, knowing he was correct, was still having a hard time getting over the feeling, but she pushed it out of her brain. This was not accomplishing what she needed. So as quickly as that feeling infiltrated her brain, she forced it out. She was on a mission and this foolishness was not helping.

"All right, Stone"

"Please call me Joe."

"Sure, whatever, may I be blunt, Joe?"

"Sure, I would expect nothing else from what I know of you."

"What exactly do you know of me?"

Teresa was not liking for a second how she couldn't remain on point. "I know you are a very dedicated and loving wife and mother, and you will and have done anything for your husband."
"Well, you're right, but how do you know that?"

"Mrs. Fabrasia."

"Teresa."

"Teresa, I am in the FBI, and even if I wasn't, you, your husband, and his men are kind of like local folk heroes around here. Kind of like Robin Hood and his Merry Men on steroids. Your love and devotion to each other is the kind of stuff dime store romance books are made of, not your normal mob couple."

"What mob? There is no mob."

"Teresa, look, if nothing else, don't patronize me if on the off chance I knew you were coming and I was wearing a wire. I'm sure you know I've saved your husband's ass by leaking confidential information and by also pulling the trigger myself because he sent two idiots to do a job we were partnering on."

"So, Joe, is that your game? You want to be my husband's partner?"

"Please—I may want to use my inside info to pad my ridiculously low salary but to become partners with Luke Fabrasia. On this short car ride, do I strike you as a complete idiot?"

"Quite frankly, Joe, I'm not sure yet, what you strike me as but I promise you, when I find it out you will be the second to know, after Luke."

"Fair enough"

"So, Joe, what are you up to? Why don't you just tell me so I can go back and tell Luke to either get more involved with you or have one of his guys put a bullet in the back of your head."

Stone knew he was going to like her and he knew she was direct, but wow! "Teresa, in due time it will all make sense, in due time, but in the meantime why don't we all just make some money together?"

"Okay, Stone, take me back. I've heard enough."

"So do we make money or should I be looking over my shoulder?"

"I told you that you'll be the second to know after Luke."

And with that, she said no more and nothing else was discussed as Stone drove back toward the federal building, but a sly smile was exchanged between the two.

Chapter 25

Lucky, always the comedian, came walking out from the cabin of the boat with a Mortadella sandwich in one hand and a fishing rod in the other—the almost comically large sandwich, with a huge bite just ripped right out of it. He spoke or spit, as the case may be, "So are we ready to fish or what?" And with that question mark, there was an even more questioning look on his face as he stared at the five coast guardsmen standing on the back of the boat. "Who are you guys and are you going to be fishing with us because we don't have enough bait for all of you?"

Chapter 26

Luke had gone from being like a caged animal to almost Zen-like calmness, now back to an almost apocalyptic state. His wife was with a known killer, and he was still having trouble dealing with Larry being dead and Sal lying half dead at a vet's office. Now, he gets a call that the Coast Guard is chasing his boat while his guys are disposing of Larry's remains. He knows his guys are good and, believe it or not, they plan for just such occurrences. Not unlike a good company, they have disaster recovery plans, problem solving meetings, and an unwritten but well-memorized policies and procedures. This is not your father's mob. There are lots of things that make Luke successful. Not the least of which is that his guys are programmed, drank the Kool Aid, so to speak. They have all spent the equivalent of weeks in the deaf room talking about how they would handle this situation or that problem. They actually have spent time talking about if they were trying to get rid of something or someone off the boat and they were being chased by the Coast Guard. Hence that was why there were readily available five-pound weights on board and plenty of bleach and ammonia to clean up messes and, of course, fishing gear and bait, so it truly could appear that they might be going fishing. Yes, his rational mind knew they were trained and they should know what to do, but that creeping little bug known as self-doubt can even infiltrate a self-confident zealot like Luke. What was driving him nuts now was the inability to do anything. He thought for about a nanosecond of calling Benny to see what was going on but then thought better of it. He could just see it now: He calls Benny and the head of the Coast Guard picks up the phone and says, "Who is this?" "Oh, Luke Fabrasia, the mob guy?" Probably not a good idea. This is why he spent all that time going over how to handle these situations. Hopefully, everything is overboard and at the bottom of the ocean. He's sure they changed directions enough to hamper the detection of Larry's remains. The boat would be cleaned with bleach before they got boarded. He knows the boat will pass inspection, and he is vigilant about that for just this situation. No reason to give them an opportunity to hang around because there's not a flare onboard or a working radio. He knows his guys are smart enough to play dumb, be polite, and answer only what is asked. Just as he was starting to talk himself into this and refocusing his concerns on his wife, almost on cue in walked the love of his life.

Chapter 27

Stone walked back to his office via the Starbucks on the corner because God knows he hadn't had enough caffeine in his system yet. He needed the diversion to clear his mind. Should he be looking over his shoulder or did the exchange between him and Teresa go well? He turned this around and around in his head. Was he too flip with her in his attempts not to seem too vulnerable? He couldn't tell. The one thing that remained constant in his mind was that he had shown his worth over and over again to Luke, who must see that now. He also must have some room of trust, if he allowed his wife to come meet with him. Stone, at this point, is literally on a different planet, walking on complete cruise control, as he rounded the corner and walked smack into Mako, hot coffee spilling everywhere and in complete unison, "What the fuck!?"

Stone is shocked and mad, although without right, since if there was a wall around the corner, he would have walked into that as readily as he did Mako. Then, of course, there was Mako's reaction as predictable as the sun rising every morning, "Stone, you fucking klutz, are you fucking nuts or what?!" Stone, still irritated from their meeting of the night before, coupled with a lack of sleep, dislike of Mako, and the overall stress of the last couple of days, just snapped and threw his coffee to the ground and went on a verbal tirade on Mako. To Stone's surprise, Mako just stood dumbfounded and listened unfazed, and when it seemed like Stone was done, Mako smiled and said, "I accept your apology," which clearly was the catalyst to set Stone off again. When Mako said, "Hey, boss man sent me to get you two more men down at the docks, Cooper and Bracket, apparently some kind of drug mob thing we—we got to go now." Stone put on his Academy Award stunned face, "No way, what happened? Dead or injured?" "Dead actually, which means we have time for a coffee—how do you take it, hothead?"

Chapter 28

"Luke, honey, any word from the boys?"

"Teresa, you never cease to amaze me. You just went and met with a guy who is a known killer because you want to give me your opinion. I've been worried sick and instead of telling me how things went, you want me to tell you what I got going on? You've got balls, honey, big brass balls, that's why I love ya. Come here, give me a hug, and first tell me what happened. If you tell me he said one thing to upset you, I'll rip his throat out myself."

"No, honey, he didn't say anything to upset me, but I got to tell you I didn't get my normal black and white indication like I normally do. He's good, real good. I got this eerie feeling like I know him, he denied it, but I couldn't shake it. So, anyway, here it is."

"I trust him, and I don't trust him!"

"Teresa, thank you for me allowing you to go risk your life to come back with that earth-shattering assessment that ought to really help." Teresa just chuckled a little, shook her head, and said, "Do you think you could give me a second to finish my thought?"

"Do I have to?" Luke never lost an opportunity to rib Teresa even in stressful times like this. "OK, Luke, let me try to explain I'm not concerned that he's working both sides as what I guess they would call a double agent. I think he has information and wants to share it so we all can make money. He's not setting you up with the FBI if that's what your concern is."

"Teresa, I kind of got that impression when he iced his own guys!" "I misspoke when I said I didn't trust him. I think he's got ulterior motives, and I don't know what they are. I'm hoping it's just that he wants to make a lot of money." "Luke, you know better than anyone, keep your friends close and your enemies closer—my suggestion is keep him on a need-to-know basis. Take his info, make some money, but you personally keep your distance until we get a bead on what his real mission is." Luke stood motionless for a moment pondering his wife's synopsis and recommendation, then just as the sun comes back from hiding behind a cloud, his expression lightened and he grabbed his wife in a waltz-like embrace, danced her around in a couple of mock dancing clichés and kissed her on the cheek. "Cardamia, you have a great way of raising the fog for me, thank you. You helped enough today. Why don't you go home now, check on the kids, then go to the spa for the day?" "Thanks, Luke, maybe I can eat some bonbons as well!" They both got a good laugh. "I need to call Benny to make sure the boat's still floating!" "What?" "I'll explain later tonight, it's complicated," he said with a smile.

Chapter 29

The ride to the docks was quiet, to say the least. Mako tried his best to edge Stone into bantering to no avail, and finally gave up. He figured he'd have plenty of time later, plenty of time. Stone was less ignoring him than going into self-preservation mode. He would only have one chance to contaminate any potential evidence because, even though he had gloves on, and he was super careful in these "CSI" days, a dribble of spit, or a lock of hair was all that was really needed. He'd played it over and over in his head since last night, but he also realized that sleep deprivation could cause the mind to do funny things. He would be less nervous if the locals were there first because they tended to contaminate the site from lack of experience. FBI guys, on the other hand, were good at reconstructing crime scenes, and especially when it was one of their own, every precaution was going to be taken. God, he wished Mako would hurry up. Every minute could cost him. That fucking pussy-whipped Cooper's wife got nervous when he didn't check in every hour and called the office to check on him. Had Stone been in the office instead of with Teresa, he might have got the call.

Stone, Stone fucking Stone, calling all fucking nut jobs called Stone! "What, What?" Stone was in another world daydreaming, deep in thought, maybe even some sort of wide-eyed sleep. "Dude, where are you? You haven't said a word since we got in the car. I know they are feds, but come on, Cooper and Bracket were pains in the ass." Stone knew Mako was fishing for a response. Mako wasn't smart enough to be devious, so a response is what he gave him. "Are you a fucking jerk or what? That could be you and I dead. They are brothers to all of us. We belong to a very special group of elite law enforcement officers. Any one of us could be killed on any given day. Cooper has a family. How could you even say that shit?!" "Hey, Stoney, calm down, you haven't listened to a word I've said since we left—like you were somewhere else. I was just checking to see if you were back. Chill out, buddy boy, speaking of, oh boy, what a fucking zoo." There were lights and a cacophony of activity at the warehouse. Stone's stomach started to turn not because he was squeamish about returning to the scene of his crime to see his handiwork and not out of guilt for what he had done, but simply out of self-preservation. He had come too far with too much on the line. Luke had to trust him now. How could he not after "AB" told him of last night's fiasco? "Let's go, Mako, and see what we can do to help."

"I'm sure we'll be of great assistance, Stoney Boy."

Stone went right into action, walking, actually almost running, to where the massacre had happened, consciously walking around each dead body scene to ensure if he, by chance, had left a bloody footprint, which he could cover up as part of his investigation. He was also committing the #1 mistake by not putting on gloves, just waiting for someone to notice and point it out to him so he could play dumb with a "mea culpa" expression and then put on gloves in front of them all to see just in case he had some prints somewhere. That was until Mako yelled in from the open door of the warehouse, "Hey, Stoney, you know better, put some gloves on, you don't want to contaminate the site, do ya, amateur?" If words could describe what went through Stone's head at that very moment, it wouldn't be printable. Stone's reaction was to coldly turn his back to Mako and theatrically snap on a pair of gloves.

The circus was continuing to grow. First, the locals, then the FBI brass, immediately followed by the press who were looking to get a film clip and interview anything that they could lead with on the six o'clock news. Then the worst of it all, Cooper's wife, showed up. What a nightmare, and there was nobody or anything that was going to keep her behind the crime tape even though no less than four FBI guys tried to contain her. It made for great TV, great for raising the level of emotion and confusion, and great for Stone to make one last search to make sure nothing was out of place.

Cooper's wife, as pathetic as the scene was, created the perfect diversion and time Stone needed to assess what was happening.

There were four forensic guys doing the CSI reconstruction bullshit, three other FBI agents, two guys from the coroners' office who had no choice but to just stand around until they got the word to start packing up the bodies. The only other person there was the chief looking half pale, half pissed, and now visibly shaken, realizing he was going to have to deal with the dead agents' families. With no way out of this one, it comes with the territory, seemingly an everyday occasion lately. As if on cue, Cooper's wife arrived and was dragging four agents behind her as she tried to make her way into the warehouse.

Chief Lew Roland was an uncompromising man of integrity. A man short in stature but large on integrity and inner strength, one of the youngest guys in the FBI to make chief, Chief Lew Roland always knew what he was going to be. As a kid he played sports and, although not always the best, was always the most competitive, always the leader. Actually, if he had to look back on all the sport teams he had played on, he would be hard-pressed not to find a team he wasn't voted captain by his peers. He was liked but never had many close friends. Too much of a straight arrow. Let's face it, kids will be kids and no matter how good they are, they all do bad things from time to time. That is everyone except Lew Roland. Kids liked him and respected him, loved to play sports with him, but seldom hung out with him, because they knew Lew wouldn't stand for shenanigans and would rat them out never thinking he did anything wrong.

This made him a man of contrast, affable yet serious. Friendly, yet a loner. Concerned yet unwavering. In a nutshell, do the right thing, great guy. Break the rules, he'll crush you.

Unlike most people who don't really understand who they are as a person, Lew knew exactly who he was, and compassion was not his strong suit. Seeing Cooper's wife, he knew this was going to be ugly but practical. Lew knew he had to keep it together; he had to keep her together. The cameras where catching all of it. Lew knew what he had to do—get control of the situation.

"Hey, guys, bring Mrs. Cooper in immediately." The agents trying to control Ruth Cooper looked on in stunned belief, knowing that this went entirely against protocol and from Mr. Protocol himself. They were in such disbelief they momentarily froze. *"Now!"* That seemed to get everyone moving.

The agents ducked her under the ropes and led, or should I say, they were dragged into the warehouse. Once in, Lew personally slammed the door shut behind her getting the scene away from the prying cameras. Lew was thinking to himself, "Please, please be done extracting all the evidence from Cooper's body because, if not, we never will after the next two seconds." His only other thought was to keep her away from the other dead bodies so as not to contaminate the rest of the crime scene. Fortunately for the scene, not for Ruth, Cooper's body was the first one in the door. If there was any doubt outside, what had happened was quickly dispelled once Ruth came upon her dead husband. She let out a bloodcurdling scream that Lew was sure was heard all the way to the docks. News cameras were still rolling with the sound fixed on the closed door. Ruth's scream told more of a story than the actual picture could have.

Most would believe that this would have had a profound effect on Stone since he was the catalyst for all of this. Just the contrary, remorse never entered his psyche. As Ruth lay over her dead husband, sobbing uncontrollably, Lew focused on her, dreading what was coming next. Stone casually walked around each and every body except Cooper's, for apparent reasons. He scanned everything for anything and unlike some cheap B movie or the all-too-convenient CSI episode. Nothing visible to the naked eye seemed to be out of place.

All the while Mako, who also seemed unpulsed by Ruth's ranting, stood a yard from Cooper's feet just watching Stone as if he and Stone were the only two people in the building.

After what seemed like an eternity but was probably only three or four minutes, the captain in his most comforting voice touched Ruth's shoulder and said, "Mrs. Cooper, Mrs. Cooper, please, we need you to move away from your husband. We need to collect evidence to help catch the dredges that killed your husband."

For a moment it seemed as if she didn't hear them, then in almost an exorcist fashion she spun her neck around glaring with a laser death look, "Who killed the father of my children? Who killed my husband? Who killed the man I was going to spend the rest of my life with? The most decent man that ever walked the face of the earth?" She kept the death stare on the captain. "Tell me! Tell me now!"

"Mrs. Cooper, at this time we don't know for sure, but it . . ." "What? Don't you dare tell me you don't know. Don't you dare say that to me—what kind of cold-blooded killer did this?" Ruth's glare never left the captain's, and Mako's stare never left Stone's. The captain's never left Ruth's, and everyone else just stared at the ground not waiting to get caught in the middle of this shit storm.

Lew was again apparently shaken by Ruth Cooper, and the truth be told, Lew's strong point was not dealing with women, which is probably why he was still single. "This is all I know for sure, I know apparently there was going to be a drug deal between the Colombians and, we believe, a Russian faction of the underworld. Your husband and his partner apparently tried to stop the deal and got caught in the crossfire, Mrs. Cooper. He acted with tremendous courage, he's a hero, he died trying to keep our streets safe from drugs and drug dealers." This was followed by an eerie silence. "You bet your fucking ass he was a hero! He was a hero to me, our kids, the FBI, the whole fucking world. Now what are you going to do about it?" "I assure you, Mrs. Cooper . . . Ruth, with every fiber in my body, I will get the guys who did this to your husband."

Ruth looked at the captain seemingly processing what he just said. She then scanned the room and all the carnage that it contained. She locked eyes with Stone. Without so much as an acknowledgment of the Captain's guarantee, she walked directly over to Stone who just seconds ago walked around the last dead Colombian. Ruth got so close to Stone's face for a second, it seemed she was going to kiss him. She spoke directly into his ear: "My husband always said you were the smartest guy in the whole building. You promise me you look me in the eye and promise me you will find the bastards that took my kids' father?" Stone, the cool calculated seldom-surprised guy, was momentarily speechless. "Ruth, I never knew he felt." "You promise me, Stone, you will avenge his death?" "Ruth, you know I will."

With that, she turned and headed to the door. She stopped momentarily and bent down and kissed her husband's forehead, whispered something indistinguishable in his ear, got up, and headed to the door. "Mrs. Cooper, this is an ongoing investigation. Please keep all the details private, thank you, and again very sorry for your loss." The words sounded as if someone else was saying them as Captain Roland spoke. Ruth didn't acknowledge the comment.

She threw open the door, the daylight blinding. All that was distinguishable was her silhouette as cameras flashed, and reporters and news crews fought for the best vantage point shouting questions from all angles.

Ruth Cooper walked up to the closest cameraman and reporter and put her hand up to signal silence. Once there was sufficient silence, Ruth Cooper spoke clearly and concisely: "My husband—Tim Cooper and his partner Louis Bracket died as heroes today as they tried to foil a drug deal between a Colombian and a Russian gang. The Russians killed the Colombians, my husband, and his partner. My husband gave his life to keep drugs and criminals off the street. We must now, as a community, not let them die in vain. We must do all in our collective power to eliminate this horrible element from our community."

Captain Roland put his head in his hands knowing what a mistake he had just made. Stone said to himself: "Home run, no, grand slam." Mako just watched as he saw an ever so slight upward curl in Stone's lips, knowing he was fighting back a smile.

Chapter 30

Almost a year had passed since the day at the docks, and as far as Stone was concerned, it was the best year of his life. Ruth Bracket's diatribe at the warehouse accomplished even more than what Stone could have wished for. Immediately, the Colombians started to extract their revenge, not only for their fallen comrades, but for the stolen drugs which they believed the Russians had stolen.

The Russians never had a chance to send a message through an intermediary that they weren't involved. The Colombians by night fall had tracked down three unsuspecting Russian gang members leaving one of their favorite haunts, kidnapping them immediately, and unceremoniously killing one of them and throwing him out onto the street to be found. The other two were tortured in order to get information about the drugs whereabouts and who actually pulled the trigger. The Russians obviously gave them nothing since there was nothing to give. The Colombians, duly impressed with their solidarity at not giving up any information, nonetheless killed the second Russian and dumped him in the street to also be found. The third Russian was apparently the lucky one of sorts anyway. He was beaten to within an inch of his life with four of his digits cut off with pruning shears. He was sent back to send a message that the Colombians wanted back the dope and the guys who killed their guys.

Vladimir Polanski, the head of the Russian Mafia, was not too pleased. Vladimir was just a big, ugly, nasty guy, nowhere the intellectual counterpart of Luke. Vladimir was just a straight ahead kind of guy. He just broke any law he wanted whenever he wanted if it helped his cause. His cause was to steal and sell anything and everything, and to become the most powerful and richest Russian in America.

Vladimir knew he didn't call the hit on the Colombians; his intention was to buy it low and sell it high. Pure business. What he didn't know was if he had a couple of entrepreneurs in his organization, who may have had an opportunity to go into a little side business of their own and not share the wealth with him. Now, that really pissed him off, and in his business you could never be too paranoid. A thief is a thief and expecting the guys to cut him in on every score, although required is seldom reality. It was critical he found out who either in his organization tried to fuck him, or who else outside his group profited at his expense.

Vladimir went on an immediate two-pronged-offensive. He sent out word to see who in his own organization was involved, promising amnesty for not getting permission. In truth, if he found out it was one of his guys, he would have to kill them not to pacify the Colombians but to send a strong message to his organization not to freelance. The second prong of offensive was after he got the message from his severely beaten soldier what the Columbians wanted. He sent back a message that, yes, two of his guys without his permission had committed the offense. He was offering up the two men and the drugs as a peace offering and apology to the Columbians. He communicated to the Columbians a drop location to hand over the money and the drugs. The Columbians clearly were either really naive, or just plain stupid, sending three guys to the scheduled drop location where, immediately upon their arrival, they were blown to bits. War on!

Meanwhile, Luke, who definitely was no one's fool, shipped the hooch to the West Coast, sold it at probably a twenty-five percent discount to a left coast family member.

Captain Roland, who never doubted the Russian–Colombian connection to begin with, had no question about what happened once dead Colombians and Russians started showing up. Not that Lew really minded all the dead Russians and Colombians other than his need to always do the right thing. A part deep down, that he would never admit to, thought that with every dead thug there was one less thug on the street, although another part of him felt uneasy that something else was amiss that he couldn't quite put his finger on.

Lew had the bureau in full lockdown mode focusing solely on the activities of the Russian and Colombian mobs. This meant, for Stone, many things, and all of them great. He pulled off the cover up with no one the wiser. Everything related to Luke was on the back burner as far as the FBI was concerned and continued to be. He was viewed as relatively a good boy in comparison to the Russians and the Colombians.

Sal lived, and although he'd probably never be good as new, he was lucky to be alive. More importantly, to him, he got "made." They must call it "made" because of the difference it makes in your life. Wow, has his life changed for the better? Respect, money, women, if he only knew he should enjoy it while he could.

Super Doctor, or should I say, vet extraordinaire, Marcus, received many thanks from Luke and the boys. He really tried to curb his gambling and get away from Luke's control, but in the end, the allure of the higher line of credit proved to be too much and like every degenerate gambler he continued to bet and lose. His debt to Luke, continuing to increase his debt in servitude, will probably be over by the time he is one hundred and ten years old.

Mike Lewis is a smart Irish kid from South Boston and Raj Kapoor, an Indian transplant, met at MIT in Cambridge, MA. MIT is not a place you get into because you're a dumb kid. You get into MIT because you're brilliant. Just because you're brilliant doesn't mean you're clean—it just means you're brilliant. Mike came from a dirty part of South Boston with an alcoholic father and a sweet mother. Raj came from an upper middle class Indian family with ambition only understood by families that have been repressed. Like all college kids, their dreams were endless. They met in a computer science class, and although different by culture, they were the same in where they saw themselves in the future—rich beyond belief, both willing to take whatever shortcuts it would take to help them to succeed. They became fast friends as freshmen and, by their senior year, best friends for life, and had already decided white collar crime would be their means to an end.

One night, as sophomores drinking heavily in Raj's room, they concocted the plan to use their computer knowledge to devise the ultimate counterfeit technology.

Mike Lewis was the one to bring the plan home first. On the edge of speaking without slurring (probably one beer away), "Raj, what's the problem with counterfeit money?!" "Let me guess . . . it's fucking illegal!" "No, you stupid Indian fuck!" Long pause. Then two sophomoric drunken kids bursting into laughter snorting and all. "No, you stupid Indian fuck!" which initiated another round of uncontrollable laughing and snorting. "The money looks too new! That's why they always get caught." Lewis finished his beer in a long gulp giving Raj time to digest what he said. "What if we made exact duplicates of old one hundred dollar bills? Never using serial numbers more than once and making them look old at the same time?"

Raj, although very drunk, immediately picked up what Mike Lewis was laying down. "Yeah, man, I know how we can copy the money, but how do we make it look old?" The drinking stopped and the scheming began, thus hatching what would become or could become the making of a life full of riches beyond belief.

Chapter 31

Fat Hands Melazia has stomach problems. Not because he eats like shit and drinks too much . . . which he does! Fat Hands has been on edge for over a year now. This whole Stone thing was bothering him, which in turn is bothering his stomach with constant agita. Some of what is bothering him is clear. Some, the unknown stuff, is more bothersome. The part that is clear is that if Luke decides to kill Stone, no doubt Fat Hands will get the call. He knows Luke, and when Luke wants someone big or close to him whacked, he wants it done the old-fashioned way, the Italian way with the life drained out of the person by choking them to death. That has always been Fat Hands' job.

Fat Hands has ended many a life with his bare hands, most at Luke's request and some just for his own edification. This guy Stone was getting in tight with the guys and it surprised Fat Hands. So many of the guys liked him. Why not? Great inside info and everybody was making money. Intuition is why Fat Hands, the quietest one in the group, was next to Luke the most introspective.

He knew at the end of Stone's usefulness, he would be the one called to extinguish the life from Stone's lungs.

Fat Hands knew this as much as he knew he needed more time right now. Killing was always risky, but killing a federal agent was bad, real bad! What bothered Fat Hands, what really was giving the agita, was the fact that he didn't know what Stone's game was. Everyone just assumed he was just a bad and greedy cop. He sensed Luke had a different feeling, had said as much to the guys by telling them not to give any info to Stone, just take the info and give him his cut after the job was done.

Fat Hands, as stated earlier, was no one's fool and even though those fat hands had drained the life out of so many, they also harvested beautiful roses every spring and summer and also were quite deft on a computer keyboard. Today was the day Fat Hands was going to take matters into his own hands, so to speak. Fat Hands sat down at his Sony wireless-aided laptop and typed in *www.google.com*, then typed into the open box: Joe Stone, FBI Investigator, and then hit enter. And so the journey began.

Chapter 32

Mike Lewis and Raj Kapoor, now two years out of MIT, were living the big life of sorts. They really don't work that much, just some piece work, computer programming that gives them both 1099s so not to raise too many eyebrows.

Mike's cover is a little more difficult because he just doesn't look like a rich kid, which is a direct correlation to how he was brought up as a working class kid.

For Raj, on the other hand, it is just the fact that he is Indian, or "foreign" as the local folks around Cambridge and MIT describe the college Euro trash—rich foreign kids whose parents send them to the best schools in the world with allowances that are higher than most hardworking locals earn. Raj could get away with being more ostentatious, but Mike couldn't.

That plan the two drunken sophomores concocted a mere four years ago turned into the most foolproof counterfeiting scam that had ever hit the United States. There were many reasons, the most notable being that the bills always looked old. Actually, if they used their program correctly, they could actually take a less circulated bill and age it to look well worn. Secondly, and most importantly, they devised a long process of chemical engineering to determine what they needed to spray on the paper in order for an iodine pen to react correctly when the bills were checked.

To say these two guys were brilliant would be the understatement of the year. From the drunken inception of the concept till the final finished process took all of three months to develop and their grades never suffered. They made a pact to work on it three hours a day, every day, which they did. One great thing about being brilliant and attending a school like MIT was that resources abounded and no one really questioned you when you were doing any kind of research or experiments. The ability to copy the bills totally took them two nights and, to be honest, any junior in high school with a good laser printer can make a passable copy to the untrained eye. They invariably always get greedy and get caught quicker than a rabbit can disappear down its hole. The real key is developing a process that can fool the store clerks by passing the iodine test and the banks by using legit non sequential serial numbers. Now, these guys aren't criminals in the commonly held belief. They were just a couple of really bright, but lazy and naive kids.

This plan from the start was to only duplicate a particular serial number once, never ever, ever more than once. Secondly, and this stayed true throughout their whole scam, they would never ever, ever let anybody, not anybody, know what they were doing. Loose lips sink ships, as the saying goes.

Hence a little bit of the problem since they had relatively little money to start with was that they could only reproduce so much. In the beginning, it was great, and in a relatively small time they would print up enough money to handle the college essentials: Beer, food, and transportation. The freedom became intoxicating, the ability to buy cool clothes, more expensive beer, college vacations, and they needed to expand their horizons.

That's what led them to their downfall. You see, since their technology was so good and their printers so small, they were literally a mini mobile department of the treasury. With all the brilliant minds that have entered and exited MIT, the infamous group that beat Vegas at their own game was the one that is most remembered. Raj, on a night after a few better beers having seen the movie *Twenty One* with Kevin Spacey, first came up with the idea,. "Why don't we take whatever cash we have, go to Vegas, buy some chips, gamble a little, trade them in, make some new money. Rinse and repeat at six or seven casinos for a week and then leave, come back once a month or so, and really take this to the next level." Mike thought about it for a second and his brilliant mind started doing mathematical gymnastics about how exponentially they could increase their cash position. Eventually they could have enough clean cash to stop and not risk getting caught.

Brilliant idea, except for one little problem. Just like there is always someone bigger, someone stronger, someone wealthier, there also is always someone smarter. Let's face it: the people in

Vegas have seen everything; hell, they invented most of the scams. It wasn't anything big that did them in, just one observant security guy that noticed two guys buying a rather large amount of chips and cashing them in just a little too soon. They tracked back the money, did an initial check, which came out clean. Then they sent the money to Washington who confirmed it was bogus. The problem was initially that these guys were so good that there wasn't a decent print to be found. Secondly, these guys were so clean that they didn't have records, therefore no prints or files anyway. Dead end temporarily, but when the case came to the Captain, he immediately turned it over to Joe Stone because he knew his men and this case had Stone's name written all over it.

Stone would never forget the day because things were really rolling with Luke, and he thought, "Shit, I really don't have time for this," but if his plan would work, he would have to continue to be diligent in his work. Stone took a flight to Vegas and spent a week going from casino to casino. Between half good detective work and half shit ass luck in reviewing tapes, he found the same guys at three different casinos. Once he found them at a particular casino, he then watched the check-in/checkout counter the day before, the day of, and the day after. Then he hit pay dirt at Caesar's. Caught them checking out. The room was registered to Raj Kaptor. Caesar's had no idea why he was looking at the tapes. Since the feds are always for looking for someone or something at the casinos, it was pretty much standard operating procedure.

Stone and Stone alone now had Raj's name and vitals from his credit card used to guarantee payment for the room.

A Caesar's employee put Raj's name on a watch list. Stone went back to the office with little more to show the captain, but a week's worth of expenses and a B.S. story of how he might have a lead from a Russian-run counterfeit gang in Chicago.

Stone had a good feeling about his one. He didn't know why but if it turned out to be a dead end, or an easy collar, he could come up with a good story later and since the boss was driven by arrests and conviction, he would be ultimately happy.

The next day, Stone started digging. By the end of the day, he knew he had something. He had found out that Raj had the same roommate at MIT all four years he was there, and he continued to have the same roommate—Mike Lewis. Both guys were brilliant, graduating with a 3.9 and 3.8, respectively. Once Stone got the info about the two of them being buddies, he decided to check both their bank accounts. He was initially upset that neither one had very large accounts. The amount, though, didn't tell the story; the amount of withdrawals and deposits told a much different story.

Stone could tell they were good, though he just didn't know how good. Another trip to Vegas was needed. Stone fed the boss another line of bullshit and hopped a plane to Vegas, this time with a mission.

Once in Vegas, Stone went back to only two of the casinos that he knew they had scammed before. Sometimes you just get lucky.

He figured smart kids don't want to be too obvious, so chances were they would travel once a month. Stone started exactly a month earlier at Caesar's and saw what he wanted, not letting on to the security guard what he saw. He went back a month earlier, searched back and forth a couple of days, and bingo. He didn't need any more. He went right back the next day, told the boss, thank god, he ran into a dead-end right away, so he came back not wanting to waste anymore of the government's money.

That night, Stone contacted "AB" and requested a special meeting with the boss.

Chapter 33

Mike, in their living room, was sitting on totally awesome movie theater type seats watching the Red Sox beating on the Yankees on their sixty-inch plasma screen TV, all of which they paid for in cash, although all their electronics, furniture, and most of all their other toys were purchased at different stores, not wanting to frequent the same stores too often for fear of calling attention to themselves.

Mike said, "Hey Raj, we have a pretty good stash of cash, now what say we take a little vacation from the printing business?" "I don't know, Mike, I kind of believe we need to strike while the iron is hot. This Vegas thing is hot, man. Remember, for years, we didn't have the resources to print five or six hundred a week, now we almost have the ability to print unlimited amounts of money and keep flipping it for good bills. I'm actually thinking we should print three or four bills with the same serial number and break our rule. We could get three times as much money every trip." "Dude, seriously, that's the rule: no more than one duplicate. Raj, no one's caught us because we haven't become pigs." "Just think, in no time we could have millions." "Yeah, a lot of good that will do us in Leavenworth. Seriously no, absolutely *no!*" "All right, Mike, chill. I won't bring it up again. We're still going to be multi-millionaires, it's just going to take longer." "Raj, I also think we need to change our venue—how about Atlantic City or the Bahamas?" "Chill, we got the Vegas thing going on now. We'll change it up in a little while." "I don't know, man, I don't know why, but my antenna is up."

Apparently, Mike had better intuition than Raj.

Chapter 34

Although Stone and Luke didn't meet often, they never met in public, too many eyeballs. They had met a number of times in the deaf room but they both felt that was getting dangerous as well. A fed frequenting a mob location meant only one of two things: either he was undercover, which Stone wasn't, or he flipped, which Stone had. Luke, although he didn't trust Stone, also knew he wasn't undercover, playing both sides, unless of course the FBI condoned killing their own.

Luke was comfortable meeting Stone in quiet out-of-the-way places. Today's meeting was on an old abandoned railroad track that had been paved over into a bike/running path. Stone would enter from one end and Luke the other end at about two in the afternoon when the track was least used. About a mile in for both of them, there was a little area that they could disappear into and not be noticed by any potential runners or bikers.

Stone showed up first, as he always did. Luke showed up about ten minutes after Stone. Luke, as was his custom with his guys, greeted Stone with a brief hug and cursory kiss on each cheek.

This felt both right and wrong to Luke all at the same time. Luke had learned to tolerate Stone but really had never felt quite right around Stone.

"So, Joe, what do I owe this pleasure or do you just like seeing my smiling face?" This brought a small courteous smile from Stone and a slightly over-the-top laugh from Johnny Gombransi. Luke, Stone, and Johnny all knew it was a kiss ass laugh, although it seemed to bother none of them, especially Johnny. Johnny was loyal to the end even if it meant laughing at not-so-funny jokes. Johnny, as much as he loved and respected Luke, also had a soft spot in his heart for Stone. When Stone contacted Johnny over a year ago, he made Johnny a hero, and Johnny never forgot that. Johnny, like "AB," and particularly Sal, whose life Stone had saved, all had warmed up to Stone. Why not, they were all wealthier having met Stone. This was somewhat to the dismay of Luke who, deep down, wasn't happy with his guys' unconditional acceptance of Stone.

"Luke, you know I can't live without my Luke fix every other month or so." This time, Johnny just cracked a smile, and since Luke was looking at Johnny, that was probably a smart move. "So, Joe, what are you doing with all that scratch you've been making over the last year?" "Just trying to pad my pension." "Another year or two like this one, and it will be a very early retirement!" "I think after I tell you what I asked you here for, we both can retire very early!" "Oh, what do you have for me? First, though, Johnny, pat down Joe to make sure he doesn't have a wire on." "Luke, how fucking stupid do I look? When exactly is this bullshit going to end?" Luke just looked at Johnny. Johnny, when he approached Stone and had Luke to his back, gave Stone a quick roll of the eyes. Stone liked the feeling of belonging that quick roll of eyes gave him. After the quick pat down and Johnny's confirmation to Luke that he was clean, Stone said, "and by the way, if you want to know where I am, feel free to call me anytime. You don't need a tracking device on my car anymore." "Joe, I have no idea what you're talking about, but I am curious how I can retire early." Stone thought, "Yeah, right!"

"Luke, I think I have the proverbial gift that keeps on giving for us." "Stone, please speak English. Where are you going with this?" "I have been put in charge of a counterfeiting case. It was a complete dead end for the Treasury department since there were really no traceable fingerprints. The reason which I will elaborate later is because the guys, or should I call them kids, are clean and have no records, therefore no prints on file. Here is the real kicker: these bills are virtually untraceable and will pass any iodine test!" Luke, clearly interested now, asked "How and Why?" "Sorry, boss, can't answer that yet. My contact at the Treasury department says whatever process they use is brilliant, the bills look used and pass the tests used at the store level. The Treasury department can tell because they have a chemical test that tests the paper, but it's too expensive to be used at the store level and even at most local bank branches." "What's in it for us? What are you thinking?"

"Here's the deal: I know who they are and I have a good idea when they will be in Vegas. I think if you give me a couple of guys, we grab them, make them think it's an FBI sting. Figure out what and how they do it. If it's easy, we take the technology and run with it. Should it be difficult, we'll recruit them and make them unwilling partners." "Stone, I don't know counterfeiting. It is a scary business that crosses a lot of boundaries including the feds." "Got that covered." "True enough, but now you got the treasury guys, secret service, homeland security. Do you think it's worth it?" "I know this, Luke. These are two really bright kids out of MIT. The best I can figure is they have been doing this for a number of years and nobody has been the wiser. All I know is that they have cracked the hardest part of counterfeiting the iodine test. There has got to be more to why they haven't got caught." "So what's the plan, Stone?" "I take three guys to Vegas on Tuesday and we wait until they show up. Then we hang out in their room until they come back and have a little Come To Jesus with them. Then we move them to a safe house which I have to assume you have in Vegas?" Luke was just shaking his head up and down, not agreeing by the way, just acknowledging. There was a long silence when Luke finally spoke. "Then what Stone, kill them too? All this fucking killing is no good for business. It's only a matter of time before it comes back to crawl up our ass!" "I never said that, Luke" "You didn't need to, I think I've come to know your style." "Luke, you're getting." "Shut up, Stone!" Johnny now could tell you how many threads held his sneakers together, not wanting to look up. Johnny had no idea where this was coming from. He knew his boss was uneasy around Stone, but what the fuck? This guy has kept him out of jail, saved one of his guys' lives, and made them a shitload of money. Stone was feeling the same and pissed off, to say the least, but he decide to just keep his cool and let Luke blow off some steam no matter what his reason.

"Luke, I'm not sure what's up, and if I did anything to upset you I'm sorry, but I truly believe this could be the holy grail!" "How about if it turns into holy shit? Huh, have you thought about that?" Stone was now silent, and he was also counting threads on his sneakers, the only difference being that Stone was doing it to temper his anger.

Luke threw a nondescript cell phone to Stone who almost dropped it because of where his eyes were pointed. "I'll call you on this tomorrow or the day after and let you know my decision. After we talk, destroy the phone—you can never be too careful." Then, with that, he abruptly gave Stone the requisite kiss on both cheeks, and just that quickly he turned and started jogging back, yelling to Johnny, "Andiamo!" (let's go!)

Stone said a quick good-bye to Johnny, put his hood up, and started jogging in the opposite direction. Johnny now had to move his slightly overweight body to catch up with the boss. Stone was jogging still, shaking his head in disbelief—sometimes he just didn't get Luke.

Johnny, now huffing and puffing, caught up with Luke who was just powerwalking. "Boss, none of my business, but wasn't you a little hard on Stoney?" "So, he's Stoney now? Just shut the fuck up!" "Boss." That's when Luke turned around and belted Johnny square in the jaw and knocked him right on his ass. Luke, now like a panther going in for the kill, had his knee on Johnny's chest and his left hand securely on Johnny's throat and his right hand cocked and ready to fire down on Johnny's face. At that split second, when Johnny even in his confused and painful state knew it was going to get infinitely more painful, Luke released his grip, got up, and extended his hand out to Johnny to help him up. Johnny, still seeing stars, and now that the shock had passed and pain quickly replacing that feeling, tried to say, "Boss." Luke said, "Shut up." Only this time there was less zip than in the prior "shut up."

Johnny extended his hand to Luke's and Luke pulled him off the ground. "Let's go, you need to pack for a little paid vacation to Vegas."

Chapter 35

Typical day for Mike and Raj: They got up at the crack of 10 a.m., had breakfast, took showers, went off to work for a couple of hours, working code for a locally funded software company. They met for a beer at about 4:00 p.m. in Kendall Square. Their regular watering hole was a sports bar called the "Dropped Ball" in reference to the infamous ball that went through Bill Bucker's legs in the 1986 Pennant championship against the Mets. The story is that the bar's owners originally were going to call the bar "Between the Legs Pub" but the Republic of Cambridge Board of Overseers killed that proposal.

The bar was your typical college town, under-thirty sports bar. Loosely based on an English pub with twenty-eight beers on tap and what seems like one hundred flatscreen TVs showing everything from horseracing to the Bruins and everything in between.

Mike and Raj were at their normal seats at the bar having a couple of seasonal Sam Adams—much better than the Natural Light Beer, which was all they could afford just a few years ago.

"Mike, are you packed for Vegas yet?"

"Raj, glad you mentioned that. I was thinking we should chill for a while."

"Mike, look, we already have non-refundable tickets, and we agreed we would take a small break after this trip.

Dude, don't worry, this trip we'll spend a little more time gambling and having fun instead of just flipping money. Come on, don't freak out on me now." "Dude, I'm not freaking out, I just don't want to fuck up a great thing by getting greedy. I just have a bad feeling. I don't know what it is."

"Look, I agreed we won't do more than one bill, and I promise we will take an extended vacation after this trip." Mike put his fist up for Raj to hit with his fist, indicating that Raj had won this battle and the partners would travel one last time to Vegas before their vacation would start.

Mike was thinking that after this vacation he was going to talk to Raj about moving out of Boston to a place where they could go and start enjoying some of their money, where people wouldn't speculate how they could afford new BMWs and maybe even a nice waterfront condo. Somewhere like Southern California, where everyone seemed to have millions and nobody knows where it came from. Mike seemed to calm down especially when he heard through his daydreaming that Raj had just ordered another Sam Adams. Mike also thought briefly that he might need to consider stopping drinking beer at four o'clock every day.

Chapter 36

Johnny's jaw was starting to swell, and he knew Luke well enough that he wasn't going to apologize, but he could see in Luke's eyes that he didn't have the same anger he did when he snapped at Stone. In Johnny's mind, to be fair, Luke had told him to shut up, and he was the boss. Therefore, as much as his feelings and his jaw were hurt, things were cool with him. That was when Luke surprised him for the second time in less than thirty minutes. "Johnny, mea culpa, I'm sorry I shouldn't have hit you."

"Boss, you told me to shut up, and I didn't—I understand."

"I know you, Johnny, you're a loyal guy, and you know I'm not big on apologies. I shouldn't have hit you. I don't know why that guy makes me so crazy, he's done nothing but help the family since he called you that day. He's killed for us, he got me out of a guaranteed jail sentence, and has made us collectively millions of dollars. I don't understand why and I don't understand why I care."

"Boss, you think maybe it's nothing more than the money?"

"Johnny, wouldn't it be nice if that was all it was . . . Johnny, my friend, my heart tells me it's different."

"Boss, money, information, the fact he's actually pulled the trigger for us more than once, he's as safe as the day is long. Now this counterfeit thing—it could be huge!"

"Johnny, I can't argue the facts, only that I know my heart, which usually never fails me. Anyway, how do you feel about a little vacation to Vegas?"

"I thought you were never going to ask." As he smiled broadly, he immediately felt shooting pains into his brain from his now swollen jaw.

"Couple of things you need to promise me. First, you are under the radar. You contact nobody in the Vegas families, no need for them to think we are moving in on their territory or to even keep an eye on you in case this thing really does turn out to be big. Secondly, I'm going to the send the brothers, no wait, just Lucky, no need to send Unlucky to Vegas, that could just be fucking ugly." They both laughed hard over that one. When they stopped, Luke got real serious, "Johnny, Sal's young and Lucky likes to gamble, and I don't trust Stone. You are my most loyal but let's face it, "You're not my most careful captain. Be smart, my friend, and be in control, va bien?"

"Sie," Johnny gave a little fist pump to Luke. They were quiet for the rest of the ride back to Fabrasia's Restaurant.

Chapter 37

Johnny went back to his high-rise condo with the beautiful view of the river. Who said crime doesn't pay? Johnny packed his best pair of white leather Gucci shoes and two of his shiny sport coats and Sansabelt pants. You really can't buy taste! Johnny got on his phone, called Lucky, and told him to pack light for a week's vacation to Vegas on the boss.

Lucky said to Johnny, "You don't have to ask me twice, Fucking Aye."

Johnny, strictly following the chain of command, told Lucky that he needed to tell Sal to get his shit together to travel with them. You see, the mob is no different than any well-run corporation. There is a clear line of who works for whom. Johnny works for Luke. Luke told Johnny whom he wanted to send. Lucky works for Johnny, so Johnny told Lucky, and Sal works for Lucky, so Lucky gave his orders to Sal. Shit clearly flows downhill, although in this case it was good shit. A trip to Vegas can never be bad, can it?

Lucky, always the curious one, said, "Why the vacation, Johnny?"

"Fuck nut, do you really think we're going on vacation? Don't get me wrong. There will be fun, but we got a little reconnaissance work to do with Stoney."

"Really, what is it, Johnny?"

"Lucky, just pack some shit, pick up Sal, and come get me so we can catch a flight." Lucky did not want to push it too far—he had seen Johnny the night before and his swollen chin. He didn't have to be a brain surgeon to figure out he must have pissed the boss off bad to get popped like that. Nobody told Lucky what happened but Lucky was with Johnny the night before and he was fine and Lucky knew that Johnny and the boss went to see Stone the next morning so two plus two had to equal four. Johnny probably pushed the boss, and since Johnny was bigger than Lucky, he didn't want the same fate to befall his chin.

Lucky called Sal, who had become somewhat manic since his close brush with death. He was clearly happy to be alive and way richer for the wear. Like most people that have a close brush with death, and the person or people who were with them did not survive, Sal had waves of guilt and more so waves of "Why was I the one spared?"

Almost no one noticed this. Sal did a great job of hiding his feelings mostly by driving around his big black Cadillac.

"Sal, boss is sending us to Vegas with Stoney for a little boondoggle."

"A what?!"

"A fucking boondoggle."

"What the fuck is a boondoggle?"

"A little vacation masked as a business trip, you dipshit, what do you live in a fucking cave?"

"Why didn't you just say we needed to go to Vegas and we can have some fun while we're there. Why is it always with the big fucking words with you?" Lucky was about pissing his pants now. If boondoggle is a big word and guys like Sal were the future of this family, they were fucked!

"Get your shit together and come pick me up, then we will go get Johnny and go to the airport." See shit definitely flows downhill. Johnny says to Lucky, "Pick me up" and Lucky says to Sal, "Come pick us both up."

Luke called Stone on the cell he had given him the day before. Stone happened to be on the way into his favorite haunt, the Starbucks near the office. You never can have enough pure caffeine, you know. Stone answered, "Hey Johnny, Lucky and Sal are going to fly out later today. I'm going to put the room in Sal's name since he's not known by any of the local guys in Vegas. I am going to put him up at Caesar's in one of the high roller suites, so there is plenty of room if you need to hold up there for awhile."

"Don't you have a house or condo or something?"

"The local guys know my place, no need to raise eyebrows. Worse come to worst, have Sal rent a house and pay cash."

"OK, I'll let my boss know I've got a hot lead and fly out tomorrow sometime."

"Stone, keep the phone. I think we can get one more call out of it."

With that, Luke hung up the pay phone, walked toward his car, and called Johnny on his cell. "Johnny, book a suite at Caesar's in Sal's name. Come by the restaurant and pick up 30Gs to make sure you've got enough scratch for the room, some gambling, and even a couple of whores if you want."

"Great! Thanks, boss."

"Johnny, low fucking profile or don't bother coming back, and Lucky and Sal are your responsibility!"

"I know, boss, no worries."

Chapter 38

"You know, Mike, we really ought to apply for frequent flyers numbers and get some free travel from all these trips."

"Raj, you never cease to amaze me! We jump through all these hoops—staying at different hotels, flying on different airlines, different airports all so we don't raise eyebrows and you want fucking free travel—are you sure you got into MIT on your grades and not from winning a place out of a crackerjack box?"

"Jesus, Mike, you need a fucking chill pill, I'm just trying to beat the tension a little. You've been wound up like a top for a week now. Chill, buddy, everything's cool. By next week, we can take a long vacation. Like you said, maybe we go to the left coast and look to set up shop there for awhile." "You know, Raj, you can be a real dick sometimes." They both chuckled, Mike a little more uncomfortably but a chuckle nonetheless.

The flight to Vegas was peppered with an awesome amount of drinking, particularly from Mike, who uncharacteristically was mixing in Seven and Sevens between his beers. There's a lot to be said for intuition and Mike was having a bad bout of it. Mike was questioning everything now—the fact that they had long stopped flying coach and started flying first class. He started feeling like there were eyeballs from everyone on the plane on him. He especially was concerned about the big fucking Italian goon sitting across the aisle from him wearing shiny polyester pants and off-white leather Gucci loafers and don't forget that Saturday Night Fever shirt opened four buttons. Does that guy know that people don't dress like that anymore? Not to mention the two goombas he's traveling with, one a little older with basically the same tailor and one a little younger with the dressing sense of a teenager, even though he was well beyond his Welcome Back Cotter days, although he looks like he could have repeated the twelfth grade five or six times.

In a flash of temporary sobriety, could Mike be just imagining all this? Raj, totally clueless, was just enjoying his beer listening to his iPod. Mike wasn't completely off base. The flight attendant was watching him wondering if there was going to be enough alcohol on the plane. They already, between the MIT boys and the I-tailyians, as she pronounced it, had to go to the back of the plane to refill her depleted stash. That's really the only reason she was looking at Mike. She had seen a thousand people before and probably would see a thousand after him that found it necessary to get shitfaced when they flew. Particularly if it was in first class where the booze is free.

Johnny, on the other hand, was looking at Mike for a number of reasons. In Johnny's mind, Mike and Raj looked like a couple of rich kids, flying in first class on Daddy's frequent flyer miles. Johnny, a self-made hoodlum, considered himself a success story—a kid from the streets who started with petty theft, and then as he grew a strong arm, finally an accomplished criminal who had made captain in a prestigious crime family. He didn't like pretty boys and people with bad work habits even though his idea of work didn't coincide with what most people would consider work, but clearly in his mind he worked hard. Mike and Raj struck Johnny as lazy pretty boys whose first priority was to party as evidenced by the amount of booze they had consumed. There was one other thing that caught his attention. The Indian kid was wearing an MIT sweatshirt. Johnny was a hardworking guy. Things never came easy to him; this had to be a coincidence. He thought he remembered and had five or six scotches to help his memory that Stone said the kids were from MIT or did he say Harvard, or was it fucking Yale? Damn, he wished he paid more attention. That, unfortunately, was Johnny's problem. His level of concentration equaled that of a fruit fly. That's when he decided he was going to make his move.

Mike had had what seemed to be a thousand beers and five hundred seven and sevens. He had to piss like a racehorse; he unbuckled to use the rest room. Mike was the type who always buckled in whether he was in a car or a plane. Actually, if he wore suspenders, he would most likely have worn a belt as well. Mike got up to go to the bathroom and while he was on his way, all of ten feet away, he let the flight attendant know he was ready for another beer upon his return. She replied with the requisite, "No problem, sir," then rolled her eyes as soon as he passed.

Sue Ann Darby was not a good flight attendant. She was a great flight attendant—just ask her and she'll tell you. She was first in her class at the Dallas Flight Attendant School she attended. She knew all the rules and regulations. She knew how to disembark a plane in the case of an emergency, she knew when to make a passenger happy, and she also knew how to shut them up or off as the case may be. She was actually contemplating shutting down the Frat boys, not because they were unruly, but because they were running out of booze. That would mean they were headed toward starting trouble. She would also shut off the I-tail-yians for the same reason and the fact that she hated I-tail-yians since she dated one in the eighth grade and he put his hand up her shirt at a school dance. That was then and this is now, and it was her profession and no need to make rash decisions. They only came back to bite you, so until the booze was gone, and if until then no one got too rowdy, let them drink. God knows they will drink plenty when they get to sin city.

Mike went into the toilet holding on with both hands as his dick was hanging over the toilet. He needed to stabilize his head as he tried to piss into the toilet. Sue Ann was getting Mike a beer when Johnny got up from his seat to stand in line for the men's room. The nice thing about First Class is there really never is a line for the men's room unless of course those cheap fucks from coach try to sneak up from coach and use the first class toilet. It probably wouldn't be a good idea that day with Johnny. Remember Johnny worked hard to afford that seat, and no cheap fuck from coach was going to use that toilet. Johnny planned the whole escapade. As Sue Ann was delivering the lazy college boy's beer, he was walking toward the restroom as Mike was just leaving the toilet to stumble the ten feet back to his seat. He clearly wasn't expecting to walk straight into six odd feet of polyester Italian stallion. Nonetheless, there was Johnny, blocking the aisle like a lunar eclipse. Mike walked right into him and stepped on his Gucci loafers.

"What the fuck! Do you know how much those fucking shoes cost?" "Uh-ih what ah-man? So-so-sorry." Now Lucky was on his feet, plane or no plane. Johnny was his boss, and it was his job to protect his boss. The funny thing was Raj and Sal both had iPods in and no fucking clue what was going on.

Johnny had already, before Mike knew what hit him, thrown him back into the men's room or actually half in the men's room, and half hanging out. Johnny understood like a predator animal knew that Mike was weak and he was going to prey on that weakness. Mike took one look at goomba Joe and just started mumbling apologies. Johnny knew he won fully and, remembering Luke's words to keep a low profile, said, after a long pregnant pause and laser eye contact, "No problem, just be more fucking careful next time, college boy, capisce?"

The weird thing about the whole surreal episode was that other than Mike, Johnny, and Lucky, no one really knew exactly what happened. Everyone in first class was preoccupied in either their books or laptops. Sal and Raj were listening to music and Sue Ann was neatly putting Mike's beer on a cocktail napkin between his and Raj's seats.

Johnny just pushed past Mike and went into the bathroom and shut the door, leaving Mike standing dazed and wondering what the hell had just happened and, just as confused, Lucky half in his seat, half out wondering the same.

Lucky, before he sat down, completely made sure he gave Mike the "I'm watching your ass" look. Mike only looked at Lucky for a half second and knew what the look was he was getting. So, not to piss him off as well, he looked immediately, completely, and uncomfortably away.

Johnny, now relieving himself in the bathroom, was smiling. He had no idea who those kids were. If it turned out that they were the one in a million shot of the two they were going to get, all the better. Should they just turn out to be two lazy college rich kids that he just made one of them shit his pants, that was OK as well. He just had a feeling this was going to be a good trip.

Chapter 39

Fat Hands' nimble fingers were flying over his keyboard, his cheater glasses lying on the top of his nose scanning the computer screen for clues. He read one article after another chronicling Stone's stellar FBI career. Had he not known differently and was just an uninvolved party, he would surmise that Stone was on the fast track to becoming inspector general of the FBI.

Fat Hands' uneasiness was continuing to gnaw with every article he read. This was his third session and probably four cumulative hours researching Stone's past. He just couldn't make sense of it. How could someone so good be so evil?

His antennae were up, not because of the articles about all of his arrests, it was Stone's personal background information—it was just too vanilla. Stone apparently came from a single mother background. Mother worked two jobs to support him. Died of breast cancer when he was twenty. Nothing else there, almost like a witness protection dossier. No, couldn't be! But then what?

"Fuck it!" he said out loud and just shut off the computer, closing the cover of the laptop. "I need a drink. Let me think on it, try to figure it out, and get back at it later." His dog looked at him, raised an eyebrow, and then went back to sleep.

Chapter 40

The rest of the flight was uneventful; hardly a glance passed between the Italians and the frat boys. Mike, scared cold sober, just sat staring out the window from the aisle seat. Once the plane landed, Mike waited for the Italians to deplane before he even got out of his seat, which clearly annoyed Raj, who was anxious to hit the tables, have some fun and make, or should I say, print some money.

The routine was always the same—the never had luggage, just some backpacks, very few clothes, a laptop, and some toiletries. In Mike's bag, he had two bottles of Johnson's baby powder; only the baby powder was replaced with two other powders of commonly obtained chemicals that were totally legal. Raj also had a few clothes, since they could easily be bought in Vegas. Raj was also carrying one bottle of baby powder that was also an easily obtainable compound that was legal. In a shampoo bottle of the size that was legal to carry in this post 9/11 world was the active ingredient that, when mixed with the three powders and water in a prescribed quantity, could be placed in a one dollar and seventy-nine cent empty spray bottle.

Since they were both still only twenty-four, they couldn't rent a car, which was a total pain in the ass. They would grab a taxi or limo at the airport, check in the hotel grab a taxi or limo to Staples and buy a small HP color printer and some expensive paper. Buy an empty spray bottle and some extra ink. They would then put the printer in a large canvas shopping bag, the kind you get at the supermarket now, only larger. They would go back to the hotel looking like they just went shopping and would go back to the room and leave the printer in the bag until it was time to hook it up to Mike's laptop.

Unfortunately for Mike and Raj today, Raj had decided that since this was going to be their last hurrah for awhile he had decided to go big. They were staying at the Rio, and Raj had ordered a limo from the Rio to pick them up.

Mike and Raj went right out to the limo pickup area. Johnny, not completely heeding Luke's advice, had also ordered a private limo to take them to Caesar's. Johnny, having the patience of an ant and wanting a smoke bad, told Lucky to get his luggage in baggage claim and meet him at the limo stand.

Johnny was already at the limo area holding up a large cement column about halfway through a Marlboro. When the frat boys exited the terminal, they beelined it toward a guy holding up a sign that read Mr. Kaptor. The limo had the Rio Hotel written across the side with a decal the length of the limo with Rio girls half naked inviting you to come to the Rio.

Raj jumped in the limo first with Mike right behind him. Just as the limo driver was closing the door swallowing the guys up behind blacked-out windows, Mike saw Johnny leaning against the cement column smoking a cigarette.

As the limo pulled away, some unknown force grabbed hold of Mike and he pressed the button to lower the blacked-out window. He stuck his head out the window, flipped the bird to Johnny and yelled, "Your fucking shoes are ugly, you stupid fucking guinea!" To which Johnny just smiled and flicked his cigarette in the general direction of the departing limo. He whispered to himself, "I'll show you, a fucking ugly shoe, I know where you live now."

Mike got his body back in the limo and shut the window now laughing hysterically. "What the fuck was that all about, you dipshit?" "Nothing—I'll explain later over a beer."

Chapter 41

"Hey Stoney Boy, hear you're working on a funny money deal. Think you could keep a couple of bags of hundreds for me if you catch them?" "That would be against official procedure, Mak," Stone said with the deadpan delivery of a comedic duo. "What's a few bags of hundreds between friends?" "Nothing except a career and some jail time" "Come on, Stoney, you know better than anybody that there is a fine line between us and them." An uncharacteristic flash of panic ran through Stone's stomach right up to the short hairs on the back of his neck. "No, Mak, I don't. What exactly do you mean?" "Come on, Stoney, the local cops they pull over some high school kids who are drinking and smoking pot. What do they do? If the kids aren't too fucked up they take the beer and pot, scare the shit out of them, take their shit, give them a pat on the wrist, and let them go. Then everyone wins, the kids get not to be arrested and the cops get party supplies for the weekend, happens every day and you know it. The more resourceful guys make a drug bust, skim some cash and drugs for their own recreational use, and still get a collar. What do you think the guys that get pinched are going to say? There was more cash and more drugs, which make them look like bigger dealers? Come on, Stoney, again everyone wins—I personally know you're not that naive." Again, that nauseous feeling sailed through his body. To quote myself, Mak, again, "No, I don't know what you're saying." Stone was now hoping his high school acting class was paying off that Mak wasn't picking up signs of his nervousness. Stone had the right to be nervous because Mak had decided that now was the time to turn up the heat. He knew Stone's game, even though everyone else at the bureau thought Stone was the epitome of FBI righteousness.

"Stoney, the difference between the local guys and us is we have more opportunity. Let's just call it better selection and the shit pay that we get, the higher risk factors we face—it's only fair we supplement our payroll." Then, Mak looked right at Stone and not with his normal asshole look, but with a serious-as-a-heart-attack look, "Stoney, I know, Stoney." With that, he spun with the deftness of a ballerina and walked away. Stone felt very faint. Stone sat still for a very long moment wondering just what he knew. Then, almost robotically, he cleared his desk, put his shit in his briefcase, and left directly for the airport. His only deviation was for an extra large quadruple Starbucks espresso.

Mak walked over to the assignment board and saw that Stone was headed to Vegas for the counterfeiting case. He put his best sad face on, went into the boss's office. "Boss, death in the family, I need some personal days." "Sorry to hear that, Mak.Who was it?

Sudden? I didn't realize you had a sick family member." "No, boss. Uncle on my mom's side, kind of like my second father. Heart attack last night." Mak, really overacting, actually had a tear in his eye. "No problem, Mak, take all the time you need" "Thanks, boss, I'll check in a couple of days, let you know when I can come back."

Again, he spun like a ballerina with his eyes drying up almost immediately, with a smile creeping into the corners of his mouth.

Chapter 42

"Teresa, how are you feeling tonight, my love?" "Luke, don't give me that bullshit. You know you're talking to me, right?" "Bella, what do you mean?" "Luke, seriously, it's me, you can't bullshit me. I know something is bothering you, and furthermore, I know who and what is bothering you. It's Stone, so stop trying to be a big tough guy." Luke's tone changed, but let's not forget it's Teresa he's talking to, so it changed to only slightly annoyed. "He is the furthest thing from my mind. Dinner with you is all I'm thinking about, so what's for dinner?" "Pasta, and you're full of shit. Luke, you can't let this bring you down, you're going to get an ulcer!" "Sweetheart, you know there's something about him that makes me uncomfortable." "But why, Luke? You know I have good intuition, and although he's not my favorite person, I've come to the conclusion that he's harmless." "Harmless! For Christ's sake!" "Luke, I mean harmless to the family. He clearly has some attachment issues, and now that he's attached himself to our family, I think he's fine, plus look at all the money he's made us, not to mention keeping your fine ass out of jail."

"Teresa, Johnny, Lucky, and Sal, as we speak, are in Vegas with Stone. According to Stone, he is on to these two brilliant kids who have figured out some foolproof way to counterfeit money that can pass the iodine test. He thinks it's so big it could make everything else we're doing look small." "Yea, so . . .""Teresa, this crosses lots of lines. It could put us into the sights of not only local guys and the FBI, but the CIA, Secret Service, Treasury, even Homeland Security." "I don't understand, Luke, what the problem is. No one says you have to do it. Your guys are there, they will figure it out, let you know, and then you can decide what to do then." The problem, my sweet wife, is I didn't think of this before I sent the guys. Should this really be the panacea, there is no stopping us, we will be committed. How can my guys see all that potential wealth there just for the taking and me tell them no? That's not how to lead" "Leading, my dear, is doing what's right for your men, Luke, and your guys know you always have their back."

"Teresa, how long do you think they will back me if I'm holding back their earning power and, more so, if it's a deal that Stone brought to the table? They know I don't like Stone, and they are going to think I squashed the deal for that reason and that reason only. Let's not forget my guys are criminals, they make their money breaking the law, and it's usually dangerous. They get a chance to just print money with little or no risk. I think you'll find Stone as the new head of the family." "Luke, don't be silly, he's not even made." Not even Italian for that matter. "I don't mean literally, but figuratively."

"Luke, chill out, let's see what it's all about, then you will make the right decision. I mean that, sincerely, you will make the right decision and, Luke, don't forget that as a last resort the fine Inspector Stone could find himself the victim of a horrific accident."

Luke was now speechless for a second, absorbing all of what Teresa said. A sense of relief seemed to be flowing from the top of his head down to his toes. At some level, he always knew that erasing Stone from the face of the earth was an option, although, until his true partner in crime and life spoke out loud what he was thinking and actually validated the idea, it didn't seem real. Now in a nanosecond, Stone just didn't seem as big a threat. Luke would just need to be super careful in his dealings with Stone in case Stone was secretly stashing information about their dealing to turn over if he ever got caught. Although the likelihood of Stone getting anything less than the death penalty for killing all those FBI guys was slim to none, Luke was starting to feel good again. "Teresa, what say we have a little appetizer before dinner?" Smiling at Luke, "Do you forget we've got children in the house? Keep that thought, though, for later on tonight. Now, go open a bottle of wine for dinner."

Chapter 43

"Hit me," Johnny said as he pounded the hundred dollar minimum table at Caesar's. A roar of approval went up from the table as the dealer dealt Johnny a five as he was sitting with a sixteen and the dealer was showing seven. "Lucky, no fucking offense, really, but Thank God boss sent you and not your brother. I just don't think we would be doing so good." Lucky, laughing, said, "I know he's my brother and I'd give him a kidney if I had to, but that guy could fuck up a wet dream in the rain. If it wasn't for bad luck, the poor bastard would have no luck!"

The whole table was laughing now, not just Sal, Johnny, and Lucky, but the two other guys at the table who until now were just minding their own business.

Sal was really happy he was with Lucky. It had only been a year since his accident when he became "made" and he really started making some serious scratch. So playing at a hundred dollar minimum blackjack table was still a little unnerving for him.

The guys were really having a phenomenal time. The scotch was flowing for Johnny and Lucky and the beer for Sal. Some guys, even when they make it, have a hard time graduating to the finer things in life. They are so ingrained with their meager beginnings that it's hard for them to let themselves enjoy the fruits of their labor and get over the guilty feelings of spending what the finer things in life cost. Sal, if he wants to kick it into high gear, will just augment his beer intake with a couple of shots of Jack. On this particular trip, Sal viewed it as a coming out party of sorts. Although he was made now, the boss was still easing him into the big time. No Jack tonight, just beer and gambling, and having some fun waiting to hear from his second hero, Luke being the first and, obviously, Stone, the guy who saved not only his ass, 'cause God knows how long he would have gone away to jail for if he got caught in that shit storm at the warehouse, although that probably wouldn't have happened anyway because he would have bled out long before anyone found him. Although he still thinks about and misses Larry, maybe they could have been a little smarter that night. Lesson learned, time to grow up and act the part. He almost had to pinch himself sitting in Caesar's in Vegas, playing and winning at a hundred dollar blackjack table, getting ready to help Stone with what Johnny called "the biggest fucking thing this family has ever seen!" He wasn't fucking this one up. Just as he was thinking all of this and hardly paying attention to his cards, the dealer hit him with a blackjack when he had five hundred in chips sitting in front of him. He jumped out of his seat and yelled for too many to hear, "Aye fucking Aye!" causing just a little too much attention for Johnny's liking. Johnny, though in way too good a mood, just gave him the look which Sal understood immediately and sat down and started stacking his newfound pile of chips.

As always, in Vegas, when a table is doing well, a new dealer is sent over and they sent over a knockout. On a scale of one to ten, she was a twelve. Sal was thinking to himself this night can't get any better. Sal and Lucky were so caught up in the whole scene they hadn't noticed Stone standing about fifty feet away leaning in a doorway coming into the casino. Johnny apparently wasn't a captain for nothing. His antennae were always up, and since he wasn't exactly sure how he was supposed to meet up with Stone, he had his eyes opened in search of him.

Johnny's eyes met Stone's, and Stone gave him the eyes up with the head point to indicate he wanted to meet them upstairs, which Johnny understood immediately and Johnny assumed correctly that since Stone was an FBI guy, he would know what room Sal was in.

Johnny now stood up before the gorgeous new dealer could start dealing cards. "Well, we must have scared them bad if they sent the prettiest card dealer in Vegas to take our money. She's too damn beautiful. I wouldn't be able to concentrate if she was dealing. That must be a sign for us to go." Sal, not learning from the last laser eye stare, said, "It's OK, boss, you can go. I don't really care if I'm winning so long as she's going to be dealing, I'll catch up with you later."

Lucky wasn't called Lucky for nothing. He knew Johnny had a reason to get up and go, and he was following. Now Sal got a double dose of laser eyes from both Johnny and Lucky. This time, Sal figured out this wasn't optional, and it was time to leave. They all stuffed their coat pockets with chips and left toward the direction where Johnny had seen Stone standing. Immediately behind them was the bank of elevators that went to the twenty-sixth floor, which was where the high roller suites were.

Sal, kind of like a puppy who had just got his nose rubbed in his own urine, was trotting behind Johnny and Lucky. Once in the elevator, Sal got up the nerve to ask, "Boss, I do something wrong, I'm sorry if I got excited when I hit the blackjack with five large on it." "Sal, we're supposed to be keeping a low profile, so yea jumping up in a casino and yelling Aye fucking Aye probably is not what the boss was thinking when he said to keep a low profile. That ain't the problem, big guy. If you weren't so intent on drooling over that dealer's tits, you might have noticed Stone showed up and if I had to guess you will be seeing him in three . . . two . . . one" and, just like magic, the elevator doors opened and there was Stone. "Thought you would never get here. Let's get down to business. Sal, where's your room key?" as Stone started walking toward Sal's room. Everybody in this group knows there are cameras in the hallways, which was why Stone was wearing a baseball hat. They didn't dilly-dally, they just all walked single file to Sal's room following Stone. Then Stone slid a card into the locking mechanism and opened the door to the great surprise of Sal and slightly less surprised Johnny and Lucky. They already knew this guy was slick.

They all went into the massive suite where Stone spoke first, "I guess crime does pay." Sal, still a little stunned, "How the fuck did you open my door?" "Oh, Sal, if you only knew all the tricks I have up my sleeve. Sit down, gentlemen, so I can bring you up to date on what we hope to accomplish in the next couple of days."

Stone went on for about half an hour describing in detail who Mike and Raj were, their graduating from MIT, and what he had figured out about their process for counterfeiting money, albeit a little sketchy, since he really only knew who they were and that they had figured out how to make a bill look old, used, and that passed an iodine test so apparently chemistry must have been in their bag of tricks. He also started telling them that he thought he figured out their schedules and that he was guessing they should be here sometime this week.

That's when Johnny interrupted Stone and asked him an obvious question, "I assume you want us to spread out to find them since we can be in four places at once." "Yea, I was going to suggest that . . ." "So I assume you've photos for us?" Stone was wondering if he had by chance insulted Johnny by going over the facts too slowly. "Sure, I wasn't quite done yet, but by all means I've got pictures for all of you." He handed them out.

"Ma Va Fungul! I fucking knew it!" "Johnny, you know what?" "Remember when you told the boss it was two kids from MIT?" "Yea." "Well, I couldn't fucking remember MIT, Harvard, Yale, whateva . . . We flew out here right across from the aisle from those two little punks, and I tell you I'm going to enjoy busting that little white rich kid's face." "You what?" That's when Lucky chimed in, "Yea, boss, isn't that the kid you gave the little push to on the plane?" Stone totally knocked off his game, "What do you mean 'little push on an airplane'? How did you know it was them and why would you push someone on a plane? Do you want Luke to blow a gasket?"

Johnny, not even hearing Stone's comment about Luke, was just really impressed with himself right about now. "I knew it, I just fucking knew it, and now I'm going to enjoy even more getting to know them better if you know what I mean." Stone, now clearing out the cobwebs, knew he had to get back in control. "OK, big guy, now that you know what they look like, we still need to find them and what hotel they're in." Stone immediately knew from Johnny's shit-eating grin that it was time for him to shut up and let Johnny puff up his chest. After an appropriate pause, "OK, Johnny, where are they?"

"The little punks . . . what did you say their names were?" "Mike and Raj." "The little punks happen to be staying at the Rio." Sal, totally amazed by all this, asked, "How do you know that, boss? Johnny, really riding the wave now, just gave Sal a little wink, waited a second, then said, "Sal, my friend, that's why I'm the boss son."

Stone really just wanted to stick his finger down his throat. He gave Johnny enough time to bask in his glory and then said, "Okay, here's the plan."

Chapter 44

Having accomplished the requisite shopping trip to Staples and secured their money machine, more commonly known as a laser color printer, the boys were ready to rock and they were getting antsy. The routine was pretty simple: one of them would go and cash five thousand dollars in bogus bills into chips. One or both of them would play blackjack almost always at different tables. They played very strict blackjack rules, never going with their gut. Betting very conservatively, they learned that playing over the course of about an hour, they would be within a couple of hundred dollars plus or minus.

They would then go to different cash windows and cash in their chips. They would go up to their room, scan the clean money into their laptops, and then print the new money. They would put the good money into a box and then go out with the newly printed money to a different casino and start the whole procedure over again. On a couple of occasions where they felt they were being watched, one of them would make a string of stupid bets and lose some money. All in all, though, very few people ever noticed them.

Although they would cash in five thousand in chips, they kept most of them in their pockets and only put a few hundred dollars in chips on the table at any given time.

Theoretically, they could operate like this all day, but being ever cautious, they opted to operate primarily at night when the casinos were busier. In their minds, the busier the better. They actually would try to plan trips around some of the bigger conventions. Less opportunity for a cashier to notice them if they were just one in a line of people cashing in chips.

In a good week, they could launder, give or take, a hundred grand. They would then pack the cash up in a FedEx box, go down to the local mailbox, etc., and overnight the money back to their apartment on their way back to the airport.

Since they were basically lazy kids, Mike and Raj started their night right at the Rio. Raj, knowing this was his last trip to Vegas for a while, was playing a little looser than normal. In the little over an hour they had been playing, Raj had made about a grand. Raj saw Mike walk by him on his way to the cashier, so he made his last bet with double his normal bet of the day. Raj had two hundred dollars sitting in front of him and bang! Blackjack was dealt to him and the dealer pushed three hundred additional dollars in chips to Raj. He thanked the pretty dealer, threw her a fifty-dollar tip, and collected his chips.

Raj went over to the cashier. He was two people behind Mike in line and feeling really lucky and full of life. Mike, on the other hand, had an uneasy feeling he couldn't put his finger on. They met up at the elevator and headed up to their room. They seldom talked unless they were in their room because they knew there were eyes and ears all over the casino, just not in their rooms, because that would be an invasion of privacy. Raj just couldn't help himself tonight when they got in the elevator. Raj proudly advised Mike, "I'm up thirteen hundred dollars. How about you, big boy?" "About even, give or take." "In other words, you suck today, and you're losing what I won?" "Screw you, Raj. Why are you being such a dick?" "Chill, Mike, I'm just busting them. I know we won't be back for a while and am just soaking it in." They had just arrived at suite 32–13. The "Do Not Disturb" sign was on like it would be the entire time of their stay. Mike slid his key card in the slot and walked in.

"I know I'm just on edge for some res . . ." Immediate pain and then darkness."

Twenty minutes later, Mike woke up disoriented but knowing his head felt like it had exploded. As he regained more consciousness, he realized he was tied to a chair in the living room of his suite, blood covering the front of his shirt from his apparently broken nose. Apparently was not the word—*definitely* broken from the feeling pounding in his head.

He painfully turned his head from left to right. When it got to his right, he saw Raj tied to a chair as well. He was also coming out of his stupor, and from the blood on his left shoulder, he had apparently been hit on the head.

"Raj, Raj, you OK, man?" "Wha . . . What? No, I mean yes, what the fuck, my head hurts, what the hell is going on?" His voice started to rise when bang! Sal's fist smacked the side of his jaw, "Shut the fuck up and talk when we tell you to talk. Too loud, and you'll never see Boston again, college punk."

Johnny then walked from behind Mike into his view, but before Mike saw him, he saw those god-awful Gucci shoes, and just when he thought he couldn't feel any worse, a sense of nausea totally engulfed him. Johnny realized that Mike was looking down at his shoes, not purposely mind you, but because it hurt to raise his head. This gave Mike a split second to prepare for what was coming next. Johnny's foot came up and he planted it squarely on Mike's chest and booted him over backward, hard. Mike actually smelled the leather of the shoes for a second and clearly, only in his mind, he thought he smelled a hint of garlic. In that same split second, he decided if he had an opportunity he would not share with the owner of the foot that it smelled like garlic-laden leather.

Smashing to the floor with stars of pain leaving every pore in his body, "Yeow." Smashing down on his mouth was Sal's hand "Didn't you hear me tell the towelhead to keep his voice down, college punk? Open your mouth louder than a whisper and you'll be eating through a straw for as long as we allow you to live, capisce?" Mike tried to shake his head "yes" to no avail, since Sal's hand had Mike's head plastered to the ground.

Sal got the message and took his hand off Mike's mouth. Sal and Lucky then lifted Mike's chair back upright so he and Raj could now be addressed by Johnny. Stone, standing out of sight, was taking this all in, letting but not enjoying the boys having a little fun. He really had a different plan for snatching up the kids away from the strip, but it became readily apparent since Johnny had such shitass luck on the plane that he had to acquiesce and let Johnny drive some of the process. He was a captain, and even though Stone had different ideas, he was still the outsider, albeit the outsider who had made them millions and with this potential little score untold amounts of money.

Although the words sounded a little funny, they were intelligible. "I'm really sorry about what I said . . . you know . . . about your shoes." Raj's mind starting to come around, just got confused again. "Shoes . . . what shoes . . . are you fucking kidding me?" he was thinking to himself, "this is all because of the story Mike told him about the guinea on the plane that he stepped on his shoes. This is surreal, it's got to be a bad dream." Mike, trying to think clearly and get him and Raj out of trouble, "We've got about ten grand, take it, please, we won't tell anyone about this. Promise. I . . . I was wrong and stupid, I was feeling pretty tough while I was in that limo, and I knew you couldn't get me . . . please take the money." Johnny, looking at Mike and as quickly as a cat, shot out his leg, planting his foot on Raj's chest and sent Raj for the same ride as Mike. Also, with catlike reflexes, Sal had a hand over Raj's mouth before Raj could scream in the obvious pain he was in. Sal put his other finger over his own mouth to signal to Raj to hold his pain in or expect more. Sal and Lucky now replaced Raj back on the chair's four legs to hold court with Johnny.

"Ten grand, oh, I think you rich little college punks have more than ten grand. How about three or four million . . . each?"

"I don't know what you're talking about, man, we're not rich."

"Really—flying first class, a suite at the Rio, apparently ten grand cash you're willing to give up so easy." Raj and Mike thought the same thought, "This should be so easy a bunch of goons we can bullshit our way out of this!"

Raj spoke for the first time, "My dad gave us frequent flyer miles, ten grand, and this room. This is what we were given by family for graduation. This was supposed to be our last gasp before entering the real world." This time Lucky, out of nowhere, busted Raj in the mouth. Stars were the last thing he remembered before blacking out for a minute or two.

Chapter 45

Luke, "AB," and Fat Hands were in the deaf room enjoying some food, cigars, and some really nice wine. Whoever says you can't buy taste apparently hasn't had a meal prepared by Luke's chef accompanied by a bottle of Ruffino Reserva Chianti followed up by a Cuban Romeo y Julieta Churchill cigar.

The Romeo y Julieta Churchill is a huge cigar but in Melazia's hands it looked almost pencil-like. "Boss, you know the funny thing is, if we ever got raided in here by the feds, we're so careful about not having anything hot around us or records or anything that could incriminate. That is, except the ten or so boxes of these Cubans that are always lying around. Wouldn't that just be a big kick in the ass to get put in the can because we're smoking some of Castro's specials."

They all got a good laugh from that comment, but Luke, with a pensive look, said, "You know, maybe we ought to have one of the boys take the labels off and buy a big humidor to store them. Fuck, Fat Hands, I was just having a good time relaxing and not thinking about that Fuck Stone and you have to go get my mind thinking about some other detail that could get me fucked, although it would be ironic to end up in the can for smoking a cigar with all the other shit we're involved in." They all chuckled a little less than last time, but a chuckle none the less.

The air was a little heavy and not from the smoke. Luke was still bothered by Stone, and Fat Hands was also bothered by Stone, more so because all of his internet research was coming up with nothing damning or, in his opinion, really good either. The stories were good as were the accolades, but to Fat Hands it was too antiseptic. "AB" was bothered because his loyalty was to Luke, but he had genuinely come to like and trust Stone as well as made some serious coin. He didn't understand Luke's inability to let his guard down with Stone long enough to see the forest through the trees. "AB" felt it was time to prod the boss a little.

"Boss, you know I would never question your judgment, but as one of your captains and your friend, I have to question what your problem is with Stone. He's kept you out of jail, he's knocked off a traitor, he's saved one of your guys' lives, and in the process kept us out of a war with the Colombians and possibly the Russians. Oh, and let's not forget the money and lots of it, and if what you tell me is true, lots more to come and without the risk we take in making most of the money we make now."

"AB," listen, I feel the same way. But he freaks me out. I hear all you're saying and no argument on any of the points except there's something." "Fungul something." "Something, what? At some point, you got to believe the guy has killed FBI agents, he ain't undercover." Fat Hands spoke up. "AB," I've been researching this guy for the last three weeks. It's weird almost like he's in witness protection. Nothing jumping out, but nothing that makes me feel like there isn't something under the rock." Luke, on the edge of his seat, interjected, "I agree, Fat Hands, there's something there, and I'm afraid that if we don't figure out what's under that rock, it's going to land on our heads." "AB," clearly frustrated, "Va Via" (Go Away) "If it looks like a duck and it quacks like a duck, it's a fucking duck!" Luke then said, "If it smells like shit and it looks like shit, it's probably shit, and I'm telling you his cologne is a la bullshit."

That temporarily broke the seriousness. Luke said, "OK, here's the deal. 'AB,' you keep befriending him, and Fat Hands, you keep digging but, I promise you once we see what this counterfeiting things turns out to be, and once Stone is back in town, we are going to bring him in and turn the screws a little to find out his real deal and move forward with him one way or the other. Should it turn out positive, great. Should he be hiding something, we will deal with it, but I'm done with not trusting him, capisce?" Both men shook their heads in agreement, but "AB" didn't like the sound of "turn the screws a little" because with Luke that could be literal.

Chapter 46

By the time Raj was coming to, Mike had just about pissed himself. Stone walked into view carrying a chair, and Mike thought, "Oh shit, now I'm going to get hit with a chair." Instead, Stone spun the chair around backward and sat down with his chest against the back of the chair.

"Boys, this has been fun, but unless you want to get the shit kicked out of you for the next three or four hours, which my friends I'm afraid would be more than happy to accommodate, we really need to get down to business." Mike and Raj were both happy to hear there was an option to getting a beating.

"OK, boys, here's the deal. If you want to speak to me, you can call me Joe. Whether or not my name actually is Joe is irrelevant, but I'd like for us to start communicating like civilized adults, and civilized adults call each other by their first names, do you both understand?" They both, not daring to speak, shook their quickly swelling heads.

"Mike Sullivan, Raj Kaptor, see how I am already acting civilized by calling you by your full names." You could almost hear the thuds in their stomachs when they heard their whole names spoken. Not knowing why this guy, who calls himself Joe, knew both their full names, but just the fact that he knew their full names could not be good. "Yea, I know your full names, I know where you live, I know where you went to school, I know where your parents live, I could probably tell you what you had for breakfast. Let me be the first to congratulate you boys on figuring out how to counterfeit so effectively. I guess someone could have figured a couple of MIT kids would figure out how to chemically alter counterfeit money to pass the iodine test."

To say that Mike and Raj's world just collapsed around them would be an understatement. They stole looks at each other and knew their gig was up. They didn't know how or who these guys were yet, but they knew they were fucked.

"Boys . . . oh, and anytime you'd like to jump in and ask a question, feel free." Mike found the courage to blurt out, "What do you want from us?" "Well, Mike . . . I assume I can call you Mike?" Not waiting for a response, Stone continued, "I know enough about you boys to have you put away for your useful lives, not to mention that my initial impression of you boys is that you're really not federal penitentiary kind of guys. So I'm going to do you a favor. I'm going to make it possible for the two of you boys to fly back to Boston and live normal nine-to-five lives or whatever it is you geeks do. That's the good news. When we let you leave is still up for negotiation. Well, I shouldn't really say negotiation since the only negotiating will be with myself."

"Here's the deal. I need you to fill in a couple of blanks for me. I know you're counterfeiting, and I know you solved how to make the bills pass initial scrutiny by passing an iodine test. That's what I know now. I assume you're copying the bills and you're using legit serial numbers. I assume you're using bad bills to buy chips, then cash in the chips for good bills, copy the good bills, make bad bills, and repeat the process. Sound familiar, boys?" No answer was really required. The look on their bruised faces said it all. That's when Raj made a huge mistake. He looked right at Stone, and said with his best eighth grade acting class facial expression. "I know you won't believe it but I . . . we have no idea what you're talking about." About halfway through his halfhearted attempt at playing dumb, Stone gave a look to Sal actually quite similar to a look Luke might have given which communicated exactly what Sal was to do. He pulled his pistol out of his pocket and pistol-whipped Raj up both sides of his head. Immediate pain shot through Raj's body and Mike was feeling Raj's pain just by watching. Johnny popped Mike from his blind side hard enough for the stars to reappear.

Johnny's chest still puffed said to Raj that in case you might want to try and lie again, I'll use your buddy as a punching bag, you understand me fuck nut? Raj could barely shake his head up and down in agreement, but his fear of getting hit again gave him the strength to do so.

Stone nodded to the boys to stand down and waited for a minute or so for the boys' consciousness to come back. "Mike . . .

Raj, I was really hoping not to have to go down this road. Let me give you fair warning, should you continue to go down this slippery slope, I won't be able to protect you from my angry friends. Now let me tell you what I think may be helpful. I'm going to have the boys frisk you two one more time to make sure you don't have an extra cell phone on you. Then I'm going to have them carry you into that bedroom and make sure you're tied down nice and tight. My recommendation would be to not try to get loose. There's no way out and I have already rented the rooms on either side of us, so pounding on the walls won't help once you two are in the bedroom and, by the way, we have removed the house phone. We will give you ten minutes to discuss with each other your options, which there are only two: The first option you have is to give us the complete rundown on how you've been counterfeiting money, including your formula, and I mean everything. Then when we know you're telling us the complete truth, you go home unharmed and promise never to come back to Vegas again. Second option, decide to not tell us or give us partial information, and your existence will cease. Capisce?" The boys, not looking very good and swelling by the second, did their best to shake their heads yes, that they understood.

Chapter 47

Mak was sitting in a coach seat on an American Airline flight heading to Las Vegas. Although he was on American, in today's day and age it could have been any airline. Mak had been thinking that thought when some nondescript flight attendant asked him if he wanted something to drink. Hardly even acknowledging her, he just shook his head no. Mak was in some serious role playing in his head. He knew he was nearing the time to really drop the bomb on Stone. Strange how everyone at the bureau thought of him as a slacker, if not a loser, with clearly no aptitude for undercover work. How they were wrong, he had sniffed out something fishy with Stone almost two years ago. At first, it was just a feeling, a sense that not all was right with Stone. He thought nobody could be that straight and good. Turned out he was right and he planned to cash in on his good fortune and hard work. Mak had been biding his time. He had enough evidence to have Stone fried a long time ago. He was tempted to blackmail Stone after the drug fiasco at the pier. He wasn't sure what Stone's take could have been, but he was sure it probably would have been enough to change his lifestyle. Typically, he would have jumped on it, but something was telling him to have patience, just to wait, and something bigger was going to come along.

He knew Stone wouldn't have gone to Vegas three times in such a short time if he wasn't on to something. Guaranteed he was going to be turning it over to that guinea Luke to run with it, he had seen it too many times over the last year. This time he was going to intervene, he was going to get the goose that laid the golden egg. The little he picked around the office was that there was someone or a group of someones that had figured out how to make untraceable currency. That was his idea of a pension.

The question was how and when to confront Stone. You see, Mak was one of the few people in the world who knew how evil Stone actually was. He had seen his handiwork firsthand. As Mak was thinking about this, he unconsciously was rubbing a sock in his jacket pocket and not just any sock, but one of the socks Stone was wearing the night of the wharf massacre. That was his insurance policy when he confronted Stone. Mak knew that he wasn't the most subtle guy, but he was apprehensive about how Stone was going to take the news. First things first, he had to be sure that Stone was really on whoever was the counterfeiter and that he was grabbing him or them for himself. Luckily, because of the board at the office, he knew where to look for Stone. He was scheduled to be at Caesar's.

Mak, not one to really think that deeply, still couldn't get his mind around Stone's gig. How does such an outwardly straight and narrow guy go so sociopathically wrong? What was even more bizarre was why hook up with Luke? Certainly, Stone would need someone or somebody's help, but why one of the most notorious criminals on the whole of the east coast, if not the country?

Mak was turning this over in his head when he also came to the realization that Stone was much smarter than he was, and he was OK with that, so long as he could just outsmart him this one time. Mak had skimmed drug money on a number of occasions and copped some stolen stuff more than once. Let's face it, the criminals were unlikely to tell a judge that there was ten or twenty grand more money that was missing from evidence. Mak knew, though, that it was small time and he really wasn't capable of masterminding a scheme like Stone had done. This was his one chance at the golden ring. He knew he was basically a miserable person, liked by virtually no one and, believe it or not, he was good with that. He had decided, though, he was at least going to be a rich jerk. Soon as he could, he would quit his job, travel the world with bought blonde company on his arm, diamond ring on his pinky, and a roll of cash in his pocket.

Chapter 48

After the boys were placed in the interior bedroom without a house phone, their cell phones were confiscated and there were no windows to escape through. Johnny excused himself to the massive bathroom of the suite. He liked and respected Stone, but Luke was his boss and Luke needed to be in the loop.

Johnny took out his cell phone and called Luke. "Speak to me" was what was heard in Johnny's ear. "We found our friends, amazing how small this town actually is." "Really, that was quick, were they happy to see you?" "Very surprised, boss, they are back in their room resting up for some fun later." "Did they tell you what they have been doing and what's planned for the rest of the trip?" "Not yet, boss. Like I said, they were very surprised and it took a lot out of them. They need a little rest before we make any more plans." "Ah, I see, enjoy their company, they are smart people, so be sure to learn from them. Have fun and call me later."

The chances of somebody listening in to their call changes from week to week or, even sometimes, day to day. They know when the feds are listening because Stone would let them know.

Unfortunately for Luke, any number of people or agencies could and do have an interest in what he's up to. The local guys always love to show up the feds, so they are constantly sticking their nose in Luke's business. Although for them to legally be listening, they need a court order, with Luke's contacts he always knows when a judge signed an authorization to wiretap him.

What they really are protecting against is the rogue cop just looking for information without authorization, or worse, a rival gang like the Russians, Colombians, or any other unsavory group of hoodlums looking to move in on some of their action.

Mike and Raj were left in the bedroom where they quickly realized that even if they could get loose of their ropes that bound their wrists and ankles, there was no way out. Their captors were clearly not dumb and they definitely knew they were not going to fight their way out of that room. As they sat silent for what seemed like hours, but was only minutes, the silence was deafening. Mike wanted to start by telling Raj that he told him so, that they pushed it too far, he wanted to lash out, but he knew that wasn't going to help. Now, it would only exasperate the situation. If they were to survive this, they were going to have to keep their heads about them and work together.

"We're fucked, Raj." "Chill, Mike, we'll get out of this." That was when the whole "we need to work together" thing went out the door for Mike. "Chill?! Chill. You're lucky I'm tied to this chair or I'd be kicking your ass right now. I told you that we pushed it too far, now these goons are going to kill us, you stupid ass!" "Mike, you may not believe it right now, but they need us as bad as we need them not to kill us." "Dude, I feel like a piñata at a ten-year–old's' birthday party. These guys mean to hurt us worse than they already have. My vote is to tell them everything and leave with our lives. ""Mike, trust me, if we tell them everything, they will have no use for us, then we could be in real trouble." "I disagree, and my face vehemently disagrees. I don't want to be a punching bag for these goons anymore." "I hear ya but I'm not sure I agree. I think we need to find a way to partner with them. That way, they will have a use for us." "Partner, are you fucking crazy? These guys don't strike me as business guys looking to merge their business with ours, if you want to call what we do or what they do a business. Speaking of which, who do you think these guys are?" "They certainly aren't boy scouts. My guess is that they are the mob, that is, except for the one who calls himself Joe. He doesn't seem like the other three of them. He's the one we need to get to. I think he can be reasoned with."

Unfortunately for Mike, and especially Raj, Stone had planted a microphone in the room and was listening to the whole conversation through a set of earplugs. Johnny had returned from the bathroom and was intently watching Stone listening in on the boys' conversation. Stone's head was just bobbing up and down, not in agreement, just in acknowledgement. When he had heard enough, he took his headphones off. Johnny waited for Stone to give him the skinny. "Mike seems to be the smarter one of the two. He's willing to cooperate. Raj thinks he's going to become our partner. I think we need to advise him that we don't need partners."

Johnny was disappointed that it was Raj and not Mike who was going to be difficult. It was personal for Johnny and he wanted to inflict more pain on Mike, but there would be time for that later. Right now, though, he needed to think about Luke and what he would want. Luke was a pure businessman. It very seldom got personal with him. Had Luke been there, he would have done only what was necessary to accomplish his goal. The goal was to convince the boys to give up how they had been successfully counterfeiting, anything beyond that would be wasted energy.

Johnny didn't need to be told what to do it. It had all been discussed earlier. The four of them walked into the bedroom, Stone with his headphones still hung around his neck. Raj immediately knew he was screwed. "No, no, wait, I was only kidding, I'll tell you every . . ." Sal stuffed a tee shirt in Raj's mouth. Mike tried to intervene, which was rewarded with a tee shirt of his own stuffed in his mouth.

Stone was still shaking his head. "Boys, do we look like amateurs? Do you think we don't know what we're doing? I told you both to come in here and decide to do the right thing, didn't I? This could have been easy—now it's going to have to get ugly. I told you two if you cooperated, both of you could go unharmed. Now, Raj, you have no one else to blame but yourself." With that, Lucky and Sal locked onto Raj's arm and held him tight. Raj remembered feeling what seemed like two huge bear clamps holding him down before the white flash of pain that raced through his body as Johnny quickly and efficiently cut off his left pinky finger at the knuckle with a pair of hefty tin snips.

Chapter 49

Mak had gone straight from the airport to Caesar's Palace. He had a choice which check-in person he would go to. He chose the buxom blonde over the slightly feminine male. He went to Lucille as her name tag stated was her name. She was looking down at her computer, finishing up from her last customer. Charlie, the feminine check-in clerk, who was standing beside Lucille, said, "I would be happy to help you, sir, if you don't mind stepping over here." Mak, not even looking at Charlie, said, "That's OK, sport. I'll wait for Lucille, she's more my cup of tea." Charlie's face, turning red half from anger and half from embarrassment, responded, "As you wish." He turned around and shuffled down the counter and into the backroom, muttering to himself, "Asshole."

"I'll be right with you, sir" "Take your time, sweetheart, you're worth waiting for, I could look at you all day." Lucille kept looking down at her computer, although now she was smiling and blushing herself. Lucille was used to dealing with obnoxious guys in her job, but if the truth be told, she was drawn to those types of guys, which was why she was so good at her job. Her boss loved her because she was such a great employee. She was a great employee because she loved her job. She loved her job because she loved to flirt with men. There were no shortage of men checking in at Caesar's who wanted to start their boondoggle by flirting with a pretty blonde while checking in. Apparently, everyone wins.

Lucille had also been convinced on more than one occasion to meet some of these gentlemen after she got off work, even though it was expressly forbidden to date the customers. She would wonder why all these men had an indentation around their left index finger. Hey, what happens in Vegas apparently stays in Vegas. She didn't mind, she was young and enjoying life with no intention of settling down.

Lucille, now done with her work, put on her biggest smile and looked up at Mak. "May I help you, sir?" Her smile went immediately to a frown when she looked up to see an FBI badge staring her in the face. Mak, trying to sound as official as he could, "Sweet thing, I'm here on official business. First, I need to check in, then ask you a couple of questions, then hopefully take you out to dinner." Lucille went from smiling to frowning to smiling all in about twenty seconds. "Why certainly, Mr. Greenwall," which she read from his credentials. "Call me Mak, everyone does. Mr. Greenwall was my father, I'm just Mak, cute thing." "OK, Mak, do you have a reservation?" "No" "OK, we have availability, so it shouldn't be a problem. How long are you planning on staying?" "Well, Lucille, I'm not sure yet, but why don't you book me for the same length of stay as my associate Mr. Stone, Mr. Joe Stone." "I assume he's staying with us, let me check his reservation. Mr. Stone is currently booked for the next three nights. Would you like the same stay, Mak?" "Why yes, I would, you wouldn't happen to have a room near my colleague, would you?" "Well, I'm a little embarrassed to admit that we are pretty slow this week, so if you want you can have the room right across the hall, or if you really want, I have the room right next door, which is a connecting room . . . well, I mean, you both have to unlock your doors for it to be connecting." "I know what you meant, Lucille. I doubt very much since we're working that we would have an occasion to have the doors open and throw a big party, but it would be very convenient to have our rooms next to each other. I'll take it. But just so you don't have any doubts about my manhood, I'll take it providing you have a drink with me tonight." The blush returning, "Mak, I'm really not supposed to fraternize with the clients." "Is that what we call it nowadays?" The blush was becoming deeper, "Seriously, I can get fired if I'm caught spending time with customers at Caesar's. "Fine, pick another location. Caesar's is for old people anyway." The blush, believe it or not, became even deeper. "Rio's main bar. I get off at 9:00 p.m. I'll be there by 9:30–10:00 at the latest." "Take your time, Lucille, I will be the guy at the bar waiting to have a drink with the hottest chick at the Rio." With that, he turned and headed to his room. Lucille, now almost purple, let out a little uncontrolled "whew."

She looked back down at her screen to finish her work, more than a little excited about her after work rendezvous with Mak, simultaneous wondering why she was attracted to guys like Mak, although she noticed for once he didn't have the telltale left index finger indentation that was so prevalent on most of her dates. This could be promising.

Chapter 50

Cold-blooded killers, yes when the situation warrants. Raj, though, still needed to be kept alive and healthy. They were far from doctors, but they needed to clean Raj's amputation. They couldn't afford sending him to an emergency room. Lucky was busy first pouring alcohol on the open wound, then quickly squirting about a quarter tube of Neosporin followed by gauze and tightly wrapped tape over the gauze to help stop the bleeding. All the while Sal, with the help of Johnny, was trying to hold Raj steady to assist Lucky with his doctor's duties.

Raj, as could be expected, was not happy, he was coming out of shock and not saying very nice things to his captors. Comments along the lines of "You stupid fucking guineas. What the fuck, are you fucking crazy, that was my fucking finger." All the time getting louder and louder. Lucky was trying to hold his arm up in the air to help stop the bleeding, with little success. Johnny let Raj go, stepped in front of Raj and calmly said, "College boy, time to quiet down and start cooperating," Raj cut him off and started on another tirade with even more colorful comments about Johnnie's heritage. The response was quick and predictable: a right cross to the jaw hard enough to knock Raj over backwards still tied to his chair and out of the grip of both Sal and Lucky. That was lights out again for Raj, which was perfect timing since Mike was waking up from his last attitude adjustment. Sal and Lucky made Raj upright in his chair again, and since shit flows downhill, Lucky instructed Sal to hold Raj's arm straight up in the air to assist in the clotting.

Stone now took over almost as if in a perfectly scripted and acted play. Johnny moved out of center stage and Stone, bringing a chair with him, swung it around backward and sat down straddling the chair and crossed his arms over the back of the chair. "Mike, look, I know you're bright, you went to MIT. You figured out how to make passable, virtually untraceable money. You clearly must be bright enough to realize we aren't leaving without knowing what you know. I am serious when I tell you, once we know what you do, and we're sure you're not fucking with us, we will let you go unhurt . . . that is not anymore hurt than you already are. Honestly, we didn't want to have to cut his finger off, but you disrespected us. We may not be MIT or Harvard grads, but don't make the mistake again that we're stupid, capisce?" Mike had been beat enough and was fond of all of his digits and didn't want to leave Vegas without them. Actually, he just really wanted to leave Vegas alive, period. So as not to do or say the wrong thing, he just shook his head up and down in acknowledgement. "OK, great, now we're getting somewhere. Now let me tell you how the next couple of hours are going down. First thing we are going to do is untie you and make you more comfortable." Johnny shot Stone a quizzical look, which Stone dismissed by continuing to speak, "Mike, I told you, we know you're smart and now I've told you we're no dummies. You already know we bugged the room, so to dismiss any question in your mind, I also have installed a number of microcameras so we can see your every move. You may be asking yourself why I'm tipping my hand. Because when we leave you and your buddy, who hasn't given us enough credit for knowing our business, I really don't want to come back in here and cut one of your fingers off." Johnny said, "I do." Johnny just can't control himself sometimes, Stone thought, he might have to talk to Luke about that at some point. Stone shot Johnny a look, but in a perverse sort of way it helped, because Mike knew in his heart of hearts that Johnny would like to not only cut off his finger, but his balls, and arms and legs and whatever other body part he could get his hands on. Stone continued, "So now, my friends and I are going to untie both of you. Then you can help my friend Sal by holding your friend Raj's arm in the air so it will clot and stop bleeding. You see, Mike, for obvious reasons we can't bring Raj to a doctor, so my suggestion is that we work together to keep his wound clean and get it to stop bleeding because if it gets infected there will be no treatment. Also, if you really get stupid and try to fight your way out, there's really no way you guys can be that stupid. Look at my friends, then look in a mirror," to which Mike was nodding his head up and down vigorously. "I think thirty minutes or so should be enough for Raj to wake up, and if you hold his arm up until he can on his own, he should stop bleeding."

Stone nodded to Sal and Lucky, and Johnny opened his switchblade not two inches from Mike's face, close enough and long enough for Mike to just about shit his pants. While Sal was untying Raj's ropes, Johnny just cut Mike's. Mike stood up slowly with shooting pains in his head, making him a little dizzy. Stone had turned toward Raj, so he was slightly startled when he felt Mike's hand clasp down on his forearm. Also taking Johnny off guard, he immediately raised this knife ready to pounce. When Stone turned toward Mike and their eyes locked, he immediately put his hand up to stop Johnny. "Joe, Joe, you said your name is Joe, correct?" "Yes." "You promise me if we teach you how to do what we know, you'll let us live, you'll let us go? Look at me in the eyes and tell me. I need to know." Stone never blinked and never lost eye contact. He grabbed Mike's forearm and said in a voice as sincere as Mother Teresa's, "Mike, get Raj under control, no more bullshit, no more secrets, full disclosure, teach us everything, and promise to stop doing it yourself, and I promise you, on my kids, you can get on an airplane and fly back to your life in Cambridge. I promise, I also promise that the next time either one of the two of you try to fuck with us, you'll be hoping that we only cut off a finger. Capisce?"

No sooner did Johnny and the guys get back in the main room than his cell phone rang. He looked at the caller ID and noticed it was Luke. He immediately picked up, "Boss, what's up?" "Same question back at you, my friend." Johnny could tell that the boss was on edge. He had only just spoken to him less than an hour ago. Johnny, still hurting from the right cross to the jaw Luke gave him before the trip. So the last thing Johnny wanted to do was to piss Luke off. Not to mention the fact that he was a captain for a reason. He had proven himself so he needed to sound confident and be positive to make the boss feel at ease. "Boss, I think they have decided to go out to dinner with us" "Really? When?" "Oh, definitely tonight." "Wow, they must be tired. I'm surprised they decided to go out tonight." "Boss, we're in Vegas, the town that never sleeps, and you know how convincing we can be when we want to." "Se, Yes, I understand, Va Bein. After dinner, play a hard eight and a hard six for me. I feel lucky tonight." "No problem, boss, a C note on each?" "Sure, sounds good, now you call me if dinner is not good, capisce?" "Capisce." Johnny was then left with a dead phone line. Luke had hung up, apparently satisfied with Johnny's cryptic conversation. Lucky and Sal had caught the end of the conversation and knew exactly what was going on. They had heard and partaken in more than a few of their own cryptic conversations. They had all learned from Luke that it didn't have to be inevitable that being in the mob meant that, at some point, you would get pinched. Even though Luke himself had sometimes gone away after being careful, this group's MO was to be über careful. This, in turn, had totally frustrated both the local and federal authorities. Cell phones have made most everyone's lives more convenient, but none more so than the police. Cell phones have been the ruination of many a formally smart underground organization.

Stone, on the other hand, went right to plugging in his headphones. He wanted to hear Mike convince Raj to cooperate. He had been bluffing about the cameras, but he was sure that in their current state they would be petrified and not questioning the cameras when they had already got caught with their pants down with the microphones. Stone had done hundreds of interrogations, and he knew he was good at it. This was totally different and way easier. They, as police officers, could only threaten violence, but how cool it was to actually use it. What would have taken him maybe days to get out of a perp, he could reduce to hours, actually even minutes. He couldn't lie to himself, he liked this side, but this wasn't a question of which side of the law he should be on, or which side liked better, it was much larger. This was a predetermined destiny. The pull right now at this moment was larger and stronger than it had ever been in his life, and it was intoxicating. Stone shook himself out of his self-induced trance and forced himself to focus in on the task at hand. He took off one of his headsets and said, "Johnny, what's up?" "I think the boss is a little on edge, but don't worry, I got it covered, providing we come back with the goods." "We will have the goods, guaranteed, want to lay money on it since we're in Vegas?" Johnny walked over to Stone and gave him a little fist pound and said, "Sure, with the money we print." They all four got a laugh out of that.

Mike, in the room behind a closed door, only heard the muffled laugh, thinking to himself, "What kind of monsters are these guys, anyway? They cut my friend's finger off, beat the shit out of us, then they sit not fifteen feet away and they are laughing? We're fucked." Raj was just starting to come back to this world, and Mike knew that he had to quickly convince Raj to play ball and not to piss the guys off again. Mike had a vision of him standing there with Raj sitting in his chair, and Mike holding his arm up like he was helping him with a question in grammar school. Although he saw nothing funny about this situation, for a split second that amused him. It also drove home his friendship with Raj. They had been through a lot, and he knew deeply that their situation was tenuous and he needed to take control of both of them.

"Raj, can you hear me?" "Yea, what the fuck, I feel like I've been hit by a truck." The realization of his cut-off pinky set in again and he became immediately agitated again. "That fucking guin . . ." Mike covered his mouth hard, "Raj, shut up and listen to me good. They obviously know about us and they are not the good guys. So we're not looking at jail time, we're looking at the end of our lives if we don't cooperate. They got the room miked and cameras watching us." "What do you mean cameras?" "While you were taking your last nap, the guy Joe told me. I really think he's going to help us out of this if we cooperate." "Mike, I don't care what you think or what they can see, they're going to kill us once we tell them how our process works." "Raj, this is the hardest thing I've ever had to do or say in my life. I am going to tell them everything because if there's any chance of getting out of this alive, I'm going for it with or without you." Raj, even in his dazed current sense of reality, believed Mike was telling him the truth. Raj always knew that, going into partnership with Mike, that he was soft, not a good poker player, and bluffing wasn't his style. Then the thought crept into his brain, maybe that's why he still has his pinky. "Mike, don't be stupid, we need to be smart about this or we'll give them what they want and still get killed." "Raj, trust me, and if you don't, you're on your own." Stone was smiling now from ear to ear with Johnny, Lucky, and Sal just able to look and imagine what Stone was hearing. Johnny just wanted to hear Mike wasn't going to cooperate 'cause he really wanted to tear him up a little more. Raj knew he was fighting a futile battle. It wasn't as if it was the Zyljian cymbal formula where one family member has half the list of ingredients and the other has the other half. Mike and Raj both knew the whole process and all the chemicals. Once Mike rolled, if Raj wasn't with him, then he really just became a liability. Raj waited a minute, knowing he looked stupid with his right hand being held up in the air by Mike. He pulled his throbbing hand out of Mike's grasp, then said to Mike, "Dude, you better be right, 'cause I'd hate to teach them our stuff and get killed anyway. Kinda like no good deed goes unpunished!" "Raj, I feel as good about this as I can under the circumstances."

Stone took off his headset and said, "Come on, boys, they are ready and I don't want to give them an opportunity to change their minds. Now, seriously, no more beating them at least until they give up the goods and we know they have told us the truth. Capisce?" Reluctantly, Johnny shook his head, with Lucky and Sal following Johnny's head. With that, they entered the room to learn the key to printing millions and making them richer than they ever dreamed. Stone then stopped them. "Wait, I'm bringing them out here." Johnny stepped up to Stone, "What are you crazy? That room is windowless and only one way in and out, too many potential problems out here. No, I can't allow it." "Johnny, trust me, I've got the guys read. I've had years of psychological training at the Fed. We've scared them, now we need to make them trust us. Johnny, stand down, I've got this. Just follow my lead."

Johnny, who had great respect for Stone, wasn't buying this so quickly. There were things they could use as weapons if they got loose, they could throw something through a window, endless possibilities. "Joe, what if one of them . . ." Stone put his hand up and stopped him, knowing he had to get Johnny to back down without losing face in front of his guys. "Johnny, did I let Sal down when he was in trouble?" Sal quickly nodded his head, knowing that had Stone saved his life. "Did I save Luke's ass not once but twice that you guys know about?" Now, it was Lucky's turn to start shaking his head in agreement. "Are all you guys a little richer since I showed up?" Now, Lucky and Sal were shaking their heads in unison. "One funky thing happens and, Johnny, you personally can crack the kids' skulls." Johnny realized he was outvoted and therefore took the out Stone gave him. "First one that sneezes funny, I'm going to kill him. Capisce?" Stone responded "Va Bien" (that's good). "Hey, when did you learn Italian with a name like Stone?" "You'd be surprised what I know. Lucky, take out your piece. Sal, take your piece out and stand in front of the door. If either one makes a move, shoot him or shoot them both." "You got it." Stone and Johnny nodded at each other, and Stone went to open the door with Lucky drawing down on the door, just in case the college punks tried to play tough guy.

Stone knocked on the door and with his most condescending sing-songy voice said, "Boys, I'm going to open the door and my friend will have a very big gun pointed at the door, so if you have any stupid ideas of playing Rambo, forget about it because I don't think your parents will be too happy to have blown two hundred thousand on an education just to have you shot dead two years out of college . . . Are we on the same page?"

From behind the door came a weak beaten voice, "Yes, sir, there will be no problem here, I promise." Stone immediately knew it to be Mike's voice, and with that he was convinced that at least he wasn't going to be an issue. "Raj is going to cooperate as well, but I think we are going to have to get him to the hospital—he's in a lot of pain." Stone wasn't convinced about Raj, yet there could always be future convincing to be performed. "God help him if he pisses Johnny off, he seems a little volatile today" was Stone's thought.

Stone opened the door slowly until he could see Mike and Raj's hands, that is ten of Mike's fingers and nine and a half of Raj's. "All right, boys, if we are going to make this happen, we are all going to have to get more comfortable with each other with some mutual trust and respect. What do you think, boys, ya think we could rewind and start all over again?" Stone went just inside the door and put an arm around each one of their shoulders and walked them into the large living room of the high rollers' suite. It was actually pretty amusing looking: Stone in the middle of the kids, Mike with his shoulders slumped, and definitely looking like a beat man, and Raj with his hand up in the air as if he was signaling a turn from the front seat of a non-existent car. Stone walked them over to the couch and sat them down. Everything seemed to be going smoothly when Raj suddenly jumped up. Fortunately for the Italians, it wasn't their first rodeo; they expected the unexpected; therefore, they expected one of the juveniles would try something.

Raj blurted out, "I'm not telling you anything until you bring me to an Emergency Room and have my finger sewn back on."

Johnny was already in motion and had covered half the distance to Raj in a nanosecond and was closing in for the kill, literally. Stone sensed Johnny's oncoming, but without turning around and breaking eye contact with the boys, he calmly raised his left hand signaling Johnny to hold off. He had it under control. As graceful as a ballerina, and without a visible break, he raised his right hand the split second his left hand went up to stop Johnny. He calmly but with incredible force squeezed the neck/shoulder muscle of Raj, very similar to the old Dr. Spock move.

Simultaneously squeezing and pushing down the pain and the pressures was too much for Raj. He crumbled back into the couch like a marionette dropped by its owner. "Now, now, now, Raj, I thought we had an understanding you were going to be nice and cooperative, and Johnny wasn't going to cut off more fingers or worse."

That was the end of it for Raj. He went from indignant to infant in about a second. He started sobbing uncontrollably, head in hands, which at some level he knew was good because at least his hand was in the air and it would stop him from bleeding to death. He began banging his feet on the ground and continued to say over and over again, "I want my finger back . . . sew my finger back on . . . I want my finger back on . . . sew my finger back on." The floors in Vegas hotels are very solid, so there was no chance of his tantrum being heard from below or above, for that matter. When a sufficient amount of time passed, which was probably thirty seconds, but seemed like a week to Johnny who just wanted to slap Raj, Stone gave Mike a look, and Mike intuitively understood Stone was giving him an opportunity to take care of his friend or suffer the consequences. Mike put his arm around Raj and said, "Hey pal, this isn't going to help us, you need to get a hold of yourself. Raj responded to Mike, "Just tell them to bring me to the hospital and have my finger sewn back on, and I promise I won't tell them what happened and I tell them how we make money," sniffling and hiccuping all the while he was saying it. Stone, for a brief second, felt bad for him, and then that thought quickly flew from his mind. Stone knew that what he was going to say next would only have one of two reactions. First, and hopefully, it would snap him back to reality, or second, it would send him off on another tantrum and he would have to let Johnny step in, which would get ugly for sure. "Raj" louder, "Raj, look at me!" Raj sheepishly looked up at Stone, who now for better or worse had his attention. "I want you to understand we are serious men who mean what we say. We told you to come clean and you opted for the wrong choice and you paid the price. Sewing your finger back on . . . that horse has left the barn. Deal with it or I guarantee you my friend over there will cut at least two more of your fingers off and probably one of your friend's for good measure. Actually, I think he wants to extract a little revenge on Mike, just for shits and giggles. Now, you have literally thirty seconds to get a hold of yourself or your little pinky problem is going to grow significantly. Capisce?"

Johnny immediately started thinking to himself, "What the hell is it with Stone and trying to talk Italian all the time? Is it part of the act with the kids or does he really think he's all of a sudden

Italian? Like he's going to get made or something?" He has got to know only Italians get made. Johnny, who was somewhat ADD, had to snap himself back into the present. Thirty seconds must have passed by now; that was the deadline he gave the little punk, right? He wasn't sure, but he knew one thing for sure, this party was over and a new one was about to begin. Stone's hand up or not, he needed to show everyone he was boss and why. His feet started moving again. That was all Raj had to see and self-preservation mode locked in.

Raj, with one of the most infamous lines from a Rock and Roll song made infamous by Meatloaf in "Paradise by the Dashboard lights," from the album *Bat Out of Hell*, put up his left hand and mightily belted out to Johnny and for everyone in the room to hear, "Stop right there!" Considering he was blubbering, just a few second ago, everybody stepped back just a little out of pure surprise.

Then Johnny got his wits about him again and started in on Raj again, "Who the fuck are you to tell me?" This time Stone knew he had to turn around to physically stop Johnny, and putting up his hand just wasn't going to do. "Hey, hey big Johnny, chill! The kid, I think, is finally coming to his senses. Let's try to handle this like businessmen." Johnny was pissed but not stupid. He knew what Luke would do and, as much as it pissed him off, Stone was handling the situation just like Luke would under the circumstances. Johnny was now pressing on Stone more for effect, then actually trying to muscle by Stone. Johnny had his arm over the top of Stone and pointing down at Raj, looking as scary as an escaped lion. "You better fucking come clean now or you won't have another hand to put up to stop me or anyone else—you got me, punk? Answer me!" "Ssssh Johnny, chill," he looked back over his shoulder at Raj, making like Johnny was going through him at any second. "Dude, dude, calm down, let's make this work, just promise me no more violence against my friend and I, cool?" "One chance, punk, one chance, you got me?" Mike chimed in, "Mister, we're cool, we're cool, just promise us if we tell you what you want, you'll let us go." "Can we trust you?" "I'll tell you what, if you don't, you're dead, so you're just going to have to trust me on that one, college boys."

Mike new it was futile to negotiate, so he decided to go with his father's philosophy of getting bees with honey. He had decided long ago, actually before the amputation, to spill his guts, and fight or flight was decided long ago for Mike. He, who was stronger than Raj, had quickly figured out that fight wasn't an option and neither was flight. Now, neither was negotiation. The only other option was to give it all up and try to hold out one chemical and use that to save their lives. "OK, are you ready?" Stone put up his hand, "Wait, let me get my laptop and a recorder, I want to make sure we get it all right, because if it doesn't work, and I play back to you what was said, there will be no mistake if you're not telling the truth. That way you'll only have yourself to blame if we have to kill both of you." Mike's stomach sank. He needed a plan B and quick.

Chapter 51

Mak had the patience of a gnat. He originally had full intentions of hanging around his room until Stone showed up. Then he would decide how to either confront him or follow him. That lasted about an hour, and he was fried. He was never good at stakeouts, and that was one of the reasons his partners hated him so much. Whenever a stakeout dragged on, he became more antsy. Then he would, believe it or not, get more annoying. On more than one occasion, he came to blows with a partner at a stakeout, or it should be said, two of his partners hauled off and hit him, one time, when he just wouldn't shut up and he was peppering his partner with questions that ranged from his childhood to his bathroom habits and ended with him asking his partner how his wife was in the sack. He was actually curious because he thought she was hot. That was when his partner hauled off and hit him in the front seat of their Crown Vic. The Crown Vic is big but not big enough for two grown men to fight. It spilled out into the street, blew their cover, and got both their asses in a sling. Needless to say, that was their last outing as partners.

The second time his partner had already had preconceived opinions about Mak. They were on their first stakeout two days into a new assignment. Mak started with some innocuous comments five minutes into the stakeout and his new partner Joe Laverne, who was a big strong guy probably six feet, one inch tall and weighing 210 pounds, just hauled off and hit him without any warning. That time they weren't in a car, they were in a rented room doing observation by binoculars from across the street of a known drug dealer. Since they were in an empty room with just sparse furnishing, it turned out to be a great fight, which, to everyone's surprise back at the station, Mak won handily.

Mak took a quick shower and put on some clothes. That is what they called them in the 1970s, anyway. Mak hadn't realized that clothes made out of natural fibers were both more comfortable and better for the environment. Not that he gave a shit about the environment, or anyone in it for that matter. So, dressed like an extra from Saturday Night Fever, he strutted like John Travolta down the hallway into the elevator and down to the palatial lobby of Caesar's Palace. Deciding that tomorrow was soon enough to deal with Stone, he was headed over to the Rio to get a head start on what would hopefully be an eventful night with Lucille. Mak kept the strut going all the way through the lobby. You see, in Vegas, the elevators are about as far away from the exits as possible. More opportunity for the patrons to make a donation either on the way to or from their room, or hopefully both.

Mak wanted nothing to do with Caesar's today. He just wanted to get to the Rio and check out the hot babes, drink a little, and wait for the arrival of Lucille. Mak, in his totally obnoxious way, was walking down the middle of the walkway, taking up at least the space of two normal men, his arms outstretched on both sides, swinging back and forth. He touched in varying degrees no less than five people on his way out the door, a couple sarcastically calling back to him, "Excuse me if I got in your way." Mak paid them no mind. One big guy turned around and called back to him, "Hey asshole, watch where you walking." Mak, only half hearing him, replied, "Yeah, whatever, go fuck a relative, oops that's how you got here." The guy only heard half of what he said and was going to go grab Mak and beat out the rest of what he said. His rather large wife, having seen this picture before, grabbed his arm, spun him around and promised him she would make it worth his while to just go back to the room. After looking at his wife, he almost decided to go after Mak, but his wife's grip, both physical and mental, convinced him to turn and follow his wife.

The valet at Caesar's was getting people into taxis like a fine-oiled machine. He was doing this unique trick with a wad of bills, presumably ones with a ten on the top. Every time he put someone in a cab, whether or not he got tipped, he would say thank-you for all to hear and flip the ten over on his wad of money. The untrained eye would think everyone was tipping him ten dollars to call up a taxi and open the door for them. A slick trick, if you weren't paying attention. I'm sure he shamed many people to tip him ten dollars for a one-dollar job. Mak let him open the door and let him in the cab, his hand out for the inevitable tip, which of course Mak did not give him. He only said to the young guy, reading his name tag, "Mark, I work for the IRS, I sure hope you're declaring all those tips. "Mark, a little stunned, but not too stunned to shut the door, flipped the ten-spot over his hand and said, "Thank you so much for that. You must be another big winner at Caesar's." Mak smirked as the cab pulled out, "Hey Cabbie, I hope you fucking speak English because I only want to tell you this once. Bring me to the Rio, do you understand me, Mahatma Gandhi?" The Indian driver who had fallen on bad times but was born and brought up in California, in his best California surfer dude accent replied, "Absofuckinglutely, dude, to the land of milk and honey it is."

Most people, even assholes like Mak, when confronted with being called out would backpedal a little. Not Mak, who just said, "then why don't you absofuckinglutely just shut up and drive the dude. I am in desperate need for a drink and a rendezvous with a buxom blonde named Lucille." The driver, disgusted with his life, disgusted with his job, and totally disgusted with his fare, just listened and did as he was told and drove to the Rio. As expected, he got the generous tip from his passenger of a whole fifty cents. As he drove away, he yelled back at Mak, "I hope Lucille gives you the clap!" Mak said back, more to himself than anyone in particular,

"It wouldn't be the first time, my little Gandhi, it wouldn't be the first time."

Mak went straight for the bar and sat where they have one of those computer poker games that sit flush on top of the bar. He figured he had about three hours before Lucille would show up, if she actually did. Wouldn't be the first time he'd been stood up. At this point, he just wanted to sit at the bar and look at the pretty women, have a couple of cocktails, eat some greasy food, and play a little poker on the machine in front of him.

That is exactly what Mak proceeded to do. "Hey there, bartender, set me up with a shot of Jack and a Budweiser to start. Bring a menu and let's get me full and shitfaced." The bartender, having heard and seen it all before, just gave the obvious East Coast Asshole his best; you can have whatever you want, sir, smiled and said, "I'd be much obliged to assist you in your endeavors, sir." "Great, then let's have it, amateur psychiatrist." That was the beginning of what was going to be a very interesting evening.

Chapter 52

Raj, who for some reason was just not getting the whole situation, asked another stupid question, which just further inflamed Johnny. "Do you mind, before we give you the benefit of all our hard work, telling us who exactly you guys are and how you found us?" Stone just rolled his eyes and Mike, who wasn't exactly sure who they were but had a good idea, also wanted to roll his eyes but instead had to leap to action. Johnny was already two steps on his way to taking Raj's head off. Even though he really wanted to pummel Mike for the shenanigans on the plane, Raj had moved clearly to the top of Johnny's hit parade, quite literally. Mike jumped up and in a pleading but decisive voice directed at Stone, "Hey, hey, you know what I . . . I mean we don't give a shit who you are. Once we tell you what we know, there is enough money for all of us and then some. My friend is just a little delusional from the pain. He apparently doesn't know what he's saying. First of all, we don't give a shit who you are, you're smart enough to find us, and obviously mean enough to hurt us. I know I may be crazy, but I truly believe and need to believe this to move forward and to give you what you want. I believe if we are up front with you and tell you all you want that we will be able to coexist. Truly, there is so much potential that we haven't even tapped into. We didn't want to get greedy and caught. We can all be rich beyond our wildest dreams. Actually, the truth be told, we're scared shit of the potential. We're just two frat boys that don't want to ever work hard. I don't know how you found us, but I suspect we got just a little too greedy, which, if this works out with us, will never happen again. We promise."

Mike, like all really bright people, is a damn good chess player. Like all good chess players, he is five steps ahead of his opponent. Hoping for the best that these guys actually let them go when they're through spilling their guts. Mike and Raj will go on with their measly existence and continue to print off what they need. These guys, though, are bound to get greedy. Just look at the guy they call Johnny. These guys won't make it six months before the feds come raining down on them. We will be long gone, change our identities. These guys have got to be organized crime. Once they are caught and put in jail, then they can start printing again in small quantities when they need money.

Johnny, looking like a raging bull, controlled himself long enough to put a finger millimeters from Mike's face, "Enough Bullshit, tell us how or you're going to become a 20/20 unsolved mystery case."

Raj quietly acquiesced and turned the show over to Mike. Stone, talking to Mike, knowing intuitively that Mike would be the one to talk, said, "OK, Mr. Mike, I got the recorder on and my laptop ready, speak slowly, clearly, completely, and chronologically on the process."

So Mike started and talked for almost an hour nonstop. Telling the boys even background information they didn't need, attempting to endear them to their captors. Truth be told, it was working. They were all warming up to at least Mike. Stone, though, was a little more apprehensive. He had seen this show many times before, during countless interrogations, where the perp was trying to become friendly in order to cop for a lesser crime. It was usually the white collar guys who thought they were smarter than everyone and, even after being caught, thought they could talk their way out of their problem. Therefore, Stone was constantly interrupting Mike and having him go over every item point by point. When Mike was done, Stone said "Okay, now let's do it again, and this time let's not forget or leave anything out."

"Excuse me," Mike said clearly surprised. "Honest, I've told you everything." Johnny jumped in being the quintessential hard guy. "Shut up, frat boy, and do as you're told or you and your friend will have matching pinkies." Stone let a brief but seemingly eternal pause go by. "Mike, you gave me a lot of information and I just want to make sure we go over it again, but this time I want Sal and Lucky to bring Raj in the other room." Raj perked up now immediately, sensing this could not be good. Why would he want to split them up? Raj now spoke for the first time in an hour. "He told you everything and you promised everything would be OK if we told you everything." He really did sound like a troubled little girl. Raj could even hear it in his own voice. "Calm down, Raj, we are men of our word. We just want to make sure the two of you have the same story. Now, please quietly go in the other room with my two associates and everything will be fine." Raj was seemingly thinking it over and happened to be looking in Johnny's direction. Johnny only flinched as if he was moving in Raj's direction and that was enough to make Raj jump out of his seat and be quietly led to the adjoining room. Stone and Johnny were now left alone with Mike. Johnny was standing sentinel and Stone was sitting down with his laptop on his lap. Stone placed the laptop on the ground, put his hands to his face, and rubbed his eyes. He then put his hands together, stretched them out beyond his legs, and kept his fingers intertwined, lowering his head as if in prayer. He paused for a moment for effect and then spoke, "Mike, let me start by saying, I'm giving you the benefit of the doubt that you told me everything, but on the off chance you held anything back because you and Raj had some sort of contingency plan if you both were ever caught, I'm going to give you a chance to first save a finger or possibly even your life." "There is no contingency plan, I swear, believe me, we never anticipated whatever this thing that's going on." "Well, Mike, I'm starting to like you, and I hate to hurt people I like. That's why you added all the extra personnel bullshit to make us like you, right?" Both Mike and Johnny's mind went to

"Boy, he's good." "No . . . Yeah . . . ahh . . . Maybe I don't know." "That's OK. I want to like you, even Johnny here wants to like you, especially if we all make some money on your genius. What we don't want is for you to withhold consciously or unconsciously any detail as small as it may be. Because when we duplicate your process, if it doesn't work, or if one of us gets caught, or if it doesn't pass the iodine test, we will not like you anymore and we will enjoy killing you and Raj slowly, very slowly, capisce?" Mike silently dropped his head, then shook it up and down confirming his agreement. He was also thinking he should have left something out because they were expecting him to do that. Now, he had nothing to give them, and they would be looking for something. Apparently, this guy Joe was a better chess player than he had given him credit for. Mike started, "OK, I know you're going to find this hard to believe, but I believed you when you told me that if I come clean and told you everything, you would leave us alone and not hurt us anymore. I'm quite fond of all my fingers, and I'm even more fond of my life. Although you said you wanted to make money off our genius, I think you guys are pretty smart as well. We've been doing this for years with no problems until you guys found us out. I promise you I told you everything." "Fine, tell us again without the ancillary bullshit, and we'll see where it goes." "How about we just make some money and go spend it—that will prove it." "Soon enough, son, soon enough. Run us through the process, then we'll see."

Mike started from the beginning this time. Joe interrupted less until Mike got to the part about soaking the paper in a tub and then drying the paper in a dryer with sneakers or shoes. "OK, explain to me again why you put the paper in a tub of water." Mike responded, "You see, in order for the bills to last any length of time in circulation, they must be waterproof. I'm sure you know US currency is not really paper, it's a kind of cotton cloth. The paper or cloth is only made in one place by one company that has been doing it for over two hundred years. You can't buy anything like it. That's why we had to create a process that first would make the paper waterproof, then we had to come up with a formulation so it would pass the iodine test, and then refine it so the chemical processes would work in unison." "Why the sneakers in the dryer?" First of all, that's why we stay in one of those huge suites—because they have their own laundry. To be truthful, we don't need a dryer, but by putting the new bills in pillowcases and throwing in some shoes, the bills come out looking and feeling more used and therefore more authentic." Stone sat quiet for a minute, Johnny and Mike waiting for him to speak. Johnny was waiting because, quite frankly, he wasn't smart enough to question without beating someone into talking. Smart enough, though, to know that Mike was not wanting to speak out of turn for fear of losing a finger a la Raj.

Stone then looked up from his laptop and said, "So, Mike, seriously, I know you went to MIT and all you guys are bright, but you're trying to tell me you and the whinny guy out there took a bunch of easily attainable chemicals from ninth grade chemistry class and figured out how to outsmart the US government?" Mike, this time being the chess player, took a pregnant moment. "Look, you don't have to believe me, just try it out yourself. We broke it down to three problems and just solved each one. First, we had to make regular paper waterproof. Pretty simple chemicals once the paper is submerged. Second, we needed to figure out how to make the iodine not react to the paper. Actually, also not that difficult. We then ran into a little issue, kind of like Edison with the light bulb, he could get many metals to burn but none not burn out in a vacuum. We could get the paper waterproof and we could get the paper not to react to iodine, but not both. Fortunately for us, unlike Edison, within four days we got half lucky and half good. After we treated the paper to make it waterproof and then treated it with our anti-iodine concoction, we just sprinkled talcum powder on the wet paper, dried it in the dryer, then printed the paper in an HP color printer." "Whoa, Whoa, wait. So you're telling me talcum powder is the secret ingredient?" "Well, not exactly, it just does something to counteract the ingredients which make it waterproof and the ingredients that make it not react to the iodine." "How?" "Honestly, I really don't know. I'm the math guy in the partnership. Raj is the real chemist." "But you both work in computer programming." "Computer programming for us is like playing men's softball after you played college baseball. Anyone who played college ball can play softball but not everyone who can play softball can play college ball. You can't even get into MIT if you're not a computer nerd. So what Raj and I do with computers, we can do in our sleep."

"OK, assuming what you tell me is correct, go over again your process for converting the bad bills into real cash." "Originally, it was truly small time, we would need to make money . . . the hard way . . . working. We would then make new money only copying the bill once and then spending a small portion of it and keeping the rest of the cash. Sometimes we would buy something big and then return it for real cash. Then we would fake the real cash and do it all over again. That was until we found Vegas."

"Okay, I got that part, now tell me the physical . . . chemical process."

"Oh, I misunderstood the question. We fill a tub with warm water."

"Does it have to be warm?"

"If the water is cold, it takes longer for the chemicals to dissipate. If the water is too hot, the chemicals dissolve too fast. Think of a newborn baby's bathwater."

"OK. Then?"

"Well, obviously, those are the chemicals with the polyethylene base. They bond to the paper and kind of put a transparent coating on the paper. Think of it as a rubber for the paper, which it keeps everything in and protects it from the outside."

"I got it."

"Then we take the paper out of the water, lay it on the counter or a table, and spray it with the solution we developed to trick the paper into not absorbing the iodine. Then you sprinkle it with talcum powder, take the wet paper, and put it into pillowcases, and dry the paper in a dryer. We've found that putting a pair of shoes or sneakers in the dryer softens up the paper a little more, which makes it feel like a worn bill."

"How long?"

"How long what?"

"How long do you dry the paper?" Stone said, slightly irritated.

"Depends."

Now Stone took on a Johnnyesque look to him and started standing up. Mike, sensing he had pushed a little too far, quickly changed his cat and mouse game.

"Chill, chill, I'm not kidding. It all depends on how much paper we are drying. You need to check it occasionally just to make sure you don't overdry it. Brittle paper is no good, you have to throw it away. On average, ten minutes is more than enough. But remember, if it's too wet, it will get stuck in the printer."

"Then?"

"Then the easy part."

"Easier than what you've told me so far?"

"Yes, because now it's only a matter of letting the computer and scanner do its part."

"Enlighten me."

"Certainly." Actually, Mike was starting to unknowingly enjoy himself. He hadn't realized how much it bothered him that he was not able to brag about his and Raj's accomplishment to anyone. What they had accomplished in what was a relatively short amount of time had never been figured out by anyone else as far as he knew. Other than Raj, to this point everyone they knew, including and especially their parents, just assumed they had wasted an MIT education. Now he was able to puff out his chest a bit, even if it was only to a Guido and some other guy who didn't act like a Guido, but certainly must be one—guilty by association.

"OK, here's the beauty. All you need is a one hundred dollar scanner. Place the bills on the scanner, scan them into a file, flip the bills over, scan them into a file, and merge them so they will print double sided. Print them, cut them, put the bills in your pocket, and you're done!" Mike, really now pleased with himself, politely folded his hands in his lap and sat quietly trying to hold back a shit-eating grin. As if a huge weight was lifted off his shoulders, he got to eat the canary and brag about it.

Then, with absolutely no warning, and as deftly as a jaguar, Stone was out of his seat, knocked Mike over backward with a right foot to the chest. He landed on top of him, with his right knee firmly planted on Mike's chest, and his service revolver cocked and pressing against Mike's temple. "Do we look stupid to you? Do we look fucking stupid to you?" Stone's glare, not wavering from studying Mike's eyes, "You're trying to tell me that with dime store chemicals and hundred dollar scanners and an HP printer, you've been fooling the US government, banks, casinos, stores . . . do you take us for fools?" Stone was pressing the gun hard to Mike's temple with a vise-like clamp, with his left hand on Mike's jaw and cheek, his glare never wavering.

Mike's body, shaking under Stone's, attempted to mutter some intelligible words.

"Wha? Wha?" "Tell me the truth or I'll kill you right here and now." Stone lightened up his grip just enough for Mike's words to be understood.

"Honest, I told you everything. Let's do it right now. Let me make you some money."

"Oh, sure, I'll let you make me some money. I'll go downstairs and try to buy chips with this bad money and I'll end up in jail. Is that your plan, college boy? Is that your fucking plan?" As he tightened his grip on Mike's face again, never losing eye contact with him, Stone loosened his grip again, just enough to allow Mike to speak, "Honestly, I'll go cash the money. You'll see."

By now, it didn't matter, Stone had his answer. The kid was telling the truth. His eyelashes were not rapid fire blinking. He had a nervous sweat but one that was from fear of dying, not one of deceit. Although you can never be too careful, Raj was going to get the same treatment and someone other than he was going to try to cash some of the new bills first.

Johnny stood almost mesmerized by what was happening, trance-like. He clearly was learning that a combination of calm questioning and a good dose of violence gave a better, more thorough response to acquiring information from someone. Then the vibration in his pocket woke him out of his trance. He took the phone out of his breast pocket, "Pronto, boss."

Chapter 53

Mak was in a very good mood and, as well he should be, he had sat at the bar alternating between Budweiser and Jack and Cokes for a few hours playing video poker at the bar. He had the bartender put a club soda in front of the seat beside him to save it for the hopeful eventuality of sweet Lucille showing up. Mak was up a cool four thousand clams and his luck seemed to be getting better and better. Apparently, the guy who programmed his machine was either a degenerate gambler and felt for his brethren or was asleep at the switch. This machine was just too good. As an experiment, he had tried to play poorly and was still winning. He was thinking he didn't need to move in on Stone, he could just stay at this machine for the next year and retire.

Actually, Mak quietly started wishing Lucielle would blow him off. This was the kind of run that you only heard about. Just then, four aces came up and another five hundred dollars appeared on his tally. Totally engrossed in his good fortune, he felt a fingernail caress the back of his neck, sending a chill down his spine. The good kind of chill, the one filled with excitement and intrigue.

"Hi, cowboy, buy a girl a drink," Mak heard from behind, recognizing immediately Lucille's voice. Poker luck thoughts faded quickly and changed to luck thoughts of a different nature.

Mak turned around and was immediately struck by her beauty and her age. The first thought in his head was, "*Wow, is she out of my league.*" Clearly, it was Lucille that was standing in front of him, but out of uniform and presented the way she wanted to present herself. The difference was night and day. While working, Lucille most days wore her hair up, which was kind of an unwritten rule at Caesar's, it made her look more in character. Tonight though, her blonde hair was flowing over her shoulders, actually kind of radiating in the bright lights of the Rio. Possibly from bleach highlights in her hair, possibly not! Her makeup was nothing like what he remembered from the check-in counter. There, her makeup was loud and gaudy, again by unwritten corporate design. Tonight, her makeup was soft and actually very ladylike.

Thoughts of confusion filled Mak. He had always been attracted to the buxom blonde, overdone up pseudo tramp look—the "I really could be a hooker" look. Now, all of a sudden, here was this woman who he thought fit that bill, and instead, she was hands down the prettiest woman that ever actually voluntarily spent time with him.

Tonight, her outfit was not Romanesque like it was at check-in. She had on a very fashionable, if not stylish, revealing dress. There was no hiding her puppies, so she had decided long ago to flaunt and not hide all her natural assets.

"Lucille, please don't say anything yet, please just spin around for me one second." Lucielle, more than happy to oblige, spun on her rather high, but stylish, stilettos. He had known she had a rack to die for, he had known that she was cute. He had no idea that her ass was as round and hard as that of a dancer. Currently, all thoughts of video poker were permanently and totally forgotten.

Mak, for the first time in his life, was speechless for three reasons. He was truly struck by her beauty. She was there to see him, and if he acted like his normal asshole self, she surely wouldn't stick around. He decided he needed to carefully choose his words, "Lucille, I thought that my luck could not get any better, and you showed up and made all my earlier good fortune a distant memory."

Lucille, showing her propensity to blush again, said, "I didn't realize what a smooth talker you were."

"Neither did I, and since I didn't think about it, apparently it came straight from the heart."

"Again, you're smooth and with me smooth talking will get you everywhere."

"Well, then sit down and let me pour on the smooth. Let me guess your drink, Cosmo, yes Cosmo. You're a Cosmo girl."

Lucille, again blushing, asked, "Is that good?"

"No, that's great! I'd be disappointed if you asked for sparkling water or a wine spritzer."

"And I would be disappointed if you pegged me as the wine spritzer type." Lucille was helped onto the bar stool by Mak who had no recollection of ever helping someone with their seat under any circumstances, and he kind of liked the sensation.

"Bartender, cash me out with five hundred dollar chips if you don't mind." Lucille let out a little "oh," showing her approval with his winnings. "But, first, mix up my pretty lady the best Cosmo you have ever made in your life, and I will tip with all my appreciation."

"Yes, boss, I feel a great Cosmo stirring right now."

"Once you're done with that, fire me up another Seven and Seven, we good?"

"No, boss, we're great!"

Lucille, now sitting at the bar, said to Mak, "I'm glad you didn't' disappoint me either." Mak, momentarily confused, kept the smooth on, "I'm glad I didn't disappoint you, but do you mind giving me a hint as to exactly what I didn't disappoint?"

"I'm just glad you didn't order a wine spritzer or a mojito or any other hundred trendy swishy drinks. Seven and Seven is a man's drink. It's what my father drank."

Mak had never really felt like this. He was running on all eight cylinders with Lucille and couldn't for the life of him figure out exactly why, but he was through thinking about that, he was just going to ride the wave. "I think I would like your dad, sounds like my kind of guy."

She smiled and said, "Let's not get ahead of ourselves, but play your cards right and you just may have an opportunity to drink with him."

"Well, darling, I'll put that on my to-do list, but right now I just want to have a drink or sixteen with you!"

Mak and Lucille got on like the proverbial two peas in a pod. They sat, drank, talked, and nibbled on appetizers. They laughed incessantly, talking about nothing and everything all at the same time. They got up and danced a number of times and Jimmy Dreggs, the bartender, who knew he was getting a big tip, watched their seats at the bar and Lucille's purse. Not that Lucille had much money in it, but a credit card and driver's license can be a bitch to replace. Mak was on a roll, and he felt pretty good that it was going to result in a roll in the hay. Thoughts of Stone and why he was there became far removed from his brain. The only stone Mak was thinking about was the rock forming in his pants. Before the night was over, that was all to change.

Chapter 54

Pronto, my ass!" Luke snapped into the phone. "What the hell is going on? What's taking so long? Do I need to fly out there now?" Johnny, still hurting from the last crack to the jaw, had no intention of pissing Luke off. Plus, he knew well enough that the boss had minimal patience at best, therefore it was always best to wait until he was sure Luke was done before interrupting him. After an appropriate amount of time, which was approximately the time it takes to inhale and exhale twice, this was to make sure the first breath wasn't just to reload his lungs to continue a rant. By the time Johnny was sure it was OK to talk, he was already out of the room and into the massive bathroom, which would serve just fine for an office.

"Boss, listen, it's going awesome. We've separated the kids and we're just getting through to the first little shit. He told us everything."

"How do you know he's not bullshitting you?"

"Well, that's the thing, boss. It seems a little too simple, but the kid sounded sincere to me, then Stone out of nowhere went postal on the guy, and the kid didn't budge from his story."

"Johnny, that doesn't mean shit."

"Boss, he offered to make some money now, and go cash it in for chips. That way he'll prove the bills are good."

"Johnny, Madonna Mia, if you were in his place right now, would you rather get pinched for counterfeiting or be locked in a room with a bunch of goons like you guys?"

"Boss, seriously, we are not that stupid, we'll keep one of them for safe keeping."

"May not be enough, kid may want to save his own ass."

"Boss, seriously, Stone's good and I've never let you down before, eh?"

"Stone's an amateur when it comes to this."

"Maybe from our way of life, but he's the best good cop–bad cop interrogator all wrapped up in one I've ever seen."

"The best, Johnny?"

"Oh . . . of course not, not better than you."

"That's not what I mean Johnny, just be fucking careful, we're not talking fencing some cigarettes here. This is counterfeiting, that's serious time."

"Capisce, we won't fuck it up."

"Va bene, call me with any updates. You may hear from me sooner rather than later."

"Sure, boss, but no need to worry. I won't make a move without checking first."

"Johnny, seriously, I trust you with my kids and I know I should trust Stone, but I don't. I can't get over why he's become so . . . I'm not sure how to put it . . . helpful."

"Money, boss, money. Plus, doesn't everyone want to be Al Capone? That is the kids who don't want to be policemen, ha-ha."

"Now that you put it that way, I'm even more convinced he became a cop and Al Capone was a mob boss!" That's the last thing Johnny heard before the click, but definitely not the last time he thought about that comment.

Luke, like all powerful people, has many powerful friends. Amazing how completely legit guys love the intrigue and danger of hanging with the seedier side of life. Luke counted among his dear friends many politicians, entrepreneurs, and more than a few CEOs of very powerful companies, some public, some not. James Eikelroth was one of those special self-made guys, coincidentally an MIT grad, poor kid on a full boat, smartest guy in his class by far, but never forgetting his street upbringing. Most likely, that's what brought Luke and James together. They met at a fundraiser, coincidentally thrown together by being assigned to the same table. They became fast friends, and weekly golf partners. James knew what Luke did from day one, and didn't give a shit. He liked Luke for Luke. Not for what he represented as an Italian, not how he made his money, but for his intellect and his thought process. They could argue for hours, or commiserate for hours, on subjects like politics in which they were mostly in lock step.

James had said to Luke on more than one occasion, "Friends don't keep score. Luke, you're my good friend, and if you ever need anything, just say the word and it's yours, no questions asked."

Luke always replied, "You're the only guy I can say ditto to and actually mean it."

Luke had to do many favors for people, but there was always a string, a return favor, whatever. Not with James. Actually, he wished James would ask for a favor, but he just apparently never needed one.

James, though, had offered up his private jet to Luke on many occasions. Only once, for a surprise anniversary vacation trip to Aruba for Teresa, did Luke ever take James up on his offer. Luke, though, asked James no less than ten times what his out-of-pocket cost was for the round-trip flight. James would have nothing of it, he was happy to do a favor for his friend. Luke, being Luke, asked around what it should cost from some of his other CEO buddies and got a good estimate of the value.

James Eikelroth was a very generous man and raised many millions of dollars for charity. His pet charity was for cystic fibrosis. He had a nephew who was afflicted. Two months after Luke borrowed the plane, he made a donation at James's annual event, for the cost of the flight plus ten thousand dollars. James knew what he did, gave Luke a stern shake of the finger at the event, but it furthered the bond between the two. The phone vibrated in James's pocket. It was already past 9:00 p.m. and James was driving home from a late meeting, when he pulled it out to see who was calling. The screen read, "big boy"—James's nickname for Luke. James answered the phone, "Let me see if I can do this right. Pronto, how are you, my friend? Are you looking for a rematch to win back some of the money you lost to me at our last golf match?"

"Fucking sandbagger, how are you, James?"

James realized immediately that the playfulness in Luke's voice was manufactured. "I couldn't be better, Luke. To what do I owe the pleasure of this late call?"

"Sorry, James, did I wake you?"

"No, just coming home from a bullshit late meeting."

"Good, I'm glad I didn't wake you. I need a favor, a big one." Luke, as most important people, loved to do favors but hated asking for them.

"Whatever you want, big guy." And James meant it and Luke knew that, which is why he could ask. "How many people does that jet of yours hold?"

"The real nice one you went on, only six, the bigger one fifteen comfortably, just a little less posh. Why, do you need it?"

"Yeah, here's the tricky part. I gotta get to Vegas for a big poker game immediately, may need it to hang around for a day or two, but seriously, I'll pay whoever to keep it quiet, though. No need for anyone to know I'm playing high stakes poker."

"Luke, listen, your reasons are irrelevant to me, you're my friend, let's not worry about money right now, apparently you need to get to Vegas tonight. Luckily for you, the big plane is fueled up and ready go to at Lawrence Airport in North Andover, you know where that is, right?"

"Sure, obviously, I do leave the city once in a while, smart-ass."

"Ha-Ha, let me call the pilot and copilot, I got their numbers in my Blackberry. Fuckers, the amount of money I pay them to sit on their asses most of the time. Tough shit if they're unhappy. Just in case, plan on being ready to leave in about an hour, but I'll call you right back. You may want to throw them a few bucks to gamble with, so they don't get pissed and fly you into a mountainside on the way there."

"Don't worry, the only hard money to get out of me is a golf bet. Seriously, James, a debt of gratitude."

"No, just a stroke a side would be fine."

"Never, ha-ha."

"I'll call you as soon as I have the pilots confirmed."

Luke thanked James again, hung up and speed-dialed "AB" who answered as if it was the middle of the day, "pronto, boss"

"'AB,' pack a quick bag with clothes for Vegas, meet me at the Lawrence Airport in no more than an hour."

"Obviously private, so no problem with hardware?"

"Actually, bring some extra for the boys, just to be safe."

"Va Bene, no problem, see you soon."

"Teresa, cardamia, pack me a quick bag for Vegas. I'm out of here in a half hour." The reply was only, "Stone?"

"Kinda."

"Be careful, your bag will be done in ten minutes"

James speed-dialed Joe Dunn, a Vietnam pilot, no bullshit kind of guy, with the social skills of an ant. Although very happy to be working for James Eikelroth, good money, great hours, seeing the world, and flying the best nonmilitary planes in the air, Joe was pulling down one hundred and fifty K a year to do a job he would gladly do for free. Happy as Joe Dunn was to be working for James, he was dead asleep when the phone rang. Wha . . . What . . . Who's there . . .

"Hey Dunnster, James here."

Waking up quickly, "Mister Eikelroth, what's the problem, what can I do for you?"

"Sorry, Joe, have an urgent matter. Need you and Mark dressed and ready to fly out of Lawrence tonight within the next hour. Headed to Vegas, maybe there a day or two. Personal favor to me and when you get back, no need to mention who was on the plane or what happens. There will be a little something extra in the Christmas envelope this year."

"Gotcha, boss, I already know Mark is home. I dropped him off about two hours ago after we shot a little pool."

"Didn't drink, did you?"

"One beer, three hours ago, and you know Mark's a recovering alcoholic, so he's fine."

"Great, you're picking up my friend Luke and whoever he has with him. You'll hang out in Vegas until he wants to come back with whoever he has with him. Give him your cell, stay somewhere nice, have a ball, but don't drink because when he wants to come back, come back so the plane's not out of commission too long. Again, Joe, you're my guy 'cause I can trust you, same with Mark. Treat this like a regular trip, no need for anyone to know who you're with."

"Gotcha, boss, we will be there in an hour and ready to leave a half hour later. Just went to Vegas two weeks ago for a trade show, already have a flight plan, just need to resubmit it."

"Great, thanks, talk to you when you get back."

The reason James and Luke got along so well was their management styles were exactly the same. They loved their people, and their people loved them. Pay a little more, show them respect, and trust. Joe and Mike would do their jobs and never say a word, no matter what they saw, and they saw a lot.

Joe called Mark and with very few words, he was on his way to Lawrence Airport. James called Luke and said, "Plane taxis in an hour and a half, be on it or wait for scheduled air."

"Thank you, my friend, I will be." And he was going there, or be damned trying.

"Back for our next match."

Luke knew there were big happenings in Vegas and he was determined to be there, convinced there was no issue with Stone as a fed, so getting pinched wasn't the issue, but the dangers of being spotted were high. Vegas had more cameras than anywhere else in the world. He would need to be careful.

Luke kissed Teresa goodnight, promised to be safe, and left quickly. He arrived at Lawrence Airport and drove directly to James's private hangar. Joe, the head pilot, was already there making preparations for the flight. He greeted Luke, who told him there would be one more passenger. Joe told him he was also waiting on one. Joe put on a fresh pot as they both waited for their respective colleagues to arrive.

Chapter 55

"That was fucking Luke Fabrasia on the phone, wasn't it?" Mike almost cried to Stone. Stone, true to his name, showed no emotion to Mike's question.

"You don't worry about who was on the phone. You worry about making sure you're playing straight with me because, one thing I will assure you, whatever bad you think will come from me, only worse can come from who was on the other end of that phone.

"Dude, I promise you I've told you everything. Please let me talk to Raj alone for a minute. I want to make sure he understands what I understand!"

"Not a chance, son, I'm talking to him alone. Depending on how cooperative he is will determine whether or not you guys get to chat again."

"You don't understand. Raj doesn't always understand our ways."

"Well, I guess if he was smart enough to get into MIT and smart enough to outsmart the Treasury Department, I'm sure it shouldn't take him more than three or four fingers to figure out not to fuck with us."

There was an awful pregnant silence. Stone did not need to break it since this was similar to a negotiation, and at the juncture when both parties are silent, inevitably, the first person who speaks loses. That was not Mike's thought. Mike's thought was how to get Raj to not be cute. Smart guys always think they can outsmart people they deem to be of lesser intelligence. That's typically because they aren't trying to outsmart serial criminals who look at violence as just part of the job. Mike was just getting ready to say something, anything when the door burst open and there was the rather large and imposing Johnny blocking the light entering the room from the main living room. Before Johnny could say anything, Stone barked, "Enough with this one for now. Have Sal bring Raj in, and have Lucky babysit this one out there while we talk to the smart ass one." Without hesitation, Johnny turned his head toward the living room, "Sal, bring smart ass over here, it's his turn."

As much as a smart ass Raj could be, his complexion went pale. He was feeling pretty comfortable out of the limelight. He knew Mike could handle himself at least intellectually. The pain in his finger (or lack thereof) was pounding, but he didn't feel as threatened with the two underlings. The other two obvious bosses scared the shit out of him. Sal was up and had his hand on Raj's left arm before Raj could get a thought in his head. Pulling him up and onto his feet, then the thought entered his head thank God he grabbed the arm that the hand with all the digits was on because a quick jerk like that on his right arm would have sent spears of pain into his brain.

Stone said to Johnny, "Have Lucky babysit this one for a while." Lucky not only heard Stone but had already anticipated it. Soon as Sal jumped up to get Raj, Lucky was already on his feet to go get Mike. Lucky had heard some commotion when the door was closed, but wasn't sure what to expect when he entered the bedroom. When he got there, Mike looked tired, scared, and had red marks on his neck. They looked like they were going to leave a permanent mark in the morning, but there was no blood. Apparently, all of his extremities were also intact. Lucky moved into the room quickly and had Mike by the arm and on his feet in one swift move. For one short moment, everyone was crowded in the smallest room in the suite, Johnny standing by the door, Stone still sitting in his chair, turning around backwards, Sal, having just entered the room, with Raj in tow, and Lucky just springing Mike to his feet.

Mike saw a small opportunity to help his cause and jumped on it. Mike and Raj's eyes caught each other for a moment in the transition. Mike pleaded first with his eyes, then with his mouth, "Raj, I told them everything, don't get cute, tell them everything. I mean everything. I trust them not to hurt us anymore. We can help them with the money and some other stuff as well!" Right then, Johnny stepped forward and smacked Mike up the back of the head.

"Shut up, college boy, speak when spoken to and if your shithead friend continues to get cute, he'll be dialing a phone with his nose. Capisce?" Mike's head was ringing but he knew he had potentially saved their lives at least temporarily by just inserting the last few words to his plea, "help them with other stuff as well." He knew that the underling thugs wouldn't pick up on it but the guy they called Joe, he was the smart one, and maybe even the other boss, Johnny, was smart enough to pick up on it. Mike obviously knew the money deal worked and once they knew it worked, they might not have much value, although, if they thought there was some other way to harness their intellectual talent, that could be their salvation.

Stone may not be an MIT grad, but he was no one's fool either. He had already figured out these kids were brilliant and although they could make millions from their counterfeit inventiveness, there may be limitless possibilities if they just took the time to think about it. Stone actually was beginning to like Mike in a weird sort of way. He wasn't going to let that cloud his perceptions. First, he was going to corroborate Mike's story with Raj's, first things first. Raj held up his hand with his severed finger and said to Mike, "Does it look like I want to lie to them?" which was greeted by a slap up the back of the head from Sal, echoing Johnny's comment and actions, "Hey, speak when spoken to, punk."

Stone said to Sal, "Sit him down and watch him for just a minute." He motioned to Johnny to step outside the room to talk to him. Lucky was escorting Mike rather vigorously to where Raj had just been sitting. Johnny and Stone went into the cavernous bathroom.

Stone asked Johnny, "What's up with Luke?"

"Nothing, why?"

"Johnny, don't bullshit me. He's called twice since we've been here, what's he saying?"

"Stone, listen to me. Everything is fine, he just gets a little jumpy, and he is not patient. Man, you wouldn't understand, it's an Italian thing."

"You're wrong, trust me, I understand not having patience, but this feels like a trust thing."

"Stone, again, don't read into this, we're a very closed group. We don't trust anybody, it's how we protect ourselves. That's why, unless you're one hundred percent Italian, you can never fully be one of us. Stone, your last name doesn't qualify you for instant access if you know what I mean."

"Whatever. When will Luke be calling back?"

"He didn't say, only that you'd hear from him soon."

"Let's go either collaborate the story Mike gave us, or remove some additional body parts until they give it to us straight."

"Cool, but Joe, once we know they came clean, what are you thinking about what we do with them?"

"Johnny, I'm hoping it works, and we can find a way to have them take the risk of converting the dough for us. More importantly,

I need to think how we can use their brains to make us even more money."

"Smart, Stone, smart. That's exactly what Luke would be thinking."

Then Johnny's mind went right to Luke's Al Capone comment.

Stone to Raj: "Look, Raj, no matter what you may think, at this point we don't want to hurt either one of you anymore, so I'll give you my word. Tell us the truth and we won't hurt you anymore. But trust me, when I tell you, hide anything from us and you'll be praying for us to kill you. Let me be clear, I don't mean answer all our questions, I mean tell us everything or whatever happens to you will be your fault. Capisce?"

"Mister."

"Joe."

"OK, Joe, seriously, one finger is enough. I didn't get into MIT because I'm a dope. What do you want me to tell you?"

"Apparently. you are a fucking dope!" Stone's voice was rising precipitously. "Didn't I just tell you to tell us everything without me having to ask questions?" In perfect timing, Johnny started over to Raj to institute some clarification.

"Stop, stop, I didn't mean it that way. I only meant from where do you want me to start?"

Stone shot back, "From the beginning, you idiot!"

"OK, OK." And so Raj started, and to his surprise as well as Stone's, Raj started from the first beer he and Mike had when the plan was hatched.

Stone's instincts seemed to be corrected. Raj recounted the whole story, without exception. Stone was reviewing his notes as Raj spoke. Every chemical, every process was in the exact order that Mike had recounted. Stone then went back and questioned every process, the exact percentage of chemicals, the washing of the paper, the drying of the bills, the shoes in the dryer, so either they had planned for this contingency or they were telling the truth and now Stone had the recipe for producing endless supplies of cash. When it was all said and done, they all three sat in silence for a moment, Johnny wondering what Stone was thinking. Then, almost the instant it happened, he knew, and Stone was out of his chair and on top of Raj like a cat, knocking him over with his hand on Ra's throat. Just like déjà vu all over again, as Yogi Berra said.

"Do we look stupid to you? It can't be that simple—now tell me the truth or I'll rip your throat out right here right now!"

Raj, struggling to speak, croaked out, "Honest to God, honest to God, that's all of it!" Stone, not wavering his eyes even a fraction, watched Raj's eyes. Not even a blink. Raj was telling the truth. Stone jumped off him as quick as he pounced on him.

Mike, hearing the commotion, his stomach sank, expecting the worst was happening to his friend and put his head in his hands.

Stone went to the door. "Sal, come get him and bring him in there. I need to talk to Johnny." Sal immediately obliged and came to escort Raj back to the bed room. Raj patted along beside like a beaten puppy. Sal, sensing that Raj was sufficiently mentally and physically worn down, just guided him to a chair near Mike.

Before they could speak to each other, Stone barked: "And don't let them talk to each other until I'm done."

Lucky responded, "You got it, boss." Johnny, hearing Lucky, his mind went immediately back to Luke's Al Capone comment. Johnny, being Italian and not good at hiding his emotions, shot Lucky a nasty glare. Lucky, having no clue what he had just said since he calls everyone boss, was befuddled at Johnny's apparent displeasure.

Stone closed the door on Johnny and himself before Stone could say a word. Johnny said, "Hey, I'm his boss, Stone. You get that?" Stone, always outwardly cool as a cucumber, inwardly was taken aback. Quick on his feet though, he calmly retorted, "I know you're his boss, he knows you're his boss and if you haven't noticed, he calls everyone boss, even Sal, who as you know he's Sal's boss. I'm just here as a facilitator, trying to make us rich, so now if you don't mind, can we discuss this?"

Johnny, taking a minute to internalize what Stone had just said, thought about it and said, "Yeah, sorry, it just hit me wrong. You're right, he calls everyone boss. So what do you think, 'Are they telling the truth'?"

Stone, without hesitation said, “Yes.” Then he paused and said, “I’m probably ninety-eight percent there. I don’t think they planned for this kind of contingency.”

Johnny responded: “Boss thinks maybe they could be setting us up that jail is safer than us.”

“Possibly, but if that’s the case, one will end up in jail and then dead and the other will end up dead right away and we will know that before we go and try to change any money.”

“That’s what I told Luke and that we weren’t stupid. I also told him we wouldn’t make a move without talking to him first.”

“Johnny, I have no intention of doing anything until we check with him, Va Bene?”

“Si, Va Bene”

“So, Stone, what now?”

“Make some money of course.”

“Really?”

“Fuck yea!”

“Should we call Luke?”

“Not yet. We haven’t done anything yet. Do you have ten grand in cash?”

“Fuck yea,” mimicking Stone. They both laughed.

Stone said, “Get the cash out of your pocket.” He opened the door and announced: “Time to make some dough.”

Mike and Raj cooperated without incident. Each had their own function, which made the job go very quickly. Raj prepared the tub and the chemicals to make the bills appear waterproof and applied the final coat of powder to make the bills pass the iodine test before placing the paper in the dryer. Mike was busy scanning the bills into the computer and using Photoshop to precisely center the bills. Twenty minutes in the dryer and the paper was ready. Since the paper isn't as flat as it is when it is new, the only slow part to the process was that they could only print a sheet at a time by hand feeding it into the copier. Mike mentioned that a more robust printer would alleviate that problem, but then they couldn't be mobile and ordering a large commercial printer in a hotel room may raise some eyebrows. They also warned Joe and the boys that the money was only temporarily waterproof, not like the real US currency. Prolonged periods of moisture like washing the money in a washing machine in your pants pocket would produce a hard ball of paper. That had always been their biggest concern about getting caught. Eventually someone would leave money in their pockets and when it came out of the wash, the money would be no good. They would then report to the bank, or wherever they got the money, that they were given bad bills, which would lead to a call to the feds and so on.

Mike carefully cut the money, and in less than an hour they turned ten grand into twenty grand. Mike, pretty proud of himself, took a hundred from the real pile, and a hundred from the fake pile and asked Johnny to close his eyes. Johnny is slightly apprehensive and more than slightly unhappy when anyone tells him to do something, in particular the little smart ass college kid in front of him. Johnny just looked at Lucky and said, "You close your fucking eyes." Stone gave Lucky a nod as well. Lucky did as he was told. Mike mixed the two bills up in his hands a few times and then carefully placed a bill in each one of Lucky's hands. "Open your eyes now," Mike said and again Lucky obliged and opened his eyes. Mike said, "Which bill is real and which one is fake?" Lucky turned over each bill a number of times making many contorted facial expressions and finally, after about a minute, he looked at Johnny and said, "Damned if I know."

Johnny grabbed the bills and started studying them and said to Mike, "Are you sure one of these is fake? Are you trying to fuck with us?" His voice and anger level was going up. Mike, sensing Johnny was getting pissed, spoke right up, "Hey, at this point, the bills have been moved around so much I can't even tell, but watch and I'll show you I didn't pull a sleight of hand." First, he grabbed his iodine pen and drew a line on both bills, and the line slowly disappeared on both bills. Mike said, "See, they both look legit." He then walked the bills over to the kitchenette sink. Stone, never let his eyes leave the bills, like he was watching a card trick at the carnival. Mike filled the sink with water and held both bills under water for about a minute. When he brought them out of the water, the real bill still looked like a real bill. The fake one, though, looked like shit and clearly no longer real. "Get me real currency paper and we can start our own bank," Mike said with a little cocky edge. Stone smiled and thought, "I really am beginning to like the young cocky son of a bitch."

Then Mike said, again uninitiated, "Let's go buy some chips and turn paper into real cash." Stone, again liking his attitude, said, "Whoa, big boy, that's not how we roll. We need to plan this out just a little better than running downstairs and potentially getting us all pinched."

Chapter 56

"Luke, do you want another drink or do you want to catch some shut-eye?"

"Sleep is not an option, 'AB,' even though this is way more comfortable than commercial. Sleeping on a plane just doesn't work for me."

"Do you mean ever or only when you have something on your mind?"

"'AB,' if you want to say something, say it. We go back way too far for you to watch your words with me."

"What are you saying, boss?"

"'AB,' be serious now, you're asking me if I can't sleep because of what's going on in Vegas and more specifically because Stone is there."

"AB" became slightly pensive because he knew that Luke, whenever he dealt with Stone, was not himself and tended to fly off the handle. He knew well what happened to Johnny on the railroad tracks and didn't want the same fate, considering they were stuck in a metal tube thirty thousand feet in the air and nowhere to go. He also knew his stead with Luke was better than Johnny's. "AB" knew he would really have to cross the line to have Luke take a pop at him. "AB" heard the whispers that, if anything ever happened to Luke, he was the heir apparent.

"Boss, let's be honest. It's just you and I here, thirty thousand feet in the air. You and I both know you have an issue with Stone, and quite frankly, I don't get it. Boss, with my own eyes I saw him take out the Colombians and his own FBI guys. He kept you out of jail, not once, but twice. We grossed millions based on his information to us and now, if he's right and this counterfeit thing is for real, we could print enough money to retire. So, exactly at what point do you become grateful and accepting of this dude?"

Luke sat with his hands together at the thumb and forefinger, resting his lips on his thumbs with his head bent down, reminiscent of someone deep in prayer. He sat there like that for a full thirty seconds after "AB" was done. To "AB" it seemed like thirty minutes. Luke, in very deliberate motions, removed his hands from his face, raised his head, and sat up straight in the beautifully upholstered leather seats. Then he spoke, "'AB,' all you say makes perfect sense and I must tell you, I really no longer feel threatened by his connection to the FBI, I really don't. To tell you the truth, I used not to like him, but he has grown on me a little. I wouldn't call him a buddy, but I no longer dislike him. To tell you the truth, I fear him, and not in the normal, '*I think he can kick the shit out of me.*' I fear what I don't know about him. Fat Hands has been doing his thing on the internet, trying to find out about his past to no avail." Luke stopped for a moment, looking to choose his words, and "AB" gave him all the time he needed. He felt for a long time that Luke needed to air his laundry.

"I guarantee you, 'AB,' as sure as we are sitting here, he has an ulterior motive, and I'm pissed I don't know what it is or how to find out. 'AB,' I've decided I'm going to get him to tell me."

"How exactly are you going to do that?"

"I'm going to get him alone, somewhere most likely in the deaf room, and I'm going to ask him man to man."

"Boss, if he does have an ulterior motive, and he hasn't shared it yet, what makes you think he'll tell you?"

"'AB,' I'm going to beat it out of him."

"Boss, with all due respect, Stone doesn't seem like the kind of guy that will crumble under that kind of stress."

"'AB,' for his sake, I hope you're wrong because after we figure out how this counterfeiting deal works, we can do without him."

"Are you saying what I think you're saying?"

"If you're saying whack him, that's exactly what I'm saying. His involvement was nice while it lasted, and we made some money and had a direct line into the FBI, but I think he's become a liability."

"How so?"

"Well, 'AB,' did you ever contemplate if he, as a fed, gets pinched and he decides to flip on us the world trouble we would be in?"

"Boss, he's done all the killing. We just made some money from his information."

"'AB,' it's all about being an accessory after the fact, the Rico statutes, and on and on, not one of us would escape an extended stay at Camp Fed."

"Boss, you especially have steered pretty clear of him."

"Yeah, but the rest of you guys have accepted him as if he was already made, shit he ain't even Italian, he can never be made."

"What nationality is he anyway?"

Luke thought for a brief moment, "Fucked if I know with a last name like Stone, he ain't Sicilian."

"Boss, personally, I like him and I think he's an asset. We can always kill him. Why not wait until we are sure we've used him for all he's worth. Plus, we don't need you getting your hands dirty. This isn't the old days anymore, you're the big shit, if you want him gone, I'll do it."

"'AB,' under normal circumstances I would agree with you, but this time it's personal."

"Again, boss, with all due respect, that's bullshit. You want to rough him up a bit, I buy that, but no need to get yourself wrapped up with murder on a fed, that's the electric chair."

"'AB,' first of all, I didn't get to be the head of the family because I'm a dope, and secondly, it isn't my plan to knock him off, throw him in the trunk of my car after six or seven cocktails, and go speeding down Main Street."

"AB" just had to laugh at that comment, which in turn got Luke laughing as well. "Boss, why don't we start with me pulling him aside in Vegas and see what I can find out from him. I have a good rapport with him. I think I can get him to open up."

"'AB,' this good rapport you have with him, that's kind of my issue."

"What do you mean, boss?"

"What I mean is," Luke's voice again rising, "You and most of the other guys in our family have a good rapport with him. I understand our guys liking the money, but he's not one of us and all of you, except me, are treating him as if he grew up with us."

"Luke, come on, he's not a hard guy to like, even if we weren't making money because of him. I'm just saying he wouldn't be a bad guy to hang out with."

"You see, 'AB,' what I mean, this guy is a fed above everything else and even if he's completely turned and I'll give you, it appears he has. The rest of the FBI hasn't turned and it's bound to turn heads if he's continued to be seen with our guys, especially you. The boys at the agency are bound to start watching him and, in turn, us."

"I see what you're saying. We are going to have to talk to him and our guys to reduce the amount of public contact."

"Actually, if this deal turns out as big as he thinks it's going to be then we should tell him to retire and start his own PI firm since he's too young to actually retire. Should he choose to stay, at the very least we will need to cut contact."

"Boss, you really think it's got to be so soon? I mean, it's only been about a year and its great information we get from him, not to mention the money we make from the information."

"'AB,' since we're on the way to Vegas, let me put this in Vegas terms. You know when you're at the blackjack table and you're on a great run, you almost feel invincible. Then, before you know it, you make a bad bet, then you double up and lose that bet, and before you know it you've lost all you've won and then some more. Capisce?"

"AB" nodded his head in agreement.

"That's where I feel we are and I feel like Stone is the hot blackjack dealer with her tits hanging out, which is clouding our judgment."

"Yeah, boss, but why would Stone want us to go down? If we go down, so does he."

"He's mesmerized by the same tits, only we're his dealer, don't you see that?"

"Boss, I agree there's a time, I just don't know."

Luke put his hand up to silence "AB." "It's time, my friend, because I say its time. Hopefully, we can knock it out of the park with this. If not, we're millions ahead of where we were!"

"Seriously, 'AB,' we may not have a choice with Stone. He's got way too much info on us. The only solution may be to eliminate his ability to tell anyone what he knows, ever."

"AB" was silent and Luke knew now was not the time to speak, it was the time to get acknowledgment, buy in, and commitment.

"Boss, you count on me for many things, commitment and loyalty first, council second, and making good decisions for the family. I will put a bullet in the president's head on national TV if you ask me. You know how loyal I am, so if you give me the nod, consider Stone done, although my council to you is, 'let's wait and see if this deal is as big as he thinks it is before we decide what to do with him'. Also, I think we ought to keep our plans OUR plans, no need to let the boys know anything until after it's all over and done with." Luke was hearing what he wanted to hear. 'AB,' first and foremost, was behind him regardless of the consequences. Luke, as much as he liked the loyalty, respected 'AB' for his ability to think first, act second. That's why he has always been the logical choice for filling Luke's shoes in case something happened to him. "Good, 'AB,' life is not always full of easy choices. Regardless, nothing will happen in Vegas, too many cameras in Vegas, they're everywhere. You brought your baseball hat, eh?"

"Yeah, hope you don't mind I brought my Red Sox hat. Those fucking Yankee fans are always wearing theirs, and I love to piss them off, wearing our colors."

"'AB,' we're not here for the World Series, ya know."

They both laughed when Luke noticed his cell phone was ringing and it was Johnny. Thank God, people don't realize their cell phones work fine in the air, because people would be in the shitter talking on their phones, all the way from Boston to LA and in between.

Luke looked at 'AB,' "Here's Johnny, let's see what kind of shit they're in now."

He picked up the phone with his standard Italian greeting, "Pronto."

"Boss, I've taken ten grand of the money you gave me for the trip and the kids made ten grand in new money, and you can't tell the difference! I swear, it's unbelievable!"

"I thought I told you to do nothing till I spoke to you?"

"Boss, we haven't spent the money or turned it into chips. Stone just wanted to see if they were bullshitting us, even though he was sure they weren't."

"Well, I guess Stone knows best?"

"No, boss, come on, you sent me out here to do this, and I am. We want to go down and see what happens when we go buy some chips. The plan is, we send Sal down with one of the kids, and I stand about fifty feet away while he goes up to cash in the chips. If he does something funny, I will be already on my phone with Lucky. Should he get cute, Lucky will slit the other kid's throat, and he and Stone will exit quickly. Sal will stick the other kid in the ribs and hopefully get out without getting caught and we will all rendezvous at Caesar's."

"Have you wiped the room down yet?"

"Not completely, but we will before we leave, we've already thought of it."

"How about hats and glasses?"

"We wore them in and won't be seen in a hallway or the casino without them, boss."

"Johnny, hold on a second."

Luke picked up the phone on the armrest, "Captain, how long to touchdown?"

"Forty-five minutes to touchdown, Mr. Fabrasia."

"Thank you, Captain," and he hung up the phone.

"Johnny, I'm forty-five minutes to touchdown."

"Touchdown, touchdown where? What do you mean?" Johnny, not always the sharpest tool in the shed, was literally confused.

"I'm landing in Vegas in forty-five minutes on a private jet. I want to see this shit happen personally."

Johnny felt a sudden and all-encompassing disappointment wash all over him. He was a captain, one of three, a big shot. He didn't need anyone, not even Luke, looking over his shoulder. He was quickly trying to process all the information in his head. Did Luke not trust him? Did he think he was incompetent? Was it Stone? What was the deal? Whatever it was, he wasn't happy but he wasn't stupid either. Now was not the time to split ranks. He could deal with Luke later. There was silence from Johnny's end of the line. Luke knew this was going to cause an issue, but Johnny was just going to have to deal with it.

Finally, "Johnny, nothing personal, this may be big and I want to be a part of it, so I grabbed 'AB.'"

"'AB,' too?"

Then Johnny caught himself and finished, "Boss, I think I could have handled this. I have so far, without a problem, but just so you know, this may be bigger than what we thought."

"Johnny, that's great, and remember you ran it to ground. I'm proud of you, but we're a family and my decision is if this is that big, we need more of us involved. Capisce?"

"Sure, boss, what now?"

"Go on with your plan, wipe the room really good, and have Lucky ready to go. Make sure you're far enough away from Sal, if things go bad and exit by a different door, capisce?"

"Sure, no problem."

"Have Sal and the kid play a little blackjack at the same table for about half an hour, cash the chips in at different cashiers, and we can all meet back at the room if all goes well. What's the room again?"

"1231, but you'll need a pass key to get to that floor, it's the high roller floor. Call me and I will come get you."

Chapter 57

Teresa was asleep but not sleeping soundly. She was never happy when her man was unhappy. He had kissed her good-bye and told her he would see her in a couple of days. She knew if it wasn't for Stone being involved, he would never be on a plane to Vegas. She had met Stone. She really was undecided if she liked him or not, but there was definitely a connection she felt when she met him, and again she couldn't decipher if it was a good or a bad connection. She just felt a connection.

Fat Hands hadn't gone to sleep yet. He was up, continuing to pound the keyboard of his Dell computer. Something didn't add up with Stone's record. What he was able to access on the internet looked almost like a person's record that was in the Witness Protection Program. He knew that could not be true. The government found people jobs, but they were low profile jobs under the radar. They definitely were not with the FBI who actually took these people off the street. Just in case, though, he ran down through all known people who have a record and have been put into the witness protection and he came up blank—nobody who even remotely looked like Stone. He then started fishing with variations of Stone's name such as Stonewall, Stonington, Stoneleigh. Nothing was jumping out at him.

He thought to himself, "Boss is out of town, 'AB,' Johnny as well. "He was the high man on the ladder left in town to make sure everything was running well. Time to go to sleep in case he was needed in the morning.

Marcus Barolo was in bed, his wife long asleep, staring at the ceiling, thinking to himself, "What a fuck up I am. I had all my debts wiped clean after I saved that Mafia punk. That Luke, though, he's a smooth fucking character. I save his guy, he wipes my debt clean, but then he raises my credit limit. That fucker, he knew I couldn't control myself, he knows I'm a degenerate gambler, now I'm into him for almost double what I owed him before. I need to quit gambling and get cleaned up with Luke. Only two ways for that to happen—I'm either going to have to save another thug or Luke's going to have to have a fatal accident."

In a weird way, he was comforted by the thought that there was a potential way out, even if it meant pain for someone or even death for someone else. Hey, it's not out of the question for a man like Luke must have hundreds of enemies. With that thought, he drifted off to sleep immediately, dreaming about hitting blackjack after blackjack.

You may or may not believe in love at first sight, but you have to believe in lust after ten or twelve drinks. Mak and Lucille had been drinking nonstop, talking nonstop, and dancing nonstop for hours. He could tell Lucille was into him by the way she looked at him. Lucille could tell Mak was into her by the way he had begun to grope her on the dance floor. Nothing is really more pathetic than two almost middle-aged people acting like two hormonally charged teenagers at a school dance with the lights turned down low, although there they were, big as life, dancing, groping, and kissing for all who could bear to watch, there on the dance floor at the Rio. Quite frankly, no one was particularly watching, which just quantifies the expression, “What happens in Vegas, stays in Vegas.” Or who really gives a shit what kind of fools people make of themselves in Vegas? They both knew where the evening was headed but, soothingly, neither one was in a great hurry, they were both having too much fun. Sex would just end the night, it was too early, and they were having too much fun to interrupt the proceedings!

Chapter 58

Time had come to find out if the kids were bullshitting or if they had really told the truth and their procedure was true. Time to find out if a couple of MIT kids had outsmarted Vegas and the US government in all their glory. Stone decided that Mike was going to be the one to go downstairs with Sal attached to his hip to complete the switch. Really, it wasn't much of a decision since they figured Raj, with his bloody bandaged hand, would attract too much negative attention.

Stone went over the plan for everyone to hear, including especially Mike and Raj.

"This is the way we are going to proceed. Mike, you and Sal are going to go down to a cashier, turn in five thousand each into one hundred dollar chips. Sal, you're going to stand behind Mike and let him convert his cash to chips first. Johnny, you're going to be standing about fifty feet from them, watching, on your cell phone with Lucky who is going to have a gun pointed at Raj's head. Now, Mike, listen very closely, 'If these bills don't pass muster, or if you try to get the attention of the cashier or a dealer or do anything that brings undue attention to you, Sal, or Johnny, Johnny is going to let us know and Raj will be shot in the head. We're not talking losing a pinky but a nine millieter to the brain, capisce?" Mike couldn't utter a word, and Raj, whose color had completely left his face, barely audibly spat out, "Don't fuck up, bro." Mike shook his head up and down but his mouth was so dry that speaking was not an option.

Stone, convinced that his message was understood, continued, "Once you have your chips, go to a fifty dollar minimum table and play a little blackjack. Then you stop playing when one of three things happens: you play for one half hour, you're up one thousand dollars, or you've lost one thousand dollars. Do you understand?"

Sal and Mike shook their heads up and down. Stone continued, "no crazy bets, just fifty and one hundred dollars at a time, and of course, if appropriate, double down, or split your cards. Again, we don't want to raise any eyebrows. Sal, do not take off your hat and sunglasses. Mike, since you never thought it was important to cover up your identity, no reason to start now. Whichever one of you is done first, say something like I've lost enough for now, or I'm quitting while I'm ahead and stand behind the other guy until it makes sense for him to stop. Now, Sal and Johnny, listen closely. If, at any time, you think our friend Mike is signaling to anyone or gets cute in anyway, put a bullet in his head and head straight for the door. We will rendezvous at our hotel after Lucky puts a bullet in Raj's head. Johnny, no need to tell you to head out a different door, capisce?"

Everyone nodded except for Raj who just about shit himself. Mike had to hold back the gag reflex, which was no easy task. They were just getting ready to head toward the door when Mike somehow processed enough saliva to speak. "Aren't you guys just going to kill us after you find out what we taught you is the real deal? Because if that's the case, you might as well kill us now, because you have the formula."

Stone, who prided himself at almost always never being surprised, was at a loss for words. Why would this kid be telling him this now? Stone was more than a little annoyed now, and time was slipping by. He knew Luke would almost be on the ground by now and if this was for real with the kids, he wanted it done and proven by the time Luke showed up. This was his deal and he wanted not to share with Luke its glory, only its bounty. "What's your point, Mike?" Clearly, there was impatience in Stone's tone. Raj, who was already reeling, felt truly faint, *"What was Mike doing? Was he trying to get us killed right now?"*

"Seriously, Mike, why are you stalling now? Is there something you conveniently forgot to tell us? Are we headed into a shit storm? Is this your way of warning us?" "*No! No! No!* I swear I . . . we told you everything . . . that is . . . about the counterfeiting, Raj and I have been working on some other high tech scams that make this look like child's play." Raj was picking up Mike's vibe, he was playing on the hope that they were greedy enough to keep them around for more than what they just got.

Raj blurted out, "like the credit card magnetic strip scam."

Mike, not exactly excited about Raj's input, was ecstatic, though, that he caught on so quick, since it added credibility to Mike's story. Johnny jumped in, "What credit card magnetic strip thing are you talking about?"

Now, it was Stone's turn, "Boys, boys, boys" and he meant all of them. "One deal at a time. We already know you're smart, so you probably do have a ton more ideas, but right now we just want to see this one work. You guys have nothing to worry about. If this is the real deal, you have my word. Now, I'm going to ask you one more time, before we leave, did you tell us everything and is this going to work?"

Almost in unison this time, both Mike and Raj responded, "Yes, sir."

Johnny and Sal put on their baseball hats and sunglasses. Johnny went out first and went right down the hall and got in the elevator to set up his position in the casino.

The Rio is set up pretty much like every other casino in the world. They try to draw you into the middle, so they have a better chance of keeping you once you get there. The main cashier is always in the middle to defer potential thieves from trying to pull a heist, although that hasn't stopped numerous penny-ante thieves as well as hardened experienced crooks on occasion from trying to beat the system and rob a casino at gunpoint. Unfortunately, for the thieves, it never ends well. By the time they make it to the outside doors, they are locked and there are a number of heavily armed plainclothes security guards with automatic weapons waiting for them. In all the years Vegas has been in existence, only once was a holdup of a major casino pulled off and just about everyone agrees it was rigged.

Johnny, as agreed, went down to the main casino floor and grabbed a slot machine halfway between the elevator and the main cashier booth. He figured he had about five minutes to kill before Stone released the kid and Sal. He settled in and pumped a C note into the slot machine that was based on a much younger Farrah Fawcett and the rest of Charlie's Angels. He loved Vegas and he loved gambling, but he hated slot machines. In his opinion, slot machines should be relegated to nursing homes. It also never ceased to amaze him how many people in wheelchairs on oxygen you could find in any casino plugged in with their frequent player cards into a slot machine. He, in a weird way, felt bad for them because, at the end of the day, they were old, sick, and next to death. Why they were out spending their social security check was beyond him. His mind then cleared for a second, and it occurred to him that he made a good portion of his livelihood from degenerate gamblers just like these old people surrounding him, only his customers were younger. He felt better now. Apparently, these types of people never learned and they will be around a long time gambling. A very perverse stroke of good fortune. Job security of sorts.

He was clearly fullfledged into a daydreaming black hole when the vibration in his shirt pocket broke him out of his stupor and back to reality. His phone was on vibrate, and he fumbled to get it out of his pocket, barely able to answer it before it went to voicemail. Caller ID let him know it was Luke. Good thing he answered it on time because the boss hated to leave messages. He would often start the message by saying, “What the fuck do you have a cell phone for if you have no intention of answering it?”

Johnny started, “Hey boss, what’s up?”

“Just touched down, should be there in thirty to forty-five minutes.”

“You sure you want to be here now before we know what’s going to go down?”

“I’ll tell you what, I’ll call from the limo when I’m outside the Rio.”

“OK, if I don’t answer right away, don’t come in until I call you. I’m going to need to be on an open line with Stone and Lucky in case the kid tries something funny and we need to deal with his friend, capisce?”

Johnny was ever mindful that you never knew who could be listening in, so saying whack or kill is never a good thing. Deal with meant the same thing in their language. Johnny no sooner hung up with Luke than his phone began to vibrate again. This time it was Stone. He flipped his phone open, "Yeah, Joe, what's up?"

"Heads up, they ought to be coming out of the elevator at any second now."

"No problem, Mr. Joe Stone, I got my eye on the elevators. By the way, boss just landed and is on his way."

"Great, like we're not under enough stress right now."

"No shit, Joe, but he's the boss and apparently you got him convinced this is a big one. Luke's a hands-on kind of guy."

"Yeah, I know the feeling."

"Hey, Stone, they are just coming off the elevator, they just stopped for a second. Looks like Sal is saying something to the kid."

"Can you hear them?"

"No, I'm out of range."

Sal, coming off the elevator, stopped short and grabbed Mike by the arm, spinning him around so he was looking at him from mere inches away. "Listen, punk, you try anything cute and I'm gonna stick you in your neck, get on a plane, fly back to your hometown, and kill your mother while your father watches, you understand me?"

"I think I got the point when your boss cut off my friend's finger."

"Well now, until we get upstairs, I'm the boss, capisce?"

"Can't you guys just speak English?"

With that, Mike started toward the cashier. He needed to prove to these goons that he had value, or he was surer than shit going to be dead by tomorrow.

"Stone, whatever just happened, it's over, they're walking over to the cashier."

"I got a good feeling about this, but that doesn't mean shit, just keep a close eye on the kid. He's smart, maybe too smart, make sure he doesn't get cute."

"Got ya, Joe."

Sal, trying to play the cool nonchalant type, spoke just a little too loudly to Mike, "Hey Mikey boy. I'm feeling lucky today, gonna turn this five large into ten." Mike, hiding his gag reflex as best he could, played along. "Yeah, then that should make you about even from yesterday." Ending it with a little chuckle, Sal, not feeling quite as cool anymore, came back with the best comeback he could think of in a hurry, "Then I guess I'll have to make it into fifteen large, ha ha"

Strangely, that actually made him feel a little better.

Betty, the cashier helping Sal, who was trained to spot any irregularities and immediately report them to her superiors, saw nothing strange, just another degenerate punk who somehow ran into money, who was planning on losing it as fast as he came into it.

"Excuse me, sir, what denominations of chips would you prefer?" Sal had to think for a second. Sal, as everybody knows, is not the sharpest knife in the drawer. He was pretty sure he knew what denomination meant but he wasn't one hundred percent sure. Betty sensed this immediately and, so as not to embarrass her customer, quickly added, "Would all hundred dollar chips be OK or would you prefer some twenty-five dollar chips?"

"Yeah, I knew what you meant, I was just deciding if I wanted to play at the twenty-five dollar table."

Mike, listening and watching, said first to his cashier, "Make mine all one hundred dollar chips," and virtually without taking a breath, said, "Buddy, you're not going to make fifteen large on the kiddy table, are you? Suck it up, be a man, get all hundreds!" Sal, turning a bright red, half from embarrassment and half from anger, was thinking to himself, "I'm going to punch that kid in the head when we get back to the room. He turned, red-faced, back to Betty and said, "All hundreds."

Betty said, "Actually, let me give you eight five hundred dollar chips and ten one hundred dollar chips. That way it's easier to carry them, and the dealer can break them into hundreds at the table."

"OK, fine, that sounds great"

Betty was counting out the chips and dropped one more pearl of wisdom, "You know, you can change your money at the table just as easily as you can here."

Mike chimed in, "Yeah, but this way when we pick a table to play at—we're ready to go! Which is right now! Come on, pal, let's go."

Betty gave them a little wave and said, "Good luck, boys" as they walked away.

Once the boys were out of earshot of the cashiers, Betty said to the other cashier, "Those chips will be back in the bank before too long." Her counterpart just nodded and said, "That's why they can pay us the big bucks."

Sal was still steaming, and as soon as they were far enough from the cage, he grabbed Mike by the elbow again and spun him around to look at him eye to eye.

"What are you—a wise ass? I'll kick your ass right here for the whole place to see, next time you embarrass me like that . . . I'll . . ."

"Hey, listen, if you didn't notice, I didn't use your name like you used mine and your bosses specifically didn't want us making any waves. I've been doing this for a long time without any problems, so just keep your mouth shut and follow my lead. I don't want to get myself or my friend killed because of you. To use your language, capisce? You may want to punch me or worse later, but right now I'm going to do my best at making you a lot of money and not getting me or my friend killed. Now, let's go over to that table, so your boss who's staring at us right now, wondering what's going on, can see us play. We don't want him to get nervous and make Swiss cheese out of my buddy."

Not even waiting for a response, he pulled away and walked over to the nearest hundred dollar table in direct line of sight of Johnny.

"Stone, there they go standing and talking again. Sal looks really pissed. I'm not sure I like . . . Hey, wait a minute, the kid's walking toward the blackjack table. Sal's right behind him . . . I guess everything is OK." Just as Johnny was saying "OK," he mindlessly hit maximum bet as he had been doing for the last twenty minutes. Three Farrah Fawcett faces came up and all hell broke loose.

"You gotta be shitting me . . . oh my bad . . . No, not now!"

Lucky could hear Johnny's voice on the other end of Stone's cell phone. Not knowing what was happening, he instinctively thought the worst, his hand tightened on Raj's shoulder, and the pressure on the trigger of his 9 mm firmed to the point of one hiccup breath would release a pulsing burning load of lead into Raj's brain. Raj, also sensing something wrong, started crying and pleading with Lucky. "Please, don't kill me, we told you everything, I swear, I swear, oh holy Mother of God, believe me, believe me."

Lucky, not knowing what to believe, raised his voice to Stone. "What, what the fuck is happening, Stone? Do I kill him? Do I kill him?!"

"Hold on, Lucky, hold on! Johnny, what's happening, did the kid freak on us?"

"No, no, I just hit three Farrahs, three fucking Farrahs!"

"What the hell are you talking about?"

"I'm sitting here playing slots, watching what's going on, and I hit a jackpot for I don't even know how much yet, but the fucking lights are going off, the bells are ringing, and everyone in the casino is heading over to me, including it looks like half the security guards . . . Oh, *fuck!* You better get down here to watch the boys 'cause I can't anymore . . . Boss is gonna kill me, Jesus, what timing!"

"Johnny, don't take off your hat and glasses, even if they ask you to take a picture. I will be right down to deal with Sal and Mike."

"Lucky, chill, no problem with the kid yet. Johnny, just hit a jackpot on the slot machine if you can believe that. I need to go down and keep an eye on the kid. Raj is tied up tight not going anywhere, right?" Lucky gave the ropes a tug or two to check, each time getting a winch out of Raj. "He ain't going nowhere, Stone."

"Good, I'll call if there's a problem. You know what to do if I call."

"Yes, sir" Another wince from Raj.

Chapter 59

Luke is not known for his patience, nor does he deal well with unknowns. Stone has been the ultimate unknown for him. Luke clearly is beginning to feel as if Stone is trying to move into his space. By space he means his family, his authority, his world, his "space." Luke continues to play this over and over in his mind. Why is Stone putting himself, and Luke for that matter, in this position for no return? Had Stone just quietly continued to pass Luke's family information, which they could act on, it probably wouldn't be an issue. Unfortunately for Stone, he continues to get more involved with his guys. A bad penny of sorts, who was making them all very wealthy. In Luke's mind, that is part of Stone's plan. Stone's making it too hard to eliminate him. He has become the goose who laid the golden egg. The decision has been made in Luke's mind: first, he was going to find out Stone's true motivation, and second, have him leave the FBI, so as not to draw anymore unwarranted attention to the Familia Fabrasia, or he was going to have a very unfortunate accident. Luke's psyche at this point, quite frankly, is his life would be better off with Stone dead.

“Boss, boss.” ‘AB’ was pushing on Luke’s shoulder. This has been an incredibly long day, and not long after Luke climbed into the black limo, he nodded off.

“What’s up, ‘AB’?”

“Hey, boss, we’re at the Rio, we need to call Johnny.”

“Fuck that, let’s just slide in, and see what’s going on for ourselves.”

“But, boss, you told Johnny we would call when we got here.”

“Yeah, and he also said he would be on the phone with Stone and may not be able to answer. Just put on your hat and glasses and let’s try to blend in as much as two big guys wearing hats and glasses can.”

“Ha, funny, boss, but the Rio is pretty big, how you guess we find them?”

“My guess is they won’t be far from the main cashier’s window.”

“How so?”

“Because, for some reason, these stupid kids, and now apparently our guys and Stone, think it’s better to turn cash into chips at the cashier than to just do a couple of Gs at a time at the table.”

“Really?”

“And you wonder why I wanted to be here, come on follow me.”

“Driver, hang out here, give me your number, I’ll call you when I need ya. Don’t go far.”

The driver responded, "Yes, sir," and handed Luke a business card with his number on it.

Luke was not fond of Vegas, although the saying, "what happens in Vegas, stays in Vegas" to the contrary was true. The place was loaded with cameras, and there were cops of every denomination there at any given time—the casinos had their own private security. Someone like Luke could hardly go unrecognized for any period of time. Of course there were the local families that didn't like anybody edging in on their action.

Gino Campanelli was the most powerful of the local gangsters. Having survived the gentrification process of Vegas, from only mobster run to almost only publically traded companies run by legal thugs, over time he has become very powerful. Gino, like Luke, was a big guy but not anywhere near as polished. Gino was known nationwide amongst his peers as being one of the most ruthless. He did not take kindly to other families making money on his turf and was prepared, at any time, to defend his turf. The families knew proper decorum was to inform Gino anytime that they, or their crew, were going to be in Vegas. Gino would make sure to show them a good time. Send over women, booze, tickets to sold-out shows, whatever they wanted. However, should they have a business dealing, he wanted a piece of the action. No ifs, ands, or buts. A family member from anywhere in the country made as little as a dollar within the Vegas territory, Gino got his twenty points. Those who tried to bypass him that got caught would end up missing body parts or dead. In more than a few occasions, both.

Luke and AB started for the entrance of the Rio. "Hey, 'AB,' we probably should have let Gino know we were going to be in town."

"Hopefully, we'll be in and out quickly, before anyone notices us. Plus, especially here at the Rio, it's a little off the beaten path."

"Let's hope so."

The thing that strikes you first about the Rio is the women that work there. They all seem as if they are carved out of marble. One more beautiful than the next, all scantily dressed in Brazilian Mardi Gras garb. Everywhere you look, behind the check-in counter, the boutiques, the dealers, and most evidently the cocktail waitresses, they seem to be everywhere wearing the least amount of clothing allowed by law. The atmosphere is almost circus-like and intoxicating by anyone's standards.

Luke and "AB" strolled in nonchalantly, not really making eye contact with anyone, trying to be as invisible as possible. There was just so much going on, even with the late hour it had become. What made the place even crazier was there was a crowd of people gathering ahead on their right. Coincidentally, it was right before the main cashier. Luke had a sinking feeling in his gut.

"Hey, boss, what do you think is going on over there?"

"Looks like someone hit something with all those lights and the people gathering around. Our luck is it will be one of our guys."

"No way, boss, you told them to keep a low profile. Johnny will make sure nothing will go wrong."

"From your mouth to God's ears."

Charlie Malone and Steve Bryant are Rio security staff that nobody ever sees. They sit in the bunker-like control room in the basement of the Rio. Actually, you can find similar rooms in all the major casinos—the army of men and women who do nothing but watch the guests' every move. They watch for card counters, and teams of people who work together to steal wallets, chips, cups of change from the slot machines, and a host of other unsavory activities. Anything that takes away from the profit of the casino and the overall enjoyment of the gambling public.

Charlie and Steve have been at their jobs for eight and seven years, respectively. Their bosses considered them competent and both of them had excellent HR files stored in the Rio's HR department. Both Charlie and Steve are good old-fashioned family guys with two young children and pretty wives. They are two peas in a pod with tons in common. The only notable difference was Charlie was a local and Steve was a transplant from Boston. Steve moved there shortly before he married Maria Columbo, who just coincidentally happens to be a niece of Gino Campanelli.

Steve was a straight arrow, which is why he loved his job. Steve, although he was never asked, had no desire or even the stomach to be involved with his wife's uncle's business. He was never asked to join in the family business, not the least reason being his stark

Irishness. Steve had had the pleasure of spending a lot of time with his uncle at family gatherings. Gino had taken a liking to Steve. Coincidentally, this happened about the same time he landed the surveillance job at the Rio.

Gino, at the christening of his first daughter, had pulled Steve aside and gave him an envelope with ten thousand dollars cash. "Steve, here is a little gift for your daughter Julia's college fund."

Steve tried to protest, knowing his uncle's reputation, but the effort was halfhearted. Gino continued, "Steve, I think you know me enough to know who I am and what I do. I make no excuses for my lot in life and what I have chosen as my career. I take care of my family and those that are close to me. You now fall into both of those categories. From now on, every month, one of the guys will come by and drop off an envelope with a little something to help pay for diapers, or to take my niece out to a nice dinner, not a lot, just to appreciate you for being part of my family."

"Gino, please, I understand the gift for Julia, but we really can't."

"Shhhhh, you can and you will, this is not an option. I know you're a proud man and you don't want charity, so don't look at it as charity. In return, I will expect a favor from you, which you may or may never pay back." Gino could see the look of confusion on Steve's face.

"Let me explain. Should you in your job ever see or hear about someone in your casino that is in the same industry as me, I want to know, capisce?"

"I think I understand"

"Good, even if you think it's nothing, call me on my private line, tell me about what you've seen or heard. That's all, nothing more or less. Nobody needs to know except you and I." Steve agreed, as if he had a choice.

On three occasions over the last seven years, he saw stuff that looked suspicious to him that he first discussed with his supervisors at work. Then, discreetly, on his break he called Gino to describe what he saw. That was it. Gino would thank him and the next month's envelope had a little extra diaper money.

Charlie said to Stephen, "Hey, we got a winner on slot 289," which popped up on his monitor as soon as Johnny hit the three Farrah Fawcett's. "Not bad for a three dollar bet, that's a quick hundred grand!"

Steve radioed to the closest security guard to get over to slot 289 and secure the winner and the area around him. "Hey Steve, look at that goomba who won. Someone ought to let him know there ain't any sun inside the casino." They both chuckled and continued to watch their close circuit screens. It is amazing how often someone wins on a slot and the guy or woman next to them or walking by them try to claim the jackpot.

Steve grabbed his radio again, "Hey Sonny, at 289, big goon, baseball hat, glasses, and Vinnie Barbarino shoes."

Charlie laughed, "Can you believe someone would actually wear those outside of Little Italy?"

"Yeah, sad part is even with the hundred grand he just won, he still will wear the same shoes, probably buy them in every color!"

Mak and Lucy were groping each other on the dance floor when all the hoopla started. Apparently, someone had won a big jackpot on the slots, because the sirens were wailing and Rio people were scurrying around to get the slot machine to identify the winner to pay off the correct puller of the one-armed bandit.

Lucy, as she was feasting on Mak's ear, said, "Looks like someone else other than you is getting lucky today." Not that Mak needed confirmation about the culmination of his evening, but knowing for sure gave him tingles in all the right places. Mak was just about ready to tell Lucy, whom he had become very fond of in a short amount of time, that it was time to move the party to his place. That's when Stone came off the elevator.

Stone walked into the carnival that the Rio casino floor had transformed. Lights were flashing, sirens were ringing, and people had gathered like flies to a light bulb. Had Stone not been called by Johnny, he would still have known it was him. He could see Johnny's slick-backed hair sticking out of his baseball cap hovering above the crowd. Stone stood there for a second with his hands on his hips, shaking his head. Had anybody been listening, they would have heard him mumble under his breath, "What are the fucking odds of that?" While he was still shaking his head, he started over toward the direction of Sal and Mike.

Sal and Mike had been doing as directed, playing blackjack by the book, nothing crazy. Sal and Mike had both eyeballed Johnny standing at the slot machine, which had made Mike very nervous. Mike had actually made a couple of stupid bets, which were responded to by Sal with stares of death, which only added to Mike's nervousness. That's when all hell broke loose and Johnny hit his jackpot. Immediately garnering everyone's attention at the table, Sal could say nothing else but, "*fuck meeee!* Boss is gonna be pissed." Under his breath.

The dealer, having seen this before, smiled and said, "Lucky guy, what did you just say?" Sal just looked up, knowing he had potentially just screwed up. "I said, Fuck me, the guy must have just pissed himself." Sal was happy with himself at how he had just covered himself.

Mike tried to stay calm and played the next couple of hands. He had decided to himself now was the time to make his move. With all the commotion, now was the time to get up and make a run for it to the closest security guard and try to save Raj. Jail for counterfeiting was better than what he assumed his captors had in store for them. He saw the crowds gathering and Johnny disappear in a sea of degenerate gamblers. Mike never saw Stone walking his way, and with Stone not fifteen feet from Mike, he had circled behind Mike. Sal was watching Stone, understanding that Johnny must have been on the line with Stone when he hit the jackpot. Sal, watching Stone, didn't pick up on Mike's intention.

Mike, with the look of determination of a raging bull, jumped up from the table and screamed: "Room 3213, Room 3213, save my friend!" He turned and started to run when he saw Stone almost directly in front of him. He bobbed left, tripped over his own feet, and sprawled to the ground. Sal, who snapped out of his daze, jumped up, pulled an ice pick from his coat, jumped on Mike's back before he could gather himself, and stuck the ice pick into the base of his skull and into his brain. Mike never knew what hit him. He was dead in a nanosecond.

Sal pulled out the ice pick and walked quickly to the exit. The whole event literally took less than three seconds. Before the dealer had processed what had happened and called to the pit boss to get security, Sal was out the door and in a cab.

Stone hardly gave a glance to what was happening but started walking toward the spectacle that was Johnny. He speed-dialed Lucky, "Pronto," "plug him, get my laptop, and get the fuck out of there, you got maybe thirty seconds."

Stone pressed end and by the time the phone hung up, Raj's last words were "No!" then Lucky blew the back of Raj's head off. Lucky grabbed the remaining piece of evidence left in the hotel room—Stone's laptop case and his bag of electronic tricks and left the room in a hurry, wiping the door knob on his way out.

Chapter 60

Lucille felt Mak tighten up and not in a good way, "Mak, what's up, did I say something wro . . . ?"

"Shut up."

"Excuse me?"

"Hey, go back to the bar, I need to go to work, I'll be right back."

"What? You had fifteen drinks, we were going back to your place or mine . . . I don't understand!"

"Honey, go back to the fucking bar and wait for me."

He whipped out a one hundred dollar bill. "Go order some champagne, I'll be right back."

Lucille stared at him like he had three heads, "Do I look like a whore to you? I don't want your money."

Mak was thinking to himself, "Why was this taking so long? It shouldn't be this difficult." That was when he decided to trade passion for financial freedom. He grabbed her by the shoulders, looked her in the eye, and said, "Lucille, go sit at the bar. If I'm not back in thirty minutes, take the money and get a cab home and don't say another fucking word."

With that, he stuffed the hundred in her cleavage and walked away leaving her on the dance floor.

Things were going crazy in the bunker far below the casino floor. The relatively normal occurrence of the slot machine jackpot, albeit an event, is an event that is somewhat controlled chaos by design. Really, no big sweat for the guys in the control room. This was different, though, because now fifty or sixty feet beyond the jackpot was another event, and this was not controlled chaos, but chaos of a different kind. Real chaos. Word had just come in from the floor that there was a stabbing. Immediately after the word had come in that there was a stabbing at or near table twelve, Steve and Charlie zoomed in from one of the thousands of cameras the Rio employs for surveillance. They isolated the camera directly above Mike, which showed his lifeless body spewing blood onto the casino rug. Neither Steve nor Charlie could get an ID on him because he was lying face down in a pool of his own blood. Apparently, the blackjack dealer was trying to stop the bleeding by holding a handkerchief on the back of his neck.

Medics had already been deployed to the scene and were arriving just as Steve and Charlie were focusing in on the action. Protocol caused them now to immediately recreate the scene by rewinding the digital recordings to try an isolate the perpetrator of the crime. Since the word came up to them so quickly, they didn't have to rewind the tape much.

Steve quickly got to the location on the tape where he saw a stocky young man stick what seemed like an ice pick in the back of another young man's neck. Now Steve and Charlie needed to back up the tape some more to see what precipitated the action and to get a better view of the perpetrator. Steve and Charlie ran the tape backward and forward a couple of times. Everything looked OK at the table, then without provocation the young kid got up, turned around, yelling something, almost ran into some guy and cut left like a running back, which gave the other young guy at the table enough time to catch him and stick him in the back of the neck and flee the building. Strange thing was the guy he almost ran into never moved out of his way; actually, he almost blocked his way. Stranger even was he seemed to look over when the kid got stabbed but never stopped to look or help, but just walked away. Then again, stranger things have happened in Vegas.

Steve said to Charlie, "You see if you can follow the perp to ascertain where and if he left the casino, and I'll see if I can bring up the sound to figure out what was said."

"Got ya."

Charlie had to switch from camera to camera to follow Sal's hasty departure from the Rio, although it wasn't hard, just a little cumbersome. He was not only able to see Sal beeline it to the main exit, but he was also able to see him climb into a cab and leave the property. The cameras are so good at the Rio that he was even able to zoom in on the cab number and cab company. "Steve, I got it. He jumped a cab, I got the number, I'll contact the police and see if they can have the cab driver tracked down."

"Great," Steve said over the noise-canceling headphones. "Charlie, I got something here as well. The kid was yelling something about room 3213. I'll let security know."

Chapter 61

Stone slapped shut his phone hard after talking to Lucky. He walked directly and decisively toward Johnny. That's when his eyes widened. Luke and "AB" had just arrived at the outer circle of the Johnny circus. Even from thirty feet away, he could tell that Luke didn't look happy. Stone walked over and stood beside Luke who was standing next to "AB." Both of them had their arms crossed. Luke saw that Stone had slid in beside him. Luke, without looking at Stone, tapped the guy in front of him and said, "Hey, what's all the hoopla about?"

The guy in front of him, without turning around, said, "Some lucky bastard just hit for a hundred grand!"

Luke rolled his eyes and then in a much lower voice, still not looking at Stone, said just loud enough for Stone, and possibly "AB," to hear, "How's the rest of the cluster fuck going?"

"Not good. I suggest we all meet at Johnny's room in Caesar's. I mean, now, this place is going to get real hot real quick. Have 'AB' text Johnny to leave the circus here ASAP." With that, Stone turned to exit away from the craziness.

That's when the real craziness began. He turned right into Mak.

"Stoney boy, fancy meeting you here, oh and you too, Mr. Fabrasia, and you too mister, I think you like to be called 'AB.' We three have got some business to discuss."

Luke looked at Mak like he had three heads and said, "I don't know what you're talking about and I don't even know who he is," pointing to Stone.

"Hey, Guinso, shut up and listen carefully, I got over a year of my life following you and your canary box over here," pointing at Stone. He then pulled out a stained sock out of his jacket pocket. At that second, Stone's life came crashing down around him. His mind in the span of a split second covered minutes, hours, days, and ultimately the last year. His mind immediately went back to the bar when Mak showed up after he killed Cooper, then the tracking device on his car, which he thought was from Luke. How could he have been so stupid? Luke was going to continue to plead his case when Stone interrupted him. "Luke, 'AB,' this is Federal Agent Mak Greenwall. Apparently, we have an issue. We certainly do not want to discuss it here. Let's all quietly, without incident, just walk out of here and leave in your limo, Luke. Best we discuss this in private."

Luke looked at Stone with a look that should have burned holes in Stone's face. He then shot a look at Mak, then finally 'AB.' "My car's outside, let's leave agent, Mak. I'm curious why you carry around dirty laundry in your pocket."

Luke and 'AB' needed not to hear anything else. they knew something was terribly wrong. Luke shot a look over to where he knew Stone had come. There was an even larger crowd gathering about seventy-five feet away, only there were no lights flashing and bells ringing where that crowd was standing. "AB" was already done texting to Johnny the message, "Your hotel. ASAP."

During all the confusion with the crowd around Johnny, he felt his pocket vibrate. He had almost forgot with all the confusion that he was there doing a job. He told the hotel official who was taking his picture with a couple of RIO hotties under each arm, holding a big check, to wait a minute. He knew enough to check to see who was sending him a text. He checked the text. It was from "AB": "Your hotel. ASAP." His stomach fell into his balls. He said the first thing that came to his mind, very loudly, "Hey mister, my lucky day! First, I hit the jackpot, then my wife texts me she just went into labor—I'm going to be a dad today!"

The crowd erupted in applause. Johnny then looked at the Rio manager with a serious look. "This is fun, but I really need to get my money and run to the hospital."

"Certainly, sir, follow me to my office." The manager, sensing the fun was over and the urgency of the situation, led Johnny through the crowd to get his money and get him on his way.

Sal wasn't the smartest guy in Luke's crew but he wasn't a complete fool either. He knew that by now they would have figured out that he had got into a taxi and what taxi company and most likely the exact taxi. He wasn't going to make it easy for himself to be tracked. He said only one word to the taxi driver, "Venetian." He nearly pissed himself until they actually pulled up to the Venetian, where he paid his fare and hopped out of the taxi. Still wearing his hat and glasses, he ducked into the Venetian. He walked to the mall area and bought the first tee shirt and baseball hat he found from a cart vendor. Then he located the first public bathroom and ducked into a stall. Quickly he changed into his new tee shirt and hat and put his old ones in the bag they gave him with his purchase. He was not going to leave evidence anywhere. Quickly, without running, he left the Venetian and walked back to Caesar's.

Lucky wasn't called Lucky without reason. Lots of his luck came from him being smart. He got into a taxi and said only two words, "Imperial Palace." Since he was carrying a laptop case and a small bag of electronics, he really didn't want to walk that far, but he also didn't want to be tied to staying at Caesar's if by any chance he had been made.

Luke and "AB" nonchalantly walked out of the Rio the way they entered, trying not to attract any attention. Mak was trailing not far behind, and Stone was on Mak's heels. Had this been a cartoon, steam would be pouring out of both Luke's and Stone's ears simultaneously.

Chapter 62

Steve, security man extraordinaire, on a hunch, had followed Stone from where Mike was killed over to where he stopped by the crowd where the jackpot chaos was happening. He had watched him make a quick call and stop next to the crowd. Nothing too out of the ordinary. He zoomed in, but the angle was a little off to get a good view of Stone's face. He panned the camera left and then right and stopped in his tracks. He knew that face, no mistaking it, hat and glasses notwithstanding. Steve was originally from Boston, and Luke was kind of a folk hero in the Boston media. Something big was either going on or could it be just a coincidence? He tried to pick up the sound but there was too much ambient noise with the crowd around the jackpot. Then it looked like Stone was about to walk away when someone else showed up. Now it was clear they were all somewhat familiar with each other. The man who showed up late pulled something out of his pocket, which Steve could not get a clear view of. Steve was watching them all walk out when he got a radio transmission in his ear about the gruesome discovery in room 3213.

Steve knew there was nothing but circumstantial coincidental evidence that they were all somehow connected. There may not be any reason to bring this up to the powers to be, but certainly his wife's uncle would be interested to know that Luke Fabrasia was in town. That was, if he didn't already know. College is expensive and a little donation to his daughter's college fund would be helpful.

"Hey Charlie, I need to take a piss and have a quick smoke, I'll be right back."

"Hey Steve, we got two potential murders and you got to take a piss? What the fuck?"

"Hey dude, nature calls, don't you know nicotine isn't addictive? I just like it." They both laughed. "I'll be quick, hold down the fort."

"No choice, big guy with the small bladder."

With that, Steve walked to the elevator and rode up the three floors to the outside smoking area. Steve walked through the back employee entrance to the outside smoking area behind the Rio. Fortunately, and uncharacteristically, he was the only employee outside at that point. He pulled his cell phone out of his pocket while he simultaneously lit a butt.

He speed-dialed Uncle Gino. He only used the letter G in his phonebook because he clearly knew his wife's uncle was bad, although you could never tell by Steve. He never saw or experienced anything overtly bad personally by his wife's uncle, only what he had read. Then again, he only saw him at family gatherings, and yes, there were those monthly envelope. Steve was daydreaming now when he was shocked into reality by Gino's voice. "Pronto, my nephew, by marriage to my favorite niece. How are you today and to what do I owe this pleasure?"

"Uncle, I have very little time, I'm on a smoke break."

"Those things are going to kill you. I will send you a box of my favorite cigars instead, they are good for you."

"Ha-ha, yeah, so I'll only get mouth cancer instead of lung cancer. Seriously, I need to get back to work. We've just had two potential murders in the last ten minutes."

"My, my, why do you think this has any interest for me?"

"I'm sure it doesn't, but what may be of interest to you is that while this was all happening, Luke Fabrasia just happened to be in the casino while it was all going down. Probably just a coincidence, but he was with another guy, both of them in hat and glasses. Then another guy walked over to him, who was literally feet from one of the stabbings. They were just getting ready to leave when someone else showed up, took something out of his pocket, then they all left. Like I said, probably nothing, but you always told me if I saw anything out of the ordinary. I thought you might be interested, so I called." Steve sensed the silence on the other end of the line to not be positive. He was quickly regretting making the phone call. He thought apparently Uncle Gino knew Luke was in town and he was bothering him. He felt foolish.

"Steve, thank you for calling, it's always a pleasure to hear your voice. I have one question, 'What exactly do you think the last man had in his pocket'?" Steve now knew his concerns were for naught. Now all he heard in Uncle Gino's voice was controlled rage.

"No way to tell, sir, someone had hit a jackpot near them. Too many people to get a clear shot, I tried. No way to hear the conversation either, too much noise."

"Tell me, Stephen, how is my niece and my grandniece?"

"Very well, sir, thank you for asking. I hope this call wasn't a bother," knowing right well that this was exactly the kind of call he had intended Steve would make some day.

"No, Stephen, not a bother at all, now that I know my friend Luke is in town, I'll have to call and invite him to dinner. I'm sure you need to get back to work. Now let me know if you sense any connection to the two murders, OK, Stephen?"

"Absolutely, uncle, see you soon."

With that, he hung up feeling somewhat conflicted. He was happy he could help his extended family in any way he could. He clearly enjoyed the extra money to help his daughter. He felt at the same time that he was betraying his employer. He knew, at a very high level, that sharing his insights from work was at the very least unethical. He also knew his wife's uncle was ruthless and the information he shared with him could cause someone harm or even death. He thought, "Would that actually make him an accomplice either in the eyes of the law or worse?" He crushed out his cigarette and went back to the mayhem.

Chapter 63

Luke and "AB" climbed into the back of the limo and left the door open. Mak climbed in shortly after with Stone right on his heels. "AB" put the divider down halfway, barked "Caesar's" and put the divider back up, and pushed the intercom off button to ensure that the driver was not going to overhear the conversation. No sooner was the divider up and the limo rolling toward Caesar's when Stone lunged at Mak with a flying right hook to the jaw. Stone was yelling something to the effect, "You no good piece of shit, motherfucker." "AB" had thrown himself in the middle of the two of them, and by now Mak was trying to get a lick in response to Stone's sucker punch.

Luke half stood up in the limo and shouted, "Silencio!" Luke was just one of those guys that, regardless of the situation, when he spoke, people just stopped and listened. Everyone settled back into their respective seats. Luke clearly had everyone's attention, although Stone was not thinking very clearly at the moment. Luke addressed Mak, "Inspector Greenwall, why don't you try and explain exactly what's going on? First, why don't you wipe your mouth with this? You seem to be bleeding." Luke handed Mak a handkerchief. Mak shook his head, took the handkerchief, and wiped the blood from the corner of his mouth.

"Thank you, Captain Ginso, let me first start by saying everything I'm telling you, all the surveillance photos and recorded conversation plus stupid shits over here's bloody clothes are stashed away in a safe spot. Anything happens to me and a friend of mine has instructions of what to do with the evidence, and all three of you will fry."

Stone snapped, "Fuck you, asshole, you don't have any friends, you're bluffing."

Luke shot Stone a "shut the fuck up" look. "Let your associate speak."

Mac wiped his mouth once more, took a deep breath, and began. "Don't ask me why but it just struck me funny that Stoney Boy took so much interest at briefing meetings about what all you Ginsos were up to. Asking lots of questions, even if it wasn't his case and all. Then out of nowhere, you are on your way to jail. Do not pass go, do not collect two hundred dollars and bam! Witness and agents dead, and off you go free as a bird. So, on a hunch, I started following Stoney Boy here and he brings me straight to you. Wow, and everyone at the bureau thinks I'm a dope." Then he looks disgruntled at Stone. "Now, I'm usually not too surprised by human nature, and I've seen a lot in my days as an agent. I thought nothing would surprise me. That was until your boy," now looking at Luke, "popped a couple of agents right before my eyes and Lurch over there," pointing his thumb at 'AB.' "Came out of nowhere and cleaned up after trigger finger," pointing at Stone. "Hey, look, I'm never one to judge, but even I draw the line at shooting an officemate. Talk about going postal. Not that I want to get hung up on that and, to make a long story short, I know about all of it: the drugs, extortion, stolen merchandise, causing a war between the Colombians and the Russians, everything. I've just been accumulating all of this evidence like a good little agent, building a case. The only difference is, unless this all goes bad, I built the case for my own gain. I guess you could call it my own personal 401K. I knew at some point, Stoney over there would lead me to the goose that laid the golden egg. Though I figured, quite frankly, I would have been happy with blackmail. That was until I saw Stoney Boy take the counterfeit case. Again, just a hunch, I followed Stoney here and guess what—the big boys show up, so call me Carnak holding Luke's handkerchief to his forehead in Johnny Carson fashion. "This is the mother load of a counterfeit system that is untraceable, am I right?"

Everyone sat silent, Stone again beating himself up, not understanding how he could have been so stupid and clueless not to have connected the dots. It was surreal that he was sitting in a limo in Vegas with two of the people he had worked so hard to gain a trusting relationship. Stone's mind was racing at warp speed. Luke would want to kill them both and take the chance it couldn't be tied back to him. No, he couldn't' chance that because if what Mak said was correct, then he had "AB" on tape as an accessory after the fact on a murder rap of two FBI agents. Luke most likely wouldn't do that, correct?

The limo, pulling up to Caesar's, shook him out of his self-induced trance. Luke broke the silence, "What's your room number, Stone?"

"1231."

"Okay, let's continue this upstairs. 'AB,' you and I will take a lap around the inside. Stone, you and your associate go right upstairs. 'AB' will call Sal and Lucky, so we can all meet in your room, 1231, correct?"

"Yeah, 1231, see you in five."

"See you when we get there, have a bottle of Johnny Walker Black waiting, capisce?"

"Sure," Stone answered in a beaten down low voice. Stone could already hear "AB" calling Sal and Lucky telling them where to rendezvous.

Chapter 64

Stone and Mak entered the hotel lobby not speaking, Mak following just slightly behind Stone. Stone led them to the lobby liquor store. He went directly to the Scotch wall and picked out a half gallon bottle of Johnny Walker Black. He was counting on this being a long night.

Mak quietly stood in the doorway, watching Stone first pick out the Scotch, then proceed to pay for it. That was when he couldn't contain himself.

"Hey, Stoney Boy, need a couple of bucks? I feel like I'm going to be in a new tax bracket soon." Stone never even acknowledged Mak was speaking, but he did acknowledge to himself that at some point he was going to put a bullet into Mak's head. He finished paying and walked out of the store, right past Mak.

"Well then, Stoney Boy, have it your way." He followed Stone to the elevator.

Stone turned before entering the elevators, "Listen, you son of a bitch, the elevators are miked, so shut your fucking mouth, we'll talk in the room."

"Oke Dokey, Big Boy."

"Excuse me, sir, can you press twelve?" Stone was already pushing twelve. Mak, really enjoying this, said, "What a coincidence—we're on the same floor!" Stone said only loud enough for Mak to hear, "Asshole."

Chapter 65

Luke and "AB" were doing just as he told Stone. They were taking a loop around Caesar's—quietly at first.

Then Luke spoke, "'AB,' did I, or did I not tell you not to get involved that night? Now, that dirty fed can put you away forever."

"Sorry, boss."

"Sorry isn't going to help us now. The family is in jeopardy."

"Not if we kill him, boss, and Stone, if we have to."

"That's always an option, my friend, but not until we understand not only what he has, but more importantly where he has it."

"Boss, you really think he got all he says he has?'

"We know he has a bloody sock, and he pretty much described your exact involvement and everything else we've done since hooking up with Stone."

"I agree, boss, I'll make this right."

"'AB,' we're a family. Don't forget you don't have to do this alone, we will handle it together."

"Thanks, boss"

"You're welcome, 'AB,' but make no mistake, they both are breathing on borrowed time. We will eliminate them, it's not a question of if, it's only a matter of when. Let's get up there now and figure out our next move."

Chapter 66

Stone and Mak had an uneventful walk back to Stone's room. Stone stopped to open his door, and Mak continued to walk.

"Hey, where the fuck are you going?"

"To my room, asshole, we've got connecting rooms. Open the connecting door."

"Motherfucker."

By the time Stone had got into his room, the connecting door between their rooms was being knocked on by Mak. Stone opened the door and the uneventfulness of the walk from the elevator ended with the turn of a doorknob. Stone pulled open the door, dragging Mak with him, and the melee began. When two grown men, who have been trained in lethal hand-to-hand combat, get into a fight, it's not for the faint of heart. Actually, it makes UFC fighters seem like schoolyard brawlers. Fists, feet, and furniture were all in play. To the surprise of an audience, had there been one, Mak yet again held his own, although, by no means was he winning the fight and had Lucky not started knocking on the door rather vigorously, someone, most likely Mak, would have gotten seriously broken.

"What?!" Stone yelled.

"Hey, it's me, Lucky, open up. What the hell are you doing in there?"

Stone got up, growling at Mak, "This isn't over yet, not by a long shot, asshole."

Mak wiped his mouth, replying, "That's right asshole, it'll be over when I'm flush and in the Bahamas, dipshit, and all thanks to you, Stoney fucking Boy."

Stone was opening the door to let Lucky in when Sal came briskly walking down the hall. Lucky immediately felt relief and also a sense of pride that this kid was going to become a valuable part of the team. The guys, including Lucky, felt that Sal got fast track "made" because of the bullets he took, even though he fucked up to take them. What the hell, the military gives purple hearts regardless of how military people get injured.

Lucky and Sal both knew not to get into a conversation in the hallway, because it was likely to be wired. Lucky stepped into the room and held the door for Sal.

Sal spoke first, "What a cluster fuck that turned out . . . who the fuck is he?"

Mak chimed in, "Your worst fucking nightmare guinea, asshole." Stone was now square in the middle between Mak, Lucky, and Sal.

Lucky, already with his gun in his hand, was pointing it at Mak. "Go ahead and shoot me, motherfucker, you'll all fry."

Stone put his hands up, "Chill, guys, I got this handled."

Mak laughed, threw the old bloody sock at Stone, "Handle this, motherfucker!"

Lucky, "Stone, what's up?"

"This asshole's name is Mak. He happens to be one of my esteemed colleagues in the FBI. Apparently, he had a hunch and followed me the night Sal got shot. He saw everything and then followed me to where I dumped my clothes and kept them to blackmail me, or should I say, us. When I said us, I really mean me, 'AB,' and Luke, but you know what I mean."

Lucky thought for a minute and said, "Shit, I don't want to be around when the boss shows up."

"Too late, he was at the Rio when all the shit went down. They met there. He and 'AB' will be here any minute."

Lucky could only say, "How the hell do I get myself out of this nightmare?"

"Just be quiet and let me deal with it, I caused it."

Mak: "No, you won't, but big guinea boss will."

Sal now piped up confused, but super pissed nonetheless, "Motherfucker, you call anyone guinea again and I'll slit your throat right here and now."

"Fuck you, you stupid junior guinea, your fault I got all this evidence anyway, you'll be lucky if big guinea doesn't ice you himself." That was all Sal needed. He went straight for Mak when Stone dove in front of him like an All-American linebacker to block him from killing Mak. The collision was as bone-jarring as any running back hitting the line. Lucky never flinched with his gun still pointed directly at Mak's chest.

Stone had Sal on the ground and talked directly into his ear, "Not now, when the time is right, I will let you know." Sal struggled a little under Stone's weight, then gave up the fight. Stone could sense this as Sal relaxed and stopped fighting to get up. Stone released his grip and slowly let him up. Once on his feet again, Sal barked, "Later, motherfucker."

Mak, "later, low-level guinea." Sal turned toward Mak again, in a halfhearted effort, leaving Stone between them who was not going to let him get at Mak. "Hey Mak, do yourself a favor, watch your mouth, we get it, you got information. You keep this up, you'll be a dead guy with information and some of us will end up in jail. Nobody wins, so we get it. Just shut up until Luke gets here. Then we will hear what you want and decide what we'll do then."

"Oh, you'll hear what I want."

Luke and "AB" were walking around Caesar's, aimlessly attempting to just kill a little time, not wanting all seven of them to show up at the same time, "AB" purposely keeping quiet, because in these times it was best to let the boss speak first, but he couldn't take the silence a moment longer. "Boss, what do we do now? I don't think killing him is the answer, if he has what he says he has."

"Well, first, I'm gonna wait to see some more evidence because if all he has is something on Stone and not you, then we have one situation with an easy solution. Should he have something more to tie you into the cleanup, we have another situation. Neither one is good but one is better than the other. Capisce?"

"I know, but how are we going to get him to give up what he's got?"

"Let me worry about that later. Right now, this town is too hot for us. We need to get everyone out of town now, including Mr. FBI Mak. Call the pilots, tell them sorry for the quick turnaround, but we will be out of town within the hour. Tell them there will be seven of us." "AB" dialed and gave the news as they headed toward the elevators.

Chapter 67

Gino Campanelli called Bruno Padaloni, his right-hand man, immediately when he got off the phone with his nephew Steve. Bruno was driving when his phone rang. Bruno saw that it was the boss and picked it up immediately, "What's up?"

"Bruno, I'm not sure, but I don't think it's good. By chance, did you get a call from anyone in Boston letting us know Luke Fabrasia was coming to town?"

"No, sir, never heard a thing."

"Well, Bruno, funny thing happened. He showed up at the Rio right when a jackpot is hit and two people get whacked, all apparently in a five-minute span."

"Coincidence?"

"Coincidence, my ass, but Luke's too smart. First of all to come to *my* town without notifying me and the fact he's here all dressed up incognito with a baseball cap, then two people get whacked! Come on, he's up to something no good and just hoped to get in and out without us knowing. We need to figure out where he's at and pay him a courtesy visit."

"OK, what do you want me to do? "

"Round up four or five guys and have them meet here at my house. Once we track him down, then we will be ready to go say hello, so to speak. Meanwhile, I will call Joey at the airport and figure out how he got to town."

"Capisce. I'll do my end and have a crew there within the half hour."

"Great."

They hung up their phones and Bruno speed-dialed one of the boys and had him call three more to meet at the boss's house. His job for the time being was done. Gino got on the phone and called Joey Strombone, a nephew of a business associate that worked in operations at Las Vegas International. He was a very respected, hardworking guy, who was a nine to fiver. Really didn't have the balls to be a wise guy, but loved the perks of being loosely associated with the Campanelli gang. Rarely, he would get a call from Gino, but when he did, he dropped everything and used his unlimited access to airline records to get information the Campanellis needed. Joey assumed he was probably trying to get guys before they left town without paying a debt. Sometimes, he would ask if he could pull a favor for an upgrade for someone, which of course meant Joey would have to pull a favor. Joey never minded. He frequently got care packages dropped at his home that ranged from cash to electronics. What Joey liked the best was the front-row seats for Vegas shows where he got treated like a big shot and, in return, looked like a big shot to his wife. Clearly, on his salary, he would not be able to afford that kind of entertainment.

Joey's phone rang. He saw Gino in the caller ID and picked up immediately.

"Mr. Campanelli, how are you? What can I do for you today?"

"Giuseppe, how are you? I only call when I need something, I feel bad."

"No need to feel bad. I call you all the time when I need stuff as well, it's all good. By the way, I like that you call me Giuseppe, only my grandfather used to call me that."

"To me you will always be a Giuseppe. By the way, I knew your grandfather. He was a great man, hardworking family man, what could be better? Now to business. I need you to check the last three days to see if a Luke Fabrasia flew in from Boston or New York and also if there is a return in a couple of days."

"OK, no problem, any chance they flew private."

"No idea, Giuseppe, my friend, that's why I have you."

"Mr. Campanelli, do you have a minute? There are only three airlines to check. This should be quick."

"Sure, I'll be happy to wait."

Joey did his magic, toggling from one airline computer system to another in a matter of three minutes, and he could confirm no Luke Fabrasia coming in or going for three days on either side. "Sorry, Mr. Campanelli, no luck."

"Hmm, that's interesting, how about charter or private?"

"Let me check."

Again in a different system that was proprietary to Las Vegas International. "Let me start with today. Twenty-two private jets came in today, bingo, one from just outside of Boston, and guess what, it just filed for a takeoff slot in just under an hour from now. May not be your boy, but it's awful coincidental."

"Giuseppe, thank you, I'll have some special show tickets delivered by the end of the week. Thank you very much."

"No problem, thank-you."

Gino was now feeling the tension that accompanies time, or more succinctly, lack thereof. He dialed Bruno again to make him aware that they needed to be on the road again in no more than twenty minutes.

Chapter 68

"'AB,' call Johnny and make sure he is on his way, even if he has to leave the one hundred grand."

"Will do, boss." They were just getting off the elevator when Luke instructed "AB" to call, which he speed-dialed and confirmed that Johnny was en route as they spoke. Luke rapped on the door to Stone's room so hard it's amazing his knuckles weren't bleeding. Sal came and immediately opened the door. "Sal, don't you even check who's outside the door before you open it? What the fuck, haven't I taught you anything?"

"Sorry, boss."

"Whatever."

Then he was quiet for a moment, almost in a theatrical way. When he knew he had everyone's attention, he spoke clearly and succinctly: "The operation today was clearly a cluster fuck. No idea what the fallout will be, whether or not they can lift prints or security camera identification. So this is what we are going to do in no more than ten minutes. Everyone will be packed and in the limo, all of you leaving with hats and glasses on. Once you're in the limo, drive around the corner and pick "AB" and me up. I don't want to be seen again with you guys, god forbid any of these photos get out and Campanelli should see me here without official notification, that would be worse than the law. We've got a private jet. We can figure out what went wrong on the way back."

Mak piped up from the back of the room, "Hey Captain Ginzo, who died and made you boss? I ain't going anywhere, I got a hot honey I've spent a week's salary on booze getting her primed and ready."

Luke, in an uncharacteristically calm voice, replied, "Mr. FBI man, Mak, I guess you call yourself, this is not an option. Either you leave with me or we kill you right now and deal with the consequences, providing you actually have what you say you have."

Mak new this was not the fight to win, nonetheless he had one more shot over to the boss: "All right, Al Pacino, but we got lots of business to discuss, lots of business." That's when Luke's phone began to vibrate.

Chapter 69

Gino was pissed. He only hated one thing more than being disrespected by anyone, in particular someone who is part of a family who should know better. That is when someone comes to his town and doesn't pay their financial respects. Gino wasn't sure what Luke's deal was. Stephen had called again and said there were now two dead guys at the Rio who were connected to each other and he looked at their check-in information and at least one of them Mike Lewis was from Boston.

In Gino's mind, at the very least, the two hits were Luke's doing. The slot machine hit—what was that all about? Had he figured out a way to rig a slot machine? That would be amazing and very lucrative. Why, though, wouldn't he just use that information in Atlantic City or Connecticut? Why bother to fly all the way to Vegas and risk having to deal with Gino? Didn't make a whole lot of sense, but nonetheless, Luke and some of his guys were in Vegas unannounced and that was unacceptable.

Gino was getting antsy now he was running out of time and needed Bruno to get here quick with the guys, so they could have a rendezvous with the Fabrasia family.

Gino dialed Bruno. "Pronto, boss."

"Where the fuck are you guys?"

"We will be there in five minutes, boss, you only called twenty minutes ago."

"They are flying out of here in less than forty-five minutes. I want to surprise them at the private jet terminal."

"No problem, boss, be waiting outside."

"Preggo."

Gino felt a little stall tactic was in order. He flipped open his phone and speed-dialed Luke. He hoped that Luke's number hadn't changed. Actually, if it had, that would have pissed him off even more. The heads of the families had an unwritten rule to make sure they all had current contact information. As stated before, the mob was like a big well-run corporation with many branches. Communication is the linchpin of any good organization, be it legal or illegal. Gino was listening to the ring of Luke's phone: one, two, and then a Verizon woman's voice came on and said, "Please listen to the music while we locate your party." Then the theme from the Godfather started playing. Some would have found that amusing, but Gino found it annoying and insulting all at once. Then Luke's recorded voice came over the phone: "Pronto, can't come to the phone now, leave a message."

Gino slammed shut his phone. He wasn't going to leave a message yet. He was actually pissed he gave Luke the heads up that he was looking for him. Now he had to move fast. Luke most likely was downtown and getting to the airport would be ten minutes faster than him since Gino's house was clear across town.

Chapter 70

Luke, staring at his phone blankly for a second, trying to remember who "GC" was in his phone book. He then wanted to slap his own head for being so dumb. How could he not put it together that GC and Gino Campanelli were one and the same?

"Son of a bitch Campanelli knows we're here, let's get out of here now before this cluster fuck gets any worse. I'll deal with him later when we're twenty five hundred miles away."

Mak chimed in, "Really, head Las Vegas Guinea knows the Boston head Guinea is in town and didn't ask permission, what's going to happen—a Guinea smackdown?" Mak began chuckling at his own benign humor.

"Inspector, you and I apparently will have some business to conduct, which may or may not end up fruitful for both of us. I guarantee you, if you choose to continue to blatantly piss me off, this will not end good . . . Capisce?"

Mak was silent for what seemed forever, but was no longer than five seconds. "Cap-issccee, big guy. I assume we are getting out of dodge?" That was apparently Mak's concession in an attempt to be a good boy.

Luke grabbed "AB's" arm and spun him around, heading out the door. "AB" and I will be around the corner waiting. All of you better be packed, have these rooms wiped down, and be out of here in no more than five minutes. "AB" and I will grab a cab and fly home with the private jet and leave you guys to fend for yourselves if we're not rolling in five, capisce?"

"Cap-isscceee, big guy."

Luke was heard by only "AB" as they walked out the elevator, "I'm going to rip his throat out with my bare fucking hands." "AB" responded just as softly, "Only if you beat me to his throat first."

Sal, for one, was not going to be left to fend for himself. He was out the door and on his way to his room to get his shit so as not to piss the boss off. Lucky stayed an extra thirty seconds to straighten the room out and bolted to get his stuff. Mak didn't need to impress anyone for the moment, so he just left to go to his room and grab his bag. He hadn't even unpacked his bag, so he was out the door in less than a minute. He figured if he got to the limo first, he could text Lucille that he had to leave quickly on business. He was surprised how much she had an effect on him in such a short amount of time.

Stone was getting back to go mode, knowing he had to think and think fast, not to mention get his ass moving because he had no doubt that Luke would be on the jet and gone ASAP. Stone finished straightening out the furniture, his bag was almost all packed, so his exit was less than three minutes.

"AB" was texting Johnny as they were going down the elevator. As the doors opened, there stood Johnny in all his Johnnyness, holding his rather large envelope of cash. Johnny insisted on cash and not a check, so with little more than a signature and a social security number, they took the government's cut and handed him seventy large.

"Boss, 'AB,' what's up?" Luke, realizing the cameras and microphones around the elevators, just shot Johnny the look he last saw when Luke popped him in the jaw on the railroad tracks. The look alone made Johnny flinch. 'AB' spoke first, understanding the situation perfectly. "Johnny, the limo outside is leaving in exactly three minutes. I suggest you, your luggage, and your winnings be in the limo, capisce?"

Johnny was getting ready to discuss the options, looked at Luke and smartly shook his head, and stepped quickly into the elevator, sensing Luke's eyes may actually cut him in two.

Sal entered the limo second. Mak had just finished texting Lucille and had pocketed his phone. Sal, not uttering a word, quickly sat himself as far away from Mak as possible, acting as if Mak was the plague himself.

Mak, never losing an opportunity, started right in on Sal, "Hey low-level guinea punk, I want to thank you very much."

Sal, not able to control his better instincts, had to reply, "Thanks for what?"

"'Cause if you weren't such a fuck up and screwed up that deal with the Colombians, I would never have seen Stone shoot his own coworkers and drag your bloody ass to safety—that and your other stupid dead buddy. Wow, what a couple of knuckleheads. I've seen smarter junior high thugs."

Mak was having too much fun to let this one go and was getting ready to start round two when Lucky jumped in. He said as he was climbing in to no one in particular, "Johnny just texted he was on his way down."

Sal, maybe because Lucky was there, felt more comfortable, barked over to Mak, "Hey asshole, I'll show you who is a knucklehead, I'm going to make sure boss gives me the honor of blowing your fucking head off, then we'll see who's the fuck up, fuck up!"

Lucky, not knowing exactly what was happening, put two and two together and decided to defuse the situation, "Hey both of you, chill, we need to get out of Vegas quick, we have no time for this." That probably would have been responded to with another barrage of epithets had Stone not entered the limo at that time. "OK, let's go."

"Hold on, Stone, we need to wait for Johnny, he just texted he should be here in a minute."

"Better damn hurry, Luke didn't seem like he wanted to wait."

"'AB' knows as well, he texted me two minutes ago."

"So long as Luke's cool with it."

Mak, never losing an opportunity in his most condescending tone, "Ou, Ou, soooo long as Luuuuuuke's coooool with it, you make me want to puke, you two-timing piece of shit! At least, though, you're a piece of shit that's going to make me rich, shithead." Stone, now with his rational thinking head back on, decided to ignore him, which he also knew would piss Mak off even more. Stone was getting antsy and it was seven or eight minutes since Luke had put the five-minute deadline on them. Stone was looking at his watch when Johnny stuck his head in the limo, banging on the divider window, "Let's go, driver, hey what the fuck happened back there? Can you believe I hit a fucking slot machine in the middle . . . Who the fuck are you?" Pulling out his gun, he pointed it at Mak, whom he just noticed mid-sentence.

"You're worst Irish nightmare Ginso. Hey, by the way, how far did you have to chase the brother for those shoes, Johnny Boy, or should I call you Luke's stupid lieutenant?"

"What the fuck?" Stone literally had to dive in front of Johnny, who was either going to shoot and then kick the shit out of Mak, or kick the shit out of Mak and then shoot him. Either way and as much as Stone would have enjoyed to watch, now was not the time. "Hey, hey Johnny, chill, this is Mak, an FBI agent, who has apparently been following me for a while and has some info on us that he wants to turn into an early retirement plan."

"Does boss know?"

"Yeah, we will deal with it in Boston. Right now, Gino Capanelli made us, or you, who knows, and we got to catch a private jet out of here pronto."

"Where's boss?"

"Right around the corner." Stone put down the divider, "Hey, driver, pull over right over there and pick up our last two guys and then get us to the airport ASAP."

The driver responded, "No problem, sir," then pulled the car over. Luke climbed in the back with the boys and "AB" got in the front seat. "AB," always the careful one, wanted to make sure there were no deviations or delays on the way to the airport. You never know who works for whom in their line of work. No need to make it easy to have the whole bunch of them Christmas-wrapped and delivered to Gino.

Chapter 71

Gino did not like to be ignored and was furious about Luke not answering his call. Luke was in his town on his turf unannounced. Should that not be enough, people were dead in his town, clearly killed on purpose, and money was being won without him getting his taste. This was totally unacceptable and would have to be dealt with accordingly. How he wasn't exactly sure, yet this wasn't just some wise guy going rogue, this was the powerful and well-respected Luke Fabrasia, technically at the same level as he. Although clearly Vegas produced more money than Boston, a head of a family was nonetheless a head of a family and needed to be treated as such. He couldn't just show up at the airport, guns blazing, and shoot them all. That wouldn't be good for business inside or outside the family, although it was and always is an option. Then there is the problem of his guys now knowing that outsiders are in town unannounced and that is not accepted in the Campanelli family ever!

Bruno had gathered four other guys, which was all he could do under the quick notice he received from Gino. Roberto "Bobby" Genari, his brother Paulo "Pauli," Geraldo "Gerry" Loubuto, and

Sylvester "Sly" Poncetta. All goons, all trigger happy, all grossly underdressed but equally overarmored. They had left Gino's a few minutes earlier with Bruno, driving Gino's Mercedes, and Sly driving himself and the three other goons in his black Chrysler 300 with the blacked-out windows.

Sly, although a goon and a ruthless one at that, probably had two-tenths more brains than the other three, a little nervous, and let his car mates know his concerns. "Hey, you know we're going to the airport to confront Luke Fabrasia and his guys, right?"

Bobby answered, "So fucking what?"

"So fucking what? He's just as big as we are on the East Coast and you know boss gets crazy about other guys in our town unannounced. I don't want to be in no fucking war with the East Coast!"

Pauli decided to help his brother with more insightful input, "So fucking what?"

Now Sly was getting nervous and pissed off, "What is that, a generic answer from the two of you? I'm just saying I'll do whatever boss wants, but I want you guys to know these are not some punks we need to shake down. They're guys like us, so just be careful, OK?"

Now, it was Gerry's turn, "OK, Sylvester, we'll be careful." That was said with dripping contempt.

"Fuck all of you motherfuckers." Everyone in the car broke out in laughter, that is, all but Sly.

Gino had been quiet for most of the ride. Bruno knew when and when not to speak. Now was the time to wait. Bruno knew it would only be a matter of time, Gino never went anywhere or did anything without a plan. Then he finally spoke, "Bruno, I know I am not always reasonable, eh?" Bruno wasn't biting, just nodding his head. "See, I know but I am consistent, no?" Again, Bruno wasn't biting, just nodding. "They all fucking know to let me know when they are in my town and what I have to do when they don't let me know, eh?" One more time, Bruno was not biting, just nodding, "Luke, he's too smart for this, there must be a reason. I will give him thirty seconds to explain—that is generous. If not in thirty seconds, you shoot first."

Now Bruno responded, "How will I know?"

That's when Gino snapped, "Can't you fucking count? I said thirty seconds, thirty secondos, if I look at you like I am not satisfied after thirty seconds, start shooting and shoot Luke first, capisce? Now call Sly and tell them to do nothing unless you shoot first. Then leave no man standing, OK?"

"Yes, boss."

Bruno, never one to piss the boss off, speed-dialed Sly's phone. "Yeah, what's up?"

"Boss says he gives them thirty seconds to come clean. If he's not satisfied, he will let me know, then I will shoot Luke first. You guys leave no one else standing, you got it?"

"Yeah, Bruno, but how will you know if boss is not happy?"

"Shut up, Sly, just follow. If I shoot, you and the guys shoot, then get the fuck out of dodge! Got it?"

"Sure, boss, no problem." Sly hung up and said for all to hear, "I think you got the gist. Boss gives him thirty seconds to come clean. If not, Bruno shoots, he shoots, we shoot until they are all dead, we good?"

Bobby said sarcastically, "OK, Sly, sure you're not afraid of the Boston Baked Beans?" That got another laugh from the Chrysler.

Sly, really crazy now, snapped, "Hey fuckheads, stay focused, we don't want to get sloppy and die here today."

Bobby responded, "The only thing sloppy here is your girlfriend I had this morning," which resulted in three hysterically laughing goons in the Chrysler. Sly thought to himself, "Maybe if I just killed all three of them now, I could join Fabrasia's family," then quickly let that stupid thought leave his brain and focused on following Bruno to the airport. Probably three minutes till go time.

Chapter 72

Luke's limo driver wheeled into the private jet terminal and with a wave the limo driver was allowed through the gate and drove right to where the plane had taxied earlier. Since they had only been on the ground for all of two hours, actually, the crew had just finished its post-flight check and was having the fuel topped off when "AB" called for the quick turnaround. To be honest, they were a little unhappy not to get some downtime in Vegas. They also knew flying a private jet for pay is pretty good work, so they weren't going to get pissy.

The limo pulled up, not more than twenty feet from the stairway of the private jet. All the guys were just going through the motions of exiting the limo except Luke. He was the only guy who seemed to have a purpose and waited to move them quickly. Luke was actually pushing Sal's ass to get out of the limo, "Hey boys, get the lead out, time to leave now before we have company."

Mak, who would be the last one out of the limo, once again, not being able to control himself, "Yeah, hurry up, the fucking IRS may show up at any minute. Hey Luke, did you declare all that money you made selling smack last year? I thought I told you to declare everything."

Luke just turned and gave that killer stare again, pushing Sal out of the car and just followed him out. Mak said, "Maybe he did declare all that money." Stone. who was next to Mak. just mumbled, "dickhead . . . fucking dickhead."

The limo driver was already loading the luggage from the car. The copilot had started taking the luggage and carefully loading the bags in the belly of the plane. Although they had never met, the limo driver and copilot had a rhythm going as if they had done it a million times before. All was going fine and it was beginning to look like a smooth exit from Vegas when Gino, Bruno, and company wheeled onto the scene with screeching tires and the reckless abandon you could expect from thugs expecting their turf had been exploited.

Luke's worst nightmare was happening. This was not going to be pretty and the hope that this was going to end well was probably not good. "Let me handle this, keep your mouths shut, and your guns ready." Stone had a different plan and wasn't going to discuss it with Luke—no time for a debate or a discussion. Stone stepped right in front of Luke, almost knocking him down. He pulled his badge out first and his gun next, "Mak, follow my lead and don't fuck up. Pilot, you keep loading luggage, no matter what they say. Boys, get on the plane now, except Luke."

The copilot seemed to be listening but the conundrum set in whom to listen to: Luke the boss or Stone, who clearly was taking over the situation. For the time being, they were all frozen in time and space.

Then the Campanelli crew was out of their cars with enough firepower to start their own militia. Now they expected lots of scenarios to unfold. The Campanelli crew had seen much and done much in their collective years. They all most likely thought that either Luke's crew would shit their pants and roll over for them or would shoot first and ask questions later. They had not expected, "Halt, FBI Agents Stone and Greenwall, put your weapons down and your hands in the air." Now if you thought Luke's guys looked funny standing like statues frozen in time, you should have seen Campanelli's guys. From an uninterested party, Stone and Mak looked pretty believable. Stone was slowly moving his pistol back and forth, fanning Gino's guys with his right hand and holding his badge straight up with his left. Mak, on the other hand, was standing to Gino's right, and alternatively fanning his gun from Gino's guys to Luke's guys again with the gun in his right and his badge in his left.

Mak spoke up, "Hey Inspector Stone, looks like we got ourselves a regular Ginso standoff here. Anyone moves the wrong way and kills Boston Ginso #1 and you kill Vegas Ginso #1." Stone was definitely wishing one of Gino's guys would put a cap in him and shut him up for good.

Stone needed to take charge again, "Gino. Gino Campanelli, you and your men stand down and there will be no repercussions.

We have Mr. Luke Fabrasia and his men in custody and are bringing them back to Boston for prosecution. Get back in your car and drive away and we will forget this happened." Gino, who had been the last to exit his vehicle for a number of reasons, not the least being that if the bullets started flying, he would be safer in the vehicle. The second is that he was the boss, and making an entrance was part of his job, his persona, his lot in life. He was a Mafia head and arguably the boss of bosses—it was Vegas and he was the last standing Don after the "Vegas Cleansing." He spoke slowly, softly, yet undeniably powerfully, "Boys, don't stand down, do not lower your weapons." Then to Stone, "Inspector, how do we know you're really FBI? This is Vegas, you know. Almost anything can be bought, including that piece of tin you and your associate are holding up."

"I assure you, Mr. Campanelli, this badge and this gun are very real and if you don't want to end up in custody with Mr. Fabrasia, you better get your men and leave now. My generous offer will not be extended much longer."

"Inspector, since I do not have a weapon, may I walk up and look at your badge?"

"I will allow you to do that but I assure you, after your inspection, you will leave or you will end up incarcerated for obstruction of justice, carrying concealed weapons, and at least thirty-two other infractions I will concoct. Mr. Fabrasia and you will be cellmates for a very long time."

"I assure you, Mr. Inspector, if I determine you are legit, we will leave without incident. I also assure you that if you're lying, none of you will be leaving here alive."

Luke, still shocked . . . no . . . pissed that Stone undermined him . . . again . . ., thought to himself, "the move was brilliant," but his ego wouldn't allow him to give Stone his due. He spoke to Gino, "Gino, kill them both, those fucking feds, kill them both. Johnny just won one hundred G's, it's yours." Mak, for the first time, was nervous. This couldn't be good. He fired a shot over Luke's head, then pointed his gun at Gino, "OK, you fucking Ginso punks, enough negotiating, we're done here. These guys are going back to Boston dead or fucking alive, and you're dying first head Ginso if you don't stand down now, fucking, capisce?"

Gino, still unbelievably calm and never taking his eyes off Mak, "Boys, lower your weapons. OK, inspector, or whatever you are, let me look at your associate's badge and we will allow you to board your plane and leave." Stone, now not taking his eyes off Bruno, knew Bruno was the linchpin, and whatever he did, the goons would follow. The goons wouldn't dare act without direction. That was just a fact.

Stone, speaking straight ahead, but directly to Mak: "Let him come and look." Mak, now quickly shifting his gun from Gino's head to Luke's back and forth, "Make it quick, Vegas Ginso." Gino calmly walked to Stone, inspected his badge and just when he seemed to be satisfied by turning away, stopped and turned back.

"Inspector Stone, one last request, may I view your driver's license as well?" Stone debated for less than a second. "Don't move an inch closer." He folded his badge, put it into his back left pocket. He then changed hands with his gun, removed his wallet from his right back pocket with his right hand. He flipped it open and behind the clear plastic cover on the inside of his wallet was his license. He held it high and straight out for Gino to view. "Joseph Stone, Grant St, Somerville Mass. Well, if nothing else, you have attention to detail, Mr. Stone, we will leave now but remember I now know what you look like. God help you if I find out this is a ruse."

Mak chirped, "Ruse, ruse, wow what a fucking English teacher you are, what's the Italian word for ruse? Rusa fucking Ginso dipshit, ha-ha" The "ha-ha" clearly sounded nervous.

Gino stared directly at Mak, "You, my friend, your face, is indelibly etched in my mind, we shall meet again." He turned, looked at Bruno . . . Andiamo, "Let's go. Luke, you better hope I'm sending you a Christmas card in jail" and walked back to his car. Stone internally breathed a sigh of relief until just as abruptly Gino spun back, "one more request, inspector."

"What, and make it quick, I'm losing patience."

"The one hundred grand Johnny won. He won't need that where he's going. I own this airport and that's your departure fee." Johnny, who was quiet until now, spit out, "Fuck you," knowing immediately that it was a mistake. Gino's eyes widened and Stone knew this was do or die. He spoke and moved quickly, "No problem, Gino." He turned, walked to Johnny and pistol-whipped him to the side of the head. He spoke to the copilot who literally had half pissed his pants, "give me that carry-on bag right there." The copilot quickly walked over with the bag. He threw it at Gino's feet, "Open it, all the cash will be there." Gino picked it up, unzipped the bag, and looked inside. "Andiamo." With that, as quickly as it all unfolded, Gino got in his car, his guys followed, and he drove away saying to Bruno, "At least we got the dough plus, if Luke isn't all over the news tomorrow, we just may have to pay him a visit in Beantown."

"Boss, no worries. Anyway, we got the money and they left town, no harm, no foul."

"True, true, but everyone needs to know if they come to Vegas, they need to let me know, and more importantly, pay if they do business here."

"They know, boss, they know."

Chapter 73

As calm as things were in Gino's car, chaos would better describe the scene on the airplane. The collective feeling was that they were all lucky to have gotten away with only a small bruise to Johnny's head and, of course, Johnny's money. They all boarded the plane similarly as a group would deplane in an emergency. Picture a group running off a plane after an emergency landing and having that caught on tape, then rewinding the tape quickly. That is how they boarded the plane.

Luke was the last to board and, as you would have expected, he moved slightly slower than the rest. No one rushed him, no one pushed him around, and no one ever talked over him. He knew at some level he would have to grovel a little with Gino. The difference is that was the Italian way to show deference to another on their turf. To be fair, Gino would do the same in return if he was in Boston. What was worse now was the inevitable call and most likely subsequent gratuity that would have to be paid to Gino once tomorrow's headlines didn't include: Boston Mob Boss Arrested. Explaining to his pal why his pilots shit themselves . . . well, borrowing his plane in the future may be slightly more difficult.

Luke, after boarding the plane, stood aside so the copilot could secure the stairs and lock the door. After he sat in the cockpit, Luke stuck his head inside and in as sincere a voice as he could muster, "Gentlemen, I apologize for all of this nonsense. I will let your boss know that you both have performed admirably today and advise him that I will personally be paying you a cash bonus for your trouble and hard work. There will be a package dropped off at your homes within the week."

The copilots, instead of being happy and grateful for the ensuing gift, could just think to themselves, "Shit, he's going to know where I live." Both pilots, still in shock, did not know how, or even if, they should respond, just shook their heads in unison. Luke, now with a little less sincere and humble voice, barked, "Now let's get the wheels off the ground!"

"Yes, sir." The pilot barked, almost too loudly, as he snapped out of his funk.

Luke turned and walked the short distance back to the plush seats of the private jet, most of which were pointing toward each other, which made it easier to conduct business while traveling. Mak had seated himself in an aisle seat pointing forward. Luke was walking down the aisle, ready to get into it with Stone, when Mak started to say something derogatory toward Luke, which Luke quite frankly did not even hear, other than he saw Mak's lips moving and the tone of his annoying voice. Before Mak knew what hit him, Luke put all his weight, frustration, anger, and inertia into a right cross that knocked Mak out cold for almost the duration of the flight home, in the process, severely bruising Luke's hand, and putting more than a hairline fracture in Mak's jaw, that was swelling not even five seconds after the blow.

"Sal, find something to tie him up and some duct tape or something to keep him quiet. Once he wakes up, I don't need to hear him anymore."

The plane had already left the hangar and was moving toward the taxi area. The pilots could not get this flight over with soon enough when Sal swung open the cockpit door, scaring the shit out of the already frazzled pilots.

"Boss wants to know if you guys have any duct tape or shit like that up here?"

Now the pilot was pissed, "What the fuck, this isn't a taxi cab. You know we need to be concentrating on flying this tube and it's against FAA regulations to be here now, you need to be seatbelted in now!" Sal was a mad man now and nobody was going to talk to him like that. He was going to teach him a lesson. Sal was clearly not the shining intellectual light of the Fabrasia clan. The copilot who had seen too much outside just wanted Sal out of the cockpit and everyone as happy, if that was the word, as could be.

"Hey, there's a bag right there to your left. It has some emergency tools and some duct tape, help yourself, but get back to your seat now or we can't take off." That sufficiently calmed the situation. Sal clawed through the canvas bag, found the tape and right before he left the cabin he gave the captain a shove on his right shoulder, which actually blipped the jet engines since the captain had his hand on the throttle. "Watch who ya talkin to, you know who I am?" The question was left unanswered, and the door was shut and locked behind Sal.

Sal and Lucky made short work of duct taping Mak's mouth shut and then taping his hands together and his feet to the bottom of the seat. Apparently, they had experience in duct taping people in the past. "Now let's see the mouthy prick say something wise," Luke quipped.

Stone said to no one in particular, "he'll probably find a way."

The plane went up quickly and without incident, which is normally the case with private jets of this kind. Once the plane reached altitude, Luke, who was burning inside on the precipice of exploding like a volcano, knew he had to hold it together, out of respect for the borrowed plane, the pilots who had already seen and heard too much and for the decorum he needed to display for his men. A leader was nothing if he could not control his emotions during a crisis. That was really what made a leader different. Want to know who should be in charge? Wait for a crisis and see who takes charge and who waits for direction. Luke knows this and, quite frankly, so do his men. Stone, taking charge back on the tarmac, was the epiphany Luke now had to deal with. Stone is a natural leader, now how to deal with that? Harness it or eliminate it. Order of business number one when he got back to Boston. Right now, it was time to backburner all the bullshit and get the lowdown on the counterfeiting and figure out what to do with Inspector Mak and, potentially, Stone. For the time being, the mafia code *keep your friends close and your enemies closer* would prevail. Luke matter-of-factly spoke to all and no one in particular at the same time. "We need to rearrange seats. 'AB,' Johnny, and Stone, let's move over to those four seats. We've got a few hours to figure out the plan before we hit Boston."

The Italian version of musical chairs ensued until all were shuffled around. All this happened without Mak moving a muscle.

Chapter 74

Luke was sitting directly across from Stone with "AB" to the left and Johnny next to Stone. "AB" and Johnny on the window, with Luke and Stone on the aisle. This was going to be a business meeting similar to the many meetings that had happened in those same four seats probably a hundred times before.

Luke was running the meeting, "AB" was taking notes, and they would have an agenda. Luke, now in his most comfortable position of acting as the band leader, "OK, here is what we will discuss and in this order, capisce?" All three shook their heads in unison. "Stone, you and Johnny will give us the complete assessment of what you learned about the counterfeiting process and whether or not it has legs. Assuming it has legs, where and how can we implement it? Actually, before that, we will need to assess whether or not we made any mistakes and left any potential evidence that could lead back to us." Again, all shook their heads. "Now quickly, before we start and before Inspector Mouth wakes up and hears us talking about him, not that I give a fuck, I'd be just as happy to put a bullet between his eyes now and take our chances." Mak, though, had already come out of his Luke-induced sleep and realized his situation. He chose to play the sleeping cat routine and keep his ears open since his mouth was already shut. Not a comfortable situation, nor a normal one for Mak, but his options at the time were limited.

Stone began, "First of all, I apologize for being so careless. I should have put the pieces together." Luke put his hand for Stone to stop, "Basta . . . stop, none of that will help now, we need to quickly assess the damage and move forward with a plan."

"I agree, but I still feel bad and blame myself, not for the position I'm in, but for the position 'AB' and the rest of the family is in."

Mak thought to himself, "damn right, assholes, I've got ya all right where I want you."

"Stone, I said enough. Now, what do you think he has on us, and what damage could it do?"

"Clearly, he saw what happened down at the docks as evidenced by what he was able to tell us at the Rio and by my bloody sock. Also, what you don't know is after the docks and after I ditched my clothing, I went to a late night bar a lot of cops frequent. I wasn't there ten minutes before Mak showed up and forced his way in to having a beer with me."

"AB," who was sitting quietly, mumbled, "motherfucker" to no one in particular.

Luke sat pensively, then finally asked, "What are the chances that he has any of this on tape?"

"Tape, what do you mean?"

"I mean film. Do you think he has any of this on film?"

"Well, the other thing I didn't tell you was that for a long time, I had a tracking device on my vehicle. I just assumed it was you, Luke, keeping an eye on me. I actually found it amusing at the time, that you thought I wasn't on my game enough to know what you were doing. Then, when there were two devices, unfortunately for me, or I guess us, I just thought it was more amusing." Mak, still being the fox in the hen house with a chicken outfit on, just took in the piece of info if he would need extra insurance. You can always argue voice recognition in court but being caught red-handed on film, that was the coup de grace for a prosecutor, although Mak knew this was never going to court.

"So, Stone, let's assume he has all he says he has, and we kill him, what do you think will happen?"

"My assumption is he has all he says he has, and upon his demise it will surface. He will end up posthumously decorated as an FBI hero and 'AB' and I will fry and most of the boys and you will serve serious time. I honestly would say sacrifice me, but that wouldn't solve "AB's" problem or yours for that matter. Mak may be a serious ass, but at the end of the day, apparently he really isn't a dope. I'm sure he's got all this all thought out." Mak actually smiled as best he could under the duct tape and, boy, did that send a wince of pain through his jaw. That Luke really packed a wallop. The pain hurt, but it was going to pay off in the end.

"All right, Stone, let's say we play ball with him, what does he really want, and can he be trusted?"

"Well, clearly he can't be trusted to do anything other than cover his own ass. What he wants is the goose that laid the golden egg. I will have to take him at his word. He wants the recipe those kids dreamt up for counterfeiting."

"What, turn it all over."

"Of course not, there's a big enough country out there that we all could get very rich and not step on each other's toes. We just need to divvy up what's his and what's ours. Clearly, Vegas is not a good place for us."

"That's if we make a deal with him, that would have to be the bottom line. He would have to agree to go somewhere far away from us."

Mak said to himself, "You bet I'll be right back on a plane to Vegas and finish what I started with Lucillle., She'll get over my abrupt departure once I shower her with some makeup gifts."

Luke finished his thought, "So we make a deal, give him his info, send him on his way, then we take our time and figure out where he's got his evidence stashed. Once we have that, then he will get the bullet he deserves."

That ain't gonna happen, that'll be the day a bunch of Guineas outsmart ole Mak.

"Now Johnny or Stone, explain to me how two kids outsmarted the United States Treasury when no one else has, and assuming they did, now that they're gone, how do we turn this into real money?"

Stone and Johnny proceeded to intermittently describe the events of the last day and a half, making sure not to leave out any details. Luke, at the end of the day, was a detail guy and wanted to know everything that happened. They knew this and obliged. Luke, the consummate poker player, never gave a hint whether or not he bought into it, just that he was listening and asking appropriate questions when they seemed they should be asked. Stone let Johnny take the lead wherever possible knowing Johnny needed to get back on Luke's good side, even though he felt it wasn't his fault that he hit a jackpot. Actually, giving that money to Gino probably helped save their collective asses. He also then remembered he needed to have a conversation with Stone about the pistol whip-up on the side of his face. It really sounded worse than what it was and he understood, but it couldn't be let go without Stone acknowledging he got away with one.

Stone took over the more technical parts of the process and assured everyone if he had forgotten anything in his description that all of the processes were safely saved in his laptop. The last few details were capsulated for Luke and then there was silence. The only sound was the hum of the jet engines cruising at a very high thirty-eight thousand feet riding the jet stream to Boston. Flights West to East were always significantly faster not having to fight the head winds traveling West to East.

Luke was sitting with his hands folded and his two index fingers pointing straight up on which he was resting his chin. Clearly, Luke was now in deep thought. Mak actually contemplated making a gurgled sound in his duct taped predicament, then thought it would be better to play possum. Luke decided enough time had passed and enough thought had been processed to understand what he had and what he needed to do.

"So as I understand what you boys had told me—those two smart ass kids figured out a foolproof plan on how to screw the government out of an unlimited amount of cash. Providing you guys didn't leave any incriminating evidence, we are the only people with the recipe. That means we can either exploit it or black box it."

Johnny looked confused, which Luke immediately noticed, "Johnny, black box it, that means put it away and not use it or share the info with anybody."

"But, boss, why wouldn't we use it? Seriously, it's easy and we can make a shitload of dough."

"Johnny, as I have said before, fucking with feds is a whole different layer of hurt that they can put on you. Not saying we won't do it, just saying if we do it, we will not be dumb enough to only do it in one place that to me seems like a recipe for disaster."

Stone jumped in, "Luke, my sentiments exactly. We could set up shop for a week in Atlantic City, then a week in Connecticut, we could even go to the islands. Our options are unlimited."

"See, now you're thinking, and this would be great if it was only us but now what do you suggest we do about this dipshit?" pointing at Mak.

Mak wanted to say if he could dipshit? I'm the dipshit. You guys are the dipshits that got caught by me, not the other way around, so I think you need to redirect that insult, although to no avail because they can't read his mind and he was still playing possum.

It was Stone's turn to stop and think for a minute, "Not much we can do. If it was just me, it would be one thing, but he's got AB as well. My suggestion is to make a deal with him to give him the recipe, providing he agrees to retire and leave Boston."

"AB" finally spoke, "He doesn't seem like the type of guy who takes directions well. What if he says no and wants to stay in Boston and make our lives miserable?"

Stone, "Trust me, he hates the cold, always bitching about it. My guess is if we give him what he wants, he just goes away."

Luke, "How about what I want? I don't like it, I'd prefer we just throw him out of the plane right now and be done with him!" Mak wasn't liking this, but he was keeping his cool for the time being.

"AB," sounding and looking beat, said to Luke, but not looking at him, because his head was hanging down between his shoulder blades. "Boss, I want you to know I will support you to the end. You feel like you need to get rid of him, I'm behind you. I was stupid, I didn't listen, you were right. I'll take the fall if you decide to eliminate him." Mak was really having a problem not squirming now he was at the end of his patience.

Stone, "I agree with 'AB.' I will support your decision no matter what."

Luke, "No need to kill him now, we always have that option. I think what we do is get back to Boston, go directly to Fabrasia's and meet in the deaf room to decide how we deal with the asshole and whether or not we black box the technology for a while." Mak almost visibly relaxed his body. He needed to be loose of his bonds before he could possess any leverage.

Luke, "Let's get a couple of hours of shut-eye while we have the time. We will call Fat Hands when we land to meet us at the restaurant." Luke got up and moved to an empty seat at the back of the plane and almost immediately fell asleep. Sal and Lucky were already dozing. It had been an eventful couple of days. "AB," Johnny, and Stone weren't so lucky. They knew they were on the hot seat and couldn't relax enough to sleep. They discussed amongst themselves the best way to convert counterfeit money into legitimate cash. The possibilities seemed endless. Mak was just taking it in. When the time was right, he would show them.

Chapter 75

Fat Hands couldn't sleep, too much stuff floating around his head. The boss seemed progressively more off every single day since Stone showed up. Fat Hands still didn't understand why. He, Johnny, and "AB" had talked about it a dozen or more times. The guy had proven he could be trusted, they had inside information, and they were all wealthier and stronger as an organization. At the end of the day, all of that meant nothing because Luke was not happy. Unlike the rest of the guys who were taking the ignore it and it will go away approach, Fat Hands was committed to figuring out what was Stone's real motivation. His plan was to figure out what in Stone's past would motivate him to want to play on the other side. To migrate from a good, law-abiding FBI man to a murdering crooked Mafia inside man. What neurosis makes a man jump that fence? Money cannot be the only motivator.

These thoughts were floating in Fat Hands' head as he floated around the internet trying to find out anything other than the vanilla facts readily available on Stone.

He had done this so many times he was truly getting ready to throw in the towel. Then he had a flash. He started writing down on a piece of paper various translations for Stone in other languages. He obviously knew Italian, Sasso. The Spanish translation was close. Having to deal with the Mexicans all the time, he became fairly fluent in Spanish. German, for whatever reason, always held a curiosity for him. He was actually one of those sick individuals that thought all things Hitler were cool. He wrote down the German word for Stone: *Stein*.

Fat Hands nimbly typed Sasso and Stone's birthdate into his search and what popped up nearly knocked Fat Hands off the chair he was straddling. He stared at the computer screen, eyes wide and mouth opened so far he hardly noticed his right hand slowly moving up to manually close his jawbone. In fact, the shock was so deep and profound it took him four or five rings of his phone to snap him out of it. He looked down to his phone and saw it was Luke. His first thought was, "Why is he calling at 5:30 in the morning?" Then he had phase two of snapping out when he realized if the boss calls, you better answer.

"Boss, are you sitting down? I've got to tell you something."

"FH, there will be time later. Right now I need you to meet me at the deaf room. We got a situation we all need to deal with now."

"But, boss, I really think you should hear this" As he was saying this, he was thinking, "News like this is better delivered in person."

"FH, unless there's an issue with my wife or kids, I'd prefer to deal with it later. It's been a very long day."

Fat Hands thought about pushing his point again and decided to delay the inevitable for another hour or two. "OK, boss, let me shower up quickly and I'll be there soon., Did you just land?"

"As we speak, Fat Hands, shower quick, big man, there's business to handle important business."

Chapter 76

The Lear jet touched down, not a minute too soon for the pilots and passengers. The copilot told the pilot shortly after leaving Vegas that he was more afraid of getting shot there in Vegas working for an innocuous corporation then when he was flying combat missions in Afghanistan. At least there he was armed and could shoot back. There, he felt like a fish in a barrel.

Luke too was itchy. He wanted to get back to the safety of Fabrasia's and the deaf room. There he could think straight and plan out how to deal with the mess that Stone and his cohort had become. On the one hand, the counterfeiting, if handled correctly, could ultimately launder enough cash that they could abandon more risky business endeavors if not all illegal activities. Imagine that, family Fabrasia legit for the first time in history. That thought made him chuckle inside with visions of the Godfather III. If it didn't work for Michael Corleone, it certainly wasn't going to work for him.

The real question was if he just killed Stone and Mak, which was his inclination, how would that play out? Dead men can't talk, but who knows exactly what Mak had in his bag of tricks. Actually, for all he knew, Stone could have evidence stashed away in case of his untimely death. Clearly, Mak had incriminating evidence on Stone a la sock. Apparently on "AB" as well. Should he kill Mak and he has what he says, "AB" might as well pack his bag and move out of the country for good. There goes the succession plan.

As soon as the jet landed, Luke was up on his feet and went to Mak whose eyes were open anxiously waiting to hopefully be unduct taped, for lack of a better expression. Sometimes you should look out what you ask for, because in one quick motion Luke ripped the tape from Mak's mouth with a sound that was only equaled by the grimace on Mak's face. Before Luke could say what he had intended, Mak spit out, "What shitty service, no hot towels and nuts." That comment was as quickly followed with an open hand slap that was almost hard enough to knock Mak out for a second time that day.

Luke spoke, "I don't care what you have stored for evidence, I've had enough of your mouth. This is your last warning, if you want to see the sun come up another day. I'm going to have Sal untape you, and we're all going to go back to my place and try to work this out. If you're lucky, we will. If you're not, remember you've got nothing on me."

"I'll be watching my mouth, but remember, I got plenty on you too, but I got enough to put number one boy, "AB" over there, away for good, not to mention your inside information Benedict Arnold."

"Sal untaped him and put him in the limo."

"You got it, boss."

Chapter 77

Fat Hands hit print on his laptop and went to his printer, gathering up his unbelievable news. He wondered what the boss would make of it. He grabbed his cell phone and auto-dialed Unlucky.

"Yeah, boss?" he said clearly through a deep sleep-induced crackle.

"Wake up and get to the deaf room pronto. Boss is back and I got a feeling there's big goings on this morning."

"You got it, boss, I got Gina here. It might take me a little bit to get out of here, if you know what I mean."

"I know what you mean, and if you're not out of your house in the next five minutes, you won't have anything for Gina ever again, capisce?"

"Got it, boss, but she ain't going to be happy."

"She'll be less happy if I cut your balls off."

"Me too. I'll get dressed and leave now." Well, that's what he told Fat Hands. Unlucky was thinking he lived closer than Fat Hands, so he still had enough time to beat him there. He made a slight detour for a quick rendezvous with Gina. That extra time put him in the wrong place at the wrong time.

Chapter 78

Luke and AB drove back to Fabrasia's together in "AB's" car. They had called ahead for a limo to bring the rest of the crew, including Mak, in the same car. Both cars were eerily silent on the drive back to Boston. Everyone in the limo knew things were not going to be good back in the privacy of the deaf room. Regardless of the unlimited possibilities of the new counterfeit technology they unveiled, Johnny was actually feeling a little bit like unlucky, shit lately, if it wasn't for bad luck, he wouldn't have had any luck at all. Hitting that jackpot could not have come at a worse time. He would, though, tell the boss even if he hadn't hit, there was nothing he could have done to predict the kid was going to snap.

Both Sal and Lucky knew they did their jobs to a T. That still would not excuse them from the upcoming wrath. They knew there was just going to be collateral damage. Sal hadn't been around at this level that long, so he had no way to know but Lucky knew, having been there before, that the boss would in time thank them for doing their part correctly, just not now because the team fucked up and in a family like Fabrasia's, you lived and died as a family.

Stone, on the other hand, knew he was the one with an issue. He was the one who had now put the family in peril and not just anyone in the family but the venerable "AB," arguably the number two guy and heir apparent. The only twist he could put on this was Mak, and Mak had zero redeeming qualities. He can and, more importantly, wants to be bought. Stone decided he was going to have to convince Luke that as much of an asshole Mak was, he could be trusted, it was just going to cost.

Mak was fuming! They apparently didn't know who they were dealing with now that he was not duct taped. Like some freshman pledge, he was going to be a force to be reckoned with when the time lent itself. He now had his eye on the brass ring, fuck the money, he had intended to ask for the recipe that was the goose that laid the golden egg. Mak decided it was time to speak, "Hey fucknuts . . . yeah you, Stone"

"What, Shit for brains?"

Mak nodded his head, "Oh really . . . shit for brains, who is the one without his bloody sock, huh?"

Disgusted, Stone decided to play, "What now, Mak?"

"Not so dumb now, am I?"

"Apparently not. You happy now that I said that? Because if you're not careful, you're going to get both of us killed."

"I don't think so. Luke ain't never going to put 'AB' in harm's way." Johnny thought he picked up on something and wanted to play along. "Hey Mak, Stone is correct, Luke would rather take his chances than be blackmailed."

"This ain't blackmail really, it's just good business."

"Then act that way and maybe you won't get yourself killed, or anyone else for that matter."

Johnny, intently watching Mak, felt good enough that Mak got the point not to push Luke. Unfortunately for Mak, he didn't get it.

"AB" broke the silence first, "Boss, I know you don't want to hear this, but at the end of the day, this could all work out for the best."

"'AB,' what exactly is going to work out? You going to jail, us having potentially to kill two feds, dealing with an asshole who wants to blackmail us for who knows how much, or for how long. Yeah, it all sounds dandy. Have you lost your mind?"

"No, boss, the way I see it is we still have our inside guy feeding us information. Now this guy Mak, for sure, is going to resign from his job and live the high life. I'll bet my life on that one."

"You might have to."

"I know, boss, but once he quits, he'll no longer . . . have the ear of his boss if he has a bad day and wants to rat on us."

"Not sure I buy your assessment. What if we kill Stone, then what does he have? I think a whole lot less."

"Yeah, but he still has me, boss."

"Not anywhere near as explosive, plus what if we tell him he has to whack Stone for us to play ball? Then we have something as devastating on him as he has on us."

"I guess that's why you're the boss. I never went there, but again why Stone? He's still the goose that continues to lay golden eggs."

"Trust me, this guy is going to bring us all down."

"Boss, death as you know is forever and the boys like all the newfound wealth, not to mention how much this new gig has potential for."

"Fungul, why does everyone want to protect this smuck? Including you, who may rot in jail for life if we don't get that evidence."

"I think we give him what he wants, watch him figure out where and what he has, then deal with him then."

"And Stone?"

"We always have the option, boss, let's just do it when it's convenient for us, plus who knows Stone is smarter than Mak, maybe Stone has stuff on us hidden with someone if anything bad ever happened to him."

"I'm quickly getting to the 'I don't give a flying fuck' point."

"Capisce, boss, but first, let's get back to the deaf room and figure this out so it's best for us."

"All right, 'AB,' but no guarantees."

Chapter 79

They all filed into the deaf room, Stone first so he sat at the far end of the table. Sal, Lucky, Johnny, and "AB" came in next and sat in that order. Mak was the last one in and sat to the right of where Luke always sits at the head of the table. Mak plopped down in his chair and leaned it against the wall, balancing on its back two legs, cocky as ever. The room was silent, waiting for Luke to enter. He had taken a short detour to his office to grab a gun in case the opportunity presented itself. He didn't like either one of these guys and could relish an opportunity to rid them out of his life. He very seldom ever broke his rule about having weapons in the deaf room, but again it was his rule and he could break it if it suited him. Luke was stalling a little because he really wanted Fat Hands and Unlucky to be present for whatever he decided was the right course of action. He was tired, though, and wanted to get going so he decided they could be caught up when they showed up.

Luke walked in and no sooner sat down than Mak started right in on him. "So this is the famous deaf room, doesn't look like much to me."

"Shut up and listen, I'm in no mood for your bullshit. I don't want to be here and I don't want to do business with you, so I strongly urge you to control yourself or I'll have to have one of these fine gentlemen put a bullet between your eyes, are we clear?"

"Not really, Mr. Big Boss, you don't seem to get it, do you? You kill, 'AB' and Stone go directly to jail. They don't cross go, they don't collect two hundred dollars, nothing. You, my friend, at the very least go down as an accessory after the fact in the deaths of not one but two FBI agents. So do you capisce?"

Stone, trying to defuse the situation, interjected, "Hey, hey, guys, everyone understands who is boss and who has what on whom. Comparing ball size won't accomplish anything. So Mak, why don't you just tell us what you want." Luke was fuming who was this idiot talking to him this way in front of his men. His grip on his pistol behind his back was tightening.

Chapter 80

Unlucky, in the colloquial sense, got lucky before he left. He gave it the old college try telling Gina he had to go. She wasn't having any of it and coaxed him back to bed for a little morning tryst before she let him go. Unlucky only had so much will power and his supply was never that high.

Fat Hands, the true soldier that he was, showered and without delay was out the house on his way to help his boss, his leader. It might also have had something to do with Fat Hands' wife, who was just named Fat and wasn't big on early moving trysts, but, nonetheless, Fat Hands would not have kept the boss waiting, and that's why he was a Captain and not just a soldier. Especially with the news he had to give, it would be a sea change for Luke.

Fat Hands wheeled his Lincoln into the back parking lot and let out a heavy breath talking out loud, "Fucking Unlucky, just couldn't keep it in your pants, could you?" As he noticed the absence of Unlucky's car in the lot, he made a mental note to deal with his lack of commitment later. Right now, he needed to see Luke and pass on the find from his sleuthing.

Fat Hands practically jumped out of the car and half jogged to the back door. Unlucky just caught a glance of his velour sweat suit disappearing as the door swallowed him up as he wheeled into the parking lot. "Shit, he beat me here, now I'm screwed."

Chapter 81

Fat Hands, almost catlike for a big man, just appeared in the door. Actually, the first to see him was Mak

"Hey, the gang's all here now, Fat Shit. I mean Fat Hands is here." That was all Luke needed to hear. One of his connecting wires snapped and before anyone knew what had happened, Luke had his 9 mm out from behind his back and pointed a mere inch from between Mak's eyes with his finger firmly on the trigger. "Shut the fuck up you hear me, asshole?" Nobody moved, not an inch, not even a millimeter. They, except for Stone, had seen Luke in this crazed state and knew not to move. Finally, Mak, at least for this moment, understood the gravity, but was still indignant that someone else, even Luke Fabrasia, could think they had the upper hand over Mak. Although, at least momentarily he understood he could be right and dead all at the same time, Mak, ever so slowly, raised both his arms with his hands palm forward in the quintessential sign of surrender, not daring to speak a word as he saw the crazed look in Luke's eyes.

Luke, slowly realizing he was on the edge, started coming back to saneness and lowered his weapon.

Fat Hands, not quite knowing everything that had led up to this madness, could easily put two and two together. He spoke first and very quietly almost in Luke's ear. "Boss, outside, we need to talk now." Luke, in ultra slow motion, never broke gaze with Mak and to Mak's defense, even in his surrender posture, never broke gaze with Luke. Luke finally broke his stare at the last possible moment to shoot Stone a last second glare as he walked out. No words were needed there. Stone felt a boulder drop to the bottom of his stomach.

Fat Hands backed out the way he came in and Luke followed him. Fat Hands walked maybe fifteen feet from the room just out of earshot. He had the look on his face that people have when they're about to tell you someone close has died.

"Boss, remember Sasso's market?"

"Yeah, so what, it's been gone for years." Luke, who was clearly annoyed, now told Fat Hands, "You understand we got a big issue here?"

"Boss, it just got bigger. The widow Sasso was your father's *butana*. She had his kid. Stone's your half-brother." Fat Hands unfolded the paper he printed, which was Stone's birth certificate, and there it was for all to see Mother Gina Sasso, Father Lorenzo Fabrasia.

Luke stared at the paper for what seemed hours, which was only seconds. His head was spinning with the memories flooding back. Every weekend he would accompany his father to Sasso's Italian Market to get fresh meat for Sunday dinner. His father was always nice to Mrs. Sasso, but at seven or eight he didn't' notice how nice. Her little boy, a couple of years younger than Luke, was always attached to her apron shy and with his thumb in his mouth. Luke's father always had candy in his pocket for the little boy. One time Luke asked his dad, "Why do you always have candy for that little boy?"

""Because he's not as well off as you, son, his mother is poor, and the little boy doesn't have a father."

"Where is his father?" Lorenzo just quickly quipped, "He had a bad accident."

The back door opened quickly as Unlucky was rushing to get in and possibly lessen the wrath of the bosses. That noise snapped Luke out of his trance, although he couldn't quite get his mouth to work.

Unlucky walked quickly by them trying not to make eye contact. Fat Hands motioned him toward the deaf room. "Wait in there." Unlucky was happy to be spared a personal meeting with Fat Hands and Luke quickly moved into the deaf room.

Unlucky, in his haste to get to the deaf room, forgot the cardinal rule to never bring a weapon with him. Fat Hands was the first to notice, but too late as Unlucky turned left into the room Fat Hands noticed the butt of Unlucky's 38 special sticking out of his belt in the small of his back. Fat Hands could not get the words out of his mouth to have him stop. It was too late, and he hoped he would be the only one to notice.

Unlucky walked in, exchanging pleasantries with the boys when he turned left to go to the open side of the table. That's when Mak saw his opportunity when he noticed the butt of the gun sticking out of Unlucky's pants. He wasted no time, jumped up, and snatched the gun from the back of Unlucky. That's when the world went crazy and everyone knew it at once. Unlucky, realizing his blunder, spun around in an awkward way which, true to his name, unluckily caused the pistol to fire, blowing off the right side of his face, killing him instantly. His last thought was Gina . . . wasn't worth being late. "AB" had already sprung to action from behind, as did Stone from the other end of the table. Mak got his footing as well as his confidence back, thinking to himself, "Now, I'll show them who's boss." Stone was rushing from around the opposite side of the table. Mak lowered the gun toward him as "AB" dove in a flying tumble if not causing, at least assisting, in the pistol firing in Stone's direction. Stone went down, hitting the ground almost at the same time, and "AB" ended up on top of Mak with the gun now safely knocked out of Mak's hand.

An explosion of pain like Stone had never before experienced raced through his body. He was wondering, "Am I dead, dying?" head spinning on the edge of consciousness.

Now, it was time for Luke to have a boulder drop in his stomach, "Stone." Luke and Fat Hands went running for the room. They entered to view the carnage with Unlucky's brains splattered on the rubber walls, "AB" on the floor wrestling on top of Mak.

Luke assessed the situation quickly. Unlucky was undoubtedly dead from the remains on the glass wall and the lifeless lump under Mak and "AB." He could see that Stone was down, but his legs were moving. He stepped over to Mak and shot him in the arm wrapped around the back and neck of "AB," which allowed "AB" to totally incapacitate Mak. He jumped over them almost pleading.

"Stone, Joe Sasso, Frattello, brother, please be OK." Stone was dazing in and out but felt himself rising out of unconsciousness into consciousness. Though, not believing what he was hearing, he must have been dreaming, how would he know?

Stone opened his eyes to see Luke looming just inches from his face. Luke spoke first, "Fratello, why didn't you tell me? All this time I didn't understand, none of it made sense, I didn't understand your loyalty. It all makes sense now, but why didn't you tell me?" Stone, not sure he could speak, was surprised how strong his voice sounded.

"I wanted you to respect me first for who I am and what I could mean to you. I didn't want you to think I showed up to just take from you."

"Brother, it doesn't matter. Why, in my world, family is family, and you're mine for better or worse."

"How bad am I?"

"You'll live, looks like he got you right over your heart but through your shoulder. Don't speak now, save your energy, we will have plenty of time to get to know each other." Luke already had his cell phone out and he was dialing his favorite degenerate veterinarian doctor.

"Hello, Luke."

"Hello, Martin, my brother and I are very hungry and want bacon and eggs."

"But you don't have a brother."

"You are incorrect, my friend, he was long lost, but he is back to stay and he is very hungry and in need of some bacon and eggs. Bc ready. We will see you for breakfast in twenty minutes."

Epilogue

Martin performed his animal magic again. He operated on Stone first of course. Actually pretty simple straight through the lower shoulder, never hit anything except muscle. Mak's was similarly simple, except he had to wait and Luke wouldn't allow any painkillers. Luke then locked Mak up for four straight days without any human intervention and no painkillers other than a few Tylenols. That put Mak in a friendlier negotiating mood. In the end, Luke and Mak made a deal. Mak moved to Atlantic City to make his fortune and floated between there, Vegas, and the islands so as not to attract too much attention. That is as much as a guy with Mak's personality can fly under the radar.

Luke and Stone started down the long road of reclaiming forty years, for the most part very harmoniously. The counterfeiting scam went on long enough to make the Familia Fabrasia very wealthy. As all good things must come to an end, so did the scam. US bills became impossible to reproduce as the US Treasury became more technological. It was a good run while it lasted. That, unfortunately, was when Mak reared his ugly head again . . .

The End and the Beginning Familia Fabrasia Act II

Edwards Brothers, Inc.
Thorofare, NJ USA
February 3, 2012